A E SPENCER

THE PINK MUTINY

A NOVEL

Published by Bliss Publishing, Sydney
www.blisspublishing.com.au

Bliss Publishing, the Bliss Publishing logo,
are the trademarks of Bliss Publishing Pty Ltd.

ISBN-13: 9780645117110

Cover design by Bibhudatta Dash
bvudatta68@gmail.com

Inspired by few women in Lucknow city of India who could defy the social norms in the 19th Century,

And

Dedicated to all the women who are still rotting in the 21st Century behind the Iron curtain of Religious Practices and so-called moral standards of the societies

CHAPTER 1

26 May 1857, Night, Lucknow, British India,
Beginning of Sepoy Mutiny
Amelia

I peek out the window as the rhythmic galloping sound of the hooves slows down a bit. The darkness of the night scares me. We are about to touch a crossroad when the coach makes a complete halt. Two other horse carts are going along the road we are about to cross. Not only Lucknow, but many other parts of India are burning. Who would be on the street at night, out of the safety of their homes? Once loyal, the Indian sepoys are showing their distrust and hatred against their masters, the British East India Company. For a moment I forget—I am also out of the house, away from the well-guarded English fort, The Residency. My pulse quickens, and I draw a cross mark on my chest. Festering wounds on my breasts come to life. No, it is my husband's home which I also called my family, until an hour ago.

I inhale deeply and try to forget the agony, forcing my gaze out the window of the coach. Beautiful sprawling mansions, many of them proudly depicting Mughal architecture in the moonlight, soften my nerves. Lights from lamps glint through the windows of a mansion. It is almost past midnight; the whole city must be sleeping. Are we in front of a courtesan's house? I press my ear to the glass window in case I can hear the songs of the *tawaifs* and the tinkling sound coming off their bell-studded silver anklets. But I hear nothing. They are all in my mind, gathered from the numerous stories I have listened to in Officer's Wives Club in The Residency.

The coach rolls again. We are probably about to leave the city. I look out to get the last view of my only favourite city outside England —Lucknow. Who knows when I will get another chance to come back to this beautiful place? The soldiers guarding the area have probably gone away. I realise the coach is moving slowly. Through the window, I notice that a sepoy is guiding my coachman toward the side of the road. My heart sinks. I close the curtain of the window, and my gaze is forced back inside at the small mirror. The dim light from the tiny lamp is enough to show my blood-drained face.

The reflection of my blonde hair makes my heart beat faster. The soldier is talking to my coachman in Urdu. I try to catch a few words to find out if the soldier is from our side or the rebel's. I notice my own smirk in the mirror. My side? Of course. My husband is Brigadier Sir Colin Lawrence, a senior commander in East India Company's army. The soldier must salute me if he knows I am a brigadier's wife. Wait a minute! What if he is a rebel soldier?

Do not worry, Amelia. Nothing to be scared of, Sona has assured me. *Indian soldiers do not attack women.*

Within a moment, the soldier's boots seem increasingly louder. He is coming to check on the coach. My heart knocks faster against my ribs. "Calm Amelia, calm. Do not show your anxiety." I mutter a prayer and realise the burqa I am wearing has slipped down to my neck. Pulling the clothing above my head, I cover my face with the mesh screen. What if the soldier asks me to lift the veil and show my face? I try to recollect a few Urdu words and start practising. "*Janab*, I am go-ing to attend to my mother-in-law in the village, she suddenly became sick."

My mouth goes dry when the soldier forces the door open. An Indian sepoy—it is difficult to know if he is still in the British army or with the rebels. His expressionless eyes don't tell me anything. *What if?* I stop thinking further. I can't even mutter a single Urdu word I have learnt with so much effort. Pushing the curtain with the rifle, the sepoy peeks inside. I hold my breath. My coachman is standing behind him with folded hands and muttering something incoherently.

Please, please don't tell him I am an English.

The sepoy pulls out and closes the door. I can hear him saying, "Go ahead. Time is not good for a woman to travel at night." I recount Sona's assurance. Relief washes through my chest.

I pull the burqa back to uncover my face and neck and realise I am sweating. The cabin is so tiny, dark, and smelly. Opening the window curtain again, I bring down the windowpane. Fresh air gushes inside and washes through my skin. No more bungalows. Only trees or open space. Thank God, we are outside the city now. I have won the first step of my escapade.

I try to get some sleep while the horse cart moves ahead. I need energy for the morning to continue my journey toward my destination. Yes, destination—which I have not figured out yet. Pulling out my diary from the bag, I open to the last page I have written. This has been my favourite pastime since childhood. Today is such an important day of my life—I have made a risky and bold decision. This I must enter in the journal before drifting into slumber.

The coach stops again. I hear the footsteps of the coachman, getting off and walking somewhere. My heart sinks, apparently for no reason. I should have given him some tips when the sepoy spared me and allowed me to move on. A dark feeling sifts through me. I pull the burqa again on my head, and my gaze goes out. He is talking to a burqa-clad woman holding a box above her head and a lantern with her hand. The sepoy's last sentence rings inside my head— *Time is not good for a woman to travel at night.*

Who would walk during the darkness of the night on a war-ravaged street for fun? It must be another helpless woman! Without thinking, I yank the door open and jump to the ground. The woman shrieks and starts running, the box bending her neck and the flames of the lantern flickering nervously. I shout, "Do not fear. I will help you." I realise I can speak Urdu. My strides become confident. Grabbing her arm, I say, "Please come with me. I will help. Are you going somewhere this way?"

The woman stops and studies me, her features guarded. She nods. I notice a hope in her eyes in the dim lantern light. Maybe she is relieved to see another woman in similar attire or someone speaking her language.

The coachman smiles. "I told you. Ma'am is so kind!" He goes back to his coach box.

I help her climb the steps of the carriage, and we both settle inside. I am careful not to talk to her much in Urdu except a few words, and I am keeping my face covered to hide my blonde hair as much as possible. The woman stumbles on something below the front seat. Light from the tiny dim lantern does not show what it is. She bows down, pulls out something, and hands it to me. "Book, your," she says in broken English. My gaze sharpens in surprise. I uncover my face and stop pretending that I am not a *firangi*. Wah! I have even started thinking in the local language, using the word *firangi* in place of foreigner. A feeling of familiarity spurts from my guts. I ask her in Urdu, "Name?"

"Sehnaz." Her voice is soft.

She sits and removes her head covering, setting the box near her feet and the lantern flickering lazily. I judge her silently. Her complexion is fair, hair long and split into two pleats. She is beautiful and young.

She is staring at the floor and says, "Going Gangapur. Mother sick." She then lifts her gaze toward me and asks, "Name? You?"

"Amelia. Amelia Lawrence."

Sehnaz springs up and yanks the door open. She is about to jump from the running carriage, but I grab her arms and pull her inside. I fail to understand why she is behaving like this. She literally cries, "No, ma'am, Rupen, not seen, months."

My surname echoes through my mind. Lawrence. This word must be the culprit. That is my husband's surname. I know Rupen Naik, chief of the army of Nawab Wajid Ali Shah. He is an excellent friend of my husband. No—instead, he was. Now they are archenemies. Fighting from opposite sides of the fence. Rupen is a leading name in the Sepoy Mutiny, and British force is frantically looking to capture him.

I regret telling her my real name. Lies always struggle to come out of my mouth. "Sir Colin Lawrence is not my husband. There are other Lawrences besides him," I lie.

Sehnaz stares into my eyes and studies me for several long beats. I have probably messed up my own safety in my attempt to help her. But it is too late now, and I doubt if she trusts me. I keep my hand on her back, showing reassurance of no danger from my side.

We don't speak much for the next hour, but I find myself smiling shyly at her if we catch each other's eye—she smiles back before gazing at the floor. Soon we arrive inside a large mango garden, and the coach stops in front of a small, dilapidated house. An old man is standing there holding a lamp. Nancy, my neighbour in The Residency, has organised all this. She has been in India for almost twenty years and knows enough people and places. I rely on her advice.

The coachman leaves after getting his dues and tips. The caretaker unlocks the house and lets us in. I pay some money to him as well, and he happily departs. I watch him until he goes out of sight—Nancy's idea. I need to get out of here by early morning so that neither the coachman nor this old man will know where I have gone. She has arranged another horse carriage to take me far from here—to Varanasi city.

"Stop here? Night?" Sehnaz looks into my eyes, and for the first time, maintains eye contact.

"Don't worry. We will sleep here and start again tomorrow morning. You will arrive at your place. Safely." I should have told her beforehand.

She hesitates only a moment before resolutely retrieving her box and lantern and exiting the coach.

I follow her, realizing that I have only a few hours to sleep. We enter the tiny structure and see that the bed in the room is enough for only one person. Silently, Sehnaz begins preparing her bed on the floor.

Acquiescing, I move to the bed, take out my diary, and start writing again. I don't write every day. But whenever I have something important, I note it. I believe one day when I am no longer in this world, someone will read this and know about my life. Since childhood, I have had a dream that I will not be like any other woman. I will be someone special so that people remember me. But I haven't figured out what that special is. Anyway, that is not my worry now.

Sehnaz's snore brings me to my senses—I am already late for bed. I notice that she has removed her burqa, but her clothing surprises me. I have seen the dress of many Indian women, including Sona, who works as my maid. Sehnaz's attire is different. A small piece of silk cloth has been tied around her breasts—something like a tight, shoulderless bodice with stitches to keep her breasts firm and round. The flower-like knot on her back confuses me. I don't understand whether that is a knot or a design. I have never seen this type of women's undergarment, even in the best fashion store in London. Also, she is wearing a short skirt, not covering her knees. I pause. Why I am worried about her dress, anyway? How can I start another journey in the morning without getting some rest?

Closing the journal, I lie down on my bed, shutting my eyes. *God, give me courage and help.* I need to arrive at Calcutta. From there, ships are going to London and even Australia. I will think about whether settling in Australia is a better idea than England. No one will even know I am already married; I can have a new life. Life? Yes. Only if Colin doesn't use his position to capture me back. I am too young to join his ex-wife in heaven.

I would have liked a few extra hours of sleep, but this morning is different. I should get out of here before the attendant comes back. I had told Sehnaz we will start before sunrise.

"Sehnaz!" I sit up on the bed.

I hear the sound of water pouring from the other side of the wall. She must be taking a shower. The old man has kept water for our bathing.

My gaze goes to her open box, and the attire she was wearing last night underneath her burqa is on the top. I am now sure she is not a traditional Muslim woman. She is wearing the head covering for the same reason I am.

Suspicion about her identity hits my guts.

I lift her clothing gently, keeping an ear to the sound of pouring water from in the bathroom. I have a few minutes only. She has sarees, salwar kameez, skirts, short blouses, and the bodice she was wearing last night. I also find a paper, neatly folded. She is literate! Unlike millions of other Indian women!

I carefully unfold the paper from a corner, which looks something like a map. I focus on it. Looks like a map of a small township—something dark threads into my mind. Sehnaz has finished her bathing, no more water sound. She will be in the room anytime. I feel like a thief, but I only have seconds to find out what this is. A picture of a gate rings a bell. Is it the plan of The Residency? Yes! This is the place I used to live with my husband until last evening, a small township housing all senior British officers of The East India Company with all sorts of security. I have no time to think. Folding the paper, I stuff it underneath her clothes and get up. Sehnaz is already entering the room, fresh from her early morning shower and wrapped in a saree.

"Good morning, Sehnaz." I rush to the bathroom before she can reply. The next coachman might arrive within minutes.

Taking water from the large bucket using a mug, I pour it over my head. But the image of the map curls like smoke through my mind. So many questions shoot through me. Is that map really of The Residency? And what is Sehnaz doing with it? Are the British families living there in danger once the diagram goes to the rebel sepoys? I have heard stories about Lucknow's courtesans helping the rebels. They are useful in collecting secret information from the British. There are officers of East India Company who regularly visit the *kothas*, the mansions where courtesans perform *mujra*, song and dance. My husband might also be one of them.

The cold water on my head brings some calmness. Why am I thinking like this when I am not sure about the map? Finishing the shower, I open the bathroom door and rush inside the bedroom, forgetting that I am completely naked. But Sehnaz is not there. Her bag is packed again. Changing into fresh clothes, I pack my suitcase, ready to welcome the new coachman. Sehnaz comes inside and greets me with a big smile; she is wearing a saree and looking awesomely beautiful.

I have tried my best to hide my unease. "The other coachman may come anytime, and we need to start soon."

I continuously look from the sky to the path to see if the caretaker is coming. Sehnaz must be surprised if she knows I, an English woman, am running away.

No, no, I am not fleeing. I am just going to a friend's place in… Which area should I say? I already made a mistake last night when I told her my real name. *Yes, I am going to Benares. No, Varanasi,* I mumble in my mind. This will be my answer.

The other coachman has not arrived yet. Inhaling deeply, I direct my gaze again at the sky and the pathway. The sun hovers yawningly over the east horizon. We should've been out before sunrise. I go inside the house and within a minute come out, hoping that some miracle might have brought the carriage. Either Nancy has not organised the transport, or there is some miscommunication. The thought freezes me. What if he has come but did not find the house, which is almost hidden behind large mango trees? I run on the pathway to the main road.

I do not see any cart, but I notice Sehnaz talking to a horse rider. I stand still as a statue behind a tree, unsure if that man is a sepoy or not. The smile on her face is bold and confident. Is the man there to collect that paper, death warrant of The Residency? Is the man there to find me and take me back to my husband?

I am confused about Sehnaz.

Everything looks blurry. I can't contact Nancy now and ask what happened to the carriage she had organised. What will happen if the landlord comes and finds that the caretaker facilitated the stay of a white woman here last night without his knowledge? How do I leave this place without leaving trace?

The man goes back on his horse, and Sehnaz returns, flashing a broad smile. "He is bringing a horse carriage for us." My mouth has formed a big O. Should I go with Sehnaz or wait here for the carriage which may never turn up? Staying back means everything might be over for me. I still have to think about that dreaded map. And I have no time to think if Sehnaz is good or bad for me. I've to pick my poison. I must get out of this place as soon as possible. Reacting instantly, I drag my heavy suitcase out.

We board the coach, and soon we are travelling once again. My gaze goes to the clear, blue sky. Dawn is here. A small patch of white clouds appears from the distant horizon. A feeling that says *you are going to be okay* tingles in my mind.

We arrive at the riverbank in less than an hour, where a boat is waiting for us.

"This boat will take us to Varanasi," Sehnaz says, mixing both English and Urdu. "Sorry, Banaras. English, no good."

"I can understand when you mix both languages. This is a new language—Unglish, Urdu cum English." I feel myself blushing at my own comment.

Sehnaz nods with a mild laugh.

As we settle down in the steamboat, I notice it is just the two of us —and the man who is steering the steamer.

"He, Sheru Pandey. He will sail us to Varanasi." Sehnaz speaks in Unglish. Opening a packet, she serves Indian snacks on three plates, one for Sheru.

I suddenly remember what Sehnaz had told me last night when I gave her a ride. "You were supposed to go to Gangapur?"

Her eyes flare open. "Gangapur? Which Gangapur?" She focusses on eating the snacks, avoiding my gaze.

You are overthinking, Amelia. I try to pacify myself, but my blood turns to ice water.

CHAPTER 2

27 May 1857, Morning
Amelia

"Your name is Sehnaz what? I mean, surname?"

She stares at me blankly. Either she is telling lies and fumbling to find an answer, or she doesn't understand my question.

I repeat, "I am Amelia Lawrence. You are Sehnaz...and then?"

"I was married as a child bride, custom." Her face darkens in a wave of sadness and possibly some memories. "I was widowed when I was a child, never remember my husband's surname. Lived with a distant aunt."

I fail to understand how the "sick mother" has disappeared, and now a "distant aunt" has come into the picture. Sehnaz gets up and goes to Sheru Pandey.

Can I just get off the boat and run away?

Taking out a book from my suitcase, I start reading, but somehow, I cannot focus. So many things cross my mind; I have made a terrible decision with my life. And now I am with Sehnaz. Is she a new friend or a trap? And regardless of Sehnaz—either I will get the life I have dreamt since I was a child, or I will go down in history as another unknown soul—like millions of other women who are born, brought up, educated, and married so that they can be a loyal wife to a man.

My soul screams. But I want to live my life, too.

I glance around the cuddy I am sitting in. There is no comfort, no one to attend. Just a day ago I was sitting in the lap of luxury—as a Brigadier General's wife. I was a VIP in the ladies' club at the Lucknow cantonment. All the other women treated me with the utmost respect. No doubt, I have enjoyed many of those moments. But really?

Women in the club proudly announce when their men either get a promotion or win a medal, but I choke. Only men can be officers, rise in their careers, and get awards for bravery. Why not me?

Sehnaz is having a conversation with Sheru. I cannot hear, sitting inside the cabin. Why did I offer her a lift last night? Is she a spy? Have I been trapped? *Amelia, do not overthink. Indian spies have nothing to do with you.*

The leftover snack on the plate winks at me. I eat the last piece. Yum. Sehnaz has cooked an excellent dish, spicy but not hot.

Spicy!

My mind again goes to the spicy gossips in the ladies' club. A new world of courtesans has opened up to me. I learnt about the *kothas* of Lucknow, the mansions of the famous courtesans. Kings, nawabs, royal family members, and even top-ranking British officers are their patrons. They regularly attend their performances, which are mainly singing and dancing.

"Spicy and hot," Nancy had told me. "Most such women choose the profession as a sanctuary for greater freedom than their ordinary world. Not only to escape the hell of a male-dominant, unhappy marriage, but also for financial independence. Women in *kothas* instead exert influence over powerful men."

I recollect Sehnaz's clothing and the confident way she was talking to the soldier this morning. Is she a courtesan? She might have some links with Rupen Naik, Chief of Army of Nawab Wajid Ali.

I had been longing to visit a *kotha* for days, but this Sepoy Mutiny started. I heard different stories about courtesans, that they are nothing more than sex workers. Deep in my heart, I would like to believe Nancy —that they are independent and educated women who have defied the traditional social rules and live on their own terms.

The ferry shakes due to high wind. I come out of my imagination and look for something to hold on to. That women's club is past now. Colin is not coming back home for almost a week; he is busy fighting the rebels, unable to hurl abuses at me or grab me by the hair.

I imagine how fast the present becomes the past. It is just Wednesday morning, 27 May 1857, around nine a.m. This time last night, I finished packing my bag. Only one bag. Some clothes, enough money to pull me for a few months and pay for a ship ticket to either London or Australia, and a few books. No one is going to the ladies' club because of the mutiny. Authorities have issued advice not to go out of The Residency. This is the worst time to flee from home.

But I have weighed all this carefully. If Colin is the frying pan, I am prepared to go to the fire. Nancy also confirms what Sona had said: Indian soldiers wouldn't harm any woman. Until a few weeks ago, most of them were loyal sepoys of the British East India Company. Why did the East India Company take them for granted? British officers treat Indians inhumanly, as if they are fit to be slaves. What was the need to force them to use the Enfield rifles, which require tearing the greased cartridge with the teeth? Any blind man can know the grease is made from fat. Cow or pig, aren't both sensitive to the native people? After being in this country for decades, if you don't understand Hindus are sensitive of killing cows and Muslims hate pork, then you don't deserve to rule them. This's where I could have made a difference had I been an officer in the Company. But I am a woman. And a woman cannot be an officer, or even in the army. Girls get an education so that they can be better wives.

Just before leaving The Residency, I stood at my only favourite location of Colin's home—the full-length mirror. I had already discarded my clothes, including undergarments. I did not know when I would get a chance again to change into a fresh, clean dress. So, I decided to put on clean clothing before leaving.

The nude woman in the mirror smiled at me. My hands ran down slowly over my neck and then over my breasts. I felt as if a beautiful young man was making love to me. Heat flowed between my thighs. I moaned and gently massaged my breasts. Suddenly my hand touched the wounds at the bottom side of both the bubbies, and I yelped. The pain from the cigar wounds was still raw. At that moment, I became sure Colin didn't deserve me. He was the monster who regularly abused Nancy, as well. Her husband, a junior officer, had no guts to protest.

I should have known this before my marriage. But did I get the opportunity to even meet him? A year ago, I was in London, and he was in India. A bride was to be exported to him in a ship. My parents convinced me that I was getting a husband who is in a senior position and well off. I was happy, sort of.

The cigar marks were prominent on the bottom side, not visible in the mirror unless you lifted the breasts. Very clever man. Who knew if his ex-wife had similar cigar marks? Antonia. I doubt doctors doing post-mortem had even noticed those marks on Antonia's breasts. A chill passed through me, and I dressed—covered myself in a burqa and was ready to run out of the hell.

I think briefly of Nancy. She can't run away like me. Poor woman. She has two small children to look after. I miss her already and send a quick prayer for her safety.

I glance at Sehnaz, still talking to Sheru Pandey. I doubt she is a courtesan. I know Colin was a patron of some courtesan. Who knows? There are so many *kothas*. He might have been going to the *kotha* where Sehnaz may have been working and has sent her to follow me. Unlikely. How would he know that I was about to flee? Even Sona didn't know. All I told her was that I plan to visit some friend and will come back before Colin comes home next week. Only Nancy knows, and she wouldn't tell anybody. Otherwise, she would be in trouble.

My thoughts go to Rupen Naik, Chief General of the nawab's army. I had seen him when Nawab Wajid Ali Shah threw a reception for my wedding. I have also seen his wife. I am sure Sehnaz is not his wife. She might be a courtesan, and Rupen might be her patron. Now she is probably helping him after the Sepoy Mutiny started and providing him with secret information. Should I not be on the side of the British in this war? I am in a dilemma as I am fighting my own battle.

On the contrary, all other English people in India are fighting against rebels. If rebels win, they have to go back to England. Let them go back! Queen Victoria is not ruling over India. It is the Company which is controlling for its own profit. I am sure that Queen Victoria, if she gets all the correct information, will side with the rebels against the Company. After all, she is a woman. If I survive and reach England somehow, I will try to contact her and tell her the ground truth of India.

An unease licks through me. I glance at Sehnaz; a serious expression has been plastered on her face.

She comes to me. "Where are you planning to go?"

I don't have a ready answer. My reply needs convincing. She shouldn't think I am any sort of informer of the Company. I already ruined the trust when I told her my surname, Lawrence. Moments ago, I was thinking about Nancy. I close my eyes and pretend I am her. Opening my eyes, I meet her gaze. "I am a junior officer's wife. His senior is using me as his sex slave—that too, with my husband's consent. And I am living in hell and fleeing. Maybe the timing is wrong. The mutiny is burning the country. But I would have died otherwise."

Was this a suitable answer?

Her gaze is fixed on me. Lasering me. I feel powerless. Last night I had helped her by giving her a ride. Today, she is assisting me in travelling alongside her on this ferry. And yet a wave of mistrust stands between us.

She turns and goes back to Sheru. I can't listen to what is transpiring, my heart whumps too loudly. She returns within a moment.

"Mutiny? Wrong." She corrects my words— "Freedom movement. Your country's people are exploiting us. Ruining our religious belief."

Relief washes over me. Thank God this is not about who I am. This is about the English in general.

"I totally agree with you, Sehnaz. They are demons. They don't deserve to rule here. The Company is ruling over India." I mix as many Urdu words as possible with English, and I seriously hope that she understands what I say.

"Hm hmm," she responds, and my nerve cools down a bit.

"You know, Sehnaz! A woman is ruling over England," I say, expecting some positive expression from her. When I don't see anything, I change my wording. "Woman. Woman queen of England. No king ruling. Queen ruling." I touch my long hair.

She smiles. "I know. We had Razia Sultana ruling over India six hundred years ago."

"Women rulers are good." I smile back at her.

She sits down near me. I feel much better and direct my gaze to the open blue sky—time to relax. My eyes follow a company of parrots flying. For a moment, I think I am free, like the birds. Suddenly I sight a small patch of a dark cloud in the distant horizon, and my heart sinks.

Sheru shouts, and my gaze follows his pointing his finger. A large boat with the Union Jack is coming our way. Briefly, I think this is my only fear. But the steamer comes nearer.

A dark feeling shimmers through me. My game is now over.

CHAPTER 3

"Are you noticing the same thing as me?" A sense of unease feathered through Sehnaz's chest.

"That is the Union Jack. I am not sure if that is an ordinary boat, or if it has soldiers inside." A quiver shot through Amelia as she stood up. Her features were guarded.

Sehnaz shot accusations through her gaze. Amelia stared at the floor like a statue, tears pooling in her eyes.

"Trust me, Sehnaz. I have nothing to do with the fight. I am running away from my own plight. I swear."

"*Firangis* are coming. Be careful, madam," Sheru yelled.

"*Firangi* means foreigner. English. Local term," Sehnaz explained to Amelia.

"I understand."

Sehnaz didn't want to delay. She had already thought about how to handle situations like this. She crouched down. Opening her trunk, she took out sarees and bangles. Within moments, she stripped out of her *choli* and skirt and started unfolding one of the sarees.

Amelia snatched a piece of cloth and held like a curtain in front of her. "You are nude, and anyone can see you." Amelia hinted at Sheru through her eyes.

A laugh blurted out of Sehnaz's chest. "Poor man has been away from his family for months and doesn't know if, after the war, he will go back in one piece. Let him get an eyeful." She glanced outside. Sheru dipped his gaze to his rudder, trying hard to hide his smile.

"This blouse wouldn't fit you," Sehnaz said and took out a piece of cloth from her suitcase. "This is a *kanchuka*—a short, shoulder-less blouse. We need to go into disguise. Save ourselves from the *firangis.*"

Amelia removed her top, and Sehnaz wrapped the *kanchuka* around her chest. "It fits you nicely. See, your chest looks round and proud now."

"I love this pink colour. Am I now looking like a courtesan?" Amelia asked.

Sehnaz looked at her in amazement.

"I am sorry. I am not aware of Indian clothing. I think we need to hide our faces from them. Let's get into our burqas."

"That wouldn't help. Your soldiers are aware of it. Many men also try to hide inside burqas, and I am sure soldiers will lift our veils and find out who we are. Better to wear sarees and look like Hindu married woman. Then cover the face with the loose end of the saree and pretend you are a woman in purdah." Sehnaz draped Amelia with another saree.

Sheru had to stop the boat. The British ferry came parallel to theirs, and a commander jumped inside, hanging a gun on his shoulder. Sehnaz and Amelia stood side by side. Amelia moved closer to Sehnaz; she was shaking.

Sehnaz whispered, "Try to stand confidently. In any case, do not show your face. If they know you are a white woman, everything will get out of hand. They will think Sheru and I have kidnapped you and may even kill us."

Sheru was pleading with the officer— "Sir, they both are from respected Hindu families. I am taking them to their in-laws' place in Faizabad. As per custom, they are not supposed to talk to outside males, not even to me. Please let us travel. We need to arrive before evening."

"Where is the map? I need it. Now. Comply immediately, or else no one will survive."

With folded hands and knees down, Sheru pleaded again, "We do not understand the word even, Sir. We have nothing to hide. We are loyal citizens of the East India Company, the British."

Sehnaz tried to stand composed. *Good lie, Sheru, do not say anything about the map. That is more important than our heads.*

The officer, without a word, began pummelling Sheru's face with his fists. Sheru didn't defend himself, only begged for compassion. Then the man scoffed and started leisurely wandering around the boat as if there were no war, and he was simply enjoying another holiday. Sehnaz noticed that a few other soldiers in the British ferry had removed their trousers, rotating them around their shoulders and dancing, showing the fingers at them.

Amelia whispered, "You understand anything?" Her voice was quivering.

"No. What are they saying?"

"They are asking this man to bring those two women, and we will have fun."

Sehnaz felt a lump in her throat. She placed her arm on Amelia's shoulder, brought her face near her ear. "We need to jump. Jump into the river."

"Do you know how to swim?"

"No. But it is better to die than to be raped. I can sleep with a man when I love him. But I cannot tolerate any man forcing me to do something. I mean anything, not only rape." Sehnaz inched slowly to the side of the boat. The men in the British vessel were shouting as if some party were going on. The officer in their boat abruptly lurched toward Sehnaz and grabbed her arm. She whimpered. *I'll rather die but never admit about the map.* She clenched her jaws, fighting back tears. *Rupen should be here, he would notice how I didn't submit to this English pig.*

"Here you go, my boys," he shouted at his men in the British ferry. "You will love this scene." He jerked off Sehnaz's saree.

The men on the English side shouted, "More, more!"

Sehnaz yanked and yipped in desperation, the darkness growing in her gut.

"Here you go." The man caught the front portion of her blouse and snatched it with such force that it ripped into pieces. Sehnaz tried to cover her bare chest with the other hand, but the man got hold of her breasts and laughed loudly as if he were holding a trophy. "Love these ripe-fruits, boys? This woman is the lover of a powerful officer of the Nawab Wajid Ali. See her destiny? Her respect is now dangling outside her blouse."

His people cheered and shouted, "Bring her here. We all will see how that trophy feels."

Sehnaz whimpered again and opened her eyes. A fire glinted in Amelia's eyes. Then she gazed at Sheru. His mouth was agape, tears rolling down his cheeks. "This is not time to cry, Sheru. Do something!" she yelled.

Someone shouted from the other boat, "A slight move, and my bullet will tear you into pieces." His rifle pointed right at Sheru.

Suddenly, gunshots tore through the atmosphere. Another boat had appeared and started firing at the British soldiers, who were caught completely unprepared. They didn't even have time to get hold of their own ammunition. Some of them were raising hands above their heads to surrender. But the rebel soldiers who were hiding in the goods ferry didn't spare any of them. Blood pinked the clean, blue water of the Gomti.

Amelia had covered her face and was crying. But before Sehnaz could help her, the officer in their boat grabbed Sehnaz and held a knife against her neck. The rebels in the other vessel all stood still.

The officer commanded, "Drop your guns, or else I will finish this woman."

All the arms of the rebels fell on the ground.

Sheru Pandey continued crying. "Sir, please let us go. We don't know who those men are."

"Shut your bone box, you bastard servant!" the officer shouted. "Motherfucker. Come and lick my shoes first. Then take the boat close enough to the other boat and collect their guns."

A trembling Sheru came to touch the officer's shoes. Sehnaz was shivering with her gaze down. She heard a growl, and the ice-cold blade pressed against her neck suddenly disappeared. She opened her eyes and saw Sheru sitting on the officer's chest, fisting him ruthlessly. The man was trying to get rid of his steel grips and attack him with his knife. But Sheru got hold of his head and twisted it violently; blood streaked down the man's face. "Go to the hell, you *firangi* motherfucker. Sehnaz's flesh isn't that cheap." Sehnaz grabbed the saree from the floor and covered her chest. She sighed with relief as her eyes raked over the dead British officer. This was the first victory in the war of freedom.

Amelia was shivering while standing in a corner. The rebels' boat came nearer, and a man jumped in. Sheru stood and saluted. The man saluted Sehnaz and said, "General Rupen Naik has sent me."

She immediately went to her suitcase, brought a neatly folded paper, and handed it over to the man. "Tell Rupen, he can now throw this East India Company into the Gomti River and free the country from the white."

Map

British-India in 1857

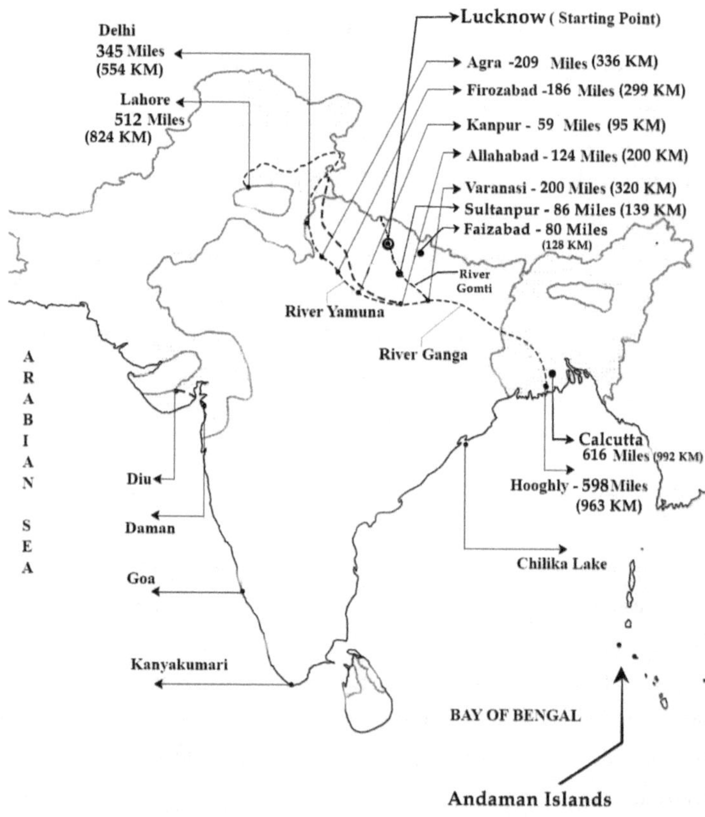

CHAPTER 4

27 May 1857, Afternoon
Amelia

My mind marvels. Who is this Sehnaz? Even the officers of the Indian Army recognise her and salute her! Is she one of the queens of Nawab Wajid Ali?

Amelia, will you ever get to this position like Sehnaz? Envy haunts me.

Sheru Pandey is not an ordinary boatman, he is a soldier. Maybe a senior commander. I don't really know. After the bloody battle in the Gomti River, Sheru Pandey advises not to travel any farther and to take a break. The fight between the Company's army and the nawab of Awadh has intensified, and the journey is not safe anymore. We take shelter in a hermitage on the banks of the Gomti, close to Faizabad.

I am yet to be comfortable with Sehnaz. I have hardly anything to hide, other than my husband, or estranged husband, is none other than Colin Lawrence. Brigadier in the East India Company army. I don't think it is me, though. Instead, Sehnaz is not comfortable with me. Last night I had favoured her by giving her a safe ride with me. Now, she feels obligated to repay me by taking me with her to Varanasi.

Travelling to Varanasi. The words bring a smile to me. I am thrilled thinking I can somehow reach Calcutta and board a ship. But I should wait until this fight is over. Otherwise, my so-called independence will be another casualty of the war.

I would have been easily captured had the British soldiers not been ambushed by the rebels. Look how the situation changes at the drop of a hat. Just a day ago, I would have empathised with the death of any English man—my own blood, own race. But I am sure now that I would have been the most excellent catch of the day. The English soldiers would have taken me back to Lucknow and bagged a fabulous prize from my husband. I know how shrewd Colin is. He would blame the rebels for kidnapping an English woman.

But the sword is still hanging over my head.

I have been running since yesterday, have hardly gotten any sleep last night or the whole day today. I am still wearing the saree Sehnaz had draped around me and covering my head with the *pallu,* the loose end of the cloth. The news that a white woman has taken shelter in the *ashram* can spread faster than a forest fire. My white skin can probably be explained—many Indian women also have fair skin, so they could be mistaken for white. Only...my blonde hair stands out.

I try to write in my diary, sitting underneath a tree on the Gomti's bank. And yes, I am also learning some new Urdu words. Ashram means a hermitage, in the local language. Holy men like hermits live in ashrams. I laugh. For Hindus, so many things are holy. Trees, rivers, cows—all are holy, and they worship them. Even women are sacred.

I have read about wars in books. Today, I had the experience of a lifetime, witnessed the combat and blood so close to me.

Experience of a lifetime? I wonder. I already have a lifetime experience of *life* itself. My mind flies back to my childhood days in England.

I was Amelia Elliott. The only sister to three brothers. I remember when I was around seven, my father would ask my brothers what they would be when grown up. I would jump in before my brothers said anything— "I will be an officer, a big officer in the army." My father would laugh, and my mother would frown. The difference between boys and girls was blurry to me at that age.

That blurriness went away when a new school session began after the vacation. We all got new books for starting education in the next higher grade. I noticed I didn't have a maths book, and I commented to my father, "You have forgotten one book for me."

"Which one, darling?" he asked.

"Maths."

He smiled. "That is not taught to girls, my dear. Maths is a boy's subject only." Dad assured me I could study maths at home.

My younger brother jeered at me, "You are a girl. You are a girl."

"So what if I am a girl? I will study maths," I complained and jumped onto him with my fists.

My mother dragged me away. "You are very young, darling. You will understand when you grow up."

It took me longer to understand that girls' education was different than boys'. I was in high school then. The curriculum for girls was music, Latin, Greek, and classes in graces and etiquette. I got angry inside at those who had decided girls can't study maths and science. After my first puberty, my mother explained to me, "Girls go to school only to become a good wife. You are lucky you are going to high school. Girls in the past just learnt how to read and write. You are fortunate, some wise men decided girls should be given high school education so that mothers can teach their boys. At the same time, they also can be better wives."

I suffocated. *Better wives?*

My father was different. He had supported me when I rode horses, learnt swimming, and even played with boys. Sometimes I had dreamt I should have been a boy. Not that I had boyish qualities, but I envied the independence boys enjoyed. I envied the attention young men of marriageable age got from families of prospective brides. I imagined myself working in an office and junior people saluting me, showing respect.

I had heard some widows in India are cremated alive along with their dead husbands. I dreamt of becoming a female knight, fighting with men and saving the unfortunate widows from being burnt alive. I would be famous for giving new lives to those widows.

But the stark reality was, I was joining the aspirant young women looking for eligible men. The qualities of a suitable girl were: she should be beautiful, she should be educated enough to take care of a family, and she should be a loyal wife.

When a proposal came from a man called Sir Colin Lawrence, a senior officer in the army of the East India Company, I agreed happily. I saw my mother proudly announcing her daughter was so beautiful and capable that she had been selected in the first instance amongst more than a dozen girls lined up for Sir Lawrence.

I started dreaming of my would-be husband as a dynamic, young, handsome knight fighting against uncivilised brown demons of India, and maybe had even saved some women from torture and death. Later on, I understood it was a propagation by churches to spread Christianity. But I dreamt to be an empowered woman from the west enlightening the lives of many women of India and keep my name in the history books. Obviously, wedding Colin would make that come true.

Colin didn't come to England for the wedding. Instead, I boarded a ship leaving for Calcutta.

It seems like yesterday—not a year ago—when I started the voyage from England to Calcutta in the bride ship. Funny, bride ship. Half of the vessel was full of prospective brides, literally imported by East India Company for their young and unmarried English employees. No one was aware of who their future husband would be except one girl, me, because my marriage was already fixed. Six months of travel time from London to Calcutta was so long that no young officers could go back to the home country and find a wife. The bride import had an unwritten rule—beautiful girls went to the high rank officers, and the others to low grade employees.

Colin received me at the Calcutta port, where we met for the first time. The man of my dream was standing in front of me, with a smile on his face. He was not as handsome as I had thought, but he was okay. He was looking a bit aged. An army officer in a hot country was bound to burn his young skin anyway. Regardless, this man and I would change the world together, and I realized I was smiling back. The next morning, I officially became Mrs. Lawrence in the famous St. John's Church. The same day we began our journey to Lucknow in River Ganga. I was literally impatient to start my dream life in Lucknow.

I was greeted with a royal reception, thrown by none other than Nawab Wajid Ali Shah, the day we arrived at Lucknow.

I spent two hours dressing. For the first time, I met Nancy. A charming lady, maybe five to seven years older than I, and with two children. She seemed to be quite accustomed to Colin's house. I found enough cosmetics in Colin's home; I didn't have to unpack my luggage and take out the cosmetics my mother had gifted me with the assurance they would last for years. She was afraid there might not be a good enough market in an uncivilised country like India for a young woman's day-to-day needs. I expressed my surprise and pleasure that Colin was so sensitive to his future wife's needs, as he had organised almost everything a young woman would want. Nancy helped me look my best, along with a young Indian woman who was working as our maid—Sona. Her husband, Chetan, was our security guard.

I remember a massive painting of a palace hanging on the wall. Sona pointed at it and said, "Qaisarbagh Palace. Reception, you going." My eyes rolled skyward—such a magnificent building! I thought, *Nawab Wajid Ali must be a wealthy businessman. Buckingham Palace is nothing compared to this.*

Colin arrived, having to prepare for the evening party. When he came to the dressing room, Sona covered her head with the loose end of her saree. Colin stared at me, head to toe. "The king would like you to wear your wedding dress."

"Wedding dress? For the reception?" I asked. "But why?"

"He is the king. No one asks *why* to a king."

"We are going to the house of a nawab, the wealthy businessman, I suppose."

Colin laughed. "Nawab means the king. He is the king of Awadh, and Lucknow is his capital."

My gaze went to the picture of the splendid palace on the wall. I was about to say something but noticed Colin's gaze was directed somewhere else. I took the time to follow. He was literally staring at Nancy's chest. She pretended to be unaware, glancing elsewhere. Sona was looking at the floor and fiddling with my worn dress which she was about to fold. Suddenly a silence swelled in the room. Within a minute, Colin came back to his senses and gazed at me. I also pretended to be unaware. I got a jolt but decided not to allow that moment to ruin my evening.

Colin went to his room to get ready himself, and Nancy helped me change into my wedding gown. I stole a few glances at her. She was beautiful with slender, smooth, and toned legs. Her bubbies bounced while walking.

Folding my dress, Sona put it in the wardrobe. I noticed women's garments stacked inside. Curiosity forced me to check them, and I got another setback. Those were worn dresses. I glanced at Sona as if she were responsible for an answer. She was the maid, must have seen this before. Her guilty gaze avoided me, focussing on the floor.

Nancy smiled. "They are his ex-wife's. She is dead."

I reacted as if Colin had committed a great sin. "He was married before?"

"Nothing wrong, Amelia. I was a widower before," Colin replied when I asked him on the way to the palace.

I understood. I tried to convince myself that time didn't permit to communicate so many things. The distance between England and India was just too much—six months of sea journey. I couldn't ruin the evening party in the Qaisarbagh Palace.

Confusion gripped me just before the reception. I had been told the British were ruling over India. What was the nawab ruling over? Colin imparted my first lesson about real India.

"India has many kings. British East India Company is alive because of infights between them. Our people are experts in keeping those differences alive. In return, the Company not only survives, but thrives. But there is news that a strong undercurrent has started against us, and it can flare up at any time. All British residents have been told to be extra careful and vigilant. And senior officials have been advised to augment their friendly relationship with the kings."

Colin probably knew the British was sitting on a volcano, which might erupt at any time.

I rolled this information over in my head the rest of the way to the Quaisarbagh Palace.

The royal reception sent me to the seventh heaven. For a girl who had never met the royals of England, it was like a fairy-tale evening. The whole palace was decorated with lights. I met the nawab and two of his four queens, Begum Hazrat Mahal and another. I forgot the name.

Had I not met General Rupen Naik that evening, my first night with Colin could have been different.

General Rupen Naik and his beautiful wife. Young, attractive, charming, tall, dark hair and ... I am not talking about his wife. No other adjective could describe Rupen.

When I shook hands with King Wajid Ali and his queens, Rupen was smiling at me from a distance. Some magical force pulled me when I reached him, and I extended my hand. He looked hesitant and stole a glance at his wife. Before I could decide otherwise, my hand was already in his. Was I such a slow thinker?

An exhilarating shiver ran through my lady bits as I stood like a statue, and my heart made a sensual flip. Two pairs of eyes glowered at me: Rupen's wife and Colin. Embarrassment washed over me. I was the chief guest of the party hosted by a wealthy king. Coming back to Colin's side, I sat as gracefully as possible. My heart sank when I focussed on

Colin. He was plump and short. Didn't I notice this when I met him in Calcutta for the first time? He was okay, until I saw and compared him with Rupen. Rupen? Oh, my! Why did I agree for a match across seven oceans, just to be the wife of a wealthy, high-ranking officer?

The silence in the horse cab was louder than the hoofbeats of the horses. Colin opened his mouth. "You are not supposed to shake hands with Indian men. This Rupen, he is a womaniser. He has concubines. Stay away from him."

The silence was my reply. I wished to ask Colin how he could stare at a junior colleague's wife—her bubbies. My mouth went dry.

Chetan saluted us at the gate, and Sona welcomed us with a big smile on the doorsteps. She guided me to my bedroom, which was decorated with scented flowers. Sona locked the door from inside, and without a word, she started unbuttoning my clothes. I was not used to this. My parents were middle-class people, and we did our chores ourselves. But I had been told I would live like a queen in India.

"Tired?" she asked.

I nodded.

Talking to me in her broken English, Sona guided me to the bathroom. Two large candles lit the room, and I noticed my nude self in the clean water of the tub. A pleasant perfume titillated me. I quickly clambered inside the bathtub and spread my legs, resting my head on the edge. Sona took a block of soap and rubbed it on my shoulders and neck. I touched her saree and said, "Wet."

She stripped her saree and hung it on the door hook, then came back with a smile and the soap, wearing only a blouse and underskirt. I closed my eyes, anticipating the indulgence while she rubbed the scented soap across my breasts, stomach, and between my thighs—virgin's flower. I fantasised about a beautiful young man. As a loyal and devoted wife, I tried my best to visualise Colin. But each time, Rupen trespassed.

Sona might have provided a similar service to Colin's ex-wife. The thought gave me a jolt. Sona's blouse and underskirt were entirely wet.

Her areolas and nipples poked through the thin, damp top. This reminded me of Colin's uncivilised gaze on Nancy earlier in the evening. "You are getting delayed. Go home now." I splashed water over the side of the tub as I stepped out.

She took a towel and patted me dry. "No sleep. Fan. All night. Hot."

I didn't understand, but I let it go because Sona had scurried to the wardrobe and brought me a new dress and undergarments. She helped me dress, and halfway through, I stopped her and asked, "Ex-wife's?"

"No, new. For you, *Sahib*."

That I understood. Colin had bought a new dress for me. He was so thoughtful toward his new wife!

As soon we got into the bedroom again, she pointed at the ceiling fan and strings attached to it. "Rope go guard cabin. Guard, husband, my, mine. He guard, all night. I pull string, night to morning. You, good sleep."

I was staring at her when impatient knocks sounded on the door. Sona carefully covered her bosom with the saree and opened the door for Colin.

This would be our first night together.

All last week, I had been travelling in an uncomfortable ferry. Now I have to be ready for my first night with Colin. Can't it wait one more day? It was already past midnight!

Grabbing my arm, Colin spun me. I whimpered in pain and smelled alcohol on his breath. He yanked my hair down and brought my face to his lips. Since childhood, I had always dreamt about the taste of the first kiss. I tried to look natural. After all, this was my first night with my husband—a moment to cherish for life. Something I could write in my diary without the graphic details. I moaned into his mouth, trying to forget the pain. His tongue pushed through the opening, and he started exploring. He was married before and must be an expert in making love. His hormones were flying wildly. I felt his erection on my groin.

Colin's hand ran over my bubbies, squeezing like they were made of dough. "Gently, please," I pleaded.

"Ripe fruits. Mine. Both are mine. Your whole body is mine." He laughed like a character in a horror drama. He was drunk.

For the first time, I felt as if I were a domestic animal, bought by my owner from overseas to satiate his desire.

He tried to unhook my frock but became impatient after two attempts. Gripping the dress, he jerked hard. My robe was torn but was still strong enough to hang on to my hips. Colin's other hand went between my thighs and pulled down my underwear. I cooperated, removing my frock, and looked at the torn part.

"Don't worry, I will buy new ones for you." Colin started undressing. Taking me to his chest, he kissed me again—this time gently. Heat pooled between my thighs. I touched him and moved my hands over him as if my dream of first love had come true. As soon as he started sucking my nipples, I moaned. "Oh, Rupen, more please."

I woke up to an explosive roar. "You bitch! That bloody Indian. He is nothing! He is not a white man. Bloody uncivilised."

I could not believe the blunder I had just done, and I apologised profusely. Dreaming about another man on the first night with my husband was a heinous sin. He stared into my eyes. I glanced down, guilt washing through me.

"You are a bitch," he howled again and pushed me hard. I fell on the bed and started weeping. He left the room and never came back the whole night.

Why did I say Rupen's name?

The next morning, he came back to the room. "You bitch, did you dream of that dark-skinned man the whole night?"

"I am sorry. Truly sorry. I didn't do it consciously. I was tired and couldn't think. Apologies," I cried. I was genuinely repenting. How could I offend my husband, who is a hero, a Brigadier General? It was all my fault. Unforgivable.

"I can never forgive you." Colin removed his belt. I shivered and closed my eyes as he swung it, each lash destroying the fairy tale marriage I had dreamt of.

"Colin, please, please! You are hurting me! I promise, I will never make that mistake again."

"Mistake?" The belt again sliced through my skin. "Sin, you committed the sin. You will rot in hell. This is the hell for you." He finally stopped when I fell on the floor and stomped out.

Sona came to the room after he left home. I was still lying on the floor. She helped me up onto the bed and applied some ointment on my wounds. "Sahib, angry. Antonia Mem, Sahib beating."

I opened my eyes and glanced at her. "You work the night shift. You must be tired. Please go home and get some rest."

"No home, Memsahib. You care... careful. This bottle—" she showed me the ointment— "hide. Antonia Memsahib got. Her. Sahib angry. Very angry." She wept as she applied the soothing salve on the fresh wounds.

So Colin beat his ex-wife, too. Despair washed throughout my entire bruised and welted body. Yes, this time it was my fault. But what did Antonia do?

"Memsahib," Sona whispered as if she were going to say something confidential. "Antonia Memsahib, letter, with me, English, no read, bring."

"What letter Sona? This ointment is good, will help me. What will I do with the letter?"

"Memsahib. I no read. Gov...govern...can't say. Yes, general. Letter. English. You read. I bring."

"Sona, please. I can't understand. I'm tired. I can't read anything now. Please."

Everything became normal after that. Or it appeared so. I cooked for him and welcomed him with a lively smile when he came back from work—the way I had been taught by my mother. We would have regular sex. I accepted all that had happened as if it were a bad dream. But only for a few weeks.

Those quiet moments were short-lived, a calm before the storm. Colin began finding fault with everything, and no matter what I tried, I couldn't make him happy. My best efforts to be a better and more submissive wife had no result in reducing his anger.

He had been having an extramarital relationship with Nancy, the wife of his subordinate. But it was not a relationship. Instead, he forced himself on Nancy against her wishes. That was what I heard from the gossips in the officers' wives club. In addition, Nancy has a five-year-old son who looks like Colin. Similar eyes and nose. I was scared to face the boy as if I were the guilty person.

Whenever he was spending time with Nancy, her husband would wait in the guard's cabin with Chetan. And I knew what my husband was doing. I would wonder, *Why did he even order a bride from England if he has Nancy to abuse and manhandle? Am I just a showpiece for the society?*

One night, he came home late. I decided to do my best to lure my husband back. Wearing sexy clothes and decorating the bedroom with flowers and candles, I created an environment for love. Sona was with me when Colin entered the home. At first, he said, "Tonight you are looking so beautiful, Amelia. I love you. Really love you," when I hugged him. I kissed him, even though Nancy's perfume mocked me from his chest.

I took the initiative for making love. I was truly hungry for that. I had compromised everything and was ready to accommodate him with anything to make my life normal. I was still angry with him for visiting Nancy, but I kept it supressed. But that night, after my repeated attempts, his shaft behaved like a sleepy snake. I didn't want him to be embarrassed and continued my effort to make it hard with my sexy touch. After a few minutes, when I met his gaze, he was glowering at me.

"You doubt my manhood, you bitch?"

I didn't understand how I had expressed any doubt on him. I still tried my best to save him from the humiliation. Removing my top, I pressed my breasts on his chest and pulled his hand to touch my nipples. "Does it feel better?"

"Are you comparing yours with Nancy's?" He shoved me, and I fell on the bed.

"I'm not," I cried. Honestly, I wasn't; I meant if his member was getting enough warm blood to harden. I got up and held his shaft again, trying to bring warmth in it.

"You do not understand a thing!" Colin grabbed my neck. Then he ran away to the adjacent bedroom, leaving me alone. I thought for a minute. I had offended him by asking the right thing at the wrong time. He felt I was comparing my breasts with Nancy's. Hers are larger than mine. Could I save the situation?

I walked to the other bedroom in another attempt to recover his mood. He was smoking a cigar. I realised late that the hot blood, instead of flowing to his love handle, went to his head and aroused the beast in him.

He grabbed my breasts.

"It is hurting Colin, please."

"Have you come here to tell me I am impotent? Huh? What is in these breasts?"

He pushed me on the bed, holding one of my breasts in one hand and his cigar with the other. I'd no clue what he was going to do. Was his penis ready now to enter inside me? I closed my eyes. A sudden burning sensation on my left breast made me jump on the bed.

"Ah! Colin, what are you doing? Leave me. For God's sake, please leave me!" I screamed, holding my breast and running to the bathroom.

Colin grabbed my hair and pushed me on the bed again. "This looks odd only on one breast, darling. You should wear jewelleries on both." He pressed the cigar on my right breast, too. I screeched. He pressed his palm on my mouth. "Stop howling, you bitch. Or else I will finish you."

Colin left the room.

I stayed alone that night, lying on the bed and weeping. I wanted to go back to my parents. At around midnight, I heard footsteps in my room. I pretended to be asleep, in an attempt to avoid another assault. When a soft hand touched me, I opened my eyes. Sona was standing with a bottle.

"Ointment. Heal. Do not cry, ma'am."

She raised my breast and rubbed medicine. How did she know?

"Antonia, ma'am. Same. No argue, live. Argue, die. Pray God."

Antonia... How did she die? Did she really commit suicide like I had heard? What was Sona insinuating? I didn't have courage to ask her. Colin might have heard from the other room. I knew then that I must behave to stay alive.

Dusk is slowly creeping in. I glance at the river. The waters of the Gomti look pinkish-blue, and a fresh wave of wind soothes my nerves. My gaze goes all the way to the gate of the ashram. An Indian soldier standing by his horse is in conversation with Sehnaz. Must be a rebel and joined the Sepoy Mutiny.

Myriads of thoughts cross my mind. I have always been told that Indians, especially women, are mostly illiterate and lead a miserable life. For example, Sati—the term they use for burning the widows alive. But Sehnaz is also a widow, and she is very much alive and lively. My childhood dream has always been to earn respect like any man in a high-ranking position, to become an officer. I would like to ride horses like men, too. Instead, I am just a housewife of an over-dominating husband. He decides when and how to have sex. I am just a female body for him. He owns me—my foot.

The soldier salutes Sehnaz and rides away on his horse. Unknown envy whips through me. I bury my head between my knees. This woman is an exception. Millions of women in this country are still rotting in the darkness of poverty and illiteracy. But all my dreams of bringing light in the lives of these women have been buried in the grave Colin has dug for me.

"You all right?" Sehnaz is standing in front of me.

"Yes, a bit tired," I reply and try to hide my tears.

CHAPTER 5

28 May 1857, Morning
Amelia

I notice a horse tied to a tree. Maybe the same soldier who came yesterday to meet with Sehnaz has come again. But Sehnaz isn't here, she has gone to the market with Sheru. Then who is here on the horse? My heart stills. I look at it carefully; it is unquestionably a warhorse.

This morning I had told myself, "Amelia, you will spend peaceful days here in the ashram before you start another journey to Varanasi and then to Calcutta."

Last night, the ashram was peaceful and event-free. The ashram is small with only two rooms. Sehnaz and I occupy the only spare space available while Sheru has settled on an open veranda. The small temple facing the river is opposite the main house. The hermit or priest is an old man, probably in his seventies. Last night we ate our first meal, cooked by the priest. Sheru Pandey was his assistant. I am told that Sheru is a Brahmin, a high caste Hindu. Non-Hindus are not allowed to cook for Hindus. Sehnaz is Muslim, and I am a Christian. We are supposed to be inferior. I remember how our English people treat non-whites as low. I laugh in my mind. Whites think brown people are mediocre, Brahmins think other castes are inferior. What sort of culture is this?

When we sat down for dinner, Sheru placed banana leaves on the floor and floormats made from dry palm leaves opposite each banana leaf. I thought this was another religious ritual of the ashram. When he started serving steaming rice on the banana leaves, I exchanged a curious glance with Sehnaz. She smiled. "Aren't you hungry?"

For the first time, I ate like native people, sitting cross-legged on the palm leaf mat. Sheru also served some thick yellow liquid on the rice. Sehnaz explained to me, this was called *dal*. There was a third item, too —some cooked vegetables. When Sehnaz and Sheru started eating with their fingers, I imitated them. Otherwise, I would have had to go to bed hungry.

There was no proper bed or mattress. Sehnaz spread straw mats on the floor, and we both lay down. She muttered, "Don't worry about tomorrow. Today we have won a battle, gotten shelter and food on our plate. We are happy."

I replied, "No, food on our leaves."

We both laughed at my comment. I would have loved to talk to Sehnaz, but my eyelids started drooping. Even Sheru's loud snore from the veranda didn't affect me. When I woke up to the conch-shell horn in the morning, Sehnaz was already awake.

"The priest is blowing conch in the temple. It is part of the *puja*, worshipping the gods," said Sehnaz.

After two days since I left The Residency, I am smelling the fresh air of freedom. We have plans to stay almost a week here, until the fighting cools down and the route to Varanasi is safe. I could not accompany Sehnaz and Sheru to the market. A white woman with two Indians will stand out clearly, and Company spies will get the news.

I am still wearing a saree and trying to keep my head covered to hide my blonde hair. The priest is always busy in the temple. I take a leisurely stroll by the riverbank; no one will get curious at my blonde hair and white skin in a lonely place. On one side, the Gomti is flowing with its clean blue waters, and on the other is the ashram and its expanse of trees. Noticing the manmade steps leading to the river, I remember I have not taken a bath since this morning. Sehnaz said she would take me to the river for a dip after coming back. I think this might be the place she is referring to. A barricade made of timber logs separates a small portion of the river for safety—the barrier to high current and maybe crocodiles.

Now, I do not have the luxury of getting into new dresses after each shower. I have given some money to Sehnaz to buy a few pieces of saree. That will be my regular clothing until I get into a ship at Calcutta either to England or Australia.

The heat of the sun pinches my skin; it must be around ten a.m. I glance around and find no one—the bathing ghat must be for the ashram use only. Removing my saree, petticoat and blouse, I hang them on the twig of a tree and take quick steps into the water. A pleasant feeling passes through my skin. Suddenly, the world looks greener again.

Soap is a luxury. Swimming is possible, but the enclosure doesn't have enough space for that. Keeping my buttocks on one stone, I rest my head on another just above the water; my legs float like a feather. I move my hand slowly down my neck and onto my breasts. My nipples are hard. I moan and imagine a man's hot mouth sucking them and tickling between my thighs. Rupen appears in my fantasy. I cannot imagine Colin. It will spoil all the pleasure, even though only he has the moral right to do such things to me. Rupen has a wife. Maybe Sehnaz is his courtesan lover. It is possible that he is also a typical husband and treats his wife like Colin does. But all I need is the face of a man in my imagination. A man who is not dominating me, hitting me for any so-called mistake. Giving me all sorts of freedom that I have wanted since my childhood, and he still loves me. Is that possible in real life?

I scream, "I want my freedom, too. I want respect, too."

The echo comes back—me, too...me, too...

Maybe I am getting a false sense of independence by staying naked in an open space, and I have gotten too excited.

I am sitting here inside the water in my birthday suit. Enjoying freedom and peace. Is this too good to be true?

I see a ferry in the river. Sheru has anchored the boat nearby. My gaze goes toward the clear, blue sky. A small patch of a dark cloud passes at the far end down the river. My blood freezes. I hope it is just a hallucination.

I wait until the ferry passes and get off the natural, free-flowing bathtub. Sehnaz has said we will be here for days. Hopefully tomorrow I can come back here to bathe, but I don't know how I'll enter the water naked when probably both Sehnaz and Sheru will be around. And I don't have a swimsuit with me.

I look for my clothes. The twig of the small tree is just behind the bathing point. My heart hammers against my ribs when I notice they're not there. I hadn't seen them being blown into the river. Who knows, they might have washed away when I was daydreaming and closing my eyes. I curse my own carelessness. *Oh, God. I asked for liberty. You gave me freedom from my clothes?*

I glance around frenetically; the clothes are nowhere. I know there is only one man in the area, the old priest. Is someone playing mischief? Will I be raped in the next few moments?

I should run to the cottage. Hopefully, he is either praying inside the temple or cooking in the kitchen. I get to my feet, my legs wobbly. An unknown fear drags me back. My gaze goes to the banana plant, and I try to slit the banana leaf with my nail, but it comes out in multiple pieces. Holding one sheet against my chest and another in front of my groin, I lope toward the ashram, again hoping the priest doesn't notice me.

All of a sudden, my gaze falls on something inside the bush. The red colour pokes out of the green shrubs as if mocking my quandary. I gently use one hand to take the blouse out, still holding one leaf against my groin. As I start wearing the top, I notice the saree behind another tree. *Thank you, God. You saved me from a lifetime embarrassment.*

I scan the sky again; the sight of the dark cloud slams me back with a punch. I stride toward the ashram. My gaze goes from the horse to the shoes outside the priest's room. A British soldier is standing inside, talking to the old man.

Despair washes over my skin. I scurry behind a tree. How long can I hide? He must come to find me when the priest admits I'm here. I notice both Sheru and Sehnaz standing at the gate, looking keenly at the horse. As soon as I catch her attention, I hint to Sehnaz to instantly come to me.

"Why is the man here?" Sehnaz casts a nervous glance at the soldier and whispers, "Has he seen you?"

"I don't think." I pull the loose end of the saree and cover my head and face. I notice the fear in Sehnaz's eyes.

"We should get away before he gets the priest to confess we all are here, especially an English woman," Sehnaz says the moment she and Sheru arrive by my side.

"I am loading all provisions in the boat, let's get out now." Sheru starts striding toward the wharf.

"Wait, Sheru, let me think." Sehnaz stares intensely at the horse, and something dawns in her features.

I move my gaze back and forth, horse to Sehnaz, before I know what she's thinking. "I know how to ride a horse."

Sehnaz shoots a million-pound smile at me. "Sheru, run to the boat," she says without looking at him.

Fortunately, our suitcases are still inside the boat. Sehnaz changes into a salwar suit and takes out a pair of male clothing—trousers and a shirt. She also wraps a turban around my head after I finish dressing in them. "Cover your face with a kerchief. And Sheru, take the boat to the first town that you see."

Sehnaz and I both tiptoe to the horse while the soldier is inside the ashram with the priest. Untying the horse, I jump onto the saddle, Sehnaz mounting behind me. Adrenaline thumps through me. The horse whinnies as we take off toward the river, but I don't look back to see if the soldier has spotted us. I urge the beast to go faster.

We try our best to stay on the riverbank, keeping Sheru's ferry in our view. We run as if Company soldiers are following us.

After almost four hours, we make a halt. Hungry and exhausted, we lie down under a tree. The horse locates a pond nearby and goes to drink the water. I have no energy left to go with it. It comes back and starts grazing near us.

"I think we are near Sultanpur, but not sure. I will go to the market and bring something to eat," Sehnaz says.

"Let the horse finish his lunch first, we both will ride to the market." I feel like I am in charge, like a man. Sehnaz, the woman, is dependent upon me.

"No, I will go alone. British spies will easily recognise you; they are everywhere. We all will have a serious problem."

I watch helplessly as Sehnaz moves in confident strides. Maybe she is not dependent upon me, after all.

28 May 1857, Afternoon
Amelia

Exhausted, I lie back down on the lawn and watch the horse munching grass. I have at least an hour before Sehnaz returns from the market.

During the last forty-eight hours, I have fled my husband's house, witnessed the brutal ambush of a ferry-load of English soldiers, and stolen a warhorse from a British officer. I have also been associated with a woman who could face court-martial for unlawfully sourcing a confidential map and giving it to the rebels—a piece of paper that could spell disaster to the British rulers and change history. Adrenaline and guilt both stab me together, making a sandwich of me.

The slow breeze droops my eyes, and I close them.

Colin's growl shivers my spine.

"I love you so much. Do you understand that? Don't you want your husband to be promoted? Will you not enjoy your life when I bring more money home?"

A woman sitting on the floor has buried her head between her knees. I can't see her face. Who is this woman?

"I am not a whore, that I will sleep with anybody," the woman screams, her face still buried.

"Sleeping with just one man will not make you a whore. He gave me the promotion. And why do you forget that you are mine? You will do whatever I want. As a loyal wife."

Colin yanked her hair and forced her to the ground. The woman's face was not clear in the dim candlelight. But I could make out that her chest was naked. She started howling when Colin grabbed her bubbies.

"Nooooo. No Cigar again. Please. Please, I beg you. Leave me."

"Leave you? Why did you write a complaint letter to the Governor General? Do you understand I will lose my job? This is what you wish to do with your husband? Send him to the street?"

"I am sorry. Truly sorry. I will burn that letter."

"Do not worry, my darling. I will burn it. I don't want your husband to end up on the street. Begging. Would you like to be a beggar's wife?"

"No, please leave me. I want to go. Go to Delhi, to my parents. You do not deserve a bad wife like me. Give me a divorce. Please."

"So you can write another letter to the Governor General? Nice plan. Awesome!"

"I promise, I will not."

"All right, darling. You will go, but not to Delhi. You will go, you will..." Colin was pointing his fingers to the rafters.

Sehnaz's voice drags me out of the horrible dream. I am sweating.

Antonia? Was that woman in my dream Antonia?

I have never seen her photo. Did she commit suicide, or was she forced to hang from the ceiling? I have heard the rumour. Through Nancy. Colin was forcing her to sleep with his boss.

I recollect Sona saying something about a letter of Antonia. She was rubbing ointment on me after Colin had beaten me for calling him Rupen. I'd brushed it off. She wasn't able to say something clearly. Something like gov, yes, gov, I remember. And general. Governor General.

Did Antonia write a letter to the Governor General? Is that the one that came to my dream just now? Was that what Sona was trying to say? Oh Sona, why didn't you learn a little better English? Now it's too late, I've already escaped!

Sona's statement echoes in my ear. "Antonia ma'am. Same. No argue, live. Argue, die. Pray God."

I force a smile at Sehnaz.

She is back after almost an hour along with food and news that Sheru's ferry is ready at the wharf for our next journey. It is nearly evening. Sheru Pandey says that by travelling at night, we are safe from British scrutiny. Darkness can provide an effective shield from the enemy.

My glance, by mistake, goes upward, only to notice another black cloud in an otherwise clear sky. I am terrified, as if some banshee is coming. As Sehnaz and I approach the wharf, my mind goes to the horse I have stolen—it has the typical cut on the ears, I am sure this is a logo of the British Army. I suggest that we hide it somewhere or take it with us. "It is only a matter of time before the British locate their stolen horse."

Sheru nods in approval. Getting off the boat, he goes to the horse and guides it to the river brink to let it drink water.

Sheru is such a nice man!

He jumps onto the ferry.

"Will you not hide it somewhere?" I smile at him.

"I will."

"Where?"

He looks at the water, but I don't understand. He goes back to the rudder and kneels down, folding his hands. I think he's muttering some kind of prayer. I have seen him doing this in the temple. Is Sheru really such a religious man?

My gaze moves between Sehnaz and Sheru. A sad smile crosses Sehnaz's face. She looks down when I try to meet her gaze. I'm confused.

Sheru gets up with his rifle. Rifle? Did he notice an enemy soldier?

The small patch of dark cloud hovers overhead. I freeze.

Sheru stands still and points his rifle toward a tree, but I can't see anyone there. Is he practising how to fire?

His arms slowly turn. I fail to understand what he was aiming at. I inhale. Deeply.

Something clicks in my head. The rifle is pointed at the horse. "Sheru. Noooooo!"

I jump onto him and hold his arm, but the bullet had already left with a roaring bang. I literally fall on him with all my weight, but his strong arms hold me.

"I am sorry, ma'am."

My gaze goes to the horse. To the blood gushing from its body. I slump down, holding the sidedeck with a loud wail as if I lost a child. The horse had fallen in the river, splashing pink water everywhere.

Sehnaz's hand is on my shoulder. "It is all right, Amelia. People die in a war."

Sheru is standing with his hands folded, eyes down.

"Sheru, it's all right," Sehnaz says. "Delaying means attracting danger. Please hold your rudder, and let's move."

She wraps her arm around my shoulder and takes me inside the cuddy. I try to take a last glance at the horse. Its body is already hidden beneath the Gomti's water. Sheru was right! He promised to hide it.

Sheru holds the rudder and starts the engine.

I breathe heavily and stare blankly at the sky. Men are strong, they don't cry. I am a woman and am now weeping. Am I not strong?

CHAPTER 6

28 May 1857, Evening, Lucknow
Brigadier Colin Lawrence

The *tabla* and the *sarangi* both played with the *thumri*. The girl was dancing as if she were doing some sort of prayer. "Nonsense. Did I come here to watch this boring thing?" Colin muttered.

"Sir, this is the most popular amongst the elite of Lucknow. She imagines herself as a *Gopi*. You know what *Gopi* means? They are virgin lovers of Lord Krishna. I have heard Nawab Wajid Ali has invented this dance form—in his Qaiserbagh palace, where every year *Rahas* is staged. Nawab himself acts as Lord Krishna, and beautiful fairies dance as *Gopis*."

Ah! This man is boring. "I know. I was a royal guest at his *Rahas* last year. King? Huh! What else does he know other than singing and dancing with women?" Stretching his legs on the divan, Colin took another sip of wine from the silver glass. The blouse of the girl seemed better than her dance. The Urdu song hammered his tired ears, and he was exhausted after weeks of handling the rebels.

Colin glanced at his assistant, an Indian soldier, through the corner of his eye. He forgot his long name, something difficult to pronounce.

The Company had decided to change the duties of Indian sepoys frequently. Who knew when a man would switch allegiance to the rebels? No sepoy should have been with any senior officer for a long time—at least not long enough to understand his routine.

For more than a week, he had not visited his home in The Residency. Cantonment was practically his residence now. Three to four hours of sleep per night was an indulgence. Finally, the rebellion had slowed down, and he had carved out some time for a treat. A man needed some spice to recharge his energy.

Convincing the seniors that he could gather the much-needed information against the rebels by befriending the courtesans of Lucknow, Colin was able to get out of the dangerous and tiring war duty. Now he was in another battlefield where beautiful girls could be potent weapons in the civil war. The only problem was finding the right girl who could provide the right information. But he couldn't decide whose instruction to follow, his exhausted brain or his bulging groin.

This soldier is an idiot. Does he really know what I need? Rupen was so much more capable! Colin closed his eyes.

Rupen. His dear friend Rupen. Life was so much fun before this war. Rupen was the second most powerful man of the Awadh kingdom. He had so many bungalows. One for his family, the others for entertaining friends like Colin. He had spent so many colourful evenings with him. Colin could never forget the last evening just before the Sepoy Mutiny started.

Hundreds of tiny lamps had lit up the hall that evening, overlooking the Gomti River. Colin was seated on a divan leaning on a large, round pillow, with Rupen at his side leaning into another pillow. A maid entered with two designed silver glasses and a wine bottle.

"Made in Awadh," Rupen commented.

"What? This wine?"

"No, these silver glasses. Wine is made in England. Imported especially for our king and his royal friends."

"Your country can't make good wines, huh?" Colin joked.

"We have better wine than this, it can come walking to you on its own feet." Rupen laughed loudly.

"What? Wine can walk?"

"Why not? Look over there." Rupen laughed again.

Colin's gaze went to the curtain opposite the divan. An ankle slowly extended through the curtain and into the room, studded with ankle bells. The toes, dazzling with nail polish, gently danced on the floor. A bare leg followed the ankle. Then another bare leg, followed by a short skirt and bare belly. Colin's eyes were licking her, toe to belly, then the breastband appeared with two large ripe fruits poking shamelessly from inside. Two beautiful hands raised the curtain, and a fairy looking girl inched leisurely inside the hall.

"I told you, Colin, I will present to you the best dance you have ever watched."

Colin was in heaven.

The girl slowly walked as if she were dancing in slow motion and approached the divan. She took the wine bottle and filled the glasses. Holding one glass, she gave it to Colin. "You are the guest of honour today, Sir."

Colin couldn't decide whether he should watch her lovely, slender arms or the wine glass. The girl gave the second glass to Rupen and bowed her head.

"This evening," she said with a sensual voice, "is for his highness Rupen and his friend Colin."

The wine was fantastic. Something started tingling Colin's skin, and he wasn't sure if it was the wine or the girl.

The girl came again to him with dancing steps and refilled the half-empty glass. "Slowly, slowly, I will tingle your senses—" she moved her slender fingers on Colin's thighs—"and elate your soul."

She went back to the dance floor before Colin could react.

Ecstasy gradually overpowered Colin's senses. He leaned toward Rupen. "She has great diddies."

"What is that?"

"Bubbies, breasts." Colin giggled. "Hidden behind that breastband, but they are swinging perfectly, in rhythm with the dance steps."

Rupen chuckled. "Want to see better?" He indicated to the girl. She didn't stop dancing but came to him with rhythmic steps and bowed her head. Rupen held the knot behind her back and pulled gently. The silk breastband released from her chest and fell, revealing her breasts. The girl giggled and immediately went back to the dance floor.

"How are they? Love them?" Rupen asked.

"Is she Sehnaz, your courtesan lover?"

"Nah, Sehnaz is much better. But she wouldn't bare her bubbies like this girl. She is different."

"Your wife has no problem, Rupen?"

"Why? I can have more than one wife. Our king has four. Tradition. We men can enjoy. My wife knows about Sehnaz. They are friends. She is happy that I am not planning to marry her. Courtesans normally do not marry."

The girl came again to refill the glass. Colin gently touched her nipples. She giggled and cast a sexy glace at him. "Hungry?" she said and went back to dance again.

"Can I have her tonight?" Colin whispered to Rupen.

"I will give you better stuff. New. Large bubbies. She doesn't know how to dance."

"You are a great friend, Rupen." Colin finished the last drop of wine from the glass. The bulge in his groin could have burst anytime. "I will gift you the latest pistol made in England. With all the knowhow, so that you can make them here."

Colin's mind came back to the present, here in the *kotha*. Rupen was now the leader of the enemy camp. Those days are gone forever. He glanced at the sepoy again; the man is enjoying the dance. Is this sepoy dependable? Should he ask him to go out? That was a real problem. His knowledge of Urdu or Hindi was not enough to communicate correctly with the courtesan. Colin felt his own tongue moving over his lips along with the girl's steps.

"Stop." He stood up.

The girl stopped abruptly. The men who were playing the *sarangi* and the *tabla* also stilled, unarticulated fear in their eyes.

"Next phase of the performance," Colin ordered.

The sepoy translated into Urdu.

The courtesan girl looked confused. "Next, what?" Her voice was polite.

Colin whispered to the sepoy.

"Sir would like to sleep," the sepoy said.

Colin felt swelling between his thighs.

The girl looked straight into his eyes and said in broken English, "Sleep? Not here. Home. Go. Sleep."

Disappointment punched him hard. *Bloody mouse acting like a tigress! Damn, this mutiny.* He took out a bag of coins and showed them to the girl. "This is advance. I will pay more."

The woman was standing straight, gaze pinned at Colin. His heart stammered. He should have gathered more information about this *kotha* and its patrons. She might have been close to someone among the nawab's top officials.

The girl said again, "Here, only song. Only dance."

Frustration thrummed through Colin, and he rushed out of the mansion. The sepoy followed. "Sir, I know another place here. They will happily take your money and provide all the comforts you need."

"How far is that, sepoy?"

"Not far from here, Sir. It is inside a by-lane in a small house."

Colin jumped inside the horse carriage, and the sepoy took the cart onto a narrow lane. It looked like another city altogether. All his life, Colin had passed through the main wide roads of Lucknow, surrounded by large mansions, palaces, flourishing colourful markets, temples and mosques. He didn't know narrow and smelly localities were hiding shamelessly behind those spectacular sights. The wooden wheels of the cart jerked over the crevices of the mud road below. Colin held the side rod firmly, but he was in a hurry—he couldn't ask the sepoy to slow down.

Within minutes they arrived in front of a small, rundown building. The lane was engulfed in the darkness of the night. Colin's innards growled at the sight as he cautiously walked along the steps; he expected a foul smell inside. The light of a single candle showed the way to a narrow counter and a half-broken chair. The sepoy crept inside as Colin crammed his fatigued, broad body on the chair. The sepoy came back after a while with a big smile on his face. "Good news, Sir, I have done a special arrangement for you. I told them Brigadier Sahib is here to show favour. The chief courtesan agreed. She will entertain you with a virgin girl who has just arrived. Her age is hardly twe—"

"I don't have time to waste, sepoy." Colin's patience was running out; his back had started aching on the broken chair. He stood, grabbed the notes, and passed them over to him. "Take your tips out of it. Where is the room?"

An old woman came out and guided him to a cabin. Colin kicked the door shut and glanced around. *Where is that girl? That virgin or whatever?*

When a faint sobbing sounded from somewhere, he noticed something like a pile covered with a piece of cloth and inched closer. It was shaking. Colin felt a gut punch when he realised the saree-clad girl had buried her head between her knees and was blubbing.

"What is this nonsense?"

The girl raised her face and touched his feet, an act of showing deep respect. "Please, Sir, I go back, mummy, village."

Colin didn't have to take time to understand that the girl had been kidnapped and sold to the prostitution ring. This was her first night to entertain a client. Boasting about enjoying a virgin was a favourite drink time story with his friends in the club. Next time he could brag of this experience.

He closed his eyes and imagined. *You will get a virgin girl, Sir.* The sepoy's message sounded like music, making his groin hot and throbbing. He crouched to the girl and placed his palm on her chest. Her heart was beating loudly. Colin grabbed her boobs and pulled her up. "Stand."

She stood on her wobbly feet and glanced at him, tears flowing down her cheeks. No resistance, but hands folded.

Colin thought for a moment. He remembered his childhood experience of a butcher grabbing a lamb from the herd and attempting to slaughter it. The lamb was bleating as if pleading to spare it and let go. Colin had asked the butcher not to kill the animal. The butcher had replied, "Every time an animal is taken for slaughtering, it whines and tries to escape. Does that mean the entire mankind will turn vegetarian?"

"If every girl acted like you, we men would literally starve!" Colin jerked the saree off her and threw it on the floor.

The girl quivered and squatted to lift the saree. Colin stooped down, grabbing her blouse, and again said, "Stand here, you whore." He started unbuttoning her top. "Tiny boobs, huh." He pulled her to his chest, shucked himself out of his jacket, and forced his tongue in, trying to explore her mouth. A faint noise momentarily distracted him, but he focussed again on the girl. After all this time, he had finally gotten an opportunity for some leisure and entertainment. High Commands had allowed him only to come to a *kotha* to extract crucial information from a courtesan.

Crucial information!

His tongue quietened inside the girl's mouth. *What sort of news can this girl provide? Anyway, tonight is just the beginning. Rome was not built in a day. I am doing an excellent service for the cause of The East India Company. If patriotism requires to enjoy a girl, that is only part of my duty.* A sense of nationalism passed through his skin.

The girl suddenly became silent, probably having accepted her fate like a lamb about to face the butcher's knife. Colin pulled the string of her underskirt, and it slipped slowly to her hips. After a brief pause, it fell on the ground.

Another noise—people were shouting outside, as if arguing fiercely. Trepidation crept into Colin's veins, and he felt a slackness between his thighs. War time. He should hurry up. He moved his palm mechanically on the girl's belly, simultaneously trying to feel if the arousal had built up. Anger toward the sepoy stomped through his chest. Couldn't he find a quieter location?

He glanced at the girl. Her eyes were closed, arms hanging loosely alongside her waist. When Colin softened his grip, she began to fall. She probably blacked out. He was filled with a moment of compassion, dragged her to the bed, and laid her there. He was looking for some water to sprinkle on her face when a sudden knock sounded at the door.

"Sir, please quickly finish, Sir. We are not safe here. We must leave immediately."

Colin growled through his teeth. "Am I eating snacks? 'Finish quickly!'" He glanced at the girl, lying unconscious on the bed—arms spread, legs wide open. His stomach tightened with an urge to flee home. Hurriedly putting on his clothes, he came out. The sepoy was still standing there.

"Sir, some of the roads have been occupied by the rebels. The road to the cantonment is not safe. Let's go to your house at The Residency. Tonight at least. Please, Sir, please."

Colin followed him and jumped inside the carriage. A heaviness swamped all over him. *Oh no, I have to go to that boring woman now.*

CHAPTER 7

28 May 1857 10PM, Colin's Home inside The Residency
Brigadier Colin Lawrence

A bolt of anger cracked through Colin.

"You both knew Amelia is missing, and you didn't even inform me?" Glowering at the older maid, he shouted again, "You old bitch. How long have you been working here? I have been feeding your family for years. Your family would be begging on the streets if I throw you out."

The old maid stood with her gaze at the floor, hands folded, shivering like a criminal just caught. Her lips twitched, trying to say something in her defence, but lacking courage.

The younger maid also stood with her gaze down. "Memsahib not missing, Sahib. She go, to friend, meet."

Colin moved his gaze to the younger maid. "What is your name?"

"Sahib, I, Sona—"

"Whatever," he growled, "you know the mutiny has spread everywhere? Or don't you know? You are Chetan's wife, right? That bloody guard at my gate? You don't know what a mutiny is?"

The younger maid didn't reply—arms frozen to her side, head ducked.

Colin eyed her head to toe. Blood kicked in his groin. He glanced at the older maid; she was watching his gaze on the younger one. A mortification of being caught by a petty maid boiled his blood. He started barking at her, "Do you even know if she's safe? If she's been abducted by bloody rebels? Do you know who I am? I am a brigadier! Rebels will do anything to take revenge on me."

"Sahib—"

"What, *sahib*! Get lost, now!"

The older maid tiptoed to the main door.

Colin shouted from behind, "You work the morning shift? Bring your stupid ass back here in the morning. Go sleep at home."

The woman stood still. She didn't understand the English slangs.

Colin loped forward and stood in front of her. "Maid *sahib*!" he mocked, bending at the waist. "Go home. Home, you know? Your home. Come tomorrow morning. Here. Understood? I talk, your bloody Indian English. Understand now? Go, you bitch."

The woman sobbed and scurried away.

He turned toward the younger maid. "What is your name again?"

"Sona."

"Sona, yes, nice name." He fiddled with his trousers' fly buttons.

Sona gathered some courage. "Sahib, you coming, no know. I go, cooking for you. Urgent. Please, Sahib. Memsahib come, seven day after. Not worry, Sahib. She, back, here."

Colin softened his temper. "Am I hungry? No, I have eaten my supper."

The unfulfilled desire in the *kotha* and the scene of the unconscious girl haunted him. Bloody virgin. All drama. Pretending to lose consciousness. *How long will you safeguard your so-called modesty? I will come again tomorrow evening. I will eat your humility and digest it, too.*

Sona was still standing there, waiting for Colin's orders. He peeked at her blouse. "Nice stuff inside. Brown flesh is tastier than white. That bloody guard doesn't deserve this," Colin muttered and grinned.

Sona noticed his gaze and pulled the loose end of the saree to cover her ample bosom protruding out of her top.

Colin leered. "Sona, hey Sona, please make my bed. I am tired and sleepy. Will you please, Sona darling?"

Sona glanced at him, mouth agape. Colin let out a sardonic smile.

"Sahib, no eating? Belly hungry, no sleep," she said.

"Eating, but on the bed," Colin said, and then mumbled, "I will eat special meat tonight."

"Sahib, what eat? I cook. Meat?"

"Nothing, go and make the bed." He attempted a smile. "I am tired. Need a good massage." Colin pretended as if he were no longer angry, and she appeared to be comfortable with his gentle approach.

Time for Sona to make him happy ... with her work.

When Sona went to the bedroom, Colin ambled after her, watching her making the bed from behind. She stooped to remove the bedsheet. Colin's eyes moved along with the movements of her buttocks. He imagined the naked virgin girl surrendering to him without resistance, and he felt the arousal.

Sona swung back and stood bug-eyed. He was standing too close—indecently close.

"Where are you going?" he asked when she started to leave after the bed was made. "Don't you get paid for the whole night?"

She pointed at the mechanical ceiling fan, strings coming through the skylight aperture on the wall. "Sahib, string go to cabin, outside. I sit cabin in. Pull string. Fan running. Here, in room. Sahib, hot. You sleep not. Not good sleep. I go. Guard cabin. Night." She paused to coin her words. "Full night, fan." She raised her arms to demonstrate the fan spinning.

Colin pretended to be angry again. "That guard Chetan is your husband, right? You both will have fun and sleep in the cabin the whole night. I pay money to you, both of you, for working at night."

"Sahib, no sleep. You see, fan rotate whole night. Fan ... not stop. If stop, cut money."

"I don't need that fan. You sit here, near my bed and do this hand fan." He pointed at the hand fan on the side table.

A forced smile appeared on her face.

"Who else is at your home, Sona?" Colin tried to make her comfortable again.

"My baby. Daughter. Five. Years. Auntie, neighbour auntie, keeps whole night. She, good. Like mother."

Colin now had no problem comprehending her language. Removing his clothes, he wrapped a towel around his waist. "Sona, you are a nice girl. I am tired. I need a massage."

She stood reluctantly. Colin stared at her. She had massaged him before, but in Amelia's presence. He relaxed back on the bed and smiled at her. "You massage me, and then you can go to the cabin, guard's cabin. Okay? All right? Fan me from there, sitting with Chetan. Your husband."

A faint smile curved Sona's lips. She nodded, sat down at his bedside, and started massaging his feet slowly.

"Nice. Beautiful. Continue," Colin said.

After a while, he started again, with a low voice. "I will tell you something, Sona. Something you should know. It's serious."

Sona lifted her gaze.

"Don't stop. Continue please." Colin took a pause and watched her from the corner of his eye. "You know this mutiny? Rebels?"

"Yes, Sahib. They, not good. Company, English, good."

"Chetan's friend has left the Company army and joined the rebels, you know?"

"No, Sahib. No know."

Colin's gaze again went to Sona's body-hugging top and undulating bosom. The air in the room was still, and the candlelight barely flickered. His eyes met hers, and she tugged her saree to conceal her bust.

"I know your Chetan is talking to the rebels."

Sona stopped, her hands still on Colin's feet. He felt the tremor in her.

"Sahib," she said, "my Chetan loyal. No rebel. Believe, Sahib. My words."

Colin laughed. "You silly woman, you don't know anything. I am trying to save your husband." He slowly slipped the towel from his waist.

Sona stood up in a jerk and crouched to pick up the towel. Colin grabbed her hand. "Sit down." His member started staring indecently at Sona. "Continue the massage," he instructed. "You know what will happen? He will get the death punishment. You know what that is?"

"No, Sahib." Her features tensed.

"He will be hanged." Colin demonstrated using his hands.

"Sahib, no," she cried, "please, Sahib. He, Chetan, no rebel. Sahib."

"Don't cry, Sona darling. I will try to do something. Come and sit here." He indicated for her to sit on the side of the bed. Sona shifted to his side. "Now press my thighs."

She placed her palm on his thigh but removed it instantly at the sight of his rigid member. She gaped at him, tried to say something, but her lips only twitched.

Colin's hormones were flying. Hungry and thirsty. He was not ready to accept *No* again, at least not tonight.

"Sahib, I, me, from good house. Reputed family. No Sahib, me, married, please."

Colin slowly tugged her saree, uncovering the blouse. "You are beautiful, Sona."

"No, Sahib." She tried to get up, but Colin dragged her back on the bed and guided her palm onto his thighs.

"I love this massage."

She sobbed and closed her eyes, her palm still on his thighs.

"You know what? If Chetan dies, you will also be in jail. For helping him. What will happen to your baby girl? She will be sold."

Sona looked up at him, mouth agape.

Colin shifted his palm onto her top, feeling the softness of her bubbies, every inch of them. She eyed helplessly but didn't dare to resist.

"Your daughter will be sold in a cheap *kotha*. She will make all men happy. She'll sleep with them. Would you like that?"

"No Sahib. Please, Sahib, leave me." Desperation clawed her throat.

"You are a good girl, Sona. Will you unbutton your blouse, please?"

She attempted to obey, but her fingers quivered. Colin grabbed the hem of her top and said, "If I jolt this, it will be torn. Your husband will notice. Would you like that?"

"No, Sahib." She slowly unbuttoned the blouse, one button after another.

"That's a nice girl." Taking the blouse from her, Colin pressed his nose against it. The sweaty smell kicked exhilaration in his chest.

He got up and pulled her head on his shoulder. "I will take care of you. Your child from me will be white. Not dark-skinned, like bloody Indians. Do not worry, Sona! I will give you a small house. Happy? Moreover, I will also give you money—every month. Happier? You will be a queen. And I will come to you from time to time. Forget that Chetan. He is just a guard. I am a brigadier. No comparison with me. Your children will not be called Indians. They will be Anglo-Indians. English blood."

Sona was literally resting on his shoulder, her body calm. Colin could feel her breath, and her bare bosom tingled his hairy chest. He moved his finger over her boobs and felt their softness. Raising her petticoat, Colin ran his fingers inside her thighs.

"No, Sahib! Noooo!" Sona jumped with a jerk and ran away, pushing Colin back on the bed. But he bounced back immediately and followed her. Sona ran to the adjacent room and closed the door. Before she could lock it, Colin forced himself inside.

"Don't worry, Sona. I am not going to harm you." A half-naked Sona was looking beautiful even in the dark room. Moonlight through the window was enough to lick her beauty.

"Don't worry, Sona. I will give back your saree—and your blouse, too. Do not shout. Your husband is sitting at the gate, in the guard room. What will happen? He will think your honour is gone. Will he accept you?"

"Thanks, Sahib. My honour."

"Nothing will happen to your honour, Sona. I will only touch them. Your *ruby-tipped globes*. You know what those are?"

"No, Sahib."

"Those two fruits you were hiding inside your blouse."

Colin slowly touched her bubbies. She stood silently, cooperating with him. His fingers slowly crawled to her belly. Her tummy pounded; Colin's fingers were thrilled—as if each part of his body had become a sexual organ, each achieving its own *sweet death*.

Colin slithered his fingers under Sona's petticoat and felt her skin, no undergarment beneath it. He got hold of the knot of the underskirt.

"No, Sahib, no further, please, please."

"Voice low, Sona, Chetan can hear."

"Sahib," she whispered and sobbed. "Not my thing, Sahib."

"Okay, good girl. Hold my whore-pipe." Colin guided Sona's fingers to his cock. "Good? Feeling good? Now you will be ready."

He yanked Sona's waist toward him and plucked her petticoat string. Sona immediately released Colin's shaft, but he grabbed her arm, and the petticoat fell to the floor. Moonlight was showing every bit of skin of the poor girl.

"No, Sahib," Sona whispered, then bellowed, "No, Sahib!"

Colin grabbed Sona's neck and put his palm on her mouth. "No shouting. Chetan will hear."

As soon as he released her mouth, she yelled again, but Colin's deadly clasp on her neck stopped her voice from going out of the room. He held Sona's waist and helped her lie on the carpet. She stopped howling.

"Good, Sona darling. Now you're co-operating. Now you will enjoy the flood of bliss from a white shaft. You will ask for it after tonight. Beg for it. You will forget that dark member of your husband."

Colin parted Sona's thighs. She didn't resist. *Is she pretending to be unconscious? Like the virgin girl in the kotha? I will not be fooled anymore.* "I will fill you up with my pearly shower, Sona."

A holler. A woman's voice. Colin tried to locate it. But all the rooms were closed, and all the doors of the house were locked from the inside. The voice sounded familiar; it was touching his heart. He was panting, sweat dripping from his torso. He realised he was naked—no time to find clothing. Urgency pounded through him. He scratched his head. Something about this reminded him of his early childhood. He started banging on the doors, one after another. All the rooms were empty. His patience had run out.

Finally, he went to the backyard. The half-moon was spreading some light. Noticing a blurred movement in a corner, he inched toward it slowly, cautiously. *Is that Sona? Still naked?* He felt his member hardening. A wave of pleasure washed through his limbs. The woman was sobbing, sitting on the ground, burying her head between her knees. He observed her. *It will take time for her to adjust to her new life—the life of a concubine. A brown woman can't be the wife of a white man.*

The sobbing sound pierced him again. This didn't sound like Sona's sobs! He went nearer and stood in front of the woman. Suddenly, a bolt of lightning out of nowhere illuminated the backyard. For that brief moment, he noticed the blonde hair of a white woman. Sona was out of the question now. *Amelia? No, her hair is not curly.* He saw a rope hanging from the tree, and a foreboding stabbed at him.

Suddenly the woman raised her head. Colin's jaws stilled. "Mother!"

He swung back and ran. How could a son look at his own mother in such a state? She was preparing to hang herself. No time to react. He needed to grab his own clothes and something to cover his mother before rescuing her. Something tangled around his feet, Sona's saree. It was enough to cover up his mother. He thought for a moment. How could he stand before his mother stark naked? He was an adult now. He remembered the towel he had slipped from his torso that evening when he asked Sona for a massage.

Rushing back to the dark bedroom, he lighted the candle and frantically glanced around. Sona's blouse was still on his bed. He desperately looked for his towel. Time was running out. A few more second's delay could cast danger to his mother's life. The scene of the hanging rope started punching his conscience. He held the blouse in front of his bare thighs and ran. Something had him, his legs refused to move. His feet were tangled in something—another saree, maybe! He crouched, tried to untangle it, but he couldn't locate the knot.

His heart started jackhammering. "Mother, please wait. I'm coming. Don't hang yourself. Mother, please." He felt his throat had been choked. He couldn't even shout loudly.

A sudden jerk woke Colin up at midnight, sweating and panting. Thank God. It was a dream. He glanced at the ceiling fan. Not moving. This was not the bed in the cantonment—this was his own bed in his home. Sweat pooled on his skin. He tried to locate his towel but found a small piece of thin cloth. It was Sona's blouse, still lying on his bed.

Confusion crammed his head. *What had happened to my mother? How did she die? Am I not supposed to know, even though I was a child and away in a boarding school in London?*

Everything was unclear. He got up and sat down. *Where is Sona? She should have gone to the guard's cabin and currently be drawing the string of the fan. But her blouse is here. Did she go without any clothes to meet her guard husband?* He knew Chetan couldn't do anything against him. He could imprison him anytime on a false allegation of having a relationship with the rebels.

Blood pounded in his head. He got up, wrapped a towel around his waist, and stomped to the gate. Chetan was alone in the cabin, dozing. Anger exploded through him. "Is this what I am paying you for? And where is your bloody wife?"

Chetan jerked to his feet and stuttered, "Sahib, no idea Sahib. She has not come out of the house."

"Then where did she vanish? You were sleeping and didn't notice she went away somewhere—you liar. Go and find her. Now," Colin barked.

He went back inside, anger still boiling in him. "First Amelia vanished, and now this woman! I will show them what trust means." He stomped through the veranda to his bedroom. On the way, his attention turned to another room. A panic squeezed through his brain.

Sona was lying on the floor. *Bloody whore, you are still sleeping here?*

Colin felt another arousal. Finally, this woman has surrendered. He entered the room and found Sona asleep. He appreciated the moonlight brightening the room. She was still naked, bubbies facing the ceiling, legs parted as if inviting Colin for another round, another *sting of pleasure*. Removing his towel, he sat down.

"I love you, Sona darling." He touched her bubbies and lowered his face to plant a kiss on her lips. As soon as he touched Sona's lips, something pushed him backwards with force. Something was wrong. Was she still unconscious?

Colin stilled for a moment and brought his face again to Sona's mouth. One hand on her soft chest. Her chest was still, cold. She was not breathing. No pulse.

His head reeled. He wobbled his way to his bedroom, dragged his ass onto the bed, and drank a glass of water. Everything revolved around him, and his vision blurred. Since earlier that evening, everything had gone the wrong way.

Colin took time to come to his senses. Chetan was the only man who could take him to prison. He was bluffing Sona before, threatening to get Chetan thrown in prison. But the truth was, regardless of Colin's high-ranking position, even if a lowly guard like Chetan were to accuse him of hurting Sona, Colin would lose everything. Suddenly it seemed like Chetan had all the power. It was time to plan, gather courage and take action. Morning would be too late. He put on his uniform, took the pistol, and stomped out.

Chetan saluted him, standing at the gate. "Sahib, she must be in some room. She hasn't come out, Sahib."

Colin didn't say anything, only growled.

Chetan shuddered. "Sahib, she is my faithful wife. Loyal woman. She will not go out at night alone. She is a woman. Danger is everywhere now. She loves her modesty."

The word *modesty* stabbed Colin hard in his chest. Time was running out. He must find something to do with the dead body of Sona. He could only save himself. Colin gathered ample strength and commanded, "I have information that your wife has spoken to a rebel's wife. You know what can happen? You can go to jail for betraying the British. Or even be hanged. I have the authority to shoot anybody who looks like a rebel, you dirty-skin. Go and find out where that whore is. Or else I will shoot you. And yes, keep that gun back in the cabin."

Chetan wiped perspiration off his brow. Casting a nervous glance at Colin, he removed the gun from his shoulder, put it inside the cabin, and dragged his feet outside the gate.

Colin sneaked inside and kneeled near Sona's body. "Why do you women not appreciate my love? Did I want to kill you? You invited your own death, Sona. You are also like Antonia. Am I responsible for her death? Why are you women forcing me to do such things which I really do not want to do? I did not want to grab Antonia's neck, nor yours. I swear, I didn't have control over my hand then. I just wanted to make love. Is that a crime?"

CHAPTER 8

29 May 1857 Early Hours
Chetan

Chetan abandoned his post at the guard cabin and scurried to his home, almost three miles away from The Residency—a village inside the sprawling Lucknow city. He knew Colin, Brigadier Colin, very well: always short-tempered. He couldn't understand how he didn't notice when Sona went out through the gate. Chetan considered himself a proud and sincere soldier. Maybe he had dosed for a minute, and Sona had gone out for something. Was she not well and went home? He remembered once when she was sick and Amelia Memsahib sent her back home. Didn't she always inform him before going out, though?

His home was locked. As expected, Sona was not there. He was exhausted, so he sat on the veranda, leaning on a wooden pillar, and thought of knocking on the neighbour's door. The old lady next door always kept his little girl when they both worked the whole night at The Residency. But he hesitated to disturb her sleep at this odd hour; it was almost three in the morning.

Finally, he decided to wake up the old lady and asked about Sona. But the poor woman didn't know where Sona was.

Chetan scratched his head. Where could she have gone at night? He was a loyal soldier of the East India Company. He knew some of his friends had deserted the Company and joined the mutiny. They thought the British had defeated so many of their kings and were ruling the country through the Company. But what was wrong with that? One ruler was always replacing another, this was the norm of the world. In fact, the East India Company was the real ruler of the country. Not only that, but they were also a hundred times better than the Mughal emperors. He had read a little bit of history. Mughal Emperor Aurungzeb had destroyed Hindu temples. He had even killed many Hindus who didn't agree to convert.

On the contrary, the British never destroyed any temples. Ordinary people like him could go to the temples or mosques and worship. Many of his friends had indeed become Christians. But no one forced them to. Instead, they were paid money to convert. *Money for converting religion? Would I change my religion for cash?*

He couldn't return to The Residency without Sona. He must find her at any cost. *Oh, God. Help me.* Chetan wandered aimlessly. When he saw an old, dilapidated mini palace, he sat down on its veranda, exhausted.

Who is the real ruler now? The British or Nawab Wajid Ali Shah? If Nawab is the real king, then what are the British doing? A confusion rose from the abyss of his mind. He had read many things about the nawab. Even though the nawab was a Muslim, he was far better than the Emperor Aurungzeb.

When the British were busy consolidating their reign, the nawab was in a different world. Having received some education, Chetan had read some Hindi and Urdu books. Of course, he couldn't read English. A warm, feelgood moment engulfed him.

He loved Wajid Ali's Yogi Avatar. On his birthday each year, he would dress up as a Yogi with saffron robes, ash of pearls smeared on his face and body, and a necklace of pearls around his neck. He had the famous *Parikhana*, in which hundreds of beautiful girls were taught music and dancing by expert teachers. These girls were called *Paries*. When the nawab would dress up as a Yogi, some of the fairies dressed up as *Jogans* (female Yogis). Chetan had once gotten a chance to escort Brigadier Colin to such a pageant and watch the nawab and the girls from close quarters. The nawab even encouraged ordinary people to dress up as Yogis and participate in the procession. But he was there as Colin's guard. *Sona, we will go together to the carnival next year, when this war will have finished. I promise.*

Sona! His head pounded again. *Where do I find Sona?*

He glanced at the sky, the moon and the stars. It must be early morning now. Still, there was time to think. A lovely thought snaked through him. *Colin Sahib is getting unnecessarily angry. Sona is safe. The Residency is so well protected. There are security guards at all the gates, and two of them make regular rounds both inside and outside. After the mutiny started, even more guards have been appointed. The weather is cold. There was no need to pull the strings of the fan from my cabin. She has friends in other houses of the colony. She may have gone to meet some friend inside the compound. I probably didn't notice.* He slapped his own cheek. *I am so stupid. I must have dozed off. She must have come back by now. Must be resting in the cabin. She knows I sometimes go to the main gate. She will not worry about me. After all, I am a man. Colin Sahib must also be resting now. Everything will be all right by morning.*

Chetan lay down on the floor. Time to take a proper nap. He stretched his legs and kept an arm below his head, attempting to get some sweet dreams and sleep.

Thanks to the British, he had gotten some education. Even though it was not enough to call higher education; higher learning meant an officer job. Still, he was happy to be a security guard with the Company. His parents had taught him to be loyal and thankful to those who had given some benefit. How could Colin Sahib say Sona had spoken to a rebel's wife? Impossible. She always came to The Residency with him and left with him.

Chetan was never in favour of Sona working as a maid. Maid? He was from a respected Hindu family! Sona had also been to the primary school. Antonia Memsahib was so impressed when she saw her, she insisted that Sona worked as the home manager. She was such a nice lady. She should not have died.

Chetan changed sides. Sleep was not friendly with him today. Why did Antonia Memsahib die?

Sona had told him Colin Sahib beat Antonia Memsahib frequently. Sona was unhappy with that. He had tried to convince Sona—what was wrong with a husband disciplining a wife? But beating his wife? Too much. He had warned Sona not to open her mouth. After all, being a brigadier, he was in such a senior position. He might have lots of stress at work.

People said she had not committed suicide. Colin Sahib killed her. Did he?

Chetan never believed that. Colin Sahib loved Antonia Memsahib so much—so what if he was beating her? He still loved her.

Sona had found a letter after her death—Antonia Memsahib's handwriting. He had no idea what was written on it, as it was in English; Sona preserved that as a memory, and he had respected her wishes. But now he wondered—what had Antonia Memsahib written in the letter?

Chetan changed sides again, now sure he would never get sleep tonight. He glanced at the moon. The dark night was almost over. Something clicked in his brain. He should have asked the head security guard at the main gate about Sona. No one could leave The Residency other than through the main entrance. The guard there knew her. He would vouch to Colin Sahib that Sona had not gone out. Lethargy took over him. *I will do this first thing in the morning. Colin Sahib must be sleeping now.* Chetan immediately felt relaxed, yawned, and stretched. *That guard at the main gate...*

A memory flicked in his brain. A chill sliced through him. His muscles jerked as he sat up like a spring. *That guard has deserted the East India Company and joined the rebels!*

Chetan recollected, just two days ago he had spoken to him in the evening. The next day, there was news he changed parties. What if Colin Sahib accused him of talking to a rebel, too? He was already accusing Sona.

His brain screamed. Why were these people suddenly making such dangerous decisions? He was aware of the developments around. He knew people doubted that the cartridges of the bullets of the Enfield rifles were covered with animal fat. Beef and pork. He was sure that it was just a rumour. He never believed it. Hindus and Muslims both thought the British sought to destroy their religions and make them Christians. What rubbish!

Chetan knew that the queen of Jhansi was also fighting against the British. He knew the Mughal Emperor of Delhi Bahadur Shah Zafer had been declared the Emperor of the whole country. The rebels were quickly progressing toward Awadh. Nawab Wajid Ali Shah and his chief general Rupen Naik were fighting against the Company. Only a month ago the nawab had invited the British officers to the *Rahas* Ceremony in Qaiserbagh Palace. What happened to all those friendships?

The night had almost passed without giving Chetan even a moment's sleep. He knew Colin Sahib was a short-tempered man. Sona must have come back. He would convince him about his loyalty. He would never join the rebels come what may.

Chetan started walking toward The Residency. He was tired but confident. He took a shortcut alongside the Gomti River. A man was coming from the opposite side. He recognised him—he was also a guard in The Residency. He was about to ask him whether he had seen Sona, but the other guard asked him, "Do you always fight with your wife?"

Chetan scratched his head and replied, "Not always. But yes. About three days ago. A minor one. Which couple doesn't fight? Why? What happened?" Chetan noticed something odd in the guard's features.

"You know the guard of Colin Sahib's neighbour?"

Chetan gave him a long, measuring look. An uneasiness feathered into him.

The guard continued, "He has become a witness that you have killed your wife."

Chetan burst into a laugh. "Brother, why do you always joke with me? This is not a funny matter. When will you grow up?"

"Joke? Why should I?"

"Don't pretend. Don't I know you always make a serious face like this? You should leave this guard job and join a theatre company. You tell me, why should I kill my wife? Will you do the same to your wife?"

"You do not understand, Chetan. This is serious."

Chetan stood still and stared at his friend. This man was telling the truth. He felt something revolving around him. He tried to open his mouth, but the tremor in his lips didn't allow him to say anything. "Oh!" He caught his head with both hands and slumped to the ground.

"Are you all right, Chetan?" His friend sat near him, grabbing his shoulders.

"No, no. You are wrong, brother. I am sure Sona has gone somewhere without telling me. She must have come back by now. I am going to ask her why she did it."

"Cool down, my friend," the other guard said, "I have seen her dead body. The police van came and took her. Please take my advice. You have no time to think and bring danger to yourself. Think of your baby daughter. She needs you. Alive. Outside of a prison. Please hide somewhere where the white police can't reach you. And don't go home, either. You will be caught."

Chetan gave his friend a desperate glance, tears rolling down his cheeks. "Can't I see my Sona one last time? Can't my baby daughter see her mother again?" He sobbed and stood up with wobbling feet.

Nervousness was building in the other guard. He was looking around frantically.

Chetan gave him a quick hug. He knew that if he wanted to stay alive, he couldn't mourn for his wife now. He needed to escape. "I know you don't want me to be caught. I am also a proud, loyal soldier like you. See how I have been rewarded? Thank you, my friend. God bless you."

Chetan started walking quickly alongside the River Gomti. Dark thoughts crawled through him. A strong desire to see Sona swelled inside him. Who would he approach for help? Colin's angry face reminded him of a ghost. Tension and confusion chased through him.

Almost an hour later, he sat down beneath a tree for some rest and inhaled deeply. Dawn was slowly creeping in, but some dark clouds in the sky were still holding back daylight. His glance fell on the Gomti River. A desire to go in the water and take a bath ran through his hot, sweating skin. Dryness choked his throat. Then something sounded from a distance. He kept his ear attuned—the sound of horses' hooves. Blood drained from his head. He couldn't see anything beyond the turn of the road, but he kept his eyes focussed. He felt as if the whole British military were behind him.

Hooves sounded louder and more apparent. Sunlight reflected on the dust, like blood spraying into the air. Chetan slowly moved onto the bough of a teak tree stretched over the water. The horses had crossed the turning of the road. He inched closer to the end of the bough, trying to hide in its dense leaves. A platoon of soldiers, all whites, was looming. Someone was pointing toward him, or so he felt. He tried to hide his face properly but heard a crackling sound. Suddenly, the branch snapped away from the tree, and before he could realise, he was deep inside the river.

It felt like everything was finished in an instant. *Am I dying?* Sona was gone. Shortly, he would also meet her in heaven. Some water went inside his mouth, but his brain was still working.

Chetan was not sure who was thinking, his head or his departed soul.

For a moment, he felt better. *Police can't chase my soul.* But the face of his baby girl haunted him. He pinched himself and found he was still alive. He forced himself above the water and sucked in a breathful of air, his vision still blurred. Throwing around a quick glance, he noticed all the soldiers were gone. He could not take a chance. His daughter's future depended upon his survival. He began swimming. Aimlessly. Then he noticed a ferry in the upstream of the river. He started shouting, "Help me, help me!" No one responded, but he continued swimming. Within no time, he was in the midriver. Finally, someone in the ferry noticed.

Not a single white skin was onboard. Chetan inhaled a sigh of relief, realising it was a goods ferry. Something clicked in a remote part of his brain. Folding his hands, he said, "I am a worker. The mutiny is burning in Lucknow. I have no job. Please give me work."

The man went inside and called to a fat man, who looked like a manager or something. He stared at Chetan head to toe as if a lifeless statue had been placed in front of him. The man smiled and nodded his head.

Chetan got a job on the ferry, which was going to Varanasi. After he thanked the man, he looked back. His favourite Lucknow was slowly disappearing. He shed teardrops, one for his dead wife and the other for his baby daughter. *Your father is alive, my child. I promise you will not be an orphan. I shall come back to you. Only God knows when.*

CHAPTER 9

29 May 1857 Night
Brigadier Colin Lawrence

A seriously sick Colin was admitted into hospital. The pain in his arms was so agonising, it was as if they didn't belong to him. Sometimes it stopped on its own. But when it came back, he felt his head spinning and his jaws clenched. Doctors repeatedly asked him where and when he had hurt his arms. How could he say it was his dead first wife's neck which twisted his nerves? Or Sona's modesty which gave the heaviest blow to his bones?

Doctors could not diagnose the disease. How could they?

Every time he fell into slumber, the sobbing of the woman pierced his ears. He would wake up sweating and panting. Colin tried to access the time. Midnight, probably. The only candle was sitting on the side table, struggling between life and death. He glanced outside. Trees stood like ghosts under the dark sky. Either it was drizzling, or dew droplets were falling from the tree leaves. Whatever. That sound was punching holes in his weak heart. He wanted to call the nurse and ask her to close the window. In fact, the nurse had shut it in the evening, but he sweltered from the heat and opened it himself.

Another chilling yelp. An emergency patient might have been admitted into hospital—another injured soldier from the war. The hospital was full of wounded soldiers. This mutiny had made the lives of the people miserable, including Colin. Perhaps he was the only soldier who was there for sickness, not a war wound.

That night was the most horrible one in Colin's life. Everything was going in the wrong direction since earlier that evening, beginning from the courtesan who pretended to be a dance performer and not a prostitute. How dare she refuse a senior English officer like him? And the second one? She pretended to be from a respected Hindu family, still trying to preserve her virginity. In the morning, when the police took away Sona's body for the post-mortem, Colin felt sick. He could have done something with her body. But that other maid! She came earlier than usual and started howling. Colin was sure she was in fact not crying but screaming, knowingly, to inform the neighbours. The erratic actions of that old maid were what brought the police to his home in the first place, forcing him to pretend this was the first he was seeing Sona's dead body, too. His performance must have been convincing, considering the police didn't even question him and immediately had asked about the whereabouts of her husband.

Then Chetan also didn't come back. He must've known Sona had died by now. Who knew if he had gone to the nawab with his complaint? It was understood the nawab was fighting against the East India Company, but he and Rupen Naik had useful contacts with the Governor General. Sooner or later, the war would be over, and a pact might be signed. Then Chetan's complaint against him could be disastrous.

The hospital had very few nurses and doctors. Most had been sent to temporary, makeshift hospitals in places affected by the mutiny. Otherwise, a nurse would have been present fulltime with a brigadier. His anger turned toward the Indian soldiers. They shouldn't have been allowed admission into hospitals under any circumstances. It was true that most of them were still loyal Company employees. But how could he know who was faithful and who was a rebel? Those who were still loyal could move to the rebel camp anytime. Better leave them un-treated so that they would die.

Black lives don't matter.

Black or brown, all are the same. Colin shouted for a nurse, but no-body responded. Must be attending that injured man from the war-front. He sat up on his bed and drank some water kept on his bedside table. Again, he tried to get some sleep. So many things were cramming his mind.

Amelia left without informing him. What was his mistake? As a husband, was he not entitled to discipline a wife? Yes, it was probably wrong to hit her. It might be immoral, but certainly not illegal. How many luxuries was she enjoying as a brigadier's wife? Yes, friends com-mented his second wife was many years younger than he. But she also got a highly paid officer as a husband. It took years to get to that posi-tion. She should have known how stressed he was with his own work. If he slapped her a few times or even hit her with his fists, she should have tolerated it as an obedient wife. She hadn't seen how the Indian servants or even the junior soldiers were beaten mercilessly. Then she would have understood the difference between discipline and punish-ment. She should have seen the penalties given to black people in Africa. Then she would have appreciated that his slap was, in fact, an expression of love.

Colin felt sleepy again. Mosquitos were humming near his ears, his throbbing head. The Company should understand how much sacrifice the English soldiers were making in a hot and humid country like this. They should have even allowed them to have slaves like the Americans were enjoying. *Oh, God! How did I become so sick that I had to come to hospital?*

He drifted back into slumber, but only temporarily. To his horror, the woman again appeared on the lawn outside the window, apparently naked. He also saw a rope hanging from the tree. Colin took the candle from the side table. His hands were trembling, but he decided to finally verify who the woman was. The candlelight was so faint it was difficult to see anything clearly. He was staggering on his feet, the lawn wobbling beneath him. The woman's back was completely bare, long hair tangled with weed flowers and grass. How could he recognise this woman?

Colin woke up again—completely wet with his own sweat, but his throat dry. He sat up in bed. Was it the worst night of his life? Probably. Why was that woman coming to his dream again and again? Who could it be? Antonia? Yes, Antonia. Her body was so heavy to lift and hook to the ceiling. He let out a mild laugh at his own dream, a brigadier being worried about such trivial things. Such negative thoughts could come when someone was not well, either physically or mentally.

He always struggled with negative thoughts, even back when he was a child.

How could he forget 1829—the year of that historical milestone? A nine-year-old boy, he was a student in Calcutta Junior Missionary school. That day saw a special gathering after the morning prayer. The Father of the church adjacent to the school was present along with the headmaster. After the headmaster briefly said, "Today is a memorable day in the chapter of British India," the Father started his long, dull speech. Somehow that day, his sermon felt exciting to Colin.

"Today is the day the Son of God, Jesus Christ, has done great mercy on this country. The iron curtain, beneath which women of this country were oppressed, has finally been thrown away. Effective and continuous lobbying by the church has finally been successful. From now onwards, women will live peacefully, no more crying, no danger to their lives."

For a nine-year-old Colin, the oppressed woman meant his own mother, who often sobbed sitting in their backyard. *Did Jesus do some magic with my dad? Wouldn't he hit my mother anymore?* The picture of his mother's sad face appeared in front of his eyes.

"This is an unfortunate country where people are still living in darkness. We, the Britishers, the enlightened Christians, are bringing light to this country," the Father continued.

The nine-year-old Colin imagined that England was not dark at night like India. He whispered to his friend Henry, "I have never seen England. After my birth, my parents have never visited their birthplace. But I have heard them discussing to send me to a boarding school in London. I will see how bright our parent country is."

"This country," the Father said, "is still in the dark age. We, the Christians, are slowly enlightening them."

"Will they bring lights from England to India?" Colin asked his friend Henry.

"You are dumb."

"The widow Hindus will no more be burnt alive. After a long fight by us, the Christians, finally, The East India Company has passed the law to abolish it. The Sati ritual is now illegal. Women will no more be tortured."

During the class break, Colin called Henry to a lonely corner of the schoolyard and said, "I think my mother will no more be oppressed. Last night my dad attacked my mom, and she was sort of crying."

"What did he do?" Henry's eyes dazzled in excitement.

"He grabbed Mom on the bed and ... and ... he was sort of biting her. Mom was helpless and crying."

Henry cast a glance at him and smiled. "Did your father wear anything? Meaning clothes?"

Colin replied, "No."

"And Mom?"

"I am not sure. She was lying beneath my dad."

"You fool! Your mother was naked, too. How were her legs? I mean thighs. Open?"

Colin nodded, then noticed a swelling between Henry's thighs. "What is that?" He pointed.

Henry laughed. "You don't get that? How old are you?"

"Nine."

"I am eleven. When you are a man, you will also get this. Your mother was not weeping, she was moaning. And your father was fucking her. When you grow up, you will also do the same."

"You are older than me. Have you ever fucked a girl?" Colin felt a tightness for the first time.

Henry noticed it immediately. "See, now your pants are also swelling."

"Then I can fuck a girl?"

"No, stupid. That is a sin. We are Christians, civilised. Not until you get married. Your mother is your father's wife. He is not doing a sin."

Colin was still not convinced. "You are stupid. The Father said about oppression against women. I know my mother is always oppressed. My father hits her. She cries, sitting beneath a tree in the backyard."

Henry's brows furrowed. "Where was your attention when Father was speaking? He was speaking about Hindu widows. They are burnt alive when their husband's bodies are cremated. Isn't it wrong?"

Colin thought for a moment. "But our maid is also a widow! She is still alive. You are wrong."

That day, Colin felt he had become a grown-up boy. He got his first erection, and he could also argue with a senior boy!

When he arrived home in the afternoon, his dad was fuming and stomping out of the house. He didn't dare ask him anything. But he decided to tell his mother about the new Sati law. As usual, she was in the backyard—sitting beneath a tree, burying her head between her knees, and weeping. Her clothes were torn; she was virtually naked, or almost half-naked.

He felt like taking a knife and... No, he couldn't do that. He couldn't kill his father. He had seen police taking people away in handcuffs who did wrong things, like stealing, killing someone's goat. Could he beat him at least? Didn't he hit Colin for any little *mistake* he did?

Like not doing homework? Not getting up from bed in the morning on time? Dirtying his clothes while playing with friends?

And Mother? She would take him onto her lap even if his clothes were filthy. Help him change into new clothes. Always patient with Colin. What mistake did Mother make that Father was angry with her? Didn't she do her own homework? No, not possible. She didn't go to school. She always woke up on time in the morning. Cooked yummy food. Why was Dad not happy with her? He was angry all the time. Apparently for no reason. Could he one day ask his dad, what was Mother's fault?

He sat on the grass in front of her and said, "Mother, the Bishop came to the school today and said Sati law has been passed. No one will burn any woman." Then he thought for a moment and said, "He was speaking about oppression against women. You will never be beaten."

Mother raised her head, and Colin's gaze fell on her chest. The red burn marks were clearly visible. She noticed his look, pulled the torn end of the dress to cover her breasts. He met her gaze. His blood pounded. "Dad is hitting you, why?"

"He wants to do something with me even when I am not well." She pulled him in and hugged him, still weeping. "You are a child, you wouldn't understand this."

The next morning, everything looked as usual again. Both Dad and Mom were talking nicely. Colin went to his mother. He wanted to ask if Dad fucked her last night, but his tongue stiffened. He turned around and noticed his Dad standing behind him.

"My boy is an India-born English boy." Dad patted his back. "He should get an education in London and become a top army officer."

Colin was happy to board a ship accompanied by a distant uncle and start studying at a boarding school in London.

Months in the ship felt like ages. Mom's sad face would haunt him, more so when he suffered from seasickness. Two things kept his spirit alive—he would study in a civilised country, and Sati law would protect his mother. The moment he closed his eyes after curling up under the blanket on his bed, he sensed his mom's warm lap and her lovely, assuring hug.

He felt enlightened from the day he set his feet in London. All white people. He remembered the Father of the church in Calcutta saying in his sermon, "We are bringing light to this dark country. Time is not far; this country will be enlightened."

The Father in the Calcutta church was right. England was not dark but enlightened. That's why everyone there was white. However, all those thoughts about enlightenment lost charm with time. Homesickness swirled in his stomach every now and then. For some time, he could draw the interest of fellow boys by telling them stories about India: Sati ritual, dark uncivilised people. He added some spice to the Sati story that he was a witness to a widow being burnt alive. Once, a boy asked him what the name of that woman was. He scratched his head. The name of the widowed maid came to his mind. "Ruma," he said, still wondering how she was not burnt, even though she was a widow. Did the Father of the church lie? *No, Fathers don't lie. He is not like my Dad, not that kind of father—who would promise Mom not to drink anymore and then go to buy the filthy country liquor from that dirty Indian guy. Didn't he assure Mom never to beat her again?*

Within two months of arriving at the boarding school, he received a letter from his mother. That was the first letter of his life, and he felt like he'd received a gift from heaven. He read and reread that letter so many times that he almost remembered each word of it. He eagerly waited for the second letter. The hostel warden once saw him weeping. He ruffled his hair and said, "Ships take six months to arrive from India, my boy."

The warden was right. Colin was always waiting for up to six months to receive another letter from his mother. She must've sent the first letter in the next ship even before Colin arrived in London. He also sent letters to her, sometimes asking if Father was still mistreating her. His mother would never mention that in the mails. Colin became sure the Sati law had, in fact, protected her.

A year and six months after Colin's arrival, for the first time, he received a letter from his dad. Only a few sentences, and the rest of the page was blank.

Your mom has died. She was sick for months. You do not worry. Study well.

Mother was dead? Only a week ago, he had received a letter from Mom. She had written she was well. She had even written about the annual fair near his house she had visited. Her message was so full of life. And love. She had filled up pages, as usual. She never mentioned she was sick. Was someone lying? Who?

Mother could never lie to Colin. No, never. Then was it his father? What is the lie, then? Her illness or death?

Colin hoped against hope—let her death be a lie. The hatred toward his dad, which was dormant since the day he left India, raised its ugly fangs like a poisonous snake. Would it bite his dad or Colin himself?

Colin wept for weeks, even went to the hostel warden and begged to send him back to India.

"Do you have your mother's photo with you, my boy?" the warden asked with a kind voice.

Colin wondered why he never bothered to bring a photo with him. The only picture he had seen of his mother was her wedding, drawn by some artist.

"No, sir," he sobbed.

The warden left but came back shortly with a thick paper and a bouquet. Asking his mother's name, he wrote on the paper in a bold and beautiful handwriting and set it on his study table against the wall. "Now take this bunch of flowers and offer them to your mother."

As if his mother became alive in that gorgeous handwriting, Colin offered her the flowers. A wave of coolness touched his heart. He even took out all her letters and kept them near the bouquet. He could feel his mother smiling at him from each of those envelopes.

"She is no more in India," the warden said. "She has gone to heaven like all nice people. And you know what?"

Colin anticipated another magical moment.

"Heaven is nearer to England and far away from India. Jesus loves people here. Do you love to see your mother happy?"

Colin nodded.

"Then you study hard. Be a good student. I am sure that is what she wanted."

After that, letters stopped coming—only money-orders from his father. He became lonely and grumpy. His stories about India didn't excite anyone. One day in 1831, after he had been at the boarding school about two years, an announcement came that the East India Company had occupied Mysore State. He was an eleven-year-old boy who didn't even know where the Mysore State was. He tried to find it on the map to get back into the limelight.

Colin thought the time after the evening prayer at the hostel would be appropriate for an announcement. He came to the front and stood facing his fellow classmates. He had already coined the words. "I have something to announce today which will make each Englishman proud. The East India Company has occupied the Mysore State after a bloody war."

"My Sore?" one of his classmates mocked from behind.

"No, Mysore."

"Where is that?"

"India."

"Oh, the East India Company has already occupied India," another student said, "you are bringing stories from the air."

Everyone laughed.

"No." Colin felt he had been surrounded by enemy soldiers with an urgent need to defend his fort. "We have fought and won the war against the brown natives."

"Brown natives!" another student mocked at him. "Look at this boy. His tanned skin. You are looking like a brown Indian."

"Yeh, really!" Another student came forward. "Colin will go back to India and work there. He will be completely brown. Even darker. Like negros."

The whole congregation burst into laughter. Colin ran out and didn't dare to come to his room for nearly an hour. For the first time, he discovered a different attitude from his friends toward him. It was as if he were an Indian and he had been defeated by the British. A dark feeling of inferiority sank into his stomach. That feeling never left his subconscious. He longed to go back to India.

At the age of seventeen in 1837, he wrote his first letter to his father, whom he hated all his life. However, he had felt the loneliness his father might have been going through after his mother's death. He received a reply after almost a year, from the new wife of his father. The letter had warned that he would be eighteen soon and shouldn't depend on his father's money. Money stopped coming. His mother would have never done this to him.

After finishing army training in London, Colin returned to India and was immediately deployed to the Anglo-Afghan War. That was 1842. This wasn't the first war of his life, but certainly the first after joining the East India Company army. Major General Sir William Elphinstone had to withdraw his garrison after being defeated by Afghan Emir Dost Mohammad Barakzai. As the battalion began its march, Afghan tribesmen attacked them. Many died of frostbite, starvation, or were killed. Some were even taken as hostages and sold as slaves. Colin survived but was severely wounded. He spent months in hospital but bounced back to life again.

Was misfortune part of his destiny?

In 1845, fortune smiled at twenty-five-year-old Colin. Probably the first time in his life that he could remember. It came in the form of Antonia. But for how long?

Antonia. That silly woman. She was the daughter of a junior army officer of the Company. Colin had always found it difficult to understand that woman. She was caring, a good cook, and beautiful. He was so happy after the wedding. After all this time, he finally had the company of a woman. The void created after the death of his mother seemed to be filled again.

His initial years with her were probably the best period of his life. Colin would impatiently wait for work to be over so he could go back home. He was a junior officer at that time. But Antonia was lucky for him—Colin's image among his colleagues improved after he started taking Antonia to the officers' club. He was on top of the world when his colleagues would watch her from the corner of their eyes while dancing with their wives. His chest would swell under a punch of emotion. He would imagine himself in fairyland, and he had received the most beautiful fairy as a prize after all his longsuffering.

His friends warned him about Brigadier Thomas Brydon when Colin had invited him for dinner one day, saying that he was after Antonia. But Colin knew Brydon was a family man with a wife and children, a man of high reputation and best behaviour. Colin laughed at the so-called well-wishers. He even joked with them after receiving an out-of-term promotion. Thomas always praised him as an outstanding young officer of the unit and his future in the British Army.

One day the brigadier's wife was sick, and Thomas came to the officers' club alone. He was sipping wine on his own and watching others dance with their spouses. Another junior officer, Albert, approached Colin and requested him to a corner. He whispered in his ear, "I will give you a mantra. 'Those who know and apply, get faster promotions.' Even the brigadier himself had done it when he was a junior officer."

He pondered Albert's words, noting that he implied the same warning his friends had. But Albert made it sound more like an opportunity than a warning. Colin immediately approached the brigadier and requested that he dance with Antonia. At first, he declined and only thanked him, but Colin insisted. Thomas was a perfect gentleman. Colin walked to Antonia along with the brigadier and proudly told her Sir would love to dance with her. Antonia hesitated for a moment but finally danced with him after casting a nervous glance at Colin.

After arriving home, he assured her it was not unusual to dance with the husband's senior. Everyone did it.

Antonia replied, "I am also an army officer's daughter. I know what happens after that. Will you be all right if your wife sleeps with another man?"

Colin replied, "I am an army officer's son, too. I also know what happens after that. Don't worry. He is a gentleman. You are my love, and no one will touch you."

Well-wishers' warnings were proven to be wrong. Even Antonia's fear was baseless. Life became so smooth that Colin felt like the happiest family man. He was no longer bitter about his estranged father and his young wife. Though he hadn't forgiven his father, he ignored his existence.

Life had so many pleasant surprises for him.

Antonia's parents lived in Delhi; Colin was posted in Calcutta. Antonia used to visit her parents, and that meant she was away for long periods of time. The same junior officer, Albert—who had once given the guru mantra to Colin—had become a trusted friend. One day, he invited Colin for dinner. Colin still remembered it. His wife, even though not as beautiful as Antonia, had better dress sense. Colin struggled to conceal his bizarre gaze at her.

Minnie welcomed him with a warmer-than-normal handshake and a *where were you until now?* glance. Her hips rolled when she walked, and she sat down with him and started talking like a long-lost friend. Colin got sort of an emotional shock when Minnie's fingers touched him while giving him a glass of water. He thought it was accidental but still felt the sensual contact. A shy Colin had hardly spoken freely with any woman other than Antonia, so it took him some time to open up with her, but he even stole a sideways glance at her mini dress. *Her name is rightly given—Minnie,* he thought.

Albert left the house for some urgent work and said he would be late. But he instructed his wife to take proper care of *Sir*. Colin had by now come out of his turtle shell. Minnie's welcoming smile when he glanced at her unbuttoned top drew blood to his inner thighs. She went to the kitchen, came back with two glasses of wine, and sat close to him. Colin inhaled sharply; blood started singing in his veins. Minnie leaned upon him, pressing her boobs on his shoulder. His groin started tickling. "Albert—" his voice quivered— "when Albert is coming back?"

Minnie laughed loudly, moving her palm onto his hairy chest. "That bastard has gone to his mistress, an Indian whore. He will sleep there the whole night."

Colin was enticingly ensnared by Minnie. He gulped down the remaining wine and stretched his hand to Minnie's bubbies. Softness bubbled through his spine. When he pressed her nipples, she moaned and started unbuttoning his pants. Colin pulled her onto his lap, exploring inside her mouth. His manhood sprang up outside his pants in Minnie's clasp.

"This feels so good," Minnie groaned, and her mouth started swallowing his manhood, back and forth.

Colin almost arrived in the seventh heaven. "Love you, Ann," he whispered.

Minnie burst into a peal of laughter. "Who is Ann? Your other lover?"

"Sorry, that is my wife. I was bit...bit n—nervous. This is my first time."

Minnie laughed again, hysterically.

Nervousness sunk inside Colin. Minnie's mouth was still teasing his member in slow, delectable thrusts. His palm massaging her swaying assets, his exhilaration rapidly going through the roof. He was about to yank her frock off when his member exploded in her mouth.

"Sorry, I am so sorry, baby."

Minnie got up and ran to the bathroom. Perspiration dampened Colin's skin. Minnie came back after washing her mouth with a smiling gaze.

"That happens. It will be better next time."

Guilt of unfaithfulness to Antonia punched Colin. He even took a shower to wash off Minnie's smell from his skin, even though Antonia was with her parents. But after his next visit to Minnie, the guilt was completely washed out from his consciousness as well.

Colin often thought about what benefit Albert might be expecting from him in return. He became a frequent visitor to his home, and Minnie also entertained him. Even after Antonia came back from Delhi, Colin found time and opportunities to visit Minnie.

Nothing comes for free. Right or wrong?

Antonia no longer resisted dancing with Brigadier Thomas whenever he came to the club without his wife. It was gratifying when Thomas would say in the presence of other senior officers that Colin was one of his blue-eyed boys. Colin felt he was a real capable soldier.

One day, Albert gave him another free piece of advice. Already, the first one had benefitted doubly on him—Thomas's personal attention, and a bonus: Minnie's love. At least he thought it was love. Albert advised Colin to invite Thomas to his home—alone. When Thomas's wife was out of the town, which she usually was, to attend to her sick mother.

"I was, in fact, thinking of inviting him. The delay happened as Antonia was not here."

A meaningful smile crossed Albert's features.

"She can cook tasty dishes," Colin added.

"She needs to cook for the brigadier, also." He winked. "She should make him happy. The way Minnie takes care of you."

Colin was unable to wrap his head around the idea that Antonia had to sleep with the brigadier. He knew she would never agree to this. His head pounded.

"What are you thinking, Sir? This is usual in our profession. War comes once in a while where an officer can prove his loyalty. This is the best way to show your loyalty to the seniors, especially if your wife is beautiful. And Sir, Antonia ma'am dazzles like a fairy. Minnie is nothing compared to her."

Colin realised he had taken months to comprehend Albert's conspiracy. And most probably he was doing this at the behest of Brigadier Thomas himself. He had been trapped. But how could he make Antonia agree?

Was anything available for free?

"You are the husband, Sir. A wife has to obey the husband all the time. Especially when her dedication helps the speedy promotion of the man. Otherwise, who knows? Another junior officer having a beautiful wife could one day become your supervisor."

Another yelp brought Colin back to the veranda of the hospital. Another wounded soldier. One more casualty of the Sepoy Mutiny.

He was missing Antonia. Very much. She should have cooperated like Minnie had with Albert. Was she not enjoying the fruits of his promotion? How hard was it to remain the wife of a junior officer her whole life and go through the hardships of a low-income family?

Colin didn't have guts to explain to Antonia what to do when Brigadier Thomas Brydon came for dinner the first time. She only knew he was coming because he was alone and bored of eating the food made by his cook. And Antonia should take care of a physically tired man.

Colin slipped out of the home within an hour of Thomas' arrival and left her to her fate, praying to God that she would make him happy. Somewhere inside his guts he felt a tinge of pain. How could his beloved Antonia warm another man's bed? Then he weighed the price and the benefit. The reward looked much better than the cost. He returned after midnight, drunk and having spent pleasant times with Minnie. The main door was open, but darkness engulfed the entire home. He was a hundred percent sure Antonia must have enjoyed this first extramarital night of her life. Albert couldn't be wrong. After all, had he not done mastery in wife-trade?

Colin tiptoed inside and lit a candle. To his horror, she was lying on the floor, clothes torn, and skin bruised. His drunkenness disappeared in a moment. The real character of a highly respected and sober gentleman, Brigadier Thomas, had been exposed. Understood, Colin was also not a clean man. But he never forced himself upon Minnie. He sat near a senseless Antonia for almost an hour, a part of his brain wondering how he could fight with the shirk if he was a small fish in the ocean. Noticing blood marks on her chest, he slowly removed her ripped top. Bite marks on her breasts taunted him.

Antonia woke up. Colin's heart sank when he noticed tears rolling down her cheeks. He gently raised her head and placed it on his lap. "I am sorry." He could hardly say these three words as he slowly kissed her bruised lips.

Was it real love? He wondered.

Thomas came again and again. Antonia succumbed to Colin's pressure and warmed the bed of Thomas. Colin thought she had become an obedient wife and didn't realise the volcano inside her was about to erupt.

Antonia should've never tried to complain to the Governor General against her own husband and also against Thomas.

Antonia had long since been gone. Colin's irresponsibility and uncontrolled anger had cast its spell. Was it his anger or Antonia's determination to resist everything that invited her untimely death?

The bell of the church rang three times. He badly needed some sleep. He sighted a hand fan on the chair. There was too much humidity in the air even though the rain had stopped. He picked up the fan, and the smell of fresh palm leaf reminded him of Amelia. She would fan him when Sona was not available to pull the strings of the ceiling fan. He glanced up—no ceiling fan in the room. But the image of Sona's dead body blackened his vision.

She was a nice woman, shouldn't have died. He could have easily supported her had she become pregnant. She could have become the mother of his child. The stupid woman didn't understand the benefits of being the mistress of a white man. East India Company was, in fact, encouraging English people to produce as many children as they could, legitimate or illegitimate, through Indian women to increase the number of mixed-breed in the country. Many officers had raped tribal women and made them pregnant. The Company even supported such rape. Tribal women did not care that much about the so-called chastity. Unfortunately, Sona was not a tribal, but from the Brahmin community. And literate, too. Colin had made a blunder. But this was not his mistake, anyway. It was all because of the rebels, causing so much stress.

You were too adamant, Sona. Why did you force my hands on your neck?

"Oh God, I will never rape an Indian woman in my life. I promise." He felt sleepy.

The bangle sound of the nurse awakened him from slumber. The nurse was Indian, wearing a white saree. She lighted a perfumed incense stick on the table. Colin glanced at her; the saree had red borders, and she was also wearing a red dot on her forehead. "How are you, sister?"

She responded with a warm smile. "I am fine, Brigadier. How was your night?"

Colin realised he spoke to the nurse with respect—it felt good. He was about to talk more to her, but an army officer arrived and indicated that the nurse should leave them alone. Colin's chest clenched tight. The air in the room suddenly thickened, tightening his nerves.

"Sir," he began, expressionless, "the police have recorded the death of Sona as murder. And—"

Colin stared at his face with mixed guilt and fear.

"And—" the officer cleared his throat— "they are suspecting Chetan as he has fled."

Colin sucked in a deep breath and closed his eyes.

"One more piece of news, Sir," the officer continued. "Amelia—" he swallowed— "Amelia ma'am, your wife, has fled also."

"I know." Colin had known, deep down, that Amelia hadn't gone to visit any friend. This was his confirmation.

"She has been sighted with a courtesan and was travelling in a boat in the Gomti River. A British boat approached them for enquiry, but the rebels ambushed them."

"What enquiry?"

"Someone has stolen the secret plan of The Residency. The courtesans might have done this to help the rebels. And, Sir..."

"Go on."

"Sir, Amelia ma'am ... she..."

"I am not going to kill you, officer. What about Amelia ma'am?"

"Sir, she probably aided in the stealing of the map."

"Anything else?"

"No, Sir." The officer left.

Collin grabbed and guzzled the whole glass of water. His throat was still dry. The information about the courtesans helping the rebels seemed to be true. What information could Amelia have passed to the rebels? Where could Chetan have gone? He knows Chetan would not get any support from the British police for his wife's death. Could he have gone to the nawab's court?

Sweat pooled off his body. Colin shouted, "Sister, sister!"

CHAPTER 10

1850, 7 Years Before Sepoy Mutiny
Sehnaz

"*Chaudharayan* has given you a new name, a lovely name. You are now Sehnaz, not Asma. A name which is one in a million. You know *Chaudharayan*? The Chief Courtesan." Gulnar winked at the naked Asma standing in front of the tall mirror.

"I am Sehnaz, no longer Asma." Asma smiled into the mirror. She didn't feel any shame looking at her own naked body. It was a part of her training for the last two months.

She noticed Gulnar smiling at her image in the mirror.

"You have the figure of a fairy." A smile played over Gulnar's mouth. "Look at your long legs. And your long hair hiding your narrow waist."

Asma was adjusting her nose-pin.

Gulnar tenderly slapped her buttocks and laughed. "You can't see your own backside in that mirror. I know how beautiful it looks."

"You may look at my backside, I don't mind. Are you finished with all your praise? Or is there still something left?"

Gulnar cupped Asma's breasts and said, "These breasts! Your nipples wink at the world when you wear the skinny silk *choli*."

Asma was lost in herself. After so long, she was finally about to get something which she had never imagined. Freedom. She could now earn money. She could spend that money. And no man would ever own—

"Sehnaz, where are you lost?"

"Who is Sehnaz?"

"You! Did you forget? You are no more Asma. Asma is dead now. Forever. You are a proper courtesan now. Each girl gets a new name after becoming a courtesan."

"Sehnaz, Sehnaz." The sound rang like a piece of music inside her brain. She again glanced at her own naked body in the mirror. A feeling of freedom and self-satisfaction tickled her skin. It was a new Asma now.

Sehnaz went to the backyard of the *kotha* and sat under a frangipani tree facing the Gomti river. A gust of wind threw frangipani petals onto her lap. The perfume engulfed her senses. It had been a long and dangerous journey for Asma to travel all this way and become Sehnaz.

She remembered when she had been caught standing naked in front of the only mirror at home.

"What are you doing, Asma? Cover up immediately. Are you insane?"

Mother's terrified look shook Asma. She covered up reluctantly and ran to her bed with tears in her eyes.

Her mother followed her. "My daughter is a fairy. Princes will be in a queue to get her hand. You looked awesome when naked."

"Then why did you scold me?" Asma buried her face in Mother's lap.

"You know Asma, I was just like you. Ditto. But be careful, you are the only girl in the house, all others are your brothers. They shouldn't see you in this condition, without clothes."

"But Mother, they are my brothers."

Tears pooled in her mother's eyes.

"Mother, Mother, what happened?" Asma shook her.

Mother hugged Asma tightly and kissed her forehead. "I was exactly like you. Standing alone in front of the mirror and watching myself. My younger sister—she was only a year younger than me, but ten years older in maturity—admonished me a few times. I never paid any heed. We had a large house. One day, that fateful day..." she sobbed, then continued, "your grandmother had been to her parents' home. I didn't realise, two of my older brothers were hiding inside the room in a wardrobe and continued watching me. They are my blood brothers. I was innocent. No, I was, in fact, stupid. When I noticed, I started screaming. But they, they both grabbed me and..." She sat down on the floor and wept.

An unknown fear washed through Asma. Thousands of questions poked to burst out of her mouth.

"Now do you understand why you have never seen your maternal grandparents?"

Asma still didn't comprehend. She was probably stupid, too, like her mother.

Mother continued. "They both forgot that I was their sister. Their own sister." Silence, the past, hung heavy in the room. "My father had to take me to several *hakims*, the local doctors. Everybody in the family was ashamed of me. It took months to terminate my pregnancy. After that, I was practically in prison. They never disclosed that my own brothers had raped me. I was forced to marry a penniless man after paying a large dowry. My younger sister married a wealthy man, another family like my father's. I am spending my life here with your poor and old father."

"Didn't your brothers get any punishment? They are the culprits."

"It is always the mistake of the females. Boys are, after all, boys. If you couldn't cover yourself properly, then it was your fault if you were raped."

Asma loved to sing and dance. Father was always serious, but mother appreciated her dance and would even comment, "My daughter will be a famous dancer when she grows up." She remembered when she wrote her first poem and read it to her illiterate mother. She couldn't forget the smile on her face. That could have never been fake. Somewhere inside her mother was hidden a desire to become like a free bird, sing and dance whenever she'd like. Mother would always comment, *A man's destiny is lying beneath a leaf, but a woman's destiny is buried beneath a stone.*

She was thrilled when she was engaged to a wealthy man she had never seen. Hardly any of her married friends were lucky to know the husband before marriage. However, Asma noticed her mother was in some sort of stress. Was it not normal for mothers to become tense when the daughter was set to leave the home forever?

She laughed when her mother said to her apologetically that they couldn't afford to host a decent wedding like others. The wealthy family of the groom wanted only the bride—a beautiful bride looking like a fairy—and they would provide everything a girl needed.

Everything a girl needed? Asma's dreams were slowly turning into sweet reality.

Asma didn't mind when her poor father sent her to the would-be husband's home accompanied by a distant uncle without any gift. Her uncle dropped her off at a small mansion on the outskirts of Lucknow and returned home. The wedding was to be solemnised the next day. The house was full of people, both family members and friends. And many young men. Her eyes were frantically wandering to find out which young man would be her dream boy. An elderly woman came with new clothes and jewellery, her face pale and eyes glowering. *She could be the groom's mother*, she thought. She threw the clothes at her and muttered, "Keep these for tomorrow, you poor girl," and went away.

Asma smiled as she left. *Poor! I was miserable until this morning. I will be a princess starting tomorrow*, she thought. Time was passing damn slowly for her.

On the morning of the wedding, another lady came and helped her get dressed. Asma's face was covered with a see-through veil. *Nice,* she thought, *I can at least see the groom.*

Asma's eyes rolled in anticipation to find out who would accept her hand. *Maulana,* the Islamic priest, took his position, and everyone assembled. For the first time, she wished someone from her family was by her side. Someone she knew could have talked to her. The sweet daydream was slowly withering away, clearing the way for an unknown foreboding. The *maulana* suddenly asked, "*Kabul Hai?* Do you agree with this wedding?"

She was gasping for breath, covered in sweat, searching frantically for the groom. An old, bearded man—the boy's father or maybe the grandfather—was whispering something in the priest's ears with a broad smile on his mouth and finger pointing at Asma. *Why is nobody bringing the groom?* Tension swelled thick in her chest.

Asma didn't comprehend when she nodded to say 'yes' as per the Islamic custom. The *maulana* suddenly announced, "*Kabul Hai.* The bride has agreed, the bride has agreed." She noticed a blend of laughter and clapping in the venue, and the old, bearded man was waving his handkerchief and shouting, "*Kabul Hai.* Agreed."

Maybe this was a custom at their place. The groom's father or some elderly man would complete the ceremony on behalf of the groom. Didn't her father send an uncle when he should have come to solemnise the daughter's wedding? So many well-dressed young boys were standing near the *maulana,* any one of them could be the groom! Who?

Asma was not a matured woman like her new avatar Sehnaz.

Within a night, Asma grew out of a girl and into a woman.

The same bearded old man came to her bed at night with a grin on his face, wearing new salwar and kurta. A stunned Asma threw her veil and glowered at him in surprise and disgust. She was going to ask him to please send the groom, then suddenly she felt queasy and shocked to her core.

"Why did you remove your veil? I am supposed to do that," the old man said.

"You," Asma stuttered, "you are the groom?"

The man sneered. "Didn't you say 'agreed' to the *maulana*? Were you sleeping when he finished the wedding?"

Asma grabbed the veil lying on the bed and covered up her face again. The husband forgot to lift the veil and instead grabbed her blouse, pressing her nipple so hard that she screamed as pain shot through her ribs. She shoved him toward the wall. The old man almost fell but quickly grabbed the side of the bed frame. Anger firmed into his features as he lurched toward her and clasped her hair.

"Your father has taken money from me for giving me your hand. Don't throw your frustration on me. I am now your husband."

Asma stood still, holding his gaze while her tears plopped and her eyes flared wide in horror. The old man didn't pay any heed; instead, he threw her on the bed. She lay motionless as agony seized her body and mind. He forced her thighs wide open and thrust inside her, forcing her to gasp with each push of his dirty penis. The heat of his foul mouth darted out onto her nipples and face.

In the morning, the old woman came inside the room, noticed drops of blood on the sheets, and called out loudly, "Come on, you have got a virgin girl. Congratulations."

Asma curled back up in the bed, no energy left to get up, groin still aching with acute pain.

The old man came rushing inside. "Allah, my money didn't go to the bin like last time."

The old woman derided him. "How much money did you pay to my father? Rather, he paid you a dowry to marry me. I was a virgin then. I shed more blood than this girl. You have never valued me as anything more than a maid."

Asma opened her weary eyes. The woman whom she had thought to be her mother-in-law was her co-wife. Neither the woman nor the man was concerned about her presence. She was another domestic animal bought from the market for amusement. Emotions roiled, tightened. An abhorrence for her own father surged through her chest.

After that first horrible night with her old husband, Asma accepted her fate. Death was the only alternative for her, which she didn't like. She became friends with the old man's first wife, who was older than her own mother, even. Her name was Jema. She also learned her husband's name, Qasim. His son, her stepson, who was much older than she, would stare at her when she was alone. Deep inside her heart, she would long to get a handsome husband like him. But Asma knew that was not possible.

There was a tall mirror in her bedroom. Mirrors were no longer her favourite. But Qasim would sometimes ask her to stand in front of it and remove her clothes gradually, one after another. The oldie was surprisingly young in mind. His libido was like a young boy of eighteen. He would stare at her breasts and comment, "They are so small. I will make them bigger. I have brought a paste. Massage that on one hour before bathing, and it will do magic. But you are too young, anyway. You know, breasts get bigger if a man sucks them. I have done that to my second wife. Within a year her *choli* became tight. I had to buy new ones for her."

That day, Asma knew she was not the second wife of Qasim. He had married six times. Some had died, and the second wife had fled.

Fled? Where is she now?

A ray of hope exploded in her.

An urge to know more about *the second wife* became fierce in Asma. Nobody would tell her anything about Qasim's second wife, not even her name. She was another number in the list of wives. Her first mission was to befriend the elderly female neighbours, those who could have known the woman intimately—some secret which had been buried inside the solid rocks of the family honour.

"Those women earn money like menfolk. They don't have to take permission from any man to do anything in life," the elderly neighbour woman told her.

Asma realized this woman was telling her the fate of the second wife. She stared at her with eyes widened as if that were a fairy tale.

The woman continued. "I was in Lucknow. The women live in large mansions there. Those mansions are called *kothas*. Every evening they perform singing and dancing before an audience, rich and wealthy patrons. The audience pays them a handsome amount."

"Do they also sleep with those patrons?"

"Not necessarily. The girls get paid for the shows, not for sleeping. Many of them are even poets. They recite their poems to their audiences. Wealthy people send their sons to them. They teach them etiquette, how to talk to dignitaries, how to appreciate literatures. They sleep, but with only those they love. Royals, senior English officers, and wealthy businessmen come to the *kothas* regularly. But they never marry. Because the moment you marry a man, the human living in that body becomes a husband. Husband and demon both are the same."

A slow, smouldering fire of hope built up in Asma's gut. Her eyes glowed as if she were one of them, those fairies.

The lady took Asma inside another room. "Stand in front of this mirror and stare at your own image. You have everything, almost everything to become a courtesan. You are still young."

Asma held her gaze. "Why you are saying this to me?"

"One day, I had also dreamt of that life. I was beautiful in my younger days. I knew a little bit of singing and dancing. But I lacked just one thing."

"What is that?"

The woman lifted her head and met Asma's gaze. "Courage."

Asma didn't have the courage, either. She didn't even dare to think of anything outside the concrete borders of a family, even after the old Qasim died a year later. She was hopeful of getting another husband: young, handsome, and wealthy. That was the dream of every young girl her age.

She got the attention of a young, attractive, and wealthy man. That man would quietly slip into her bedroom at midnight and wake up her yearning. He would quietly unbutton her blouse and tingle her nipples. When Asma would sense his bulging member under her palm, heat flowed to her groin. But a part of her grappled with a fantasy which could never be a reality. That man was Asma's stepson. She could have never married him. When his mother Jema came to know, she became furious. She was practically the head of the home after Qasim's death and started treating Asma like an unwanted domestic animal.

Asma approached the neighbour auntie, and a rude shock slammed through her. Jema had already finalised a deal for her. She would be sold to an old man in Lucknow for her second marriage. She was petrified, imagining an ugly face of an old man with a white beard, wrinkled skin. Sweat started beading on her forehead.

Auntie laughed. "This is your golden chance, my child. If you have a little bit of courage, you can do what I couldn't do and am still regretting. I know somebody who can help. That man will follow when you are taken to Lucknow to be sold. You decide whether you would like another life."

"Sehnaz, Chaudhurayan is waiting for you," Gulnar was standing near her, "you will do the final rehearsal in the costume and be ready for your first performance before the audience."

Sehnaz's heart pounded. *I will dance before the audience!*

CHAPTER 11

28 May 1857 Evening, After Boarding the Ferry
Sehnaz

Sehnaz's heart sank.

She and Amelia started their second boat journey from Faizabad to Varanasi. Amelia's features crumpled as she gazed at the dying horse, shot by Sheru, with an imploring look in her eyes. Tears rolled down her cheeks. Sehnaz hadn't seen her that upset even when a boatload of British soldiers was ambushed and the Gomti River wore a red blanket of their blood. After two nights of togetherness, the two women had become somewhat like close friends.

Amelia powerlessly slumped to the floor of the boat, consternation creasing her brow. Sehnaz's heart crunched. She glanced at Sheru, who was calmly manoeuvring the rudder of the ferry as if nothing had happened. She couldn't blame him. Her safety and life both were in Sheru's hands until they arrived at Varanasi. She had to trust him.

Sehnaz looked at Amelia. She had stopped sobbing, accepted the horse's destiny. Who knew what she was going through? It was not an easy decision for a woman to leave the safe haven of a family home—until that turned out to be worse than hell. Why didn't Sehnaz ask Amelia before? Why did she make such a precarious decision with her life?

Sehnaz sat down with her, hugged her shivering body tightly against her own. A current of soaring power stirred deep inside her. She felt a kind of energy in her veins. Sehnaz was no longer a helpless woman surviving on the mercy of a husband or any man. She was independent, living on her own terms.

Amelia turned her head and glanced up, semi-dried tears still glistening on her white cheeks.

"This is a war, Amelia ma'am. Rulers and kings start the fight, but it is the innocent who lose everything. The innocent horse was another victim of this war. Sheru didn't kill the animal for fun. He wouldn't even kill a bird for his own amusement. He is a Brahmin and a strict vegetarian. British could trail us effortlessly had it been left alive."

A shy smile pulled on Amelia's mouth when she hugged Sehnaz and said, "Thank you. And please don't call me ma'am. Just Amelia."

Sheru was still sitting tight, holding the rudder.

"Can I help?" Amelia went to him and asked.

Sheru glanced up. "Ma'am, I am sorry. For the horse. Both ladies, please go to sleep. I will row the whole night, it's safer than the day."

Sehnaz spread a bed inside the cabin. Both women deserved a night of peaceful sleep.

Amelia's squeal sliced through the dark night; the ferry was shaking. Sehnaz woke up and glanced outside. Sheru had vanished. The wind slapped waves against the boat. A roaring chill of foreboding whipped through her. She sighted Sheru's head—he was standing in neck-deep water and tying the ferry to a bough of a tree. They were already near the riverbank.

"We can't proceed farther in this storm." Sheru's loud voice was almost drowned out by the sound of the storm. "So I brought the boat here. Let's see if I can get some accommodation for the night."

"Which place is this?" Sehnaz asked.

"Looks like Sultanpur. I can see a large house there. Let me see if the owner agrees to spare a few rooms for a night or two."

29 May 1857 Morning

Amelia was sleeping. Sehnaz stared at her face in the dim light of the small oil lamp. A childlike innocence blended with lots of pain plastered over her beautiful face. She had never gotten a chance to talk to her about her family. She had known English people didn't like to discuss personal matters with outsiders. That was one of few etiquettes she had been taught when she started as a courtesan. Had it not been such an unusual time, she could have easily gathered data from inside The Residency.

She had not been able to sleep, wondering whether the map safely arrived and Rupen received it. The British had more money and arms. All the kings together couldn't defeat them unless they used the same tactics as the Whites. Deceiving and betraying. Divide and rule, which they had successfully applied in India. The rebels were not organised. Everything seemed like a mysterious puzzle. *Will Rupen survive the war? Will the good old days come back again? Can Nawab Wajid Ali continue as the ruler of Awadh?*

Sehnaz left the room and ambled to the riverbank. They were planning to stay here the whole day and start again before evening. Sehnaz glanced at the river. Stormy waves were still lashing the riverbank, and the sky was a mess of dark clouds. The anchored boat was swaying as if wincing in pain.

So many memories started haunting Sehnaz's soul. Amelia's ashen face reminded Sehnaz of her mother's look when she saw her for the last time. She was going to her would-be husband's house with lots of daydreams which her mother probably knew were all false. Like any other devoted wife, her mother had swallowed all her sorrows.

What could have happened to Amelia? Sehnaz's brain said not to trust an English woman when a civil war was burning the country. Her heart said she was innocent and a tortured soul. She had experience in what happened when a woman was trapped in a wrong marriage. Only another woman who had faced such a harsh life could understand her situation. Asking an English woman to reveal her personal problems might be rude. But Sehnaz could talk about her own past with Amelia. She could talk about how her father sold her to an old man, and the society called it a marriage. Amelia might open up about her problem. She remembered her own poem, based upon the theme, *Men think through their brains and women, through their hearts.* Sehnaz had to prove her heart was smarter than her brain. Could she?

The storm had stopped and the Gomti was flowing calmly, like an obedient woman.

Sehnaz got up to return to the room. Amelia had already gotten up; Sehnaz had watched from a distance as she had meandered from the house—probably to go to the river ghat for bathing. She was about to go inside, but Sheru approached her.

"I have some confidential information for you," he whispered.

Sehnaz stilled. A panic flickered through her stomach. Millions of questions hounded her. *Did Rupen not receive the map of The Residency?*

Sheru came close, as if even trees had ears. "Amelia ma'am..." He carefully glanced around. "We have been trapped in our own game. She might be, in fact, a spy of the Company. I saw her talking to an unknown man outside."

Lack of sleep had already jammed Sehnaz's brain. Confusion rattled through her. "Where is she?" she asked. "I will talk to her and clarify."

"You are going to ask a cobra if she would bite you? Highness Rupen has given me the responsibility to take you safely to Varanasi, and he will meet you there. If a white woman comes with us, British spies will notice."

Sehnaz regarded him in silence. Tension swelled thick in the air. No woman would flee from the family home unless there was a real danger to her life. She had done it once and could feel what might have gone through a woman in such a situation. She regretted not taking Amelia into confidence earlier. Conflict tightened in her guts. There was no time to enquire about her life. A quick decision could help the rebels or destroy them. She was no longer another courtesan or a mistress of the General of Awadh kingdom, she was managing the information network for the rebels on behalf of Rupen Naik. A single white woman on one side and the destiny of millions of patriots who did not wish to be ruled by a foreign power on the other—she had to make the decision. Within minutes. Before Amelia came back.

Sheru immediately brought all of Sehnaz's belongings from the room, and they both ran toward the anchored boat.

"I haven't told you something important because she was with me all the time," Sehnaz said.

Sheru's hand stilled on the tiller and he fixed his gaze on Sehnaz, consternation creasing his brows.

"Her full name is Amelia Lawrence. She said she was of no relation to Brigadier Lawrence, but if what you're saying is true, then I think she lied to me about her last name."

"Our master is fighting against Brigadier Colin Lawrence, and his wife is travelling with us? We passed on the map of The Residency in full view of her, and no doubt she was passing on the information to the East India Company. If Rupen fails to capture The Residency, there is little chance of our victory."

Sehnaz didn't reply but glanced blankly at the sky. *Women think through their hearts...is that wrong?*

CHAPTER 12

30 May 1857 Early Hours
Chetan

Chetan failed to understand why the world was continually collapsing under his feet since the night before. Swimming in the Gomti River holding on to a log, he had little time to think what went wrong with his life. He was a peaceful man, had never thought of joining the rebels. He rested for a few moments. At least the current of the river was not overpowering, and he was lucky enough to find a log immediately after the boat—on which he had received employment only hours ago— went into pieces after being hit by a large cannon bullet.

He heard a shrill sound. Someone was shouting, "Help, help!" Chetan gazed around, but the morning sunrays made him partially blind. The holler was coming from that direction.

He started pushing his way toward the sound. "Wait, brother, don't panic. I will be there shortly." His voice didn't have depth, and he doubted whether the man could hear him. He shouted again, "Brother, where are you? I am on my way. Please hold on to whatever possible and try to remain afloat. I am coming."

He noticed another log. *Not everyone is as lucky as I am to find support.* It was a plank of the destroyed boat. He changed his direction and swam toward the floating plank; it was heavy, attached to something larger underneath. Chetan struggled to yank it with all his force. He shouted again, "Brother, are you all right?"

No response. Urgency prickled through Chetan. He immediately started swimming toward the direction where the sound was coming. How come there were so many people in the boat, and no one knew how to swim? He increased his pace, vision still partially blocked from the sunlight. He noticed a man floating at a distance, not too far. "Hold on, hold on, brother. We both can fit on this one plank. Don't lose hope."

Chetan approached him. A pleasant laugh blurted out of his mouth at his own success. "Come on, brother, I am here. Hold on to this. The riverbank is not far away. We will be there in no time."

The man didn't respond. Chetan came closer. The man's eyes were open, hands severed. Chetan's eyes flared widely. How big could the bullets have been that the limbs of a man could be separated? Something dawned in him—*then who was shouting for help?* His pulse kicked. "Hello, where are you?"

Chetan became worried when he didn't get a response, so he shouted again, louder. A faint reply propelled him to swim faster, only to find disfigured bodies floating. How could he believe, only a few hours ago, those bodies were his work colleagues? He had even made friends with a few of them.

A bellow blurted out of his mouth. *Oh, God, what type of test you are doing?*

Only a day ago he had jumped into the water to escape the British police, and he had been rescued by this ferry. He had no rowing experience but was ready to work in whatever capacity possible. A hungry stomach could push a man to any extent. He told the crew he was a soldier of the East India Company but worked as a guard to the brigadier. He wanted to lie, tell them he was a rebel to emanate some sympathy.

Patriotism was racing high in the blood of the natives. But he couldn't. Regardless, the crew were happy to accommodate him and pay some wages. Chetan got the duty of a nightguard.

The whole night before the attack was peaceful. Chetan had spent most of his time in the engine room with the pilot. The previous night's events were still raw in his mind. He planned to get some time alone during the day for some prayer and meditation.

Many people have already lost their lives, and many more will suffer. This is a war. So what is the big deal that you also lost something? Your wife? At least your daughter is alive and safe. You are living, too. Everything has a purpose.

It was as if God came in his heartfelt prayer and told him something that touched his soul. He clearly saw Lord Ram in his mind's eye, giving him some peaceful air and consolation. After arriving in Varanasi, he could send a letter to the neighbour auntie that he would be back one day. The war would be over sometime anyway. Nawab Wajid Ali and Brigadier Colin were friends; they would definitely make some agreement, and peace would be back. His heart assured him—he would go back to his daughter and start a new life.

Chetan had gazed at the clear, nocturnal sky. One of the millions of stars twinkled at him. He saw Sona's face in it. Tears slipped down from his eyes. The pilot standing nearby noticed and asked him whether everything was all right. Chetan pulled a smile on his lips and said, "All good, brother. Something got in my eye. Dirt, maybe."

It was just before dawn. A military ferry appeared from nowhere. The sight of the Union Jack sent his nerves into the alert zone. The flag, which he was saluting just a day ago, created panic in him. A sudden urge to flee punched his guts. He was confident they were following him only. Yesterday he had escaped from the police and jumped into the water. He knew the British were the mightiest in the world, probably next only to God. How long he could evade them?

The goods ferry was in danger because of him. Guilt washed over his skin. He didn't want to endanger the lives of the very people who had rescued him and provided shelter. He mentally prepared to surrender and go to prison.

As the boat came closer, he realised the pilot had already alerted the captain, who scurried to the machine room and ordered them to move faster. Chetan tried to convince him that the British were in fact, after him, but the captain didn't pay any heed. Instead, he commanded Chetan to go inside and wake up all the sleeping people. Chetan hurried inboard without any further argument.

Only one day into his new job, he was unaware of the many stairs and floors of the large ferry, and mistakenly arrived at the cargo side. His eyes flared open when he saw the consignment: rifles and bullets. He lifted one of them. It was an English-made Enfield stolen from the British arsenal! He swung back and climbed the stairs again toward the cockpit, without awakening any of the sleeping crew. Suddenly the exchange of bullets sounded. The war was on. A crew member scurried past him. He promptly asked him what was happening.

"We are carrying weapons for the freedom fighters. Follow me! We need your help," the man screamed and lunged up the stairs. Chetan followed him without even knowing where he was going. Soon they arrived at the rear of the vessel. His gaze fell on the giant cannon mounted on the enemy's ferry and a soldier inserting a massive cannonball.

His baby daughter's face suddenly flashed in front of him. Chetan screamed, "This is the end! They will blow out the whole vessel. Save your lives first."

Within a fraction of a second, he had found himself inside the river. An unexpected force of water pushed him deep down. Chetan struggled to look for a way out, but all he could see was a vast reddish glow —it was beyond his comprehension. He muttered a short, final prayer, surrendering his daughter's fate to God. But the next second, he was up above the water. The vessel he was in had been broken into thousands of pieces floating on the blood-soaked, pink water. The Union Jack was proudly moving away with the armed British ferry beneath it. He was lucky to catch hold of a plank to stay afloat.

It then dawned on him that no one else in that goods ferry was alive. The ruthless British cannon blew up everyone in one shot. A chill of foreboding trickled down his spine. The little energy he had left drained from his body. *Am I a cursed man? So many people died because of my ill omen!*

The shrill of the helpless man was still echoing in his ears. Chetan raised his head and glanced around: blankets of dense forests covered both sides of the Gomti River. He didn't notice a single house on either side. The possibility of facing wild animals frightened him more than the waves of the Gomti. He continued floating on the plank and shifted slowly in the current. Hours passed, but the forest appeared endless. His stamina withered away further. He had no other choice but to rest on the piece of wood and stare at the sky. Everything was silent around him.

After a while, he noticed houses alongside the river. His plank was already ahead of the locality, and he would have to swim against the current to come back. But hunger slammed him in the stomach. He twisted on the floating wood, hauled his hand to change direction, and forced his way against the current—which spun hard beneath him. A tiny hope kept Chetan's eyes focussed on the small locality, and he slowly moved toward the bank.

The bank came closer, and the tiny houses looked bigger. Only a few hundred gauges left. Finally, Chetan touched the riverbank. He got off the floating wood and gave it a kick. The plank fell back into the stream and drifted away in the current. He trudged toward what looked like a small village, but his stomach was flat, empty. He couldn't drag his feet any farther. Chetan slumped down on the grass next to the narrow, unpaved pathway and peeked around. He could knock on someone's door and beg for food.

Beg! His conscience struggled within. He could be impoverished, but he couldn't be a beggar. Even when the goods ferry had rescued him from the river, he didn't ask for anything free; instead, he requested to work. How could he beg now?

Chetan stretched his legs and arms on the wild grass, eyes asking for sleep, but stomach demanding food. Clouds in the blue sky, birds flying in droves, everything looked hazy. Suddenly his eyes flicked up at the sight of something yellowish hanging on a tree, leaning toward the river. Chetan got up and hobbled toward the only mango tree he could find. Gathering all his strength, he climbed up. This was the only way to survive starvation without begging. The fruit he found was raw; he ate that in one bite. Sweet, but tiny.

His gaze fell on a bough hanging directly above the water of the Gomti. Yellow, rounded mangoes swinging pulled saliva out of his mouth. He inched toward them, the current of the Gomti flowing beneath him. Chetan picked one mango and hugged it, dangling his feet and resting against another branch. He thanked God for providing him with something to keep him alive. His gaze wandered as he ate the fruit. The plank he had kicked away was still there, trapped in a mangrove. A mild laugh blurted out of his mouth.

The plank was a severed door from the destroyed ferry. Chetan hadn't noticed earlier. The picture of Lord Ganesh was crafted on the top portion of the door. He plucked another mango and threw it toward the plank. "Oh, Lord, you secured my life. I am sorry I did not notice you earlier. Please forgive me. This fruit is in your honour, my offering. Namaste."

Chetan failed to comprehend whether the plank was struggling to free itself from the tangle or if Lord Ganesh had a plan to stay there for a while.

Suddenly his gaze fell on a horse tethered to a stump in the distance. He wondered how he didn't notice that earlier. An unknown worry stabbed into him. Within no time, a white man came out of the house and approached the horse. Chetan stopped eating the mango and lay flat, grabbing the branch tightly as he had been taught in army training. He tried to calm himself down and focus on the floating door in the water. *Oh, Lord Ganesh. Please save me.* Chetan, who only two days ago was a proud, loyal soldier of the British army, was now petrified at the sight of any white man.

The horse snorted as the man, who was in an army uniform, mounted the saddle and started moving. Chetan drew a breath and muttered, "Thank you, Lord. He didn't notice me."

As if he had heard his voice, the man instantly stopped his horse and started scanning the area. It didn't take him long to discover Chetan hanging from the bough. "Hi," he shouted, "what are you doing there? What are you watching?"

Chetan shivered but didn't reply. The man got off the horse and ran toward the house, screaming, "A spy! Hello all. Come out immediately! A spy is watching us from above the tree, bloody Indian rebel."

How could Chetan convince the man he was watching his own cursed life?

Panic stabbed Chetan's guts. He tried to get off the tree and flee, but sweat and nerves both slackened his grip. The man had already disappeared inside the house. He could hear the clamour. Within no time, a group of angry soldiers would appear and shoot him down as if he were a wild animal. Chetan tried to hurry. His shaky grip refused to oblige, and he plummeted into the Gomti. The plank with the sculpting of Lord Ganesh was awaiting him patiently. He dragged himself out of the water and grabbed the plank tightly. Within no time, he swam to the other side of the mangrove and stayed put, holding onto a twig. Around ten British soldiers came shouting out of the house and swarmed the area.

"He was here, hiding in this tree," the man who had noticed him first yelled. "Must be somewhere here. Can't go far in such a short time. He is a secret agent. Spread out and find him. Just shoot that brown dog."

All the hateful words torpedoed across the shrub and stabbed Chetan's ears. *I am still a loyal soldier, running because of a misunderstanding. Why is there so much hatred for us?* Bitterness flooded into his heart.

The group scattered on the opposite side to hunt him down. It wouldn't take long to come back and look for him in the water. Chetan let himself loose in the current of the Gomti. *Lord Ganesh, you were waiting here because you knew monsters would come back for me. I didn't recognise your plans.* He folded his hands. Emotion warmed his heart. Within minutes, he was a safe distance away. It seemed like his journey was to be through the river, and with a brief stopover for a lunch break. He blurted out a laugh. Again, whispering chill flushed through him. He must find shelter before the evening. Ripe mangoes could energise him for almost a day.

A day?

The sun was getting warmer. Chetan was thrust back to his childhood when his father would take him to the River Ganga and train him in swimming. "This river is a goddess," he told him, "and the goddess will save your life."

He never thought of this day then. "River Gomti has also joined Ganga. This is also another goddess. She has saved my life twice today and will save it many more times." Floating on a river and without any plan where to go, he still felt protected by Lord Ganesh on the plank and the river goddess beneath his body. Stress and fatigue buckled his muscles. Chetan curled up on his plank and drifted into a deep slumber.

When he woke up from a sweet dream, yawned and stretched, the soft and warm sunlight was slowly massaging his tanned skin. The day had already tilted toward dusk. A mild panic whispered at the edges of his mind. He tried to sit up, but slipped off the plank and fell into the river. He couldn't spend the whole night on the water. And hardly any daylight was left. Moments after, he sighted a city at a distance. Getting up on the wooden door, he started rowing with his palm. He doubted whether he could arrive at the destination before darkness covered him with its blanket. A proper oar could have helped speed things up. He did the last salute to Lord Ganesh and discarded the plank for the last time. Swimming almost an hour, he arrived at the riverbank, hungry and exhausted.

I will not tell anyone I am a soldier. This place must be far away from Lucknow, and police will not recognise me. I will pretend to be an ordinary worker and ask for some work. This army job is not for me. My father was a farmer, and I should have been a farmer, too. Once the war is over, I will take my daughter and move to my ancestral village. I will do agriculture in my village's farmland and lead a peaceful life. I will also complete the religious rites for Sona. She deserves it as the wife of a pious Hindu.

The city was at a distance, but Chetan noticed a few houses and also a temple nearby. The temple would be the place to get food and shelter for the night. Begging for food in God's house was not against his ethics. A narrow path alongside the river led the way to the temple through orchards and scattered dwellings.

Chetan ambled toward the shrine. Dusk was almost paving the way to the darkness of the night. Fatigue crumpled his body. *I am not a soldier anymore. I will not be afraid of any white man here,* he thought. The pathway forked at one point, and he noticed a woman standing beneath a tree watching the orange hue in the gentle ripples of the Gomti. Chetan thought he could ask her the shortest way to the temple. He approached the saree-clad blonde woman from the side and felt a sparkle in his own eyes. *The British pride themselves for being white. They should come and see this village woman. Her white skin and blonde hair!* He realised that he had yet to see her face. But his brief fear of the white skin vanished, and he approached the woman.

The lady swung around, and both stood face to face. Something whispered and crackled around his mind. The woman was Amelia. Sweat beaded on his torso. He knew that Amelia Memsahib had gone out for a week to meet a friend. The British soldiers must be guarding her as she is the wife of a brigadier. He blathered as tension snapped across his stomach.

Chetan swung back and ran away as far as possible, knowing very well that going away from the city would make him starve, but staying there would bring sure death.

CHAPTER 13

30 May 1857 Early Hours Until Midday
Amelia

I increase my pace toward the house. Locating a large tree, I hide and breathe hard, exhausted. I had seen only a glimpse of Chetan, but I'm sure it was him. Maybe I'm wrong. If he was Chetan, then he would have saluted me with his usual trademark smile and asked in his accented English, "Amelia Memsahib, how are you?"

I think he muttered something—he probably said my name and then ran away. That man always prides himself for being a loyal soldier of the East India Company. I am jumpy. Colin must have information that I've fled and am hiding here in Sultanpur. I know the East India Company has a good information network; Colin had once told me that they could even locate a pin in a haystack. British have planted thousands of informers. Has he used those informers to find me? Otherwise, what is Chetan doing here?

I was sure we would spend a few days in this house, as Sheru Pandey had told us that day journeying in the river is risky. British could quickly locate us. I was also averse to being found by the British, for my own reason. In the morning when I came out of the room, I noticed Sehnaz strolling on the banks of the Gomti. She looked absorbed in her own thoughts. I felt relaxed and ambled toward the road, thinking that we had the whole day ahead of us. A chipper feeling started tingling my skin. I was already far away from the feral environment of Colin's home. Varanasi was not far away, and within weeks I would be boarding a ship to London. A local man saluted me, and we exchanged pleasantries. Suddenly an urge to practise the local language overwhelmed me. I forgot that I should have concealed my identity. I overlooked the fact that I am a white woman in a brown country which is ruled by the white British. I ignored that my actions could endanger the lives of Sehnaz and Sheru, besides compromising my own safety. I indulged with my chats for quite some time and calmly returned.

Entering the room where both Sehnaz and I had slept last night, I noticed her suitcase was not in its place. I blamed myself for leaving the room unattended. Someone might have stolen her belongings. Immediately I opened my suitcase and checked if my money was intact. Yes, it was. Relief and guilt both wash through me. *Poor Sehnaz, she has lost all her money to the thief, all because of my utter carelessness.* I scurried toward the riverbank but didn't find her. My eyes scanned everything around me. Then I realised the ferry was also missing.

A chill sank into my bones. How could Sehnaz abandon me when we were sort of close friends? I had helped her on a cold night when she was walking alone on the war-ravaged streets of Lucknow. I had felt the warmth of her heart when she hugged me last evening on the boat. I walked on the banks of the Gomti in hopes of getting a glimpse of the ferry. So many boats were sailing in the river, but none resembled the one we were in. I felt like crying. But I kept my gaze fixed in case she changed her mind and came back.

I realise that I'm still standing behind the tree. Chetan has gone since long. Unknowingly, my eyes scan the sky; no remote dark cloud comes into view. A faint hope ignites my soul. Chetan might not have noticed me. Or perhaps the man I saw for a moment was someone else. Again, the word *if* starts chasing my perception. What if that man was

Chetan? Colin's trusted guard is here, and that can have only one meaning. I must do something right now. I scurry toward the house, breath rasping, as if it could shelter me like a fort. My legs suddenly want to give up, energy drained from my blood.

I slump down on the grass beneath a tree. The small distance between the riverbank and the house feels like miles to me. Sweat drips from my forehead, throat dry. It is so difficult for a white woman to hide even though the country is so vast. Rebels would doubt I am from the British side. For those faithful to the East India Company, I would be a prize catch. I should have thought of this before setting my feet outside Colin's house. I might end up like his first wife, or even continue living in hell—which is worse than death. A ghastly scene of an imaginary Antonia hung to the ceiling blurs my vision.

I arrive at the room and pack my suitcase. I need to go somewhere where Chetan can't find me. But where? Dragging the suitcase, I come out on the road, covering my blond hair with the loosened of the saree.

As I continue walking, I encounter a smiling face on my way. Not knowing how to react, I stand quietly. My heartbeat quickens. Ignoring her, I start pushing myself again down the road.

The woman asks in English, "Hiding? Husband beating?"

I still as if her voice has a commanding power. But I avoid meeting her gaze, hoping she will go away and let me go, but where would I really go? Unknowingly, my gaze goes to the sky, and a tiny block of pinkish white cloud smiles at me. A calming thought suddenly soothes my nerves. Strength comes back to my limbs. If I have to face Colin again, so be it.

"How do you know?" I dare to ask her.

She touches her snow-white hair and says, "Gray, see? Not in sunlight." She points at the sun. "Please come with me."

I do not understand what she meant, but I strangely feel mesmerised and quietly follow her. I have no other options—starve until I'm caught, or follow the woman. A man from the British police might be waiting in her home to capture me and be awarded a handsome prize from my husband. *The man who can't control his wife doesn't deserve to control a battalion*, I have heard my husband saying in the past.

The pinkish white cloud is still winking at me. Is it a sign of something opening up for me?

The woman's stride is confident. I follow her with my suitcase on my head, which helps me to partly hide my face. A white woman walking on a road holding a box on her head could be an unforgettable scene to the brown natives. We pass through a few uncrowded roads and an orchard before we enter a large brick house. The woman helps me offload my suitcase in her front room in the front yard, and I stand before her, awaiting further command. A beautiful smile unfurls on her mouth. She is an old lady in her late sixties, but still retains lots of charm from her youth.

"Please sit down on this chair, you must be tired. Let me go and fetch a glass of water for you." She disappears into another room.

She walks gracefully and knows modern etiquettes. I hadn't noticed any police or horses outside her house. Anyway, I have already surrendered myself to the circumstances. I draw a cross on my chest. Within minutes she comes back with a glass of water and a plate full of some dry Indian snacks. I remember Sona cooking similar items but do not recollect the name.

"You must be hungry." Her smile is assuring.

Exhaustion has stolen all mannerisms from me. I curl my weary feet on the chair and start eating with gusto. The cold water eases away my tight muscles and soothes my mind. I don't know where to go or look for another shelter without Sehnaz or Sheru Pandey with me. I had never even gone to the market alone in Lucknow.

"I am Bibi Khanum. I was a courtesan. Retired now." She meets my gaze, poise glowing in her eyes.

Before I can reply, a female voice calls her. Bibi gets up and exits the room, heading into the main house.

I sit tight. So many thoughts cross my mind. Bibi must have had high ranking British officers as clients in her younger days.

I close my eyes. Colin's voice floats up to me. "We, the British, have planted hundreds of thousands of moles among the stupid Indians. It is so easy to buy these poor natives. Throw a piece of stale bread at them, they will start licking your feet. Bloody dogs."

Bibi Khanum is neither impoverished nor stupid. I am torn. How much might this intelligent woman have received from the Company to spy on the rebels? I am not against the British occupying this country. My fight is only against the force, which has denied me a decent and respectable life. I wouldn't mind if each Indian became loyal to the East India Company and the Sepoy Mutiny finished tomorrow. But I'd hate to be a captive between the rivals.

Bibi is still inside talking to some female in a hushed voice. Is something cooking?

She comes back to the front room in the front yard. "You can stay with me," she says and herds me inside. A young girl comes and carries my suitcase. We walk through a large open courtyard full of native flower plants and step onto a wide veranda. Bibi stops in front of a crafted door. I flick a quick glance; the figures of dancing males and females in compromising poses throw cocky winks at me. Bibi blurts out a laugh. "You will know about them later."

The massive and heavy door opens with a creak. We enter into a large bedroom with a tall *palank* bed. I notice the orchard through the open window. "This is your bedroom. I am sure you will love that cupboard for your clothes." Bibi proudly opens it for me.

"Wardrobe," I correct her.

"She right." The girl giggles.

My bedroom? I wonder. For how many days?

I peek through the window. The fence wall is high, like that of a small fortress.

"Yours is a beautiful bungalow," I comment as the girl leaves the room.

Bibi lets out a smile of appreciation. I steal a quick glance at her while she straightens the sheets on the bed. Her skin is flawless even at this age, her breasts proudly peeking through the thin saree she has draped, exposing the bare navel of her slim waist.

You look gorgeous. I think of complimenting, but something tightens my mouth.

"Please take some rest. You can freshen up in the bathroom in the courtyard. We will meet at lunchtime." She leaves. Sitting on the bed, I ponder if I can escape everything and enjoy the solitude. I hear a faint noise and realise that the only heart beating in the room belongs to me.

When I left The Residency, I had never thought I would travel with Sehnaz. Why am I worried now that she deserted me? Maybe God has chosen a different path for me. I try to steal a nap, but unknown angst keeps me awake. I come out of the room and ask for the way to the restroom. The maid girl takes me to the courtyard—a large, open space with a well, a stone bathtub, and a stone bench to relish the luxurious bath. The maid has already kept enough water for me in two large tubs. It has no ceiling. I can see the branches of a mango tree extending over it. Anyone climbing on it will have a beautiful view of the woman bathing inside. I glance around to make sure no one is watching from above. A gloomy mood pervades my mind. I pour some water to ease my nervous skin and rush to the bedroom, wrapped in a towel.

30 May 1857 After Midday
Amelia

"I will now take you to my dressing room," Bibi announces after lunch.

Thank God she didn't announce of the arrival of the police. I force a smile and follow her to a spacious room. Almost a dozen lamps brighten the perfumed interior. As soon as I enter, I see my reflection on a half a dozen tall mirrors.

"Awesome," I compliment.

Her gaze penetrates my eyes. A smug smile unfurls on her face. "Take off your clothes," Bibi says, her voice low and quiet, but commanding.

I stay still, feeling like a soldier standing in front of a senior officer and striving to execute the order. It's awkward for an unknown person to be asking me to remove my clothes. For a moment I hesitate. Then my hands move to my back to unbutton my frock. I make sure to plaster on a smile. The skin-tight dress struggles to fall on the carpeted floor.

"Persian carpet, clean."

I glance at the expensive flooring under my feet and then look at the mirror. I am standing with only my undergarments. Bibi will probably give me some clothing from the wardrobe to wear.

"Remove the rest," Bibi says.

"Rest?" I mutter, then slowly and hesitantly unhook my bodice. Bibi takes it from me and gently deposits it on a stool. I watch my breasts dancing to the tune of my heavy breath in the mirrors and notice a seductive smile unfolding on her lips.

"Everything," she reminds me.

My underskirt touches Bibi's Persian carpet. A dozen naked Amelias stare back at me.

"You have a lovely body," she remarks. "Did you ever dance when you were a kid?"

"Yes, I did. And still remember some steps." I think about telling her I have never danced naked. But my lips don't open.

Bibi inches to the large wardrobe and opens the doors. My eyes expand at her vast collection of clothing and pieces of jewellery. She asks me to lie down on a cot and widen my thighs, and she calls out for the maid. I bite my lips and glance away when the girl comes inside. She shaves my groin, underarms, and legs. Sona used to do this for me, as Colin loved my body clean all the time.

Bibi takes out a dark coloured dress. "This is called *lehnga*," she says. "This is like the skirt English girls wear. I think dark will suit your white skin. You know, Amelia ma'am—"

"Bibi, please call me Amelia, no ma'am."

"Sure, and you also call me 'Auntie.' In our culture seniors are never called by their first names."

"Bibi, umm ... sorry, Bibi—Auntie, you were saying something, and I disrupted."

"Yes, Amelia ma'am—pardon me, Amelia," she laughs, "I love if a woman selects dresses matching in colour. Take this *lehenga*, and I will give a matching *shaluka*."

A wave of trust and familiarity suddenly touches my skin.

She selects a *shaluka* for me, a short version of a blouse. I like the lovely pink colour of the robe. I wear both to cover my nakedness. The skin-hugging *shaluka* hardly covers three-fourths of my breasts. Bibi also gives me a scarf, which she calls a *dupatta*. I try to hide my semi-exposed chest with it, but it's so transparent I literally look like a sex goddess in the mirror.

"Now I'm looking like a courtesan." I blurt out a hearty laugh, forgetting that an hour ago, depression and panic had engrossed each cell of my body.

"You *are* a courtesan." She laughs with me, but her eyes regard me intently. "I mean, you need some training."

"Courtesan?" My eyes flare in the mirror. "I am an educated woman, why should I be a prostitute?"

Bibi's eyes bore into mine. "Courtesans are not the same as prostitutes, they are artists. They sing and dance on a stage. Don't you have actresses in England performing on the stage?"

"Yes," I answer like a student.

"Do you call them a call-girl?"

A long silence hangs between us. The maid, probably feeling the heat in the room, leaves.

"A man can become an officer, police, or even a worker in the field. But a woman can only spend life as the servant of a male. They call it 'wife,' a decent term to keep us women happy. Stupid women are content with this. A courtesan, on the other hand, is a dancer or a singer.

Many of them are renowned poets. Some become teachers and teach etiquettes to children of wealthy families. You earn your own income and do not depend on the charity of a husband. You own property. Get status in society."

"Then why do people call them sex workers?"

"Who says?"

"My husband." I don't want to say Colin's name unless I'm asked.

"He must be going to some cheap call-girls who call themselves courtesans. Does your husband love music? Does he like to watch dance programs?"

I scratch my head. "Do the courtesans marry?" I ask instead.

"They can if they like. But many of them have tasted abusive marriages and have already fled their secure home. When the home bites them like a wild dog."

I ask question after question, and I finally say, "I will not sleep with anyone." I realise my childlike negotiation.

"That is up to you. Many courtesans have lovers. As long as you are not the wife of a man and you have your own income, men will respect you. And Amelia, you know what? A life without self-respect is worse than hell."

Self-respect has been a rare commodity for me after my marriage with Colin. The life of a courtesan looks tempting.

I change into my regular clothes, but I don't glance away while removing the courtesan clothing.

That evening, I open my diary for the first time after many days. The room, with four lamps, is as bright as daylight. I don't write that Sehnaz has abandoned me. Somehow, I still remember the warmth of her hug in the boat. That was the first and probably last hug from her. God knows if we will ever meet again. But that was also the first hug I received from any brown woman. I have met many Indian women, but they've always treated me like I'm from another planet. Admittedly, we white people are from another world. That is the reason, even after ruling over them for so many years, we haven't won their hearts. And now some of them have joined the mutiny against the British.

I think over what has happened to me during the last twelve hours. Sehnaz has left, and I have somehow not met any disaster. I have a shelter, and if I undergo training from my new brown auntie, I will survive any assault by Colin or his formidable British spies.

But what about boarding a ship at Calcutta? The way I'm meeting one disaster after another, there is no guarantee my money will last long enough to buy a ship ticket. And with the direction the Sepoy Mutiny is heading, I should take a break from my adventuresome journey.

I get up and run to Bibi's dressing room. The *lehenga* and *shaluka* are still lying on the Persian carpet. I grab them and stride back to my room. Slamming the door behind me, I rip open my frock and throw it on the floor. Standing in front of the mirror, I stare at myself, which I have not done in ages. I cup my breasts gently; they swell inside my palms. The proud, protruding assets have since tilted a bit, showing signs of ageing or...or Colin's brutal handling, his bite marks. I squeeze my nipples and elongate them. Then I move them from side to side. The cigar marks are still hidden beneath my bulges. My glance traverses all the way to my tummy and navel.

I bend over to pick up the *lehenga* and *shaluka*, both pink. I haven't seen so much pink colour before and can't describe how much I've fallen in love with this colour. I feel like proudly swimming in an ocean of pink. Putting the clothing on, I stand again before the mirror. My lips turn up into a sweet smile, something I haven't done in ages. First, I mutter under my breath, then slowly, my voice rises. I start to laugh loudly and announce to myself, "I am the first White Courtesan of India."

I come back to my senses when a knock sounds on the door. The maid is calling me for supper.

I saunter toward the dining room still in the courtesan clothing. Bibi gazes at me in awe, a friendly smile brightening her face.

Before she can say anything, I announce, "Besides teaching etiquettes to wealthy children, I can also teach them English."

Bibi lets out a soft laugh, admiration glinting in her eyes. "Your new name from tonight is Amelia. I will be your trainer. I will teach you to dance and speak Urdu. The rest, you already know."

"Amelia? But that is my name already!"

"Right," she says, "but don't forget you are absconding from home. Your husband might be in an influential position in the East India Company. And there must be police or even moles looking for you. Everyone knows courtesans never keep their original, parent-given name. With the name Amelia, everybody will think you are another woman, not really Amelia. I will announce that you are from an Anglo-Indian family from Calcutta and naturally don't know Urdu. You will stay protected."

A deep, gruff voice sounding from the entrance slices through the quiet evening. Bibi presses her ears, darkness twisting through her face. "Take one plate and throw it in the backyard, inside the bushes," she commands the maid, her voice low, but firm. Then looking at me, she says, "Please go to your room, now, and stay in this costume. Cover your face with a headscarf. Stay calm if I call you out."

I turn and tiptoe to my room, heart thumping against my ribs.

CHAPTER 14

31 May 1857 Morning
Chetan

Waking up on the riverbank to a predawn cold breeze, Chetan gazed toward the summit of the hill and the temple on top. The Gomti's mild waves slowly lashing on the brink soothed his nerves. He glanced around. Reflection of an orange-coloured sun from the Gomti water welcomed him, and the bell of the temple sounded hope in his ears. The mild wind soughed through the trees, stirring the branches. The susurration of the Gomti brought a relief inside him. He thought he might get a reprieve from the struggles of the last few days that were still crackling like a fire inside him.

He surged up and moved along the perimeter of the hill to find a way up to the temple. The food offerings to the deities could make way to Chetan's plate and provide some energy to his tired muscles. He had noticed a city nearby while floating in the river yesterday but didn't know the name of it. A glimpse of Amelia ma'am on the riverbank was enough to keep him away from any city for a long time. There must be villages around. Could he get a job as a field worker?

Finding a way to the temple was difficult as tall, thorny bushes surrounded the hill like an armed fort. He drew air deep into his lungs. God had been making everything tough for him, testing his resolve, even while he was so near to God's abode—the temple. It looked amazingly close to him, but he could not find the route. Glancing desperately at the riverbank, he shot a mental prayer at the Gomti, imagining her to be a living and loving goddess who had saved his life and brought him here with a purpose. *I am too exhausted to swim again in your waters, please bless me. And thank you for saving my life.*

His gaze went to a man coming from the river ghat. Chetan let out a yell without a second thought. The man moved his head a little toward him but continued walking. Chetan studied him for a few long beats; the man looked like a tribal—dark skin, a loincloth covering his groin only, hair long but clean-shaven. The man came closer. Chetan stared at his muscled forearm, broad clean chest, and long legs.

"Brother, can you please guide me on how to go to the temple?" Chetan asked him in Hindi.

The man continued walking; he probably didn't know the language. Chetan had learned sign language in the army. That little education helped soldiers lost in deep forests communicate with local people to find a way out. He lurched forward and stood before the man. With some signs he had almost forgotten since his training days, he tried to ask him for help.

The man stopped for a while and suddenly started running, shouting something in his language. Another man appeared holding a bamboo rod. Chetan was tired of running away from everybody, but his pulse started to race. *I can't run anymore.*

The other man came nearer and asked, "What do you want in the temple? There are so many other temples in the city where you can go to worship, why this one?"

"I am hungry and looking for food. I thought I could get food in the temple." He started to think about what he would say if the man asked the next question. Like who he was and why he had come there.

The man moved his glance over Chetan, head to toe, and smirked. "You look like a strong young man. Aren't you ashamed of begging? Look for work."

The word 'begging' punched Chetan hard in his guts. He would rather die than stretch his arm out for money or food. Asking for a plate of food offerings in a temple was considered auspicious, not begging. He forgot that he had planned to seek work as a field worker in the farmlands. "I can work as a security guard," came out of his mouth, when suddenly he realised it and bit his lips.

A warm smile on the man's face blossomed softness through Chetan's chest.

"Security guard?"

Chetan stilled. "Yes." It was too late to rescind what he had already admitted.

"Come with me." Both men instantly turned back and started walking.

Chetan followed them.

Part of him knew he shouldn't have done this, yet he was mentally incapable of making a rational decision. He folded his hands and shot a quick prayer to the temple on the hilltop, requesting to safeguard him. Walking with the two men to the other side of the hill, Chetan noticed winding stone steps snaking up to the temple and a massive steel gate blocking the view further. They stopped at what looked like a small, dilapidated house, but the first man kept walking without a word.

"This is an ashram and temple of goddess Kali." The man pointed toward the hilltop. "My name is Raghu. You will be watching the ashram from here, twenty-four hours. Do not allow anybody other than *Daita* or his wife beyond that gate, that large steel gate you can see. All right?"

Chetan inhaled deeply. A security guard for a temple? Something was not adding up. "Thank you, brother," he said. "I will go to visit goddess Kali and start my job right away."

"No way." Raghu's voice was hoarse—bitter, but low. "Nawab Wajid Ali Shah's order. No man is allowed inside the temple, except this *Daita*. He is the only male allowed inside. That is only because Mata Radhe has allowed him. This is an ashram only for Hindu nuns."

Relief washed over Chetan. He became sure the British had no authority over the ashram. He again folded his hands in the direction of the temple and muttered, "Bless me, Ma Kali. I surrender myself to you."

Raghu allowed him to occupy one of the cabins. "You don't need any uniform," he said when they arrived inside the room. "You can also cook here. I buy provisions for the nuns and will bring for you, too. The other guard was too old and left. I was temporarily working as the guard for some time. I live in the nearest city with my family and visit once a day."

"City?" Chetan asked.

"Sultanpur. You don't know Sultanpur?"

Chetan noticed a gun hanging on the wall. Removing it from the hook, he examined it.

"You know how to use a gun?" A contented smile unfurled over Raghu's face. "Good, I don't have to train you." He crouched and took out a bag from a cupboard. "Here is some *poha*, flattened rice flakes. You seem hungry. Eat them."

Chetan literally snatched the bag of *poha* and swallowed a mouthful. "Thank you," he said while chewing.

"Do you know why we call him *Daita*?" Raghu asked Chetan with a familiarity, as if they had been friends for a long time. "He is a tribal but looks like a demon with his tall, dark, muscular body. The meaning of demon in colloquial dialect is *Daita*. You have noticed he hardly wears anything, only a small piece of cloth just enough to cover his male parts! *Daita* also has a wife and a four-year-old girl. I am sure she might have gone to the ashram. None of them understands our language. But the man is good in nature."

"How is he allowed in the ashram of women? He is practically naked!" Chetan asked.

Raghu's eyes fluttered with an amusing smile. "The nuns do tantric rituals, sometimes at night. Every dark moon night, a big fire is lit on the other side of the ashram facing the river, when they ward off the evil spirits."

Chetan wasn't convinced by Raghu's answer. But he got shelter as well as a job, so why would it matter if naked Daita visited the nun-only ashram?

Something wobbled in Chetan's chest when Raghu left for the day. The room was nice and warm. He ran to the river to have a bath and start his new life.

He was allowed to go beyond the steel gate. There was a level of tall hedges planted around a hundred meters below the ashram. Beyond that level, only *Daita* and his wife could go. *Why did Raghu smile when I asked about the nuns?*

He sat down for a morning prayer after returning from the river, Sona's death and hounding by the East India Company forces still raw in him. Chetan tried to keep his focus on the flag on the temple top, but it looked blurry, and images seemed to float. The sight of the temple felt hazy and confusion blossomed in his heart. He lay down on the floor with a heavy head and slowly retreated to blackness.

CHAPTER 15

**30 May 1857 Evening and Weeks After,
A Kotha In Sultanpur
Amelia**

"You look a little bit like a *firangi*," a patron remarks when I finish my *thumri* dance and am about to get off the stage in the small auditorium.

Firangi! I think. Any white person here is called a *firangi*, a foreigner. I bend down to rearrange my *ghungru*, an ankle bell that is tied to the ankles of the dancers. I am tired after a long dance. Suddenly, I notice the man who made that comment is licking his lips. I cast a sideways glance around, still bending over my ankle. Dozens of pairs of lips are touching, eyes focussing on something. My gaze goes to my breasts, peeking through the upper portion of the tiny blouse I am wearing. I pull my *dupatta* onto my chest and stand straight.

Meeting the gaze of the enquiring patron, I reply in chaste Urdu, "*Janab*," I address him instead of sir, "my mother had a *firangi* lover. I have never seen him, though. I have gotten a bit of his skin colour only, nothing else. Even my mother has light skin."

Bibi's advice starts whispering at the edges of my mind. I should not talk much in Urdu even though I take pride in learning that language within just one month's training.

That momentous afternoon scraps a new life out of a bewildered one.

I jot it down in my diary.

Had I not gotten a glimpse of Chetan, I wouldn't have run in desperation, and Bibi Khanum wouldn't have come into my life. That could have been a hallucination. Sehnaz's decision to abandon me had jarred my conscious. Chetan might not be following me, but being a white, it is nearly impossible to hide from the public's gaze. But Bibi does not know the word impossible.

A month ago, when I stood near Bibi's dining table with full courtesan costume and was about to join her for dinner, a deep male voice sounded at her main door. Bibi smelled the danger and asked me to go back to my room. An urge to flee again churned in my stomach. Dark thoughts serpentined through my head. That room was a bit far from the main door, so I couldn't hear what was transpiring. The only thing I was confident about was that she wouldn't hand me over to the police. I waited anxiously and tried to practise as many Urdu words as I had learnt in case I needed to answer something.

After a while, a few knocks on the door sent my heart lurching into my throat. I dragged my feet from the bed and opened the door.

"I said to be inside the room, not to lock it from inside." Bibi was standing before me, her voice soft.

I tried to read her eyes, but fear blurred my vision.

"E...everything okay?" I asked.

Bibi's gentle smile cooled down my nerves. She held my arm and guided me to her dining table. "Faiza, serve another plate for Amelia. We both are hungry."

She started eating as soon as our plates arrived. Silence descended in the room.

"This Sepoy Mutiny," she started, "has made a big loss to our business."

"Which business?" I glanced at her frequently when she spoke.

"*Kotha*—I mean, the patrons in the *kotha* are now lesser than they used to be. You know both English and Indians are our patrons, and now that they are on either side of the war, who will come here, then? Only those who have nothing to do with this rebellion!"

I failed to understand. Was that man shouting at the door only saying this that business was going down? I stopped eating and stared at her.

She probably read my eyes.

"He was a police havildar. They are suspecting us, the courtesans. They think we are sending secret information to the rebel camp and are really angry. The English feel betrayed. They, too, are our patrons. Only a few months ago both sides were enjoying *thumri* together in the courts of Nawab Wajid Ali Shah."

"I know. I have seen them together in the *Rahas* dance program in Quaserbaugh." Suddenly I realised I had told her something which I had tried to conceal until now. My own stupidity whammed in my gut. "I, I a—am," I faltered, "I am the wife of a brigadier."

She laughed. "I know. Colin Lawrence. I have seen you in the court of the nawab."

I swallowed, then pick up a glass of water and gulped down half of it, staring at her through the rim.

I shot a direct question— "Did that man come enquiring about me?"

"Yeh." Bibi's glance was focussed on the plate. "I told him he must have received some false information. But I know they might have kept watch at my house. But don't worry. My fence is tall enough so that no one can just jump inside. I have even fixed broken glass pieces on the top edge. Anybody trying to play mischief will lose his limbs or get seriously injured."

I put the plan of going back to England on ice. From the next day onward, my training started. *I will be a dance performer. I will teach wealthy kids English, manners in royal courts, and how to talk to senior persons in the East India Company or the courts of nawabs and kings,* I convinced myself.

Every day since then, I have gone to the *kotha* in a horse cart to undergo education directly from Bibi, who is the *Chaudhurayan*—the chief courtesan. She owns the business, recruits girls, and solicits patrons. She also is teaching me Urdu. I've come to know each courtesan is not of the same level. Their level not only depends upon the young age and beauty of a girl, but also their ability to dance and sing, their figures...everything is taken into account. There are poets, too. I even met some courtesans who write speeches for the top royal officers. My theory that courtesans are sex workers has faded into oblivion. I feel I have some importance in society. I have also been able to receive respect like a man does from the community as a bread winner.

Sehnaz's name is well known in the courtesans' circle, even though she is from Lucknow. She is the girlfriend of Rupen Naik. I also dream of getting my charming prince—not an Indian one, though. Hardly any courtesan prefers a married life. They can dictate a man as long as they are not married to anyone but stay only as a lover. That is a position where they can influence the critical decisions taken by top royal officers. Sehnaz's confident face appears in my imagination. I am going to get all those men I had imagined when I was in school, but with one compromise—I have to stay as a courtesan.

My dance education is always in an empty auditorium. Other courtesans, musicians and servants are my audiences. Almost a month has passed. Bibi has coloured my hair, and I became a brunette from a blonde. Exceptional performances have been announced for the patrons. Fashion designers have already stitched a *lehenga* and a pink-coloured *shaluka* precisely for me.

My first night of performing, Bibi introduced me to a hall full of audience members. That evening will forever remain in my memory.

She announced the arrival of a new, fairy-looking, fair-skinned beauty in Sultanpur who would do a *thumri* dance for them. Her name was Amelia. I entered the stage to the tune of music and claps from the viewers. I swiftly glanced around. The auditorium was dazzling with hundreds of candles covered by pink glasses, my favourite colour. When I noticed that there was not a single English patron in the hall, my heart jumped in excitement. No one would expect a perfect Urdu. Everyone knew courtesans always discard their birth names. No one would even doubt the courtesan Amelia is same as Amelia Lawrence, wife of Brigadier Colin Lawrence.

A new dawn in my life has lightened my soul. But for how long?

I have moved out from Bibi's *haveli*. With my enhanced knowledge of Urdu, I write the word *haveli* in my diary instead of *mansion* and smile at my own achievement.

Twenty courtesans live in the *kotha*. Out of them only five are treated as star courtesans, and I'm one of them. I am special being the only white, even though I have been introduced as an Anglo-Indian. Only a few courtesans in the *kotha* know that I am a real English woman and not an Anglo-Indian from Calcutta. I even have the luxury of getting the most sought-after room in the building, on the top floor of a three-storey mansion with a balcony facing the Gomti on one side and a hill on the other.

Madhuri is my personal assistant and is probably the only woman in the *kotha* to whom I have opened myself up. She knows my background and spends most of her time with me. Each star-courtesan has been provided with her own personal assistant, but Madhuri is, in fact, more than that. She sits with me for hours, either in my room or on the balcony. I narrate to her my childhood days in England—my competition to be on par with boys, so much that my friends called me a tomboy. Madhuri is surprised by how I was a tomboy in my childhood. She says she doesn't find any symptom of manhood either in my body or my nature. Madhuri and I have become friends, no more master and servant. She slowly opens up with me—all in a matter of a month.

Starting now, all star-courtesans will be required to have one milk-honey bath a month to rejuvenate their skin. On the day of my first bath, I am thrilled. A tribal man fills up the bathtub in the large garden with water. Madhuri pours milk and honey into the tub.

"How can someone bathe in the open?" I glance hesitantly at Madhuri.

"Don't worry ma'am, I will draw curtains around when you are bathing. Anyway, no outsider is allowed in the backyard."

"But a man is pouring water!"

She doesn't reply, just winks at me and goes away. Coming back with a small bag of beauty materials, she guides me inside the tub and pulls curtains all around. I can still gaze at the sky. The balcony of my room is visible, and I can see the Gomti River through the slit of the curtain. Madhuri asks me to remove my clothes, which I instantly abide by.

Just as I am about to step in the tub, I notice the reflection of the tribal man in the water, and my gaze swings back. He is standing on the steps of the bathtub, wearing only a tiny piece of black cloth around his waist and groin. A shriek erupts but stalls before it explodes through my mouth.

Madhuri blurts out a mild laugh and whispers, "He is trained to do this job, and does this for all the beauties living here. Don't worry, he will not rape you."

"You are saying all this in his presence?" I fumble whether to cover my breasts or vagina.

"I will bring a new dress for you when he finishes his job. He doesn't know Hindi or Urdu. Enjoy the milk-honey bath." Madhuri swings back and leaves with my clothes.

I sit in the water which goes only up to my waist, leaving my rounded bubbies totally exposed as a visual feast for the man standing before me and looking at me without expression. I glance at him helplessly and wait, wondering what will happen next. He crouches and pulls my feet out from the water. I mumble, about to say something, but he wouldn't understand anyway. He takes a round object from the bag which looks like dried fruit with bristles. Dipping that inside a pot of oil, he starts scrubbing my feet—between the toes, and the heels—while warm morning sunlight trespasses through the slits of the curtains and glimmers on my feet. A yin-yang feeling whispers all over my body.

I take a closer look at him. A tall, muscular man without any hair on his chest or legs, he has skin darker than most Indians I have seen. He is dazzling, as if the oil has been liberally massaged all over his body. His strong hands manoeuvre tenderly around my toes, heels, and bottoms of my feet, scrubbing off the dead skin. My glance slowly traverses to his waist and his minuscule waistcloth covering his groin. His long jock is hardened and poking through the thin and damp cloth as if struggling to burst out. I look at the clear blue sky and notice tiny fragments of white clouds slowly passing through. A wave of unknown pleasure washes through me. My clitoris starts tingling as his palm moves progressively up my calf and touches my thighs. He slowly opens my legs, revealing my lady parts. I follow his gaze, a straight line from his retina would penetrate my vulva instantly.

I fight an overwhelming urge to get up and hug him tightly as his fingers sway through my inner thighs. He is now inside the tub, his loincloth drenched, and his expanded hard member radiating warmth onto my skin. I can even feel his erection on my thighs when he leans over my tummy to massage my chest. I moan as silently as possible when his stiff fingers circle around my nipples. I close my eyes and savour the moment, awaiting my paps being squeezed.

A soft footstep sounds near me. My eyes refuse to open and end the heavenly pleasure I am relishing. "Your new clothes." Madhuri's voice fills my ears.

I open my eyes as a smiling Madhuri stands beside the tub. The tribal man slowly gets out of the water and waits outside the container, gaze directed at the floor. As soon as I step out, he takes a soft towel and rubs it against my over sensitised skin. I gaze into Madhuri's eyes with a serenity inundating my soul. After so long, I finally am getting pleasure from a man without actually doing anything, and from a man who can never be my companion.

Madhuri hands over the new clothes to him and mutters something I can't make out. I guess the man's name is Himu. He takes one piece of cloth from her and starts wrapping it around my bubbies. I understand it must be a breastband. It has cups precisely fitting my bosom. After tying it behind my back, he takes the other piece and ties it around my groin—the same way he has his loincloth.

"Is this all?" I mutter at Madhuri. "Am I going to perform in this?"

"None of the courtesans face the audience like this. He will come to your room and massage lotion on your body. You may sit on your balcony the whole day until evening, watching the waves of the Gomti. We make the lotion from the herbs sourced from the Himalayas."

As I walk to my room, the tribal man follows me with his bag of lotion.

Lately, the performances have been suspended when British and Indian rebels fight on the streets of Sultanpur. The whole city looks like a ghost locality. No patron turns up at the *kotha*. The British have deployed people to keep watch on those who come to see the performances. There was even a ban on all staff of the East India Company from attending any program by us, the courtesans—British and Indian employees alike. As a result, I never see a white patron coming inside, and I am delighted with that. Even though others frown upon the loss of their income.

One evening, Madhuri and I are sitting on the balcony and watching the moonlight reflecting on the waters of the Gomti. She asks me, "I have seen your husband, Brigadier Colin Lawrence. I have heard

English men have longer members than Indians. He must be keeping you satisfied?"

I think about how to answer. Then an idea strikes me. I go inside the room and bring the lamp. Madhuri stares blankly at me. Removing my top, I lift both of my breasts and ask her to see. Her eyes flare, and her mouth drops. "This is his love symbol. Now you know how much he loved me?"

A thick silence hangs in the air. I try to lighten the mood. "Tell me, Madhuri, how do you know English jock is longer than Indian? You must have tried both. Which one is better?"

She laughs. "I am not as beautiful and talented as you courtesans. Otherwise, I would have also performed on the stage. Once you dance before the audience, you can get both British and Indian. Both will dance to your fingers."

I try to ponder this, but Madhuri continues. "I had the impression British people are more educated and treat their wives like princesses. But all men are similar, white or brown, it doesn't matter. As long as you are just their lover and they know you will never marry them, you are a queen. The moment you cross the line and become a wife, you are a slave. Whether a man will dance to your tune or you to the man's, depends upon if you are a wife or a mistress."

I sit back and consider what she's said. The war has taken momentum and is turning against the rebels. A gloom has pervaded all over the *kotha*. Most courtesans have lovers who are top-notch royal officers of Awadh Kingdom. They don't have any news whether their boyfriends are doing well or have succumbed to the war. The human mind is strange. Even if many have denounced their marriages and have vowed never to remarry, they have still developed emotional bonding with men in their lives, each praying for the wellbeing of her prince. No one is willing to perform. Bibi is also absent for a few days. Being a British citizen, I wouldn't like the English-controlled East India Company to lose, but an absolute win by them could go against my own safety.

Meanwhile, I have already made friendships with many Indians and have developed a soft spot for them. I would love a middle path, some sort of agreement so that Nawab Wajid Ali continues as a ruler and the East India Company continues its trade. Unfortunately, I am not a decision maker. I'm a woman.

7 July 1857. Having had no work for the last few days, I spend most of my time sitting on the balcony and watching the blue waters of the Gomti. Madhuri, when she finishes her daily chores, accompanies me and we talk endlessly. I have enhanced my skills in Urdu and Hindi. She is also learning English from me. The temple on the hilltop, visible from my balcony, fascinates me. In the evening, I notice a faint light coming out of it. Madhuri says that the public is not allowed to visit the temple. Nawab has organised strict security around the hill for trespassers.

Today, Madhuri takes me to an underground room. "This room is forbidden for others, Amelia ma'am," she says. "I have received special consent from Bibi Khanum for you."

She lights several lamps, and a whole new world opens up before me; it's not just a room, but a hall, and it's filled with stone sculptures. I check one of them while holding a lamp. In the statue, one woman is positioned bending at the waist with a man's penis in her mouth, another man penetrating her from the backside. Two other men and two women are standing and watching. *Bedroom scene in public!* I snicker.

"This is the reason this room is not allowed to the public!" I say, "This is obscenity."

Madhuri lets out a hearty laugh. "This is only a stone replica of thousands of such scenes from the temples of Khajuraho. There is nothing secret there. Anyone can visit the temples and witness those erogenous sculptures. This is part of the ancient Hindu culture."

An erotic surprise punches me. What type of religion is this where sex is considered auspicious?

Without waiting for Madhuri, I move with the lamp and explore more such sculptures. The erotic figurines blow my mind away. My nipples tingle. The variety of sex scenes and poses these statues have been displayed in is beyond my imagination. The women portrayed in them are with their full bosoms and curvaceous bodies, perfection in beauty.

"You know Kamasutra?" Madhuri asks.

"Who is Kama—and then?" I can't pronounce the word correctly.

"Not 'who,' what, what." She giggles. "That is a book, written thousands of years ago by a sage. His name was Vatsyayana. Please do not try to pronounce it. You can't. It is a book about sex knowledge. It has—" she closes her eyes and thinks more deeply— "it has, I think sixty-four types of sexual acts one can try during love makings. Many of them are beyond the capabilities of ordinary people unless you do yoga regularly."

My eyes snap open. "Vat, Vats, whatever something...something," I chortle, "I need that book. Can you please get one for me?"

"That is not available in English. But I can arrange one Hindi book for you. But you will see the pictures, at least. Then you don't need a translated book."

This is material for my diary. Vat, Vatsya... I falter mentally. "All these are right. But I fail to understand how racy artifacts are allowed in places of worships."

A smile cracks on Madhuri's face. "According to Hindu belief, Kama is divine and an essential part of human life."

"Kama?"

"Means sexual pleasure."

My gaze falls on a large door just behind me. I touch it. "What is this, Madhuri? Something too costly or confidential that is secured by a steel door?"

She ignores my question and instead guides me to another end of the hall. "This is a special one. A beautiful image of Lord Shiva and Goddess Parvati, his consort."

"These are your deities? How can someone depict the gods in an erotic pose?" I remember the sermons I had heard in churches both in England and India ridiculing Hindu deities, saying that these people are still in the stone age and far from the civilisation. I don't wish to offend Madhuri or her religion. If some people believe in stone-age culture, let them. The fact that I am enjoying what she is taking me through is enough for me.

"Look at this." Madhuri shows me some inexplicable piece of stonework. "Do you know what this is?"

"Lovely," I comment, not knowing anything about the sculpture, and watch her saluting it. I try to focus on it, but there is nothing. A small cylindrical pillar, the bottom side of it has been buried in an oval-shaped something.

"This is *Linga*, means the male sexual organ, and it is inside the *Shakti*—that is a female sexual organ, or even 'infinite energy.' The infinite energy has created the whole world with the help of *Linga*. The *Linga* denotes Lord Shiva, and the *Shakti* or infinite energy signifies Goddess Parvati. She has another name, that is Kali."

A memory swirls inside my mind. Sehnaz and Sheru had visited a temple on the way. Sehnaz, being a Muslim, had stayed outside, but I went with Sheru out of curiosity. Inside, the deity was a naked woman's statue with a sword in her hand.

"That is goddess Kali, a symbol of the infinite energy."

Something punches my brain. "That is terrific, Madhuri. I have always believed that God has to be a male. We always address God as HE. But you have a female God, and she is called Infinite Energy, that means Supreme Power. Then why are the women of the world so weak? Always depending upon menfolk for basic survival?"

I am thrust instantly back to my school days in England. Only boys could study mathematics, ride horses. We girls got enough education to become an ideal wife or a better mother. My mind revolts. Why is God not a woman?

It's already late, time to go to bed.

"These are very unique historical statues," Madhuri says as we leave the room. "People believe they were buried in the ground to protect them from the destruction of the Mughal attack during the reign of Emperor Aurungzeb. Bibi discovered them while digging the land for laying the foundation of this mansion. In the past, British people have tried to steal them and take them to some museum in England. Bibi doesn't allow anyone there. She is somehow extra pleased with you and allowed me to show them to you."

We come back to my room. I don't feel like going to bed and head directly to the balcony. It is a dark-moon night. I glance up at the stars as if they could lend some light in the absence of the moon and I could still watch my favourite scene—the blue waters of the Gomti. To my amazement, I notice the reflection of bright light in the river. My gaze follows the source—the hilltop. I scream, "Fire, fire. Madhuri, there is fire on the hilltop temple!"

Madhuri is about to go to her room, but she comes back. "Don't worry, ma'am," she says in a strange calm. "Every dark-moon, a ritual is done in the hilltop temple. This fire is part of that rite. It will continue until the wee hours. If you want to see that, I can take you. But it is already past ten at night, and you go to bed early."

"Don't worry, Madhuri, I can sleep late once. I would love to see the waters of Gomti from the hilltop while the fire is still going," I insist as my gaze is mesmerised. Everything looks like a picture-perfect postcard.

I follow Madhuri. We again go to the underground hall. "Madhuri, we are planning to go to that temple on the summit of the hill. Why are we coming here?" I ask on the way.

"Shhh." Madhuri stops abruptly, finger to her lips. "Many here don't know there is a level beneath the ground floor. Bibi has made me your personal assistant, and I was Bibi's deputy."

I quietly follow like a subservient person. She takes me toward the end of the hall near the massive steel door, asks me to wait, and goes back. This's the same door I'd asked Madhuri about earlier and she'd ignored. I stand there like a statue holding a lamp. My gaze goes to a small figurine near me. Trying to recollect what Madhuri told me only an hour ago, I inch closer and examine it. It is the *Shiva Linga*, a penis inside a vagina. The eternal symbol of creativity at the cosmic level. The sermon of the fathers in the church blares in my ears. *This is a culturally backward country. We are bringing light to this nation.* I get a desire to shout and call all such enlightened priests, *Please come and understand the philosophy behind this little but probably the most potent symbol of the universe!*

A strange idea snakes into my mind. If God can be a female, why can't a woman be trusted to work as an officer in the East India Company? Why were my subjects in school intended to make me a better wife and not a better officer?

Madhuri comes back holding the lamp and an extended key in the other hand. Putting the light on the floor, she inserts the long, heavy key with both hands in the keyhole. After struggling for nearly a minute, the lock clicks and the door booms open, the sound vibrating through the large hall. I peek inside. The light of two lamps shows steps going up. We have already descended three levels of stairs to come down. Are we going back to my room on the top floor again but through other stairs?

Holding the lamp again in one hand and the key with the other, Madhuri enters. I follow. Once we both are in, she closes the metallic door with another boom.

"Careful, ma'am. The steps are steep."

I follow Madhuri, holding the other lamp. I don't understand. Maybe these are hidden stairs in case there is an emergency. The steps are so steep I take breaks to ease the pain in my back and knees.

"By this time, we should've reached our floor already. Why are these stairs taking so long to get there?" I ask, still breathing hard.

"Ma'am, it takes time and energy if your destination is higher than the one you're already at."

I glance up. Madhuri is smiling. A personal assistant suddenly has become a philosopher for me. I try to comprehend, but the blood from my brain has been drained to my tired legs. We start walking again. I don't calculate the time, just follow her.

"We are going to the hilltop temple. Bibi had given permission to take you there, but I thought you might not be interested in visiting a Hindu temple. It will take a while, but you will love the scenery. The view of the Gomti water on a dark-moon night with the fires on the hill is stunning."

"Thank you." I am now mentally prepared to walk for hours to arrive at the temple.

"The deity in the temple is the goddess Kali, the symbol of infinite energy," she says, and we arrive at a place where I can feel the cold wind. The steps end on a stone floor the size of a room. We stop and sit down for a rest, and I get a glimpse of stars through a cleft.

A vague thought comes to my mind. "Madhuri, you have female Gods, but not a single female ruler in hundreds of kingdoms in the whole of India. On the other hand, people in my country believe God is male, but England is being ruled by a queen." A sense of triumph tingles my nerves.

Madhuri smiles. "We had one Razia Sultana ruling over the country hundreds of years ago. She had to fight her way to the throne and finally died from fighting the male supremacy. England got a woman ruler because the king didn't have a son."

Right. Sehnaz had also told me in the boat.

We continue walking up in the tunnel. "This tunnel was built by some king hundreds of years ago so that only serious devotees can visit the Kali temple," she says.

After almost an hour of sweating and panting, we finally arrive at the front of a mansion. "Is this the temple?" I ask.

"No, this is the place called *ashram*, hermitage. The temple is behind this. Gomti is on the other side." She knocks on the door.

When no one responds, she knocks again, louder. We hear footsteps approaching, and something clunks inside. As the large wooden door opens and light from many lamps disperses, my eyes roll skywards. Four naked women are standing in front of me, each with a lamp—one of them is Bibi Khanum, with the full glory of her womanhood, defying the age.

CHAPTER 16

3 July 1857 Early Evening
Sehnaz

Sehnaz's heart thumped to the flicker of lights from the boat sailing at a distance. She stood up to find out if Sheru had noticed the same. The attack from the British naval ferry a couple of months ago was still raw in her bones. Without a surprise appearance from the rebel boat, she could have well been kidnapped by the East India Company soldiers and used as a sex slave.

The boat they were travelling in was in the mid-river, whereas the other one was still close to the riverbank. It looked like it had just departed from a nearby jetty, but it was unusual to begin a journey at night unless forced by circumstances. Holding the boom pole near the mast, she stood still, gaze focussed on the burgee—the saffron flag showing a picture of Lord Hanuman. Many boats had saffron flags, so the British shouldn't think of them as rebels. Last time, they probably watched a white woman standing and displaying her long, blonde hair. British have powerful binoculars, Rupen had warned her—which she should have remembered.

She shouldn't have let the womanly compassion take over the pragmatism of the situation. Amelia shouldn't have been with her, travelling in the same vessel. The cause for which the rebels were fighting was much more important than a woman's personal struggle with her own troubles. After all, she was also white and British. Her own people always looked down upon the brown-skinned Indians. Had God made a rule, white skin would always be superior to brown or black?

The subconscious guilt of leaving Amelia alone was still haunting Sehnaz's guts. She was always battling with herself since they decided to sail alone without even informing her. She relaxed her hand from the steel pole and forced her gaze to the moon rising from behind the peaks.

Sheru would continue sailing throughout the night, reducing the chance of detection by the British. Good decision. She appreciated his dedication, experience, and intellect. As the chief general of the Awadh kingdom, Rupen found a competent soldier to carry his paramour throughout this freedom movement.

Or in the language of the white—Sepoy Mutiny. What mutiny? Anger surged in her. *This is our country. They are interfering in our country in the name of trade. Which trader keeps its own army? This is all fake. They have almost occupied the whole land, leaving our kings and nawabs with limited authorities. Now is the time Nawab Wajid Ali's army should give a fitting response and show them their real place. Do business or go back to your own country. Stop meddling in our traditions and rituals.*

She got to her feet and went inside the cuddy. Another flicker from the other boat attracted her gaze. It had a pattern, a combination of colours, and the ferry was nearing them. Sehnaz noticed a man in a military uniform holding three different colours of oil torches, waving them and standing on the deck. A dark feeling rippled through her, and she lurched toward Sheru. He should think quickly and manoeuvre the ferry elsewhere.

"We have nothing valuable with us," she muttered as if the wind would carry her words to the other vessel. Sheru's eyes were focussed elsewhere. All she saw was his hairy bare chest, sweat dazzling on his tanned skin, muscles gyrating to the movement of the rudder in his hand, sending tingles to her skin. Sehnaz stilled. The other boat was still at a distance, and she realized that her fear might have been unsubstantiated.

"Sorry, ma'am, I didn't notice you here." Sheru gazed at her, tension visible in his eyes. "You said something I couldn't hear."

"We have nothing valuable with us," Sehnaz said again.

"Yes, we have one. You."

A mild laugh blurted out of Sehnaz's chest. "That is not what I mean, you idiot."

"I know. But the man in that boat is probably asking for the map." He pointed to the other boat. The flicker had since stopped.

"Map?" Shock slashed through her. "But why? How? We have already handed it over a month ago!"

Sheru's face looked pale. "Did we give it to the wrong man, then? Did Rupen Sahib give any codeword before trusting someone?"

"No codeword. Everything happened so hastily. I had to leave Lucknow in a hurry after sourcing it, and there was not much time to communicate with Rupen. But I don't think we have given it to the wrong person. You saw how the rebel boat ambushed the whole British troupe. They can't just pretend to be rebels and working for the English. In that case, they wouldn't have killed the English soldiers."

Sheru scratched his head. "I don't understand. Maybe the man who took the map sold it to the British."

"Bloody traitor. So many Indian soldiers are leaving the British and joining the rebellion, the English must have opened their treasury to all double-crossers. Some people will do anything for a few coins."

"Not always, ma'am. The British are not raw players in the war game. When they sent a ferry-load of soldiers to snatch the map from you, don't you think there might have been other boats watching them? They must have noticed with their powerful binoculars what happened to their soldiers and followed after."

"Oh, yes. You are probably right, Sheru. But no one attacked us after that incident."

"Why should they? You handed over the diagram, and the binoculars must have done their work. The British must have followed the other boat which took the map from you. Do we know what happened to them? Are they still alive? The map might have fallen into the British camp, if Rupen is sending another boat because he still hasn't received it."

Sehnaz's pulse kicked. This was the only hope for Rupen to lodge a successful attack on the enemy. Without enough firearms, there was hardly any other avenue to win the battle.

She peeked into Sheru's eyes. "Two things. Either the man sold it himself, or another attack for the map was successful."

Sheru responded with a sad smile. "Let me see what this boat is after."

The other boat was sailing close to theirs. The man holding the torch gave a thunderous shout at them. Sheru manoeuvred the ferry closer.

"Hello, friend," Sheru shouted, "what are you after?"

"Map," came the reply.

"We have already given the map, weeks ago. Rupen Sahib had sent the boat to collect it from us."

"We know. He had sent people to collect the map. But somehow it has not reached him. He thought maybe no one could contact you, so he sent us again to confirm."

A chill suddenly crawled under her skin.

"They ambushed a ferry-load of British soldiers before getting the paper from us. That was more than a month ago. I think it was the twenty-seventh of May. Yes, I remember. The twenty-seventh of May. It is possible that the British attacked them again," Sheru said.

There was a moment of silence as both boats absorbed this information. "We're going back then. Will inform Rupen Sahib you've already passed on the map. This's devastating for all of us."

The boat returned empty-handed, creating a massive vacuum in Sehnaz's heart.

"We shouldn't have trusted that white woman, ma'am. Imagine why suddenly at midnight a white woman's cart stops, gives you a lift, and makes such a drama that next morning you felt obliged to bring her along."

Sehnaz didn't dare to meet Sheru's gaze. She looked at the sky; messy clouds had imprisoned the half-moon under their blanket, and the moon was struggling to free itself from the dark clouds forming ominous shapes.

The twenty-seventh of May, 1857 would always remain an unforgettable day for Sehnaz. So far, she was thinking she was lucky the rebel boat arrived in time and saved her from the assault of the barbarian British. Little did she know, Amelia, the goddess of all deceit, was acting as her friend and was a witness of the ambush of the English platoon and also the exchanging of the map. And Sheru had noticed how Amelia was talking to an unknown man in Sultanpur. Could she go back and ask Amelia what she did?

The whole night Sehnaz's mind heated up with new sources of disaster and danger. The more she tried to let them go and relax, the louder her inner voice told her what could have gone wrong or what blunder she might commit. The night was the longest one in her life.

A conch-shell horn from a riverside temple awoke Sehnaz.

"We have now touched the Ganga," Sheru announced. He had held the rudder the whole night.

Sehnaz rubbed her eyes and came out of the cuddy. The water beneath the boat chuckled and whispered. River Gomti flowed since time immemorial, always onward, toward its destiny. Each drop of its placid waters headed for its larger avatar, feeling the welcome touch of coolness and watching the eddies in the current disappear in the holy river, Ganga.

She approached Sheru. "I am wondering why Rupen didn't wait until we arrived at Varanasi, but sent someone to take the map in the midriver."

"So many possibilities, ma'am." Sheru's sharp eyes focussed on the swirls in the water. "Varanasi might not have been a safe location anymore for handing over the important piece of information you were carrying. The British spies must have spread even to the cities like Varanasi, where we thought was a safe place. And we also don't know how far the rebel army has proceeded. Maybe waiting until our arrival would have been too late, and the map would have served no purpose."

Sehnaz wondered how much stamina Sheru had that he was driving the ferry the whole day and night without rest. He was determined to finish the journey by the evening. Lazy sun had slowed down the progress of the day. Each passing cloud was mocking Sehnaz and reminding her of her failure in handling the map.

As the sun sank lower in the horizon, draining the light of the day, Sehnaz noticed hundreds of oil lamps floating in the river. A calm stillness hovered around her conscious. Absorbed in the soothing breeze, she let the gentle energy of nature wash in. Sheru was muttering some prayer with eyes half-closed. Bells of the temples at the ghats of the holy city Varanasi invoked a comforting warmth in her heart.

"Rupen has given me the address of a house—" she came to Sheru and unfolded a small piece of paper— "which our location will be nearer to this. We will anchor the ferry accordingly."

Sheru paused.

"That was more than a month ago, ma'am," he replied politely. "Time has changed. The British might have already gotten hints of the arrangement."

"So, what do you reckon?"

"I am thinking of the Kaal Bhairaav temple."

"You think that is a safer place?"

"This is a temple of Lord Shiva, and people think he is the protector of Varanasi."

"And you think Lord Shiva will protect us from the wraths of the British?" Impatience twisted inside Sehnaz. "And you know I am a Muslim. I will not even be allowed, despite being General Rupen's close associate."

"The British also know that you are a Muslim and will not be allowed in the rooms of a Hindu temple." Sheru got up to moor the boat. "But the priests in the temple do not know who you are, or your real name."

"Will it not be wrong?"

"Nothing is wrong in war or love."

She smiled. "I have to think of a Hindu sounding name then. I had a friend called Sanju. How does Sanju sound to you?"

They pretended to be a couple—he as Sheru Pandey, and she, Sanju, his wife in Hindu married-women's attire. Sehnaz already had a saree and bangles in her suitcase. They arrived at the temple guest house and finally, their room. Varanasi was a pilgrim city, and most temples had rooms to accommodate people.

Sehnaz glanced at the River Ganga through the small window of the room. Sheru had gone to the river ghat for a holy bath. She got up and made another bed on the floor for Sheru. She knew the animal inside him would be aroused, having a beautiful woman in the same room. Sehnaz was the paramour of his boss, and she had hidden a sharp knife beneath her pillow, in case.

When a knock sounded on the door, Sehnaz got up and opened it. Sheru entered, accompanied by a beautiful aroma. "What have you got? Smells so nice!"

"Lord Shiva's *prasad*, food offerings. Dinner for you. When I offered a prayer, the priest asked where you were. I told him my wife is not well."

"Your wife?"

Sheru stepped back but gave a don't-act-a-fool stare. "Just acting, ma'am. In a time of war and espionage from both the sides, we shouldn't trust anyone. Not even the priests. They are dealing with the public. They can pass on information to anybody. We should be careful."

"I know, Sheru. Just joking. I am the woman who had planned how to set up an espionage network for Rupen. Didn't you see how I could organise to draw a map of The Residency? Rupen Naik is not a fool who spends so much time with me. For outsiders, he was coming to spend time with a courtesan."

"I understand, ma'am. The food is getting cold. Please finish your dinner."

Sehnaz took a bite of the roti, but it didn't go past her throat. *What happened to the map?*

13 July 1857
Sehnaz

It was almost midnight, and Sehnaz was still struggling to sleep. Not used to wearing a saree, she felt the heat of the Varanasi summer. Sitting up on the bed, she pulled the curtain of the open window. A silver moonlight spilled into the room—not enough to bring the view of the blue waves of the River Ganga, but enough to show the rising and falling of the muscular chest of Sheru Pandey. She could hear each of his breaths with ease. A tingle crept onto her skin, and she simply let it sit there.

His ribs were like steel traps. His strong arms—a little rough from hard work as a soldier—stole the air from her lungs. She yanked the saree away from her torso, and it dropped onto the floor. Moving her palm gently to her blouse, she felt the sweat and unhooked the buttons.

Her large mammary glands sprang out in pride. A gust of mild breeze whispered like a lover, placing warm kisses on her bosom, which slowly crept onto her belly and thighs. It had been more than two months since Sehnaz had the company of the man of her life. Here was another man who was silently and unknowingly touching her heartbeat.

Sheru changed sides. A sense of guilt whispered at the edges of her mind. She belonged to Rupen Naik. How could she even dream about another man? That was a sin. She leaned over the edge of the bed and grabbed the saree from the floor. A mild laugh erupted in her mind. How could she become so devoted to a man who could never become her husband? Pulling one loose end of the saree onto her naked chest, she lay flat again, staring at the beams of the roof. A few minutes later, she felt her focus diminish. Images from the events of the last few days seemed to float aimlessly around the pools of her thoughts. They all looked blurred as if viciously blown away by a hurricane. Sehnaz slowly retreated into wallowing darkness.

CHAPTER 17

30 May 1857 to 15 July 1857
Chetan

Chetan jerked awake. He lay dead still, trying to figure out what disturbed his sweet sleep. His own daughter's naughtiness snaked through his memory when a child's voice outside tingled his ears. He sat up and stretched his arms. Staring through the window, he noticed a little girl playing all by herself.

Chetan got up to go out and play with her. Raghu had told him hardly anyone would come here. He need not be alert all the time. His presence was enough. The large iron gate and thorny bushes around the hill were enough to stop intruders. Also, the locality nearby knew nuns did tantric rituals; that was enough to scare most people away.

As soon as he came out to the open space, a bolt of current shot through him. A tall, dark, and muscular woman stood, showing her yellow teeth and wearing hardly anything. Modesty punched him hard as he swung back and ran toward his room.

Inhaling deeply few times, he took a break and scratched his head. This must be *Daiti*, *Daita's* wife. Raghu's laugh sounded in his conscious—*these are not their real names*. Nicknames were given by Raghu himself. Standing partially hidden near the window, he watched the woman. A breastband covered her breasts, but only partly. The large breasts were struggling to hide inside the thin and narrow piece of cotton, nipples protruding through the damp cloth, the flesh dancing merrily as she walked. Another similar piece of cotton covered only the front of her lady parts, her backside completely bare. Sweat beaded on Chetan's forehead. This woman was not civilised and couldn't even talk in the local language. She didn't feel any shame. But how could Chetan, being educated and bearing high moral character, move outside the house?

He sat on the floor and closed his eyes. His gaze refused to move despite hindering his vision. It left his pious body and jumped out the window to travel slowly up the length of *Daiti*. He felt arousal. Pleasure and heat thrummed through his blood, matching each beat of his heart. *Mother Kali, please save me from this scandalous thought, this sin.* He could force his mind inwards, but only for a few moments. His fingers started touching his aroused member unknowingly, and he felt a wetness in his organ. He yanked his arm out of his thighs and ran toward the riverbank—the bathing ghat.

Jumping onto the second step in the water, he sat submerged up to his neck. Cold and mild waves of the Gomti cooled his passion. He stayed there almost an hour in a meditative pose, praying to the Gomti as if she were also a goddess. *You saved my life from the hands of the ruthless British, please also protect my modesty,* he thought again and again. His blood cooled down, and his brain started working again as usual. He would ask Raghu to give some salary in advance and go to the nearest market to buy some sarees. Civilised people always must help the less fortunate see the enlightenment. These tribal people had not known how to cover themselves, as they had lived in jungles. Now that he was here, it was his moral duty to teach them the benefits of wearing clothes. Could he?

Something sounded nearby. Chetan didn't wish to open his eyes and disturb his meditation. He listened to the chuckles of the Gomti's waves lashing mildly against the stone step on which he was resting. Another thought snaked into him. This woman was regularly visiting the ashram and must have been meeting the nuns. How had they never tried to ask this woman to cover up? This world was full of devils.

Hunger twisted through Chetan's stomach, time to go back to the cabin and cook a meal. He finished his meditation and finalised his plans for educating the woman. *Daiti*. He gently stood up. He had no towel to dry his torso.

Chetan was about to walk to the cabin when a plop in the water swung his head. Gazing at the bathing ghat, his mouth quivered and pulse quickened at the sight in front of him. *Daiti* was sitting on the stone step hardly a few feet from where he was seated, legs in the water and clothes deposited on another stone.

"God, help me."

Daiti got up at his words and stood facing him, her massive, naked mammary glands poking fun at Chetan. A gush of blood thrummed through his veins, and he started running as if a wild animal were behind to swallow him.

Raghu laughed when Chetan told him what happened and his resolve to teach civilisation to this tribal couple.

"I have tried several times. Even my wife has brought a saree and tried to wrap it around *Daiti*. But after wearing it a couple of hours, she yanked it away and again moved around only in a pair of tiny clothes—a breastband and a napkin," Raghu said.

Chetan asked again why the nuns had never tried to impart enlightenment on them, and a funny smile curved around Raghu's lips. *What is funny about this?*

Days and weeks passed.

Chetan gradually got used to the way of living of *Daita* and *Daiti*. He would walk freely, even if *Daiti* bathed without her clothes. Their little daughter became the consolation of all his troubles. He would try to find his own daughter through her, playing with her whenever possible. *One day, when this girl grows up, I will make her a civilised being.*

Even if I leave this place to go back to my own family and to my own daughter, I will certainly come back and make this girl a normal and civilised woman, he vowed.

A comfort swayed through him. The area, though not far from Sultanpur, was still away from the dangers of the Sepoy Mutiny and its effects. One day the war would be over, and he could possibly go back to Lucknow to bring his daughter and live here permanently, between the serenity of the Gomti and the hill.

In his spare time, which he had plenty, he would watch the stone steps snaking their way up to the hilltop. He would go to the last point he was allowed—the tall hedge outside the ashram—and would watch the Gomti's waves from there during gardening work which he volunteered to do. The orchard surrounding the ashram was his greatest attraction, where he would collect mangoes—taking care that he didn't cross the danger line beyond which only the tribal couple could go. He had never seen any nun, even from that close proximity. *Do the tantric rites demand strict isolation?*

15 July 1857.

Chetan was busy gardening when a soft crunch of dead leaves sounded in his ears. He stood still, waiting for the arrival of a deadly beast. He had never seen any animal on the hill except for rabbits or occasionally a deer. But the footstep sounded different. He inhaled with mouth open; a different kind of smell dispersed in the wind. He regretted not carrying his gun all the time with him.

Finding a bamboo stick, Chetan held it in position and moved slowly to the other side of the bush. As a security guard, it was his duty to safeguard the nuns from any types of danger. Gathering enough courage, he inched slowly forward. His gaze went to something that looked like a woman's bare foot. Dusk was slowly swallowing the daylight. It might be possible that he didn't see that clearly. The foot-like thing moved slowly ahead, and he notice that the waist down was totally bare. It couldn't be *Daiti*; she was dark-skinned, and he had already seen her going back to her cottage. Curiosity haunted him. *Is this a ghost?*

The unknown tantric ritual haunted the edges of his mind. There was no time to go back and run. Deciding to face and fight if required, he lurched ahead and stood before the animal.

Chetan swallowed and felt blood draining from his head. The bamboo stick fell on the ground; a naked young woman with waist-length hair was standing before him. He held a tree branch for support and slumped down on the grass. The last word he could utter before closing his eyes was, "Ma'am."

CHAPTER 18

7 July 1857 Before Midnight
Amelia

As I stand near the ashram door with Madhuri, I try to supress my surprise at all the naked women standing and welcoming me.

"Welcome to the Kali temple, Amelia." A senior-looking woman with a million-pound smile comes forward to hug me but halts abruptly. "I hope you will not mind being with us, a group of fully naked women."

Back in London, I had read about some area in India where people remain without clothes. The sermons in the church also discussed uncivilised people in this country and how they are making lots of sacrifices to reach those inaccessible terrains and spread the lights of Christianity, bringing civilisation to their doorsteps. This woman in front of me is speaking in immaculate English. Midnight is at the doorstep. Am I dreaming?

The woman is staring into my eyes with the expectation of some reaction. Bibi is standing next to her, also unclothed, and a weak smile is curving her mouth. Bibi probably didn't expect me here at this time. A sullen silence swells around. I understand. The British are considered the rulers of this nation, despite the local kings. I am English, white, and superior to them. Or at least that is the impression I'm getting. My approval or disapproval has a lot of significance here. Stepping forward, I hug the woman. I have to say something nice to save the situation. I remember Madhuri had told me about the *Shiva Linga* and *Shakti* hours ago. "I don't mind what you are wearing or not. You are part of *Shakti,* or infinite energy."

Bibi gives the woman's introduction— "She is Mata Radhe, head of the Shakti Ashram."

"The doors of Kali temple are closed for the night." Mata Radhe guides me to the other side of the ashram, where the large bonfire is still dancing, flickering flames throwing gold light onto the Gomti waves down the hill. This's stunningly beautiful.

Almost a dozen people are standing around, watching with folded hands. One of them is reciting some verses loudly, competing with the crackle of the flame. With each completion of a stanza, another woman pours some liquid into the fire.

"That is *ghee,* molten butter," Mata Radhe explains, "and that woman is reciting Sanskrit verses, holy hymns. This will continue for another half hour, at least."

Glancing around, I discover Madhuri is not with me. The reciting of verses doesn't ignite any interest in me, so I excuse myself and quickly move toward the far end of the yard, fenced by meter-high flowering plants, and watch the Gomti waters. Its blue waves shimmer red and yellow with the flame's light. This is my purpose of coming here, of fascinating my senses with this rare scene dancing on mild blue waters of the river on a dark-moon night. A vague idea comes to mind —if somehow this scene could be captured alive and played whenever I'd like, there wouldn't be a dull or depressing moment in my life.

I don't know how much time I spend standing alone and cherishing the scenery. The recital gradually lowers its volume. The reflection of the flame on the water fades slowly. My eyes are still greedily focussing on licking the last bit of it. A soft and warm hand rests on my shoulder. My head swings to the side; Madhuri is smiling at me. "The ritual is about to be finished. Tomorrow there might be a dance performance. There is news that the war has slowed down, and some patrons would like to come tomorrow evening. You need to do a rehearsal in the morning. We should leave now."

My glance moves from her head to her toes, and I whisper, "Where are your clothes, Madhuri? You, too...?"

Madhuri's eyes dance with mirth. "I like to stay like this whenever I come here. This is so liberating. I will bring you again sometime. You will know everything."

Bidding goodnight to Mata Radhe, we return through the tunnel. Going down the hundreds of steps is not difficult. "Did Bibi mind that I suddenly came here without informing her?" I ask on the way.

"She should have told you earlier. Everybody in the *kotha* knows about this Shakti Ashram and that Bibi is a close friend of Mata Radhe."

"Maybe because I saw her stripped, though," I say when we are about to arrive at the steel gate of the *kotha*.

"No one in any *kotha* minds if anyone shows up unclothed if there is no male around." She stops at the first floor, leaving me to head up to the third floor alone. "Goodnight."

"See you again tomorrow morning for the rehearsal." I trudge up the stairs, heading toward my room.

8 July 1857 and Weeks After
Amelia

Waking up to a severe headache, I lie on the bed to the sound of crows cackling. Dark clouds smirk at me through the ajar window on the balcony side. The mantle brass English clock sitting on the alcove is teasing me, showing its hour hand hovering above five. *Amelia, you need some more rest.* A silent curse comes out of me for the uncivilised crows. Couldn't they find another spot for this morning?

I try, but I can't get up. Staring at the clock, I am instantly thrust back to my bedroom in Colin's house. This clock would greet me every morning. That is the only precious item, gifted by my father, that I had packed when leaving his house. Recounting my weeks spent outside his home, I realise, in my failed pursuit to go back to England, I have come a long way. If I write them down, that can be a thrilling memoir. I have not written anything in my diary in a long time. So many incidents are knocking at the door of my memory, seeking a niche in my journal. Everything jumbles in my mind: the secret basement of the *kotha*, the hidden tunnel stairs to the Nude Ashram—sorry, the Shakti Ashram, the naked nuns, replicas of erotic arts of Khajuraho, and finally the female God denoting the infinite energy. Did I forget anything?

Pulling the sheet up to my eyes to block out the little light sneaking through the dark clouds in the ajar window, I try to steal some more sleep. Today will be a tiring one, as a long rehearsal will be required to make up for the lack of practice. My savings is dwindling at the bottom of my piggy bank, due to the war and the *kotha* closing down dance performances.

Sehnaz's betrayal, Colin's ghastly face, Sheru shooting the innocent horse—all are lodging attack on my conscious, and my determination to make a beautiful, meaningful life is swaying away from me. I glance at the messy dark clouds again. *How will this day be for me?*

A knock sounds on the door. Must be Madhuri. "Come in, door no lock." My voice sounds flat. I sometimes use broken English to communicate with people with no or little English. But Madhuri speaks English better than many.

A maid comes inside. "Morning good, madam." She smiles at me. "War going, more. No dance today. Madhuri sent."

"Lovely." I am still lying on the bed underneath the sheet.

"Madam?" She sounds alarmed.

I get the point. She doesn't know what *lovely* means. "Good. Thank you." This much any Indian who has ever come within ten feet of any white man understands. I suppress a giggle.

The maid goes to leave. "Please close the door," I say.

She swings back. I remove my arms from underneath the sheet and signal to close the door.

Madhuri comes around nine a.m. when I am still in bed.

I ask, "Can we get out for a stroll on the banks of the Gomti today? I think this will freshen my mind. Something is pinching me from inside."

Her soft smile takes away half of my headache. "No strolling outside. Bibi has only coloured your hair black. But it's difficult to tan your skin to look like a native."

I regard her in silence, something unreadable winking at me in her eyes.

"British police might come into the *kotha* to look for something. You know the East India Company suspects that courtesans are informers of the rebels? It is not good for you to stay here today."

Time to flee again? How? Sehnaz has deserted me! Where do I get another boat to take me up to Calcutta? And secretly, too?

Madhuri probably reads my tension-filled face. "Don't worry Amelia ma'am, the police who will be enquiring are our patrons. It is they who have informed us to be careful. You wanted to be in the Shakti Ashram one more time anyway, so why not today? Bibi has excellent contacts both with the British and the nawab. She will manage everything."

Thank God. I don't have to flee. "Thanks, Madhuri. You always bring happy news."

Two crows perch on my balcony and cackle. This time, though, it sounds like music to me. I immediately take out some *poha* snacks from the cupboard to throw at them. They savour the snacks while I look at them admiringly until they finish the food and fly away. My soul becomes light as if ready to fly to the hilltop ashram.

Within an hour I am ready, and we are on the stairs of the secret tunnel again.

"Who built this tunnel? This is magnificent," I ask while climbing.

"Don't know. Must be a thousand years old. The Khajuraho replicas were discovered buried beneath this land when excavation was done for the construction of this building. We believe that they were buried to hide from Aurungzeb, but no one knows the reality."

"I have always been fascinated with the kings, emperors and nawabs of this country, but never got an opportunity or the time to learn more about them. I have been to Nawab Wajid Ali Shah's palace a few times. But I don't know much about him, though." I take a sharp breath.

We take a break on the flat surface—the same one where we had rested last time, having a cleft opening to the Gomti River.

"Wajid Ali Shah's ancestors were lieutenants in the Mughal Empire. When the empire became weak, they occupied the Awadh kingdom and declared themselves nawabs, same as a king."

"Awadh or Oudh?"

"Both are one and the same," Madhuri says. "When he was a young boy, an astrologer told his parents that he will become a yogi or ascetic. To counter the effect of the evil stars, he advised dressing the boy in a saffron robe, similar to the monks' clothing. When Wajid Ali himself became a king, he kept the tradition alive. He would dress up as a yogi in a saffron robe, smearing his face and body with the ash of pearls, rosary beads in his hand, and a pearl necklace around his neck, and walk into his court along with two *paris* dressed up as yoginis."

"*Pari?*"

"Means a fairy. The nawab has established a *parikhana*—an abode of fairies. Hundreds of beautiful and talented girls were taught music and dance by expert teachers. The most talented and beautiful girls are named things such as *Sultan Pari, Mahrukh Pari,* and so on. Gradually, he made it into a spectacular annual fair in which citizens of Lucknow are encouraged to participate."

"I know. I have heard about the fair, something called *Rahas*. The Sepoy Mutiny started; otherwise, I could have visited Qaisarbagh to watch the famous show."

"That is different. The nawab himself is dressed as the mythological character Lord Krishna, and the fairies are dressed as Krishna's girl-friends."

"I hope this mutiny finishes and some sort of agreement is arrived at with the nawab so that one day I can see the *Rahas* dance."

Once again, we are at the locked gate of the Shakti Ashram. Mata Radhe welcomes me back and asks if I can spend a few days with her. That is what I want, too. To be away for a few weeks.

Unlike my first visit, the nuns are not always without clothes. They cover to protect their bodies from cold and sun. Mata Radhe is wearing only a shawl on her shoulders today, that's all.

Days pass by.

I get opportunities to interact with Mata Radhe and learn her views about life, nudeness, everything.

"We practise becoming comfortable with our body. But the outside world will never understand us. Some will think we are yet to become civilised, others will plan how to exploit us because we are all women here," Mata Radhe said. "Amelia, you will be surprised to know that Naga Sadhus in the Himalayas roam naked without any hesitation. But they are all male. They do not hide anywhere."

I also learn that Nawab Wajid Ali was a patron of this ashram. Sometimes I wonder what would happen if he is deposed after the war. Tension snakes into me, thinking about this beautiful place one day being discarded if the missionaries bring their so-called enlightenment to this monastery and force the western civilisation here. Sometimes I sit in meditation pose in front of the statue of goddess Kali and dream one day God will not be addressed as *he* or *him*, rather *she* and *her*. Is this just a daydream? Would God as a woman think of courtesans differently as God as a man would?

One day I ask Mata Radhe if becoming courtesan is a sin. She says, "Singing and dancing is not a sin. If you make love with a man out of your own will, that is also not a sin, even with more than one man. But if you are selling your body, that is a sin. Even for a short period, you are transferring ownership of your body."

Ownership of my body?

These four words strike my guts hard. Is this the reason some Hindu women are forcibly sent to the pyre of their dead husbands because the men own their wives, even their soul? We, the British, pride in making laws and imposing restrictions to curb the *Sati*, even though I have heard it is not the practice in all parts of this country. Only a few people committed *Sati*. What about my own country? I have been educated so that I can be a better wife. I was denied maths as that is only for boys who will work in offices. And maths probably can't contribute to the making of a good wife. Who owns me?

I get a feeling that now I own my body and soul. I am now confident enough to shed my clothes and feel comfortable with my own body. I have danced in front of an audience, but I have not slept with anyone. I am not loyal to Colin, but like my days in England before my wedding, I still believe I will get a prince in my life whom I can love. At least I have got my dream back because of Mata Radhe.

Madhuri and I both share a small room in the ashram. One day she says to me, "Let's enjoy the holiday until the war is over, or at least until patrons start coming in."

I continue to stare at the ceiling from my bed.

Madhuri moves her palm before my eyes. "Where are you lost? Come, I will show you something you will love."

I blink and look at her. "Are we going out?"

"Sort of," she replies.

Sort of, I think. I am in a *sort of* prison because of my skin colour. I don't dare leave the *kotha* for fear that the British police will find me and hand me over to my husband, who owns my body. *Sort of!*

I walk with Madhuri. It has been almost a week since we've arrived at the ashram, and I still have not explored the hill we are all living on. Most of my days are spent helping in the kitchen and watching the Gomti. I haven't noticed any boats in the river exploding due to fighting, but the war is still going. The time is not right to go back to the *kotha* or resume the performances.

My gaze suddenly goes to a man inside the ashram complex. "Madhuri, look there," I mutter, squeezing her arm.

A tall, tribal-looking, dark-skinned man stands wearing only a loincloth—similar to the man who gives me my milk-honey bath. Standing near a tree, he removes his loincloth and hangs it on a tree branch. His eight-inch-long manhood springs out in the open and swings freely. I watch him through the corner of my eyes.

"He is the only male allowed inside," Madhuri whispers. "Do you know why? Because he doesn't have any inhibitions. He has been brought from a far-off tribal area. In his locality no one wears clothes."

Whatever I have heard about this in England is not entirely false. The man enters the ashram holding some bags.

"Guards protect this ashram and stay at the bottom of the hill. Those guards are not allowed to come here. They buy provisions for the ashram. This man carries them inside. He lives with the guards."

We go across the hedge-like flower plants that surround the ashram like a natural boundary wall.

"There is another such natural barrier toward the bottom of the hill, tall thorny bushes surrounding the whole area," Madhuri says as we move to another side of the hill.

After crossing over a narrow and dry nullah, I notice a small waterfall. The height of the fall is hardly ten feet. As we enter the knee-deep water, my toes wriggle in the golden sand, and droplets of water glitter like jewels on my naked skin. I sit down to bring the water at least to my chest height. "Are you sure there will be no one else here other than us two?"

"There might be," she answers casually and moves ahead.

I get up and splash in the water toward her. "Why didn't you warn me? I could have covered myself. I don't want the whole world to see my naked and so-called liberated body." I feel a sudden heat in my breath. She is a friend, but she is also my personal maid. Unknowingly, I start behaving like a boss.

"Don't worry, Amelia ma'am. Anyone else will also be without any clothes."

I stare at her and then follow her smiling gaze. Two women of the ashram are going hand in hand ahead of us.

"See, they are also wearing nothing. Only ashram residents come here. Today it is neither cold nor hot. Why do we need clothes, anyway?

She takes me far behind the waterfall, where natural rock walls are on both sides and water falls from above. We walk through a narrow nullah and find a spot to sit—a rock as big as a bed. Water splashes over my shoulders and flows through my breasts, belly, and thighs before touching the sandy bottom.

"Do you like this place?" she asks, sitting close to me, her breasts touching the back of my right shoulder. I enjoy the warmth of her body.

"Absolutely." I splash water with my hand and wriggle my toes in the soft, golden sand dazzling inside the shallow stream. "Had it been on the other side of the hill facing the river, I would have spent whole days here."

She doesn't respond, but slowly moves her arms around my shoulders, then cups my breasts. My nipples harden. She rolls her thumb on the nipple, elongating it. I still and think about whether to reprimand her. My heart rules over my head. I feel the sensation all the way to my inner thighs. I moan. She instantly plants a kiss on my cheeks.

I giggle. "I am a woman. Like you. Can't satiate the heat of your body."

"So what? When you don't get a full meal, you manage with whatever you get. Just imagine I am a man."

I don't understand. Madhuri's fingers move progressively to my thighs, slowly caressing and creeping forward.

"Those two women are still here, somewhere around. They might come this way anytime."

She is not bothered by my warning. "They might be doing the same thing. Like us. Don't you miss the man of your life? His hard member inside you? His hot lips sucking your ruby-tipped globes?"

"A man can't be a man of my life just by marrying me. All those things are still in my dreams. All my experiences are from reading romance books. All that man has given is me…" I stop abruptly. "You have seen the cigar marks beneath these bubbies you are caressing."

"Don't mind. I had a husband, too. He loved me. I was a princess to him."

I swing my neck a little and try to stare into her eyes. All I can feel is her hot breath on my neck. "Then?" I don't want to spoil this moment. The moment I have always wanted from the prince of my dreams is now coming from a woman. Although I know it can't go to that level.

"Five years after the marriage, I couldn't give him a child. His mother insisted on bringing another daughter-in-law. I was also not averse to the idea. After all, a child is required to continue the family tree. I even arranged his second marriage with one of my cousins. I was willing to share everything, even my man."

I know polygamy is common in this country. Even Nawab Wajid Ali has four wives.

Madhuri's finger is now caressing my thighs, slowly moving toward my clitoris.

"He was still making love with me, at least two days a week. But my mother-in-law didn't like this. 'Making love with you will make his liquid thin. The new wife will also not conceive.' That was her thought. She even told me. No, she threw those words at me as if I were a bitch who was eating away the prospect of him conceiving a child. No, not a bitch, but a witch. She even got a tantric to remove the witch in me.

My husband stopped talking to me. Even my cousin, who is his second wife, treated me as an outcast. My reputation for being a witch had spread to all the nearby villages. When he threw me out on the road, I had nowhere to go. My parents could have probably supported me, but they were dead. My sister-in-law was pregnant, and she told me I would be a curse to her unborn child. People in the village took their children playing on the road inside their homes to save them from my spell. I ran away and came to Sultanpur, where nobody knew me."

"Then?" I ask.

A moaning sound comes from the other side of the rock wall.

"Then," she giggles, "there is this beautiful white woman beside me with her large bubbies and gorgeous body. I am her maid and have to keep her happy!" She moves her fingers closer to my labia. I feel her hot breath on my breasts as she sucks the nipples. I start to moan softly, trying my best not to let it go behind the rocks.

"Don't mind," she mutters, still keeping the nipple inside her mouth, "everyone here does the same. Men are not living in the ashram, what are we to do?"

Her fingers caress my clitoris. *I am so selfish,* I think and move my palm on her thighs. I can't just swing and take her nipple in my mouth. I don't want to suck her anyway, but she should also get some pleasure from me. She must be missing a man in her life like I do. And something is better than—I cry out louder, and I can't think further. All I can imagine is a muscled, hairy chest holding me tight, and my moan shoots through the rock walls. I fear it will even be audible to the ashram. I forget that a woman is caressing me, but a strong male hand gently circling my clitoris. I hear an unknown man's voice in my ears, *Love you, Amelia.*

"Love you, too, love you soooo muuuch." I giggle and cry louder. My breath is ragged. The hand moves down my waist, cups my other breast and comes back to my clitoris. A finger slowly goes inside and comes out, continuing the movement. I dream that my man's hard member—similar in length to that tribal man—is moving in and out, in and out, again and again. I cry louder and hold the imaginary shaft tightly. "I have got it. I felt it, the first time in my life. This is the climax. I love you, sooo." I realise I am not holding a long penis, but Madhuri's fingers.

"Thank you, Madhuri," I whisper as I also plant a kiss on her cheeks. "I owe you the same."

"Never mind." She gets up. "Time to go back. Time for noon *aarti*."

"*Aarti*?" I glance at her.

"Yes, you have attended the worship when food is offered to the goddess?"

I understand. Moving a lamp of ghee in a rhythm and beating the drum before the statue of goddess Kali. Singing hymns, I never understand.

We walk toward the temple. On the way, I hear a strange sound. A hoarse sound of a man talking comes from the bushes. "What is that?" I ask.

"You want to see?" Madhuri changes the path without waiting for my answer.

It doesn't take long. The scene steals away my heart for a moment. The tribal man whom I had seen earlier is sitting on a piece of rock with two women of the ashram. One woman has clambered onto his lap, dancing in a rhythm. The man is squeezing one of her bubbies and fingering the other woman's inner thighs who is standing behind him, holding him tight and pressing her breasts on his back.

We stand silently. Madhuri's breathing sounds harsh, and her nipples harden. A guilt washes over me. I have gotten the pleasure of a climax with her but haven't reciprocated. I am still feeling uncomfortable doing this with a woman.

The woman lap dancing on the man moans louder and starts pulling his hair before stopping suddenly. "This is called *orgasm* in English," I mutter in her ears as if I am repaying something.

Soon the woman dismounts, and the other woman comes to the front and sits on his lap. For a brief minute I notice his long penis, still hard and—oh my, must be a foot long. Maybe in my admiration, I am exaggerating a little bit. There's no way to go and measure his member.

"Can he still do?" I ask when we leave that place.

"He is like a bull, can do with several cows in a day. But not everyone gets a regular chance." Madhuri walks toward the temple.

I see a woman I have never seen before—a dark and naked woman with a little girl near the temple.

Before I ask, Madhuri says that she is the wife of that tribal man, *Daita*. Her name is *Daiti*.

"Poor woman doesn't know her husband is cheating with two other women."

Madhuri laughs loudly. "You, British people, judge everything as per your standard. She very well knows what her husband is doing. No secret. Men can do with more than one woman. Didn't I arrange a second marriage for my husband?"

"What happens if the women here become pregnant?"

"Daiti makes a paste out of some herb and applies to his penis before he comes inside the ashram, to ensure his sperm has no power." Madhuri giggles again.

Silence. Time to wait for the completion of the noon ritual in the temple. The aroma of food is banging in my stomach.

"In our country, we call it *tribade*, this female to female," I whisper to Madhuri while eating lunch. "This is counted as sin."

"I know. Same here, too. If someone is hungry, he must steal food. You call it sin or whatever."

15 July 1857

Spending some time alone is like a hobby for me. The last few weeks have felt completely liberating. I go out for a stroll on the outer garden, beyond the first layer of the flower-plant boundary but before the gate. A feeling that I am away from all the dangers of the world thrills my nerves. Am I still daydreaming?

How beautiful can the world be without men? I think.

No, not possible. No children would come into this world, and mankind would perish. My gaze goes to the tribal man and his wife sitting outside the temple on the floor with banana leaves laid before them. Madhuri is serving rice and curry and is talking to the man in sign language while his wife is busy feeding the baby daughter. Madhuri might be fixing a date for herself inside the bush and on the sex-rock.

My thoughts change direction.

How would it be if men would serve women like their wives? Like women would be husbands and men, their wives?

Lots of mango trees are here. I collect some mangoes but realise I can't carry them. Wearing a frock would have helped in wrapping a few fruits in the hem, but I haven't touched any clothing in days. Gathering some leaves of a teak tree, large enough to cover my bare buttocks, I place them on the grass and sit down between a mango tree and a tall, bushy plant I don't recognise. A layer of cloud blocks the warm sunrays, and the wind sighs, brushing over my skin like a soft, friendly touch. I lie down, keeping my buttocks on the leaves to stop insects from crawling inside my vagina—following Mata Radhe's sermon from time to time, the golden rules of nude life.

I hear a sound, like a movement on dry leaves. I freeze, listening in-tently. Something is moving. An unknown fear curls into me. It is not always safe to walk carelessly on the grass. This is part of a forest, any-way. I don't hear it again. Inhaling deeply, I indulge in my dream once more. This area might have snakes, but I am safe from the police and my husband's powerful, legal arms.

Another sound. Again, it stops. I listen more intently. It's coming from the other side of the bush. I stand up and look for some stick. There is nothing. I try to look through the bushes, but nothing comes to my sight. I tiptoe and peek around the other side. Nothing. Nobody. I notice a stick sort of hanging—maybe stuck to the thorns of the bush. Bending gently, I extend my hand to grab it.

Suddenly a man stands before me. Before I can react, he mutters, "Ma'am," and slumps down on the grass. A shudder runs through my body. This is Chetan again! Swinging back, I run to the ashram, cover-ing my groin with one hand and breasts with another. I am not safe even here. Colin was right. Spies of the East India Company are every-where. They can find anything, anybody—only a matter of time. Where do I hide now?

Madhuri is smiling, standing on the steps of the ashram. "I was looking for you."

I look at her helplessly, not knowing what to say.

"We need to leave now. We got a message. You have gotten an invi-tation from a wealthy businessman to perform at his riverfront bunga-low in two days. Congratulations, you have gotten a wealthy patron."

"Who is he?"

"Hari."

"Thank you. Let's go back to the *kotha*." I go inside to wear my clothes.

Hari. Wealthy businessman. Riverside bungalow. Patron of my own. How much time will I need to arrange enough money and steal a journey to Calcutta?

CHAPTER 19

25 July 1857
Sehnaz

Days passed. Sehnaz was practically alone in the temple. Every morning Sheru went out and would come back in the evening, tired. He had organised food to be delivered to the room so that Sehnaz wouldn't have to step outside. People in Lucknow knew her as Rupen's mistress. Anyone could inform the local British police, and the message would fly to the East India Company army like the wind.

Sheru would always come back with depressing news about the mutiny. No, not mutiny. It was a freedom movement. More and more areas the rebels had occupied had been snatched away by the British forces. The Indian side could lure away many Indian soldiers from the British army, but they were short of modern armaments.

"What else do you bring from outside, Sheru, other than the bad news?" Sehnaz asked him.

"Money."

"Who pays you?"

"I was a soldier in the army of the East India Company, you know. After joining the rebel force, my income stopped. I lift heavy items at the jetties for the commercial boats, and they are paying me some money. How else would I survive?"

Guilt whispered through Sehnaz. She had never thought about how a poor man without any savings survives a calamity. She was also poor once, but that was ages ago. She was a wealthy woman now, in her own right. She had even planned to buy her own mansion in Lucknow and spend her time writing poems and teaching young courtesan aspirants. "You should have told me, Sheru. I could have given you money. You are a soldier and shouldn't work as a daily labourer. This is beneath your dignity."

Sheru Pandey stood silently, his eyes lasering hers, something unspoken glinting in them. "I am sorry, ma'am." He folded his hands. "I can't accept money from a woman. This is beneath my dignity. Instead, I would prefer to die from hunger."

The bell of the temple rang—*Aarti* time. Sheru quietly slipped out of the room to attend the evening worship ritual of Lord Shiva, the deity of the temple.

Sehnaz slumped on the bed and recollected a poem she had frequently recited in her early days as a courtesan. *Male pride, it is like a dried bamboo stick. Even though it has hardly any strength left, but it wouldn't bend, rather break.*

Sheru was poor. He had to work hard. At least he was free to go out openly. Sehnaz didn't have that freedom. The price of being Rupen's mistress was high.

Next Day

"Can I go to the temple with you this evening?" she asked when Sheru returned from his daily work.

Sheru stilled in awe, features guarded and mouth tight.

"What happened, Sheru? Is something wrong? I am a Muslim and can't go to the temple?"

"Ma'am, please. Even the walls have ears."

"I am Sanju, your wife. Do you remember?"

"Not real wife, ma'am, but yeah, ye—yes."

"Lower your volume, Sheru, even walls have..."

Sheru laughed.

"Yesterday evening, when you went to attend the evening ritual, I quietly slipped to the main gate of the temple and met an old woman. She told me about Kaal Bhairav," Sehnaz said with the excitement of a child.

Sheru stared at her, awaiting her to continue.

"Kaal Bhairav means both 'Death' and 'Fate.' Even Death is afraid of Kaal Bhairav. And you know what? He is the protector of Varanasi. No one can enter this city without his permission. He is the fearsome manifestation of Lord Shiva."

"You really wish to join me for *aarti*?"

"I know the name Lord Shiva," Sehnaz said, "Rupen is his devotee. I didn't know that this is a Shiva temple."

"Ma'am, you will disclose your identity if you talk to anyone like this. Who will believe a Hindu woman, who has been living inside the temple for more than a week, doesn't even know this is a Shiva temple? Did you say your name is Sanju or Sehnaz?"

"She didn't ask me. Look, Sheru, it is so depressing to sit inside a room for the whole day. Until you are back, there is no one to talk to me. I am afraid to talk to anyone in the temple as they would easily find out I am a Muslim and unlawfully staying in its compound. You should have taken me to the prayer every day. At least I will know the rituals and behave like a real Sanju. I can also pray for the victory of Rupen in the war."

The evening bell rang—time for *aarti*, the evening ritual. Sehnaz followed Sheru to the temple as his wife Sanju and watched the ritual.

The priest moved the ghee lamp in a synchronised motion to the chanting of a Sanskrit mantra. Sheru bought some flowers from the shop outside, and both offered them to the deity.

Afterward, Sheru said, "Let's go back to the room ma'—sorry, Sanju. The worship is over."

"Can we please spend some time here? On this stone floor? I am suffocating inside that room."

Sheru agreed and sat near her. Sehnaz turned her head toward the sky and whispered to the stars above, "Lord, Allah, Shiva, whatever name you prefer, please help us to learn your ways. Your creation is divine, and please teach us to cherish it. The powerful enemy is going to crush the patriots. Please help them. And yes Lord, I don't know if I have done right or wrong, leaving Amelia. Please help her wherever she is. Amen."

She heard a noise. Some people rushed inside the temple with slogans like, "Hail, Lord Shiva."

"Is there some festival?" Sehnaz asked Sheru.

"No."

"Then what is this?"

"Looks like these people are celebrating something."

Slowly, the number of people in the temple grew to more than a hundred. She could hear other slogans like "Down with the *firangis*!" and "Go back, *firangis*!"

"It is not about any festival, ma'am," Sheru said, "something different."

"Sheru, I am Sanju. Who is this ma'am?"

"No one can hear what we are saying in such a noise. Let me go to them and ask."

Sehnaz got up and went to a corner as even more people gathered inside the compound. Within a minute Sheru was back wearing a broad smile on his face. She had never seen him so happy before.

"Did they tell you a joke?"

"Better than that. The map... The map!"

"What happened to the map?"

"It has finally reached its destination. I think. Lord Shiva has answered our prayers."

"How do you know, Sheru?"

"Rupen Sahib and his Awadh army have sieged The Residency. It is not long before the English will pack their baggage and go back to the island they have come from."

Sehnaz gazed at Sheru in disbelief and then turned her head toward the deity inside the temple with folded hands.

Did you wait for the day when I would fold my hands?

CHAPTER 20

Those five words fill up my chest and hammer inside my head.

The. Residency. Has. Been. Sieged.

This morning when I wake up, I say to myself, "Amelia, this will be the best day so far on your quest for a new life."

Finally, I have my own patron—a man who owns an island in the Gomti River and has his own luxurious mansion. Madhuri says he is wealthy like a king. Even nawabs and kings compete among each other to be his guests. Had it been another time and not the Sepoy Mutiny, some king from any state of India could have attended my dance performance. I am thrilled and start daydreaming that I am earning so much money. I am travelling back to London and opening my own theatre company there. No one in London has ever watched the Indian style dances—*kathak, thumri*. Maybe I could bring some musicians from Lucknow. That would be a superhit there.

Madhuri continues to dress me in my best. New *lehenga* and *choli* were stitched for me by an expert tailor in just two days.

"Exact size is required for a perfect fitting cup of your blouse." Madhuri says. "The courtesans who dance before kings always wear special costumes. These cost a fortune. But Hari is no less than a nawab or king. If he is impressed, heaven is not far away from you."

"The *lehenga* is translucent and has so many slits, will it not expose me?" I cast a nervous glance at Madhuri.

She replies with a smile. "Don't worry, ma'am. You will wear a near-invisible undergarment. It will hide your things properly."

Once the tailor is gone, she confides that he stitches designer breast-bands and fitting tops for many British women, too. Some days, more than a dozen English women line up in his shop to shed their tops and get their breasts measured for exact fitting blouses and breastbands to keep their husbands happy. He also has a shop in Lucknow with a large British clientele.

I recollect the ladies' club gossip in The Residency at Lucknow, and women talking about their sexy garments reserved for special nights with their husbands.

The. Residency. Has. Been. Sieged.

Again, those five dreaded words pummel my heart. Here I am standing in front of the mirror wearing the most attractive, sexiest costume I have ever known and am ready to do a performance that might change my life, when my acquaintances and friends are probably spending a sleepless night at The Residency. I have heard of the massacre at Saharanpur and Seetapure, the wholesale slaughter of European inhabitants. I have seen with my own eyes the carnage of an entire ferry-load of British soldiers in the Gomti River at the hands of the rebelling sepoys.

When I saw Sehnaz concealing the map of The Residency in her suitcase, I should have realised how that could be used in the mutiny. I could have begged Sehnaz. I should have snatched it out of her box and thrown it in the waters of the Gomti.

I take out my diary from the cupboard and start writing. In case the fort is destroyed and only the remnants are available, my journal will provide some information about the strong fortification the British had constructed to rule over a part of India. I start drawing the main gate and a few features which come to mind. In case the native kings and nawabs win this war and the British are entirely thrown out of this land, my diary will serve as the history of an English landmark. I am not worried that the English rule will be finished in this country. But my heart cries for the innocent families living inside The Residency whose only fault is their husbands or fathers are fighting against the lo- cal sepoys.

Madhuri comes in; time to start. As I stand before the mirror, my heart thumps in my chest. I am in a dilemma—whether it is stage fright or the anticipated fate of my country people facing the wrath of the se- poys. I get the sense of a cage closing in, sealing any viable exit. I notice the dull ache in my eyes and wonder if I still look beautiful. My knees buckle. Can I impress my new patron with my looks and dance?

"Madhuri, you once told me the tailor who stitched this costume for me also has English clients in Lucknow? What if he discloses that a white woman is working as a courtesan here? What if the police come here to look for me? They will take me back to my husband."

"That monster's fate is now sealed inside the fort in Lucknow. You should be happy."

"He is a brigadier. I don't think he was sleeping when the sepoys surrounded The Residency. He must be in the cantonment or some- where else fighting the mutiny. It is the innocent women and children whose fate has been sealed."

Madhuri comes and stands in front of me, meets my tense gaze. "Rebels will not kill the innocents among the hostages. They may only use the women and children as bargains, not take their lives."

Bargains! Another thought crosses my mind. I know The Resi- dency has underground storages. It has enough supplies of food and ammunition to sustain for months. My lips must not open to say any of this. Another piece of information could help the rebels as potent ammunition. When only one person from more than a hundred thousand British is after my life, the rest are all my own countrymen.

The thought of Antonia floats before my eyes. I still doubt she committed suicide. I don't want that to happen to me. I must gather strength to impress Hari in my performance.

My determination flashes a confident smile in the mirror. "Madhuri, are you sure with this revealing outfit, Hari can control himself? He will not force me onto his bed?"

An assuring smile unfurls over Madhuri's lips. "He is a gentleman. He was the patron of a sweet girl from our *kotha*. The poor girl died from malaria. Since then, Hari has never visited us for the last two years. He is again showing interest. Who knows? He might be your star patron."

Covering ourselves head to toe in a burqa, we both sit in the horse carriage, slightly opening only one window.

"We will avoid the city route and take the road alongside the river," Madhuri instructs the coachman. "I have sent the musician and instrumentalists ahead of us."

My heart is already in my stomach. *Can I perform well today? Will this Ha—I forget his name, again and again—appreciate my dance?*

Hardly anyone is on the road. The mutiny has cast its spell of fear equally among both the locals and the British.

When the cart touches the unpaved road stretched alongside the river, I peek through the little window. We are travelling in the opposite direction of the river's flow. I struggle with the heat inside the long, black robe. Madhuri opens the door for me, and wind gusts inside, cooling my nerves. Finally, I see some human faces—people bathing in the river ghats. "One day I will also bath like this, openly," I mutter to Madhuri, "but there should be some female-only ghats."

She blurts out a laugh. "If a white woman bathed like this openly, that piece of news would be all over the country." She peeks out the window. "We are almost there. This is the private road for Hari's island mansion."

As we approach the narrow but bricked road, trees on both sides look like a natural fence. Realising that we are outside the city now, I get a sense of security soothing my nerves. I notice the small island and get a glimpse of the mansion through the dense trees around it. But the luxury ferry anchored in a jetty doesn't escape my gaze. Our cart moves left and enters the pathway leading to the island.

"Do we have to sail through a boat?" I ask.

"No, the island is close to the riverbank, connected by a small bridge."

The carriage stops in front of a large mansion, built in a similar style as those back in England. Two Gurkha guards hanging rifles on their shoulders open the massive steel gate for us.

I clamber out of the carriage gingerly, fixing a smile. "Does Har... Hari know I am British?" My voice is fevered and anxious.

Madhuri cast a don't-be-so-stupid glare at me. "No. You are Amelia from Calcutta, and you are the daughter of a courtesan who had an English lover. Don't you remember Bibi has planned this reply for you if anybody asks you about your heritage? Like any other courtesan, you have also changed your name, and your new name is Amelia."

I jolt out of my inadvertency.

I follow Madhuri up the marble steps with my heart in my throat. A maid opens the main door and guides us through a long corridor decorated with lots of antique bronze and stone statues on the recesses of the wall with an oil lamp lighting each of them. It is not even midday. We go inside a room with beds, a large mirror, and a bathroom attached. My inner goddess appreciates the modern taste of this Indian businessman. He must have visited London, hence has built this mansion with the latest design and interiors.

"Mr. Harry will arrive shortly. Please freshen up and let me know, I will serve you snacks," the maid says in Hindi.

"I am not hungry, please get something only for Madhuri."

The maid leaves, and my mind instantly goes into a whirl. Did she say, Hari or Harry? Have I made a blunder by agreeing to perform here? I should have waited until Bibi came back from her daughter's home. Will this open new doors for me or close whatever is already available?

"Madhuri, are you sure his name is Hari?" A sudden panic squeezes my brain as the maid returns with the snacks.

She replies, "What is in a name, ma'am? Harry or somebody else? In fact, I have never seen him, only heard of him." She takes a bite of the snacks.

Accepting such an offer to perform without consulting Bibi is probably going to result in a blunder. The thought suddenly tightens my gut. I can't do anything now but prepare for the dance. I am not worried anymore about my concert. Let him get up and leave halfway through.

Coming to the corridor, I notice the musicians already eating their snacks in another room. There are four of them, including one who sings—an old man in his sixties. He stops eating as I stand before him and look into his eyes.

"Can you please sing the same song we rehearsed two weeks ago?"

"But ma'am," he swallows, "that is a sad song. You have already practised for today with another song. This one can jolt up a depressed man." He smiles with his half-broken teeth darkened by chewing *paan*, the betel leaf stimulant.

"You are right, *ustadji*—" I remember to address him correctly instead of *master* as per the local custom— "but I feel I can perform better with that one, the sad tune."

"I will," he said hesitantly.

Coming out of that room, I let my eyes wander around. The end of the corridor is covered by a screen. Warm daylight slips through it, illuminating the veranda. Curiosity winks at me as instead of returning to the room where Madhuri is waiting for me, I walk and raise the curtain. The corridor opens to a large terrace overlooking the Gomti.

"Wah!" I scream without checking if anybody is there. I stroll across the balcony and stand at the edge. The sprawling green lawn with small flower plants goes all the way to the riverbank. My skirts and waist-length hair blow in the wind. After a while, I realise I am in a dancing costume, against the custom. A dancer needs to cover with another long, full-body robe before the performance starts.

A feeling of being watched sends a chill down my spine, and I swing back to face a man standing near the door of a room off the terrace. My gaze stills for a while at his features: tall and slim, all shoulders and muscles. He looks at me with a smirk while moving his fingers through his unruly golden hair. As I stand panting, my blood rushes through my veins, skin tingling. No one has seduced me like this before. Suddenly another face appears, lifting the curtain of the corridor. Madhuri is there looking for me. I jolt and sprint through the terrace, almost tumbling over her. "Let's go to our room," I gasp.

"He is Hari, your new patron."

"He? Hari?" I falter. "He looks like a European—might be English."

"Don't know. The maid said Hari has come, so I just guessed."

His name is Harry, the maid confirms. I am hung between two strong magnetic fields on both sides—Harry's attraction, and the fear of being caught and returning to hell. Can I go back now?

As I arrive with Madhuri in the small private auditorium, I notice Harry is already seated on a throne-like chair as if he were a king. Two young maids are standing beside him. I meet his gaze and bow my head in the traditional custom. Quickly I move my gaze around; the musicians and the singer have taken their positions. All the windows of the hall are closed, leaving no room for either daylight or breeze from the river. Hundreds of candles are blinking at me from inside the recesses of the walls. I swing myself around in a dancing style and find dozens of Amelias around me. Then I realise, those numerous candles are mere reflections of a few dozen, in reality.

Isn't the room stuffy?

Harry immediately orders one of his maids to run the ceiling fan connected with a rope. *Can he read my mind?*

I am nervous to meet Harry's gaze even though I long to look at him properly. Suddenly the sound of the *tabla*, the twin hand drums, fills up the serenity of the auditorium, and my ankle-bell-studded feet start moving automatically to the tune. I make a full circle around myself keeping one heel fixed to the floor, and the mirrors show my *lehenga* dancing freely, revealing my thighs. The other instrument, the *sarangi*, joins the *tabla* when the singer reveals the magic of his wonderful voice that drifts on the wind.

"Today you are weeping, do not stop please. Shed the tears as long as your heart is heavy. This is your flower offering to the God. HE will bestow the heavenly blessings on you and will bring the million-pound smile on your face."

I focus on the words of the song and struggle hard not to make any mistakes. Yes, The Residency is in danger. But my performance should be enough to siege the mind of Harry.

I feel my eyes pooling.

The dance finishes, and I kneel to the host with the *namaste* pose, but my eyes are closed. I'm not sure how I have done.

When Harry stands up and claps, I guess that I have done well. I raise my head and glance around. Almost everyone is in tears. Harry comes and stands before me, breathing warm against my skin. Not knowing how to react, I stand, meeting his appreciating gaze, resisting a strong urge to hug him tightly against my chest. An intoxicating masculine perfume from his body gently massages my nostrils.

He takes a gold necklace from his pocket and hangs it around my neck. "I had stopped coming to the *kotha* after Rambha's death. You have again aroused that flame. I am your fan now." He speaks in chaste Urdu.

"Thanks." I don't know what else to say.

"It is not even lunchtime. I would love it if you joined me for a drink and lunch after that. In my room." His voice is so calm and mesmerising.

"Sure."

"Please stay in this costume. You look like a heavenly dancer to me. I will draw a picture of you," he whispers, coming closer.

"Thanks a lot for inviting me. Where are your family members?" I continue talking while walking alongside him, up the stairs to the top floor.

We arrive at the penthouse, surrounded by flowerpots on all sides except the riverside. Harry sits close to me, close enough that I can smell his scent and feel his warm breath. I steal my gaze at his chest hair peeking through his top-unbuttoned shirt. Then I feel the warmth of his stare on the round, protruding cups of my *choli*. A wine bottle and glasses sit idly on the side table, awaiting our touch.

"I have no family here." He starts the conversation in English. "I mean, I live in the city for my business and come here occasionally for leisure. After Rambha's death, I didn't come to this house for almost a year. I even thought of selling this. Nawab Wajid Ali was interested. But then this mutiny started."

I am mesmerised by his voice. Did I dream of this man as my prince during my days in England?

Harry starts again. "Rambha was not her real name. She had told her name to me. Only to me. You know."

I jump in. "Courtesans never disclose their real names. But my parental name is Amelia. People think I have changed my name."

I open up to him about everything—almost everything. I'm not aware of when I took Harry's palm inside my grip and rested it on my lap, on my half-naked thigh. Two of his fingers are even touching my thigh through the slits of my designer *lehenga* and slither on my skin. I inhale deeply as hot desire surges through my nerves. This should be my ideal man, and this room should be where I have my first intimate night with him—a perfect full moon night in full view of the River Gomti. But unfortunately, I am not Rambha.

"You should have taken a new name," Harry mutters, "Menaka. The other heavenly dancer as per Hindu mythology. Rambha, Menaka and Urvashi."

"You know so much about mythology?"

"My mother's mother was Indian. She is thus an Anglo Indian. My father was British. He is no more. Mother has remarried a prince in Bengal. A Hindu prince." He gently squeezes my hand. His other hand moves on my bare belly, trying to discover every inch of it. I am literally under his spell. I would love for his finger to wander through my whole body, including whatever little bit is hidden beneath the slits of the skirts and the tiny blouse. I get the urge to peel open his shirt and run my nose along his muscular chest.

Harry starts again. "Most courtesans do not marry. But Rambha had different plans. Will you, Amelia, ever think to be a wife?"

Suddenly my heart is in my stomach. If I say I am already married and running away from my husband, for whatever reason, everything will be over soon. I want to enjoy this moment to the fullest. Keeping mum is the only way. Is this just a daydream and about to be over?

"I would like to tell you something." He pulls me against his chest and plants a hot kiss on my lips. I blush. His fingers start unbuttoning my blouse.

As a knock disrupts my erotic reverie, Harry releases me and opens the door. The security guard mutters something to him. Harry comes back, urgency shadowing his face. "I need to go to the police station for an urgent matter. Sorry we couldn't have lunch together. Please wait, and my maids will serve food to you and your staff. We will meet again soon."

I freeze. Dark thoughts snake through me.

After Harry leaves in a hurry, I lurch to my feet and arrive on the ground floor. Madhuri has just started her lunch. "Can we—" I struggle to mask the tremor in my voice— "can we leave as soon as possible and eat in the *kotha*?"

She stares at me in shock. I scramble upstairs and change into the burqa lying on the bed. Madhuri leaves her plate and follows me. Within minutes, we both are in the horse carriage.

I close the window and mutter, "Harry has gone to the police station."

Madhuri lifts her veil. "You spoke to him in a complete British accent."

"That is the only accent I know."

"Bibi has told you to speak in Urdu only. Pretend you are an An-glo-Indian. You became like ... like, someone did magic to you, and you forgot everything." Accusations glint in her eyes.

My lips are tight; anything can happen to me now. Chetan is following me and already knows my whereabouts. I can't even hide in the Shakti Ashram. Will I be treated as an accomplice to Sehnaz for providing the map of The Residency? Will I face charges for conspiring with the rebels against my own people?

CHAPTER 21

Brigadier Colin Lawrence

Colin was hospitalised for almost a month. He was seriously sick after Amelia fled from home without his knowledge and Sona died because of her own insensitiveness to Colin's needs. Doctors treated his physical sickness, but he could never talk to them about the enormous emotional trauma he was enduring. His condition didn't get better. The ghost of Sona haunted him day and night. And the death of his own mother who he now believed had committed suicide—hanging herself when he was in the boarding school in London. Otherwise, why she was repeatedly coming in his dreams? Once healed, he would have to go back to the haunted house. Scary. Two women had died there. How could he dare to face so many ghosts in his own home? He couldn't do his duty in a time when his army needed him the most. A sick soldier is a liability in times of war.

"Bastard natives. They deserved to be blown up. They don't deserve humane treatment."

Colin reacted to the death of countless natives when nine ordnance officers in Delhi blew up the British arsenal fearing a rebel takeover. He couldn't have done anything else sitting on the hospital veranda and talking to his personal assistant. The East India Company had finally taken care of its hospitalised senior officer. Colin had gotten a personal assistant in the hospital even though his case was not a war injury. A physical injury would have been much better than the damage inside his mind.

"Bastard?" Joseph muttered as he felt the heat in Colin's words toward the natives.

Realising what he had just said, Colin gazed at Joseph. "You are almost like..." He was thinking how he would describe a man with brown skin but having some British blood. Colin plastered a large smile on his face. "Even though you do not look white, you still have some European blood in your body. You can be trusted by the East India Company. How else were you appointed as the personal assistant of a brigadier?"

Colin badly needed that news even though it was depressing. He had never envisaged a fight could get to such a level. Regiment after regiment of Indian soldiers joined the rebellion. Somewhere in his subconscious, he believed that the British could finally defeat the natives and re-establish its hold over the country.

"Sir, the rebels have declared Bahadur Shah Zafer the Emperor of India," Joseph said.

"Nonsense. He is a weak king. People think he can rule over such a large country as he is a Moghul and his ancestors were mighty emperors. I know Indian history very well. The East India Company should appoint me as an advisor to draft policies on how to deal with these kings and nawabs. This Bahadur Shah is a toothless emperor."

"I am sure you can, Sir. But please do not forget you are still in the hospital, sick."

"Huh."

"Sir, Emperor Bahadur Shah is not as simple as you think. Rebels have captured fifty of our—" hesitation was in his voice— "our people. I mean, British taken as prisoners. The emperor ordered death punishment to all of them in a summary trial. He has retaliated against the killing of the civilians in the explosion of the arsenal."

"Huh, emperor. He is emperor only for a few months. We will fight back and take over Delhi again. This is totally inhuman. To kill the British soldiers without giving a trial in a British court!"

"You are right, Sir." Joseph smiled. "I have done some research about the history. The Sikhs will never accept Bahadur Shah as the emperor. For centuries, the Sikhs have fought against the oppressive Islamic rule of the Mughals. Many Sikh gurus have been slain especially by Aurungzeb, a past emperor. Rebels have made a mistake in declaring Bahadur Shah as the emperor of the country."

"Brilliant, Joseph, you know so much about the history. Instead of creating unity, this action will divide the rebels, and the mutiny will be weak. All we have to do is make a strategy—divide and rule." Colin considered himself adept in the war diplomacy and was confident in himself. He should not be sent to dangerous war zones. Instead, he would be helping the British Raj from the confines of the secured English forts.

"Yes, Sir. Our information network needs to be stronger to avoid the siege and massacres."

"Oh, yes. Joseph, do you know about the Bibighar massacre at Kanpur?"

Joseph took a paper from his pocket and unfolded it.

"This is the report, Sir. I have got this for you. It was all due to a lack of credible information. When the sepoys besieged Kanpur town, Major General Sir Hugh Wheeler, the British commander, sought the help of Nana Sahib in fighting the rebels. On the contrary, Nana Sahib assumed the leadership of the rebellion."

"Nana Sahib?"

"An exiled king from Maratha, Sir. The East India Company was giving pension to his father, Peshwa Baji Rao II after his kingdom was annexed to the British Raj. Nana Sahib is his adopted son. He was angry as the Company stopped the pension.

"The British garrison remained under siege for three weeks, until their resources were almost finished. Wheeler agreed to surrender, provided the women and children would be given safe passage out of the city. Nana Sahib accepted. The British were about to board a boat at Sati Chaura Ghat to sail to Allahabad when rebel sepoys attacked. The ferries were burned, and many British including Major General Wheeler died."

"Damn it. So many inhumane acts! What else is written in that Goddamn paper, Joseph?"

Joseph gazed at Colin with awe. He again buried his head in the paper. "Almost two hundred women and children survived the attack. The rebels took them to Bibighar. It was a small residence without any facilities in the cantonment magistrate's compound with a large courtyard and a well. The sanitary conditions were so pathetic that some of them died of cholera and dysentery. Nana Sahib attempted to use the captives as negotiating chips. But news arrived that General Henry Havelock was nearing Kanpur with his troops, and the order was issued that all British women and children were to be killed."

"Nana Sahib ordered?"

Joseph looked up. "No. I mean, he probably didn't know."

A shiver chased down Colin's arms. "Who was the bloody bastard who ordered the murder?"

Joseph's features were guarded. He read from the paper again. "Begum Hossaini Khanum. She was a courtesan in Nana Sahib's court."

God. Let that not happen to the hostages of The Residency. Colin gulped down a glass of water.

"Are you all right, Sir? Should I call the nurse?"

"No, no, Joseph. I am much better now. Doctors should release me at any time. I must help the army in whatever way I can."

Joseph again read from the report. "Some say that he was not aware Begum Hossaini ordered the murder. But the sepoys were reluctant. Hindu sepoys think it is against their religion to kill women and children. One of the guards fired only a single volley and refused to do more. Annoyed, Begum asked her lover Sarvur Khan, a Pathan, to finish the task. Armed with knives and hatchets, Khan and his allies butchered the English women and children. The walls were covered in bloody handprints, and the floor littered with human limbs. The butchers threw the dead and those were still dying in the well of the courtyard. When the well was filled with the bodies, the remainders were thrown into the River Ganga."

Joseph neatly folded the paper and put it in his pocket.

"Finished your report? Anything else?"

"Yes, Sir." Joseph lowered his head.

"What, Joseph?"

"Sir, Sir... Amelia..."

"I know she is a bitch. Tell me what she did."

"Sir, there is an intelligence report. She was with a courtesan called Sehnaz. In a boat. Sehnaz was carrying The Residency map, and our soldiers were following her. Rebels killed all the soldiers in the river, and they escaped. Another English boat was watching them from a distance, but they didn't have enough strength to face them. It might be possible Amelia madam helped in providing the map to the rebels. And this woman Sehnaz is..."

"I know, she is Rupen 's lover."

Revenge swam through Colin's stomach, and a quiet determination calcified around his heart. A real soldier can fight from anywhere. Even from hospital?

A physically weak officer just recovering from hospital could not be sent to the war. But Colin's brain could be used to provide support to the East India Company's efforts to repress the rebellion. He was appointed as officer on special duty.

He offered his three-point action plan to the Company headquarters.

Divide and Rule, that was plan number one. Hindus and Muslims should not be united. Plan number two, *Courtesans*. They were the primary informers of the rebels. Buy them at whatever price. They were double-edged swords. And finally, plan number three—*stop the missionaries from propagating the so-called enlightenment, at least temporarily*. Would these plans supress the rebellion?

Colin created more arsenals from his brain.

The rebels were making grave blunders by these genocides. Let them. *One should never disrupt an enemy when he commits mistakes.* A vast section of locals would never support these indiscriminate killings of women and children and would switch allegiances.

There were many other senior officers in the army to think and strategize to win back The Residency. Colin had his own worries. Whisper already circulated that his wife could have passed on the insider information about The Residency. Colin had a detailed map at home, which he had never thought would be a piece of confidential information. He was not the only officer to have that. Many other officers had that information. But because of Amelia, he had been in the focus of suspect.

Chetan was the other worry. Colin knew Chetan was not that clever to help the rebels with insider information. He was a stupid loyal man, hiding because of the false accusation of his own wife's murder. If he were to be caught, the police would quickly know he had no knowledge of the siege, and even his innocence in Sona's death might be proved. It would also be a source of trouble for him.

Amelia and Chetan were hanging like the sword of Damocles above his head. He would be in serious trouble whether they got caught or not. Colin couldn't think of a way out of this problem. Confusion tightened around him, encircling and trapping him inside out.

Could his fertile brain design plans for getting rid of Amelia and Chetan?

25 July 1857 afternoon

Back at the Sultanpur Cantonment, Colin snatched The Bengal Gazette newspaper from his colleague, a Sergeant Major, and read it again and again. *Nuns in Indian Hermitage Living Naked.*

"This is all bullshit. This must have been copied from The London Press."

"How do you know, Sir?" the Sergeant Major asked.

"This news is about something happening in India where the Indian newspapers don't have a clue. And our great journalists sitting in London have got extra powerful telescopes! They can see thousands of miles away and even penetrate the walls of the hermitages that nuns are living naked? First of all, a nun must be a Christian. People in England wouldn't understand so they have written the British way. And this newspaper in Calcutta has copied everything blindly. They should have typed 'Female Monks Live Nude in Ashrams in India.' And you know what? This is one of the conspiracies of our great missionaries. They are spreading this fake news so that the British parliament will exert pressure on the East India Company. Allow them to propagate Christianity so that they can make these nuns civilised. They should know how a cartridge of the Enfield rifle has ignited such a large fire of the Sepoy Mutiny, and we are still struggling to get hold of it. Why does it matter if some female monks decide to stay nude as long as they are inside their hermitages? Why are our great missionaries worried about them? Do they worry that we all stay naked in our bathrooms? Or while sleeping with our wives?"

Sleeping with wives...

He was about to start his new life with Amelia after a long period of time. Antonia's death had left a lengthy void in his life. He could never understand that woman. He had always dreamt Antonia had come back to life and he had stopped forcing her to sleep with any senior officer. A new life of love and trust. He even promised himself not to push his new wife to make any senior officer happy.

He had never repeated any such mistake with his second wife, Amelia. Having already been a senior ranking officer, he had juniors competing among each other to push their wives into pleasing him. Yes, few times he had been angry with her and even hit her. But didn't she instigate Colin each time? She was the one who made Colin a mad dog and forced him to bite her. She should have understood how much stress a senior army officer goes through. She was supposed to be an obedient and charming wife. Her parents must have taught her how to be a better spouse. What happened to all those teachings?

The army intelligence had sighted Amelia with a courtesan who was none other than Rupen Naik's lover. Then this attack on The Residency. The rebels knew precisely where the British were storing the ammunition. They knew where to hit to inflict maximum damage to the Company's supplies and not affect the families who were living inside. Now that the families are hostages, they are in a better position to negotiate. Maybe the Awadh kingdom will declare complete freedom. Nawab Wajid Ali will be the sovereign ruler.

Colin had spent his time collecting data of the number of influential *kothas* in Sultanpur and a list of officers who would visit them as new patrons. The local English officers who were excellent in Hindi or Urdu would lead the action plan. They would praise the poetries they recited and attend dance performances, to find out which courtesans had influence in Nawab's Court. Then try to replace the existing patron by sheer money power.

"Sir, the only English man still having a relationship with the courtesans is here to meet you," the officer said.

Colin glanced up. "Only one man is going to the *kotha*? All other English people became saints?"

"Sir, authorities banned all English from attending courtesans' performances."

"Bloody loyal idiots." He frowned. "Why didn't that one man honour the prohibition?"

"Sir, he is not an officer. He is a businessman from Calcutta. Harry is here waiting to meet you. He is a wealthy businessman and has excellent contacts among courtesans. You can explore your plans with him."

Colin was getting up from his seat when another officer came rushing inside and said, "Sir, we have arrested a sepoy who was a security guard in the nude ashram."

"Nude ashram?" Colin smirked.

"Sir, he has admitted the ashram has only female monks, and they all stay mostly naked."

"Sorry, I am not interested in spending my time helping missionaries spreading the religion. They are inviting more problems for the East India Company. There was no need to arrest that man."

"Sir, Chetan admitted to having seen an English nun in that ashram. We thought that might have some significance in the information you are after."

A sudden bolt of fire cracked through him. Things didn't add up.

Chetan? English nun in the nude ashram?

Colin felt he was sweating.

"Some serious conspiracy is going on. I am going to personally take care of that man, Chetan. Please organise my return journey to Lucknow, today, by a ferry. Urgently." He was going to meet Harry but again stopped. "And yes, nobody else will interrogate that man. Let him cool his heels in the detention."

How could he get rid of this fool, Chetan?

Colin proceeded to meet Harry at the office, which was in a marketplace close to the palace of Nawab Wajid Ali Shah. Nawab had gifted the land to the East India Company during the honeymoon stage between the British and the kingdom. The British promised to provide law and order to the capital Sultanpur, but Colin knew this came with a hidden agenda of keeping an eye on the ruler's activities.

Harry stood up and saluted Brigadier Colin. Harry, being white, was not taken to the interrogation room. Instead, he was made to sit in the meeting room with a glass of cold earthen-pot water and a local attendant cooling him by waving a handmade fan. When Harry indicated for the man to go out of the room, Colin asked him to stay and continue waving the fan. "He doesn't know English, and it is so hot anyway."

Colin had forgotten what to ask. He glanced out the window at the emptied road. A chilling fear of the war had already sent out its tentacles throughout the busy locality. After some time, he realised he was tapping his forefinger against his thighs and his feet against the floor while Harry eyed him, amused.

"All right, Mr. Harry, how long you have you been in India?"

"Always, Mr. Lawrence." He straightened his back.

"I mean, when did you come from England?"

"Never. I was born and brought up in Calcutta."

"So similar! I was also born in this country, only went to London to finish my studies. Otherwise, I am almost a native except—" he pointed at his skin— "that I am white."

"I am a full native. I have Indian blood in me. I can even speak Bengali fluently. Same with Urdu and Hindi." Harry spoke comfortably and with familiarity, like a friend.

Colin glanced outside. His mind wandered to Chetan, how soon he could take him to Lucknow and get a quiet time to interrogate him. But he had a task to do.

"All right, Mr. Harry, have you seen the nude ashram in Sultanpur? Nuns—I mean, Hindu nuns live in that ashram. And any white nun there?"

Harry looked bemused. "I haven't even heard of it."

The London Press is circulating fake news to help the missionaries. He looked outside at the sun dipping slowly behind the peaks. Chetan must be taken by him, him alone before he spills the beans. Colin's pulse raced at the thought. He got up from his chair and lurched to the door, "Goodbye, Mr. Harry, it was nice meeting with you."

What could he do with Chetan?

CHAPTER 22

25 July 1857, Afternoon
Chetan

From the moment he was taken into custody, Chetan had not eaten anything. For hours he was interrogated at the cantonment. Not a single question was about the allegation of his wife's murder—he couldn't have answered that anyway, other than refuting the charge. He indeed had not joined the rebels against the East India Company.

"Sir, I was always a loyal soldier of the British. Never even thought of joining the rebels."

"Loyal British soldier? Good," the havildar who caught him said. "Good to know there are some dark-skinned soldiers who are still loyal dogs. Where did you eat the thrown-away, stale bread before this, Chetan?"

Chetan scratched his head. He clearly noticed the policeman was mocking, but he didn't understand. "Sir, I have not eaten anything for hours, Sir. I am hungry, Sir."

"Don't worry. I will feed you enough. So much that you can't get up." He clasped his stick. "I am asking where you worked before."

"Lucknow, Sir. Lucknow. Guard. As a guard." He was weighing whether he should say he was working as a guard in Colin's house. Probably not.

"Will you tell me exactly where you worked in Lucknow? Or my stick will bring out the truth."

"Sir, with Brigadier Colin. His house."

"Then why did you leave? Did he throw you out?"

Chetan was in a dilemma. He had been framed for Sona's murder. He couldn't say that. Sure, he would get the death punishment if he couldn't prove himself innocent. But he was a poor and less educated man. Who would help him in legal matters?

"Sir, I was sitting in a boat and that boat drowned. I swam to the riverbank. Survived. Got a job in the Shakti Ashram."

"Did you steal the map? The Residency map? And give it to the rebels?"

"No, Sir. I swear on the name of Ma Kali. I would never bite the hand which is feeding me."

"So you will not tell the truth. Okay. Stay here. We have other means to find out." The havildar left the interrogation room.

From the day Chetan started work at the Shakti Ashram, he had never ever visited the markets of Sultanpur. He always had a fear that the long arm of the British law would get him. The senior guard Raghu always helped him buy from the market. In return, he was doing extra hours to cover Raghu's duty.

The unexpected encounter with Amelia in the ashram jolted him out of his shell of the so-called culture and civilisation. Amelia ma'am was roaming freely in the park without a shred of cloth on her body, comfortably, as if it were perfectly normal. Finally, he surrendered to nature's law. For the first time, he started communicating with *Daiti*, albeit in sign language. Gradually, her naked youth became usual for Chetan. He spent his spare time with the baby of *Daita* and *Daiti*. She had no name. Chetan called her baby, who to some extent made up the absence of his daughter.

One day he dared to go out as Raghu was sick for almost a week. Mata Radhe called for him from the gate of the ashram and asked him to buy provisions from the market of Sultanpur. That was the first time he saw Mata Radhe.

He went to the market with unknown fears in his mind. As if the whole world were looking only for this one man, Chetan. When he noticed a police officer coming in his direction, his inner voice warned him. He had only moments to decide where and how to hide. That was not enough. But when he tried to hide behind a tree in full view of the officer, that was enough to draw his attention. Within minutes he was in handcuffs.

The havildar came back after a while. "Get up now. Now I will see how long you can hide the facts."

"I will—I will admit, Sir. I will tell the truth."

The havildar stopped, and a victorious smile widened his lips. "Throw up."

"I have committed a great sin, Sir. That's why Ma Kali is punishing me. Handed me to the police. Sin. Unforgivable sin."

"Be clear, man. I am losing patience."

"I cast an evil eye to the hands that were one day feeding my family."

The havildar lifted his steel studded bamboo stick.

"Sir, Sir. I am telling the truth. I saw her. Naked. In the Shakti Ashram. I ran away to my cabin. But after that I have had sinful thoughts about her. I tried to resist. But it came back to me. That thought. She was in the temple of Kali, the goddess. Ma Kali never spares anyone who commits a sin. I am guilty, Sir."

Chetan glanced up. The havildar was holding his head with both the hands.

"Did I say something wrong?"

CHAPTER 23

25 July 1857 Evening
Brigadier Colin Lawrence

Colin thought the time was perfect, the dusky sun spooling gold beams on the blue waves of the Gomti. Chetan had been handcuffed in a small cabin near the stern of the ferry. When the boat left the jetty, Colin was flouncing on the deck, fiddling with the keys of the handcuffs. The Gomti was flowing smoothly, and they were travelling upstream. He moved his gaze toward the riverbank and then to the dipping sun. *The bank is still at swimmable reach. And the sun is moving down at an abysmally slow pace.*

Colin went to the helmsman. "Is the weather always like this? Calm and quiet?"

The man saluted him. "Not always, Sir, sometimes we have to stop sailing because of the bad weather conditions. But today is much better, Sir, you will get a comfortable sail."

"Are you sure? No storm tonight?"

The helmsman's eyes wandered around looking for a large dark cloud building up in the horizon. Colin followed his gaze.

"Sir, sailing at night is anyway, not safe. If that cloud comes this way, we will see wild waves. If you wish, Sir, we can go back and again sail tomorrow morning."

"Are you afraid of stormy weather?" Colin glared.

The helmsman gave him a measuring look. "No Sir, we are all used to sailing in odd weathers. I was thinking about your comfort, Sir."

An unease was gradually feathering into Colin. He had carefully and diplomatically avoided any other soldier, both British and Indian, from accompanying him to Lucknow.

When the dark cloud vanished after a while, Colin wiped the perspiration off his brow with his sleeve. Anxiety ignited deep in his belly and began to burn hot. The darkness of night had already crept in. Knowing that the ferry was already in the mid-river, he tiptoed to the small cabin where Chetan was handcuffed and unlocked the door, his hands quivering.

Chetan was sitting on the floor. Colin removed his handcuffs. He stood up and saluted him with a shaking hand. "Go... Good... E... evening, s...s...s...Sir."

"Sit down," he commanded in a low voice, almost whispering, and stood holding the door. Faint moonlight was spilling into the tiny space. He could see frustration crinkling in his eyes. "How are you, my boy?"

"Y... your g...g...grace, Sir," he replied.

"Lower your voice, Chetan, I don't wish to alert others. Our loyal soldiers are so angry at you that they will beat flesh out of your skin. They don't yet know that a traitor is handcuffed here. You were working with me for a long time, so I have some compassion for you, irrespective of what you have done."

"Sir, Sir, I swear to God, I have not killed my wife."

"Again, loud voice!"

"Sorry, Sir," Chetan whispered.

"I don't know what you have done or not done," Colin said, "but detectives in Lucknow are suspecting you are the culprit. And they think you have even provided the map of The Residency to the rebels. You know The Residency has been sieged? So many women and children are hostages inside?"

"Sir, I swear to God again, I have no idea."

"All right, I will ask something else which I am sure you have not done, but you might have noticed. Here is a chance to tell me the truth. I may even help you if you tell me the truth. Remember…"

"Yes Sir, I will tell the truth, only the truth, only if I know."

"Good."

A pause.

"Have you seen the nuns staying naked in any ashram in Sultanpur?"

Chetan's shoulders dropped. "Sir, I have promised you, I will tell the truth."

"Go on."

"Sir, I was a guard there. I mean, I am not allowed to go near the ashram. My cabin is—" he swallowed— "was near the foot of the hill. The ashram is surrounded by bushes and trees."

"How did you notice then?"

"Once, I had been to the mango garden outside the ashram. Normally the nuns stay indoors. But somehow, I could see her, roaming outside."

"Who? Do you know her?"

"Sir, one nun maybe. I saw one nun. Only one, Sir. Later on, Raghu told me all nuns stay naked. But I haven't seen others."

Colin met his gaze. He was still concealing something from him and trying to hide the look.

"You still haven't told me everything. Did you know her?"

"Who?"

"You told me you saw *her*. Meaning, who?"

"Sir, I saw a woman." Chetan focussed his gaze on the floor.

"No Chetan, the way you said it, it seems you know her. Who was she?"

He raised his head, wariness snapping through his eyes. "A... Am... Ame—"

Colin grabbed his face and muttered in anger, "Chetan, do not hide. This may be your chance to survive the death punishment, I can promise you."

"Sir, Amelia ma'am."

"Amelia? Here? What is she doing here?"

"No idea, Sir."

"What was she wearing?"

"N...no...nothing," Chetan stuttered. "I mean, Sir, I just saw the face. I do not e...ex...exactly know, Sir."

"Anything else you know?"

"Sir, that's of no use for you. The letter."

"Letter? Which letter? Whose letter?" Colin stared into Chetan's eyes.

"Antonia memsahib, Sir. Her letter."

"What is in that letter? How did you find?"

"I can't read English, Sir. Sona had kept as a memory. Memsahib liked her so much. I will give that to you when I come home."

Antonia's letter! That woman's ghost is still hiding in that letter! I thought I had destroyed that letter, but did Sona snatch it away instead? Maybe it is a different letter?

Colin gave a short, mirthless laugh. "You have probably told the truth this time. I will ask you one more question. I am sure you know."

Chetan stared at him in fearful expectation. Perspiration dazzled on his skin.

"How did you escape from Lucknow?"

"I saw armed people coming toward me and jumped into the Gomti. God saved me."

Colin laughed. "So you are a good swimmer."

Chetan stared at the floor.

"Can you swim from here to the riverbank?"

"No Sir, that is a long way. I got a log luckily that day. I would have died otherwise." He folded his hands. "Sir, I have a baby daughter. She has already lost her mother. I am the only hope for the little girl. Please save me. God will bless you. I will remain a loyal man to you until my death. I swear, Sir, in the name of God." Silence shimmered between them for a while.

"I will tell you a secret since you have told me the truth."

A gratuitous smile curved around Chetan's lips.

"You know John Nicholson?" Colin asked.

Chetan scratched his head. "I, Sir, I don't think."

"He is the cruellest officer I have ever seen. You probably do not know what happened after you left. Someone said the soup in our regiment had been poisoned. John Nicholson was in charge of the enquiry." He stilled to see the reaction in Chetan's eyes. "The man didn't do any investigation but arrested all the Indian cooks. He ordered their hanging without any trial. And that is the man who is in charge of your case. I will have to hand you over to him once we arrive at Lucknow, even if I don't want to."

Colin could feel the thickness of the tension in the air. Chetan was quiet, his features guarded. "I am leaving you without handcuffs, Chetan, and I don't wish you to rot in this tiny cabin. You will die of suffocation by the time we arrive at Lucknow in the morning. I know you will not flee. You think about how to save yourself and stay alive for your baby daughter. And yes, do not just jump into the water and swim, this may not be the best idea. Please do not tell anyone I have told you the secret."

He got up, leaving the cabin door open. The waves of the Gomti were chuckling.

A thunder sounded after a while. Colin looked back; Chetan had jumped into the water. A laugh burped into his chest.

Chetan is finished. Now what about Amelia?

CHAPTER 24

25 July 1857 Night
Chetan

His wrists were still aching from the prolonged confinement in the handcuffs and then the paddling in the water. Chetan felt stiffness in his arms and legs.

I shouldn't have panicked, Chetan thought while floating in the water helplessly. For a full day, he had not eaten anything and had drunk water only after diving into the Gomti, hoping to escape the wrath of a wounded East India Company. The British were on the path of taking revenge against anyone who even remotely thought against the Raj.

Muscles of his arms and legs refused to cooperate even though the Gomti was calm like a saint. The dazzling assemblage of glittering stars glistened on the soft waves. Raising his tired head several times, he tried to find the riverbank. Either the light was not enough to guide him, or his hungry stomach could not provide enough energy to his weary eyes. When his fingers felt the touch of something tangible, it was like invisible light in the darkness. "Mother, please help me to learn your ways." He muttered a small prayer to Kali, addressing her as the divine mother, goddess of doomsday and death. Hope beaded on his skin, and it slowly radiated to soothe his nerves. *I can see my daughter, my baby.*

Looking to touch the banks of the Gomti, his exhausted legs started to kick again, and his arms paddled. He was thinking of riding on a log again and using it as a drift. As he tried to get a better grab of one, his fingers got stuck in something. Something that felt like a leather belt. A bolt of consciousness shot through his skin. Moving his hand around, he tried to see anything possible in the dark-moon night. He felt the torso, and the hand, and the leg, and finally, the head of a man. Must be a dead soldier—a rebel, tied to a log. A shiver ran through his spine, and he pushed the body away. "What kind of a joke, oh God?" he heard himself shouting. There was no one to listen to him there, probably other than God.

Within moments God gave the reply; it crept into the logical side of his brain. *My body will also float like this if I do not use the log attached to this body. Friend, you died for your country, but even after death, you are helping someone. I can only pray to God for your salvation. Thank you.* Chetan grabbed the body. He attempted to free the body from the log, but couldn't find the knots in the darkness. He finally acquiesced and rode on it.

He tried to find out the time by looking at the stars. His empty stomach had stopped generating any further energy to his brain. If only he could survive until the morning.

Noticing the silhouette of a boat upstream, Chetan rubbed his eyes and glanced again. Yes, it looked like a boat. Hopefully, someone would rescue him. His voice wouldn't go that far. He waited on the log until the silhouette grew larger and appeared more clearly. Yes, it was a boat, but moving slowly. At this rate, he wouldn't be near it probably until morning. Chetan paddled to change the direction upstream, fought against the current, and allowed the ferry to get close enough to hear his yell. Struggling for almost an hour, he could finally see the boat clearly.

Chetan yelled, raised his hand and yelled again, using all his strength. No one appeared to have seen him. Anxiety whipped through him when the ferry passed through, ignoring him. Unable to let go of this opportunity, he swam nearer and yelled again, and again, and again, until he could not. He didn't even notice anybody moving onboard. Possible—the people might have been asleep. But the oars? They were swinging from the oarlock, unattended. He glanced at the vessel again. Something was wrong—no, seriously wrong.

Maybe it had somehow been released from its anchor and was floating freely.

I can own this boat. I will hold this boat. I am the owner of this. I will take it and keep it with me. So many times since Sona's died, I have survived because of this Gomti River. From today onwards, I would not have to swim for survival. I will travel in my own vessel.

Silent energy emanated from him in waves. Speeding to the boat, he almost touched it—his possession. Almost. If only he could go inside and control it. There must be something he could hold on to and clamber inside. Chetan didn't know what that something could be other than a hanging rope. He slowly circled around and moved his hand along the starboard until something hard came in his grip. While trying to grab it tightly, the log slipped away from him. He struggled, hoping to find something to help him get inside. Trying hard to set his foot on it and somehow jump inside, his feet slipped, and he fell in the water again. The vessel moved ahead in the current, and an exhausted Chetan scrambled to float.

Chetan's body was becoming heavy, some invisible force was pulling him inside the river. He should have never thought of getting onto the boat, which was nothing but a mirage. Or a curse which came as his doom for some grave sin he might have committed. Since Sona's death, everything was going against him. The intermittent survivals could be, in fact, the taste of hell he was destined to suffer, and finally, God was kind enough to rescue him from this cursed life. He conveyed his last prayer to the goddess Kali and requested she help his daughter survive.

Once the prayer finished, his legs stopped kicking and arms stopped paddling. *The sooner death comes, the better*, he thought. Slowly his body would be engulfed by the current. He might have to struggle to find breath, but that would be only for a minute or two. Then everything would end. He had finally surrendered to the supreme will of the infinite energy, goddess Kali.

Suddenly Chetan felt something warm as if he were passing through a fire pit. Impossible. How could fire come inside the water? *Maybe this is how death starts unfolding itself.* The fire slowly went inside him and settled in his gut. The warmth of the fire oozed across his arms, then the torso, and then the legs as if someone planted a momentum in Chetan's limbs. He swam at full speed for around a mile. Circling the boat, he located the anchor chain, and within no time he was aboard.

The energy that came inside him was gone the moment he rescued himself. Hours of swimming and daylong hunger had taken its toll. Stretching his legs and arms on the cockpit, he inhaled deeply. Next job would be to find food and water. He needed to rest for a few minutes only. His eyelids became heavy, his nerves slackened.

26 July 1857 Morning

The first sunrays of dawn woke Chetan from a deep slumber. Glancing at the sky, he folded his hands into a namaste position. This was his daily routine when he woke up; today was nothing different. Today he was not sleeping on his cot but on the deck of his newly acquired ship, or whatever he could call it. He was the owner, anyway.

Hunger clenched his stomach. He did not even know if he could really find food. His arms and legs were aching. His legs had no energy to help him sit up. He spent some more time lazily stretching.

Turning sideways to get up, Chetan noticed many other men on the deck, all sleeping. Mysterious tension snapped across his chest. His jaw dropped. No wonder no one could hear his yell last night and the oars were swinging idly. He had heard of the massacres but had never seen them. Out of complete silence, an agonising cry arose. Each unknown soul in the Gomti stilled to listen. He stood up raising both arms to the sky, complaining to goddess Kali by letting out one long, mournful yell to the heavens. Within his heart, he longed for his wail to be loud enough to reach the ear of the goddess of death and doom.

The bodies were all lying in a pool of dried blood. The deaths appeared to be fresh, not more than a day or even less. He found a piece of paper half inside a soldier's trouser pocket. Yanking it out, he realised something was written on it. Unfolding it, he held it in front of his eyes—hands trembling out of hunger-driven weakness, anger, sorrow, and everything. It was not just a piece of paper, but a letter written by the soldier to his young and recently wedded wife.

Chetan started reading.

My dear Kavita,

I am sorry I had to leave you within days of our wedding. You were right, I had been sanctioned one-month holiday for the marriage. You know what? My commander was not happy to approve the month-long holiday. I had to do his personal chores, worked like a slave, and tolerated all the nasty abuse he showered on me. I badly needed this holiday so that I could spend quality time with you and we both can get to know each other. Finally, he sanctioned my leave, with a remark, a bloody brown dog is going for his wedding. Other white officers laughed out loud when he handed me over the sanction letter with this rude comment, as if I can't hear, or my heart would not sink, or I don't even have a soul. The fact is that this is my country, and they are here for making the trade. Yes, they were not supposed to rule us. East India Company is a company for doing business in India. For importing goods from England that are not available here, and exporting goods to England those that are available in our country.

Our kings were fighting among themselves. These firangi people took the benefit of the infight. They made one king fight against another, and in turn, went on grabbing more and more lands for themselves. Many kings didn't even realise the British became the real ruler of their state while they were enjoying their royal lifestyles inside their palaces.

But finally, some of them woke up and decided to fight back. Soldiers like me who were serving the whites thought enough is enough.

This was the time my skills as a soldier would be of any help to our motherland. Before, I was working for money. I was really a pet dog of white English. A dog who goes with its owner to prey. I deserved those abuses hurled at me. I have even chewed the leather made covers of the Enfield bullet without questioning the English bosses. I have committed a grave sin. I promise, once this freedom fight is over, I will come back home for a long, no, the most extended holiday. I will do religious repentance as per the scriptures to wash my sins. Then I will spend a full month with you. Take you, Mama and Papa to temples.

I will tell you something about this freedom struggle. Indian kings and nawabs have defeated the English in most of the cases. Some of our soldiers have committed grave sins. They have taken the British women and children captives and even butchered them. British soldiers have also done the same with many Indians, finished many villages, including women and children. I hate such things. I can promise you neither I nor my battalion has made any such blunder.

I do not know when this fight will be over. Maybe one more month, or even more.

Give my respect to Mama and Papa.

Your Mohan.

Chetan's eyes glimmered with watery tears. The whole world was about to crumble before him. He was not the only victim. Dropping to his knees, he cried with all his might, holding the letter in his hand. He felt Sona's absence in his bones. There was no one to console him, leaving him alone in a big world. He folded the letter neatly and kept it securely.

Glancing around helplessly, he thought about what he should do, then he realised the boat was still floating aimlessly. He took charge of the oar and also found something to satisfy his hunger and keep him alive. Goddess Kali had given him another life, and it should have some purpose. Only he didn't know what that was. Chanting a prayer in the name of the goddess, he rowed the boat, letting the feelings of fear and grief ebb from his system.

Not knowing how long he was rowing and with no one to chat with, Chetan kept talking to goddess Kali and stopped planning. *You decide what my next destination is, I leave it to you.*

Chetan didn't know where to go, but his destiny was being guided by Kali—a symbol of energy. And she knew it, crystal clear. Chetan noticed another river, much broader and more massive than the Gomti flowing across. The Gomti had arrived at its destination. He stopped rowing for a while and saluted the holy River Ganga. Then eyeing the bodies of the soldiers, he said, "My friends, your boat has saved my life. I owe you. I will arrive at Varanasi soon, and I promise I will do the cremation of each of you as per the religious ritual. You have served our motherland, and heaven is awaiting you."

My next destination is Varanasi.

CHAPTER 25

26 July 1857 Morning
Amelia

The war between the British and Indian rebels have brought more idle days to the courtesans all over Sultanpur and Lucknow. Courtesans didn't know the word *holiday*. For them, the *kotha* is both their workplace as well as home; the colleagues are their only family members, and vacation means accompanying the lover to outstations.

I have taken time to adapt to my new life. For most courtesans, the *kotha* is the ultimate destination, even after they retire from dancing. Not for me, though—I am the exception. I am still dreaming of going back to England, far away from the deadly clutch of Colin, and settling into a new life. After facing enough hardships in my life, I have become a stronger person. I am not only the first white courtesan of India, but there will also be many firsts in my life when I start a theatre company in London which will show Indian classical dance.

Meeting with my new patron Harry yesterday has given me new hope. He is handsome, wealthy, white, and moreover, he liked me. I know this cannot be a long-time love affair. Here wealthy men do not marry courtesans but keep them as concubines. Like Sehnaz with Rupen Naik. I am not someone who would like to live as a mistress.

It is my day to have a milk and honey bath, the only time when the almost naked tribal man Himu will massage my naked self. Sometimes I feel like grabbing him and asking him to kiss all over my body, to engulf me in his muscular thighs and make love. I know that is not possible in the roofless bathroom in the backyard of the *kotha*—hardly any privacy. And moreover, I can't communicate with Himu. He doesn't even know Hindi. And I don't want to start a love affair with such a dark-skinned man, almost like a negro.

After taking my milk-honey bath, I go to the terrace to dry my hair under the warm sun. The empty streets of the once-busy market of Sultanpur mock me from one side of the balcony. The other side is my favourite, the river view. Standing close to the riverside terrace railing, I watch the birds flying above the water and boats cruising. A small patch of dark cloud appears from the horizon of the clear, blue sky. I focus on it.

Yesterday the police had called Harry when our new romance was about to take off. Dark thoughts, unbidden, curl like smoke in my mind. Running downstairs to Madhuri's room, I don't find her there. Then I run to the backyard to the milk-honey bathtub, in case she might be there. Finally, I locate her sitting beneath a large sacred fig tree, covering her face with the loosened end of her saree, weeping. Sitting down on the grass near her, I squeeze her shoulder. "How are you, my friend?"

Raising her head from between the knees, she glances at me and holds my hands. "I am sorry, Amelia ma'am."

Nowadays she addresses me just as Amelia, not ma'am. I look into her eyes in case I can get some clue and probably solve her problem before she speaks.

"Sorry for what?"

She again buries her head between her knees, her breathing ragged between the sobs.

All along, I have thought I am the only person having heaps of problems. I don't understand how to help her.

She raises her head again. "Bibi is upset. I shouldn't have introduced you to Hari—sorry, Harry. He is white, and Bibi thinks your life is in danger now."

My jaw tightens; it is not her problem, but mine. "Harry? What is wrong with Harry? He is such a nice person."

"You know why the police called him just after you finished dancing in his mansion? To get information about you. Bibi had done so much to hide you from the British. She was away for a week, and I messed up everything. Who knows if he told them you are here? And you have already told him you are Amelia."

Now it is my turn to bury my head in my folded knees and sob. For some time, I don't even know Madhuri is shaking my shoulder and trying to say something. I am already in another world where everything is rotating and hammering inside my head. I snap out of my stupor to Bibi's voice. She is there standing before me, something dark entering her face. She holds my hand and pulls gently, helping me to stand. Following her to the front side of the *kotha*, Madhuri and I clamber inside a horse cart. We are finally going to Bibi's home. I feel the thickness of tension in the cab, surrounding me and my existence. Bibi stares at me in silence. I hold my gaze down.

Within half an hour, the cab enters Bibi's bungalow. As the large gate opens and then closes, she clambers out, and then Madhuri. I follow both in silent steps like some guilty person being guided inside a court for sentencing.

Bibi asks her maid to go inside, and we all settle in her front room. I eagerly await what will come out of her mouth with my heart in my throat.

"The Residency," she says and then stops, eyeing me in silence.

"I know. I was living there. With Colin. Brigadier Colin. It has been sieged by the mutineers—I mean, rebels. So many women and children are inside as captives. Rebels should let them go. I know they will let them go. Rebels are religious, both Hindus and Muslims, alike. They are only against the British army, not the innocents."

"Do you know of Bibighar?"

"Yes, your home. I knew in Hindi *Ghar* means a house."

"You are too innocent, Amelia." Moving closer to me, Bibi places her loving arm on my shoulder and gazes at me. "I was talking of Bibighar in Kanpur city. It was also under siege by the rebels. The fact is, the rebels have multiple leaders. Each king is a separate commander. Anyone who can command over a hundred Indian soldiers is a leader and making his own decisions."

"What happened in Bibighar?" Madhuri asks.

"More than two hundred women and children were hostages there. They were all butchered by some mad rebel and were thrown inside a well in the compound, the Bibighar complex. Both dead and those who were dying. The deep well was buried with bones and flesh of women and children. All whites. English. When the well was full, the rest were thrown inside a pond."

I blow out a chestful of air and close my eyes. All my friends and neighbours inside The Residency appear before me, begging for life.

"Someone has stolen a map of The Residency and passed it on to Rupen Naik, the chief general of Nawab Wajid Ali. And the British now knows who has done this."

My mouth is now tight. I have no courage to ask.

"I have seen a map with Sehnaz. The woman who helped me out of Lucknow."

"Sehnaz!" Bibi jumps off her seat and stares into my eyes, consternation creasing her brow. "I know her. She is Rupen's mistress. That might be the reason she fled from Lucknow the day she got hold of that fateful piece of paper. Oh my God!"

Madhuri jumps into the discussion. "Bibi, you always supported the rebels against the British. What happened?"

"I support them now, too. But I do not support involving the innocent women and children in the conflict. Not even innocent men, who are not fighting the civil war."

Silence descends inside the room.

I thank God that Sehnaz has deserted me. The long arm of British law must be looking for her. I would have been taken as her accomplice. "Are the police looking for Sehnaz?"

"I don't know. But I know courtesans in the *kotha* where she was a dancer, and Rupen was her only patron. And Amelia, you said now that you were with her. You need to go underground. Immediately."

She glowers at Madhuri. "You shouldn't have taken Amelia to Harry's mansion without my permission. He is white, too. And he might support the English. He had been called yesterday by the police. Can you imagine why? They must have enquired about Amelia."

"I thought his name was Hari. I didn't have any idea he could be an English with an Indian sounding name. Harry and Hari, both sound so similar. I know I am stupid."

"Chetan," I speak up, "he has seen me in the Shakti Ashram."

"Who is that?" Bibi asks.

"He was our security guard in The Residency. I don't know what he is doing here. I have a feeling he is following me... That means, means, I'm going to be caught. I should've changed my name from Amelia to something else when I became a courtesan."

"You need to go underground somehow," Bibi contends. "How, I don't know. You stay here, and Madhuri, you go to the *kotha* and pack her bag. No one there should know what we are doing. The British have become smarter now. They are now paying girls in the *kothas* to buy information."

Immediately Madhuri heads to the *kotha*. Bibi also leaves, but I don't know where she's going.

Underground—the dreaded word spins around me and resonates in the hollowness of my mind. All my dreams of going back to London and starting a new, independent life disappear in the turn of events. I walk to the same room I was staying in when I had met Bibi. Sitting on the bed, I glance outside the window. Bibi's backyard is full of thorny and ugly weeds. Where is that beautiful greenery? The dry leaves on the ground move; something is crawling beneath them. A deadly snake?

The word *underground* oscillates inside my brain. Is it the underground hall where Madhuri had shown me the replica statues of Khajuraho? I weigh two situations: fleeing again to some unknown place, or hiding in that dark hall. But my brain refuses to analyse, and my synapses start to shutter. Each of my limbs becomes heavy, and my heart slows down to a serene beat. I stretch my legs and back, and cuddle into bed.

26 July 1857 Noon

"You are an accomplice to this ghastly massacre," the prosecuting attorney reads out from a piece of paper. "Hundreds of English women and children were brutally murdered by the rebel sepoys. They knew exactly where the secret tunnels open and targeted the area. They used the ammunition hidden in the secret spots inside The Residency because the map you had provided pointed to everything needed for the enemy to siege the fortress that we, the brave and intelligent British, had built to rule over the uneducated brown people of this country."

I impatiently look for my lawyer. I have assured him that I would organise to pay his fees when I go back to London, as I have nothing left with me at the moment.

"Please reply to my questions, Mrs. Amelia Lawrence. What are you waiting for?" The attorney's eyes pierce mine.

"The defence lawyer, Sir." Ice forms in my blood.

"No lawyer will work for you without fees, Mrs. Lawrence. You are a housewife and have no income of your own. Your husband, a loyal and senior army officer, is supporting the East India Company in the Sepoy Mutiny. Unfortunately, you have to argue your own case, Mrs. Lawrence."

The entire court bursts into a loud laugh, and a sense of aloneness haunts me. I sneak a glance around the courtroom. Only men. There is not a single woman other than me. Mr. Colin Lawrence is also sitting in a corner and glowering at me.

"Sir, I will write to my father back in England, and he will send money. I am sure he will not disappoint his only daughter. Please wait for a few months until my letter arrives and he sends money to me."

The prosecuting attorney swings left and focuses his gaze on the judge. "Your Honour, this is a court martial. We do not waste so much time for such cases. Now that the rebels have set back and thousands have been arrested by the army, we will have piles of cases."

The judge clears his throat. "Mrs. Lawrence, it is not possible to give you any extra time. The hearing will continue."

The prosecuting attorney starts again. But before he can read the next sentence, I speak up. "Your Honour, I have not provided any map of The Residency to the rebels. In fact, I didn't even know that such a map existed before I saw it with Sehnaz, a courtesan who helped me escape the cruelty inflicted by my husband..."

The attorney interrupts me mercilessly. "Now you have admitted your crime, Mrs. Lawrence. Sehnaz is the lover of Rupen Naik, the dreaded general of Nawab Wajid Ali, who managed the siege of The Residency and directed the massacre with the help of that piece of paper. That Sehnaz has been nabbed, and she has admitted to having sourced the map with your assistance. The learned judge has kindly awarded the death punishment for her ghastly crime against the Raj and also against mankind. She will be blown from the cannon."

Blown from the cannon? Her body will be scattered into pieces?

"Besides," the attorney continues, "there are many other serious allegations which, though they are severe, might not attract a death penalty."

A wave of consolation rolls off me. I will not get the death punishment. Poor Sehnaz.

"You have stolen money and expensive pieces of jewellery from your husband's home and have fled at a time when he should have been focussing on fighting the rebels. Besides stealing, which is a grave crime in itself, you have also inflicted severe mental injury on your husband, crippling him so much that he was unable to go to the war."

"Your Honour, he has also inflicted injuries to my... my... brea... breasts," I mumble, realising I probably haven't used the appropriate word.

"What did you just say, Mrs. Lawrence? Breasts? What happened to your breasts? Did anyone bite your breasts?"

The male crowd sitting in the court chuckle and giggle at me. I can't say Colin has burnt my breasts. How do I prove that I am not a criminal, but a victim? I cannot remove my clothes in full public view of all males.

The judge comes to my rescue. "Honourable Attorney of the Prosecution, you can't use any vulgar words in the court. A woman deserves all the dignity, even if there are allegations of crime against her."

"I am sorry, Your Honour." The attorney bows his head. "But I have more serious allegations against Mrs. Lawrence, even though they are not grave enough to attain the death penalty."

I inhale deeply. Thank God I will be spared of the gallows, at least. By the time this case goes to a higher court, I might even receive money from my father to hire my own defence attorney.

"Mrs. Lawrence." The prosecuting attorney swings toward me. "There is an accusation—no, solid evidence that you have been in the Shakti Ashram where Hindu nuns live completely naked. And we have a witness who has seen you roaming completely without a shred of cloth in the garden, in full public view. The security guard Chetan has testified this. You, having come from the highly civilised and culturally advanced country of England, have forgotten all the manners of the modern civilisation and lived like a barbarian, forgetting modesty. And there is a serious allegation with evidence from the Catholic missionaries, that you have been doing prostitution. You have joined a *kotha* in Sultanpur."

"You are wrong," I scream, "the courtesans in the *kothas* are not sex workers. They are dancers, and singers, and poets, and even teachers who teach poetry and literature to the young boys. It is wrong propaganda by the British against the courtesans, as they are supporting the rebels. I am a witness to this, Your Honour; the courtesans do not solicit anyone for selling their bodies. I have only danced, and have done nothing else. Don't we have dancers at theatres in London? Are they all doing immoral things, Your Honour?"

The judge clears his throat again. "No need to discuss the allegation against Mrs. Lawrence about the nudity or her becoming a courtesan, Honourable Prosecuting Attorney."

He takes a pause. *Here a gentleman is coming to my rescue again. Saving my respect in a gathering of all men.*

"The court has thousands of war crime cases to solve, and we are short of time," the judge says. "We are here to give our judgment against the war crimes only."

The attorney quietly goes back to his seat. Relief washes softly through me.

"Taking all the pieces of evidence tabled before this bench," the judge continues, "and considering the grave crime committed in the siege of The Residency, I pronounce Mrs. Lawrence guilty of committing the crime of abetting the massacre. And I award the punishment; she will be blown away from a cannon."

A raw chill slices through me. Suddenly I am drained of all my energy. I eye Colin helplessly, who is sitting quietly in a corner of the courtroom. He levels a mocking glare at me. Finally, he has eliminated his second wife without even lifting a finger.

An officer is advancing toward me with handcuffs. Closing my eyes, I shudder; my heart beats in my throat, and sweat dampens me completely. Everything reels around me, and I start wailing.

"Wake up, wake up," the man coming to handcuff me says, but in a soft tone. He holds my wrist. How can a man's touch be so soft and his voice so feminine?

I wake up. Faiza, Bibi's maid, is shaking my wrist. "Ma'am, you are crying in your sleep. Do not ever sleep resting the arms on the chest, you will see only ghosts in your dream."

I blink and look around the room, then back at Faiza. She is smiling. "Ma'am, you must be starving. Please come, I have cooked food for you."

I get off the bed, completely soaked in my own sweat. I am about to enter the dining room when Bibi and Madhuri both enter from the other side; Madhuri is holding my suitcase.

"A group of monks will be sailing to Varanasi this afternoon." Bibi looks exhausted but confident. "And I have arranged your travel with them. Madhuri will dress you as a Hindu married woman, wearing saree, bangles, and a red dot on your forehead. You will stay in a temple lodge for some weeks."

Faiza serves hot food for all three of us. As we start eating, I ask, "Is the death punishment here being blown from a cannon?"

Bibi and Madhuri both stare at me.

26 July 1857 Afternoon

I arrive at the jetty wearing a saree, my head covered by its loose end. Bibi comes to see me off. I am the only woman in a small boat crowded by monks. Sneaking a peek through the slit of my headcover, I notice the vessel is, in fact, overcrowded.

"There is not a single woman among the passengers," I whisper to Bibi.

"That is good, monks normally do not talk to a woman. Anyone who talks to you will know you are white, English. You should remain quiet until the end of your journey. I have written a letter. One of the monks will take you to the temple lodge, and you will stay there."

They both go back, leaving me alone for my next journey. *Underground*. Everything looks dark to me. Hopefully, The Residency has only been under siege, nobody has been massacred. Sehnaz had said she was on her way to Varanasi. I would love to see her again and plead—no, rather send a request to Rupen Naik. Please do not kill the innocents.

Time to go inside the boat. Sitting quietly in a corner, I keep my head covered. Then monks start singing in a chorus. I can understand a few words; it must be some religious song. I wish to go to the helmsman and ask him how long it will take to arrive at Varanasi. I'm sure that without a steamboat, it might take days. Without a single cabin, the whole vessel is an open area, without even a toilet. Reality slams me with a punch. If I have to sit in a corner like this for days without relieving myself, I might as well be dead by the time the boat arrives at the destination. Sitting on the floor keeping the suitcase to my back, I notice a small packet tied to the box and remove it. A sweet aroma wafts out of the pack. I imagine the fluffy paratha Faiza made for me whenever I was in Bibi's home. It was always my favourite.

When the songs reduce to a deadly tranquil, I can hear the Gomti chuckle and whisper, but my vision is blocked by the purdah, hiding my British identity. That is only for a few moments until the boat starts to shake slowly. Grabbing the handle of my suitcase, I sit tight, and a sense of foreboding crosses through me. A gust of wind pierces my thin saree. Shortly after, the boat shakes vigorously, and I jump to the screams and shouts of all the monks. Removing my purdah from my face, I look at the sky; a massive storm is going to break. Two crewmembers are trying to pacify them and direct the vessel to the riverbank.

I try to do a mental calculation of how long it will take to touch the bank. But a giant wave surges toward us, and the vessel tilts and climbs the steep mountain of water. When I try to grab the wooden deck rail, my shoulder slams into it. The monks all collectively scream and shout at the crew, pointing fingers toward me. A crewmember clambers in my direction on his knees and calls something to me, but I can't hear him. I guess everyone is trying to help the only woman in the boat. I can't imagine such people could ever massacre captive women and children, must be a different breed. Wolf hiding among the lambs—no, holy cows. With another giant wave, the crew and some monks are swept into the tons of white foam. I shut my eyes. I know swimming, but in a pool or a calm river. Suddenly, a bolt of consciousness cracks through me like fire as I yank off the saree from my torso. A strong desire for survival sweeps through me, overtaking all panic.

Another giant wave comes. Before I can realize what's happening, I find myself inside the river, whirling and circling along with the massive force of the water. I scramble to get out of the petticoat, but it seems impossible. Darkness envelops me. My arms and legs kick desperately as the white foam swirls around me. I don't know how long I fight like this, but I am still alive. As I get out of the whirlpool and strive to swim, rain lashes my face, blurring my vision. I don't see anyone floating around me, not even the vessel.

After a while, everything is quiet. The storm has stopped, but it is still raining. I notice a ferry coming toward me. Raising my hand, I yell. There's no doubt that my voice is not loud enough to reach the boat. But I notice a man standing near the bow of the ship waving his hands. Two strong men jump in the water and swim over to me. One of them throws a rope. He pulls me toward the ferry and guides me to a rope ladder hanging from the deck. I drag my feet onto the wooden rung. The two men follow me up the ladder. As I clamber up, my gaze goes to the man in the cockpit. My chest clenches tight when I guess that I have been rescued by a British man. This might be an army ferry. Only a few hours ago, I felt the horror of facing the court martial through a dream. And that dream is going to be a reality soon. My plan for going underground in Varanasi is now doomed.

CHAPTER 26

26 July 1857 Afternoon
Amelia

Amelia, you have been caught. Drowning in the Gomti would have been much better. Indulging in self-pity, I lament, but only for a few moments. I am determined to fight with my destiny until my last breath. Who knows if any of the monks travelling in the boat survived? The two Indian men who brought me onto the deck are standing at a distance, heads buried on their chests and gazes focussed on the floor. The white man I had noticed has vanished.

Looking intently at the two men avoiding eye contact with me, I wonder why they are behaving like this. Then my gaze goes to my own torn clothes plastered to my skin, revealing every minute detail for the whole world to notice. I had discarded my saree the moment I was thrown into the water when the boat capsized. With a short blouse which is hardly covering my breasts and the torn *lehenga* which is displaying more of my thighs than it is concealing, I look like a stranger in my own eyes. Water is dripping from my clothes. I'm sure most of these people will be English and male. What do I do when more men gather on the deck and stare at me?

Noticing an empty cabin, I lurch inside and close the door behind me and realise there is no latch. I continue to stand pressing my back against the door as if I could stop Colin getting hold of me at any moment. Colin's angry face, when he was hitting me, appears before me. I close my eyes in trepidation and feel his hot breath all over me. When I open my eyes, everything looks dizzy. *Amelia, you will be all right. You will survive this.*

When no one pushes the door, my dizziness slowly cools down. I am now standing near the only window and watching the blue waves of the Gomti, which only less than an hour ago was trying to swallow everything that came in its contact. Rivers can also be angry sometimes, and when they do, only a lucky few survive. Hopefully, the cool breeze will dry up my scanty wet clothing, and they won't remain glued to my body.

I know only a few moments are left before my doomsday starts. But this is my moment, and I cherish it, inhaling the breeze to my heart's content and wandering my eyes aimlessly. The flock of birds in the sky lightens my mood. I see a beautifully choreographed dance above the blue waves, hundreds of sparkling souls swooping in the air—the essence of life floods into my exhausted limbs. Standing near the window, I watch the birds circling. Within moments they are about to vanish into the horizon, and my eyes follow them. Suddenly I sight a small patch of white cloud. Is it a sign of fortune smiling at me?

I don't understand how being captured and taken to Colin is lucky. Maybe I was lucky an hour ago. My life has been saved despite falling into the water during a deadly storm. Is it the calm before a fatal storm in my life?

Suddenly, I get the feeling of being watched, and the awareness that my clothes are still wet and clinging to my skin haunts me. As my heart lurches into my throat, I try to cover my chest with my palms to conceal my nipples—which are shamelessly exhibiting themselves to the public—and then spin around, panting. I don't realise when my palms move away from my breasts and start rubbing my eyes. Harry—my dream man, Harry—is standing, hip cocked against the doorframe. I gape at him, dumbstruck.

Thrill, nervousness, and relief all flood together inside me. I lurch forward and hug him tightly, kissing his face madly. He smiles, his pleasant perfume filling my nostrils. Coming back to normal, I see I have already torn his shirt and scratched his hairy chest red with my nails. He takes his shirt off to cover me.

"Come with me," Harry whispers and swings around. I follow him, wrapping my arm around his shoulder and hiding my waist behind his back. We walk downstairs and arrive at a corridor. *This is his lavish yacht*, I guess when I swiftly glance around.

We enter a bedroom. His bedroom. Huge and opulent. He shuts the door, and we both are in total privacy. Three lamps are radiating light. I remove his shirt from my body. Beneath, my scanty clothing is still wet and will start stinking if not dried soon. Undressing, I hold the *choli* and *lehenga* in my hand and ask, "Where is the window? I must dry these."

Displaying a sweet smile, he clambers onto the bed, puts his finger in a small hole on the wall, and pushes sideways. The window opens to a scene of fish swimming on the other side. Coming back down, he takes my damp clothing, lays them on a chair, and hugs me tightly. I feel his erection on my thighs. "They can't dry here, and there is no female clothing in my yacht, unfortunately." He plants a kiss on my cheek. "I didn't have enough time. When I came to know that you were leaving, I came back to my island bungalow and noticed the storm slowly coming over the Gomti River. I followed your boat in a hurry. But it was too late. Your boat capsized, and this yacht was nowhere near. I had lost all hopes of getting you back alive."

"I was wearing a saree and had to remove it to swim."

"Thank God you can swim. You are alive now."

"And all the monks died. Probably." My subconscious does not allow me to enjoy the comfort and accept the deaths of monks at the same time.

"You must be starving, let me go and bring something for you to eat."

I realise that I am standing completely naked with no guilt or shame. "I hope you do not count me as uncivilised. I have been trained by Mata Radhe in the Shakti Ashram to feel comfortable with my body even though I did not choose to remain naked here."

Harry smiles and leaves, closing the door behind him. I hear him saying no one should come into this room.

Within hours, the yacht is anchored at the jetty adjacent to Harry's island bungalow. He orders all in the vessel to disembark and go away while I'm still inside the bedroom. After a while, he comes and asks me to come out with him. I yank the bedsheet from the cot to cover my body. Harry smiles at me. "Don't," he says, "there is nobody to watch you, other than me."

Holding a lamp, Harry guides me to his mansion. There are just the two of us. We enter his massive and lavish bedroom on the first floor, facing the river. Hot food on the table radiates aroma. Consciousness about my nude state spirals into my mind, and I pull the sheets tighter to me. "You said there is no one, did the ghost serve hot food for us?"

Harry smiles. "There is only one maid, and she is downstairs and will never come here. I can bring some clothing for you, but they belong to the maids, old and used. I can get you something nice tomorrow morning from the market, not tonight, unfortunately. You may use the sheet as a saree if you wish. Whatever clothing you are in, you look stunningly beautiful to me."

I wrap the bedsheet around my chest. I can't pretend to be like Mata Radhe or her disciples for the next twenty-four hours. I remember her preaching. *People lose interest in a woman's body if they get used to seeing her naked most of the time. That ensures safety to a woman.* Now the opposite is true for me. If I remain without any clothing, Harry might not be attracted to me—but I am already in love.

"Can we sit on the balcony and have some wine?" he asks.

"Sure, I would love to." The opportunity to view my favourite Gomti and its calm, blue waves thrills me. It is beyond my imagination that only a few hours ago, this river was a threat to my life, and I am enjoying its view now.

Harry brings the wine bottle and fills up two glasses. "These are all imported from England. I have a collection."

I admire his taste. He feels like a dream too good to be true. A man who has never seen England and is only partly English, he almost fits all the points I think would make a perfect life partner. The most ideal husband I could have imagined.

I go on sipping wine and continue watching the water without saying anything. For some time, I am totally swallowed in my own thoughts without even realising Harry's presence. When I know, I notice he is sipping from his glass and his eyes are on me, watching me silently.

He pours another glass for me. I have been drinking wine for a long time. It is not unusual to have English wine in a *kotha*. But due to the civil war, it is nearly unavailable in the market.

He goes inside and brings me a towel. "The sheet must be awkward to wear for a long time. I think you can wrap yourself better with this."

I stand to change into the towel—a thin cotton towel, and comfortable. The bedsheet is knotted tightly on my chest, and I struggle to open it. As Harry unties it for me, his fingers touch my breasts, and my eyes shoot up to meet his gaze. He lets out a sexy and lazy smile, and titillation washes over my body. The sheet falls on the floor, but Harry does not waste a second. Instead, he picks up the towel and wraps it around me, making a small knot above my chest.

"Do I have to wear this until you get clothing for me tomorrow?"

"Unless you decide to wear my trousers, but I think that they will be oversized for you. But you can stay anyway with or without clothes on the first floor. The maid will never come here unless I give permission. And no man will dare stare at you."

The alcohol in the wine slowly engulfs me. A gust of wind removes a loose end of the towel and exposes my belly downwards. When my hand goes to rearrange it, I find Harry's hand is already there. My eyes again shoot up to meet his, but I feel his breath on my face. A seductive scent enters my nostrils. Inhaling, I come closer to him, leaning over his chest. My fingers push through the button gaps and crawl over his muscular, hairy chest while the other hand frantically unbuttons his pants. Never in my yearlong married days with Colin had I been inclined to explore his body.

Soon I discover the towel has dropped on the floor and Harry's fingers are slinking over my hair. Slowly his hands glide down to my neck, teasing me. Exhaling a sharp breath, I imagine my first night with the man I adore. As his fingers crawl down, my nipples pucker. My breathing is now shallow, and I force his pants down. Grabbing his neck, I push his lips apart with my tongue and press his pelvic area with my thighs.

Harry pulls his tongue out from my lip lock and starts licking my neck, sluggishly moving to my breasts. His lips creep onto my belly and stay for some time on my navel.

I moan and wonder, *What next?*

He places his palm beneath my buttocks and lifts me. He is probably planning to take me inside his bedroom, but I am dying to have everything under the moon and stars. A light breeze ruffles my hair and covers part of his face. He sneezes, and I moan and laugh at the same time. "Please, Harry, here, no bedroom please," I mutter while licking his earlobes, gently biting.

"I love you, love you, Amelia." His volume is so loud I hear the echo.

"Harry, please, the maid will hear."

"She is asleep. But I don't care what she thinks. She knows that I am bringing you here and must have guessed what we both are doing. Don't worry. This will be a memorable night for both of us."

I don't know where we are going. The sensation is entirely new to me. Colin had never aroused me so much. All he was concerned about was his own pleasure. Even in my wildest imagination, I had never dreamed of so much delight. The moon and stars are all winking at me, and a bunch of white clouds are playing hide and seek. Harry is right. This will be a memorable night for me.

"Harry, I beg you, please do it fast."

Harry lets me lie flat on the wooden bench nearby and moves his finger slowly around my clitoris. I mewl and close my eyes. Parting my legs with one hand, he leans over me, touching his lips on my clitoris. I move my fingers over his impressive length. Suddenly he plunges inside my thighs. My breathing is now rugged, and the echo of my loud moan comes off the Gomti River. His delicious shaft moves up and down, pounding me with his handle. I convulse around his shaft and call out his name loudly with each moan. Moments after he pauses, I stop. He grabs me tightly and pushes his tongue into my mouth.

"Love you, Harry. You are the man of my dreams," I mutter, pulling away my tongue as he continues thrusting.

This is the climax. Orgasm. Much better than I had experienced with Madhuri. I cherish these few moments that I can describe as the best moments life has offered me so far. It feels like my body has become so light that I could probably fly in the sky. I have heard monks in the Himalayas do so much meditation that they become light like feathers. Can sex be like that? Can I reach super consciousness from sex?

"Are you tired, Amy?"

I wonder whom he is addressing. Who is Amy? He is gazing at me intently. *Is this my new pen name?* I wonder. *Amelia in short form is Amy.*

He gets up, and we both go to his bedroom, leaving our clothing on the balcony. Harry gives me a powder from a bottle and asks me to swallow. "What is this?"

"To avoid unwanted pregnancy."

He must be bringing women here and knows what to use in case...
I swallow without further questions.

"This was last used by Rambha." He is watching me intently; he
probably read my mind. "No other woman has come here after her
death."

One thing is sure now—I am replacing Rambha and am going to
be his mistress. I regard him for several long beats. Am I destined for
this? I am not Rambha. I am Amelia. One day I will cross over seven
oceans and start a new and independent life in London. But again, let
me enjoy whatever God is giving me on the way. But for how long?

A good night awaits me on the chest of the man of my dreams. "I
love you, Amy." Harry kisses me again, and within moments he is in
another world, deep in slumber. At least he is using my real name to
make out a short name, not naming me *Menaka* or *Urvashi*—the two
other heavenly dancers he had mentioned when I first met him.

The cockerels call to declare the dawn, and the sun opens up like a
flower through the slits of the curtain. Harry is still sleeping. I glance at
his face, as innocent as a child. I stretch my hand to place it on his chest
but withdraw instantly. Let him enjoy his slumber. Everyone is not an
early riser like I am. This is the time to stare at my dream man to my
heart's content, even though deep in my heart, I know this is temporary. His hairy and muscular chest is rising and falling with the sedative
qualities of a lullaby. I raise my head and shift my gaze slowly to his
bare belly and then to his naked thighs. A morning erection starts
winking at me and arouses me. As I keep staring at the elongated shaft
dazzling in the morning sunrays, hot desire starts pulling in my belly.

Harry changes sides and pulls me toward his chest. "Good morning, Amy." His voice is mesmerising. He takes me inside his thighs, and
his shaft rests on my clitoris.

Will he do it again this morning?

He doesn't, only caresses my hair and neck. My breasts are pressed
on his hairy chest. I am about to start roaming the heavens again, but

some dark thoughts creep into my mind. Even though Harry is in love with me, I might as well be like a second-rate citizen. Just a mistress.

"Your wife will not mind you spending so much time outside your home?" The words slip off my tongue before I can weigh them.

His fingers still crawling on my scalp, he lets out a shy laugh. "She is dead," he says.

Murder or suicide? These two words hover around my mind and punch my conscious. As if there is no other way for a married woman to die. Colin's first wife had either been murdered or forced to hang herself. I inhale deeply when Harry brings his fingers to my lips. My sharp breathing must have hit his chest.

"She died five years ago, complicacy during childbirth. There was no Rambha in my life then. I had built this island mansion for her. But she couldn't enjoy this."

Grabbing him tightly against my breasts, I keep my head on his chest. Nothing comes to mind on what I should say. Should I condole with him or remain silent?

"The maid will come upstairs to serve breakfast," he says.

After taking a bath, I wrap another towel around me. Harry, after having breakfast, goes to the market. He has not forgotten that I need clothes. I adore Mata Radhe. She and her disciples stay nude only when the weather is average, neither too hot nor too cold. I remember Mata Radhe's preaching—*Clothing had been invented to protect humans from the vagaries of the weather, not to hide your body from others.*

When I come to the balcony, reality starts punching my guts. *What next?* I wonder. Do I contact Bibi Khanum and ask her to organise another trip for me to Varanasi? She might think I'm still on my way and will be arriving there sometime today. Does she know the boat has capsized and so many people have been swallowed by the River Gomti? Whatever happens, my future here is in the dark. I am being hunted by my own countrymen on the allegation of helping the rebels, a serious offence which could court-martial me.

Harry returns before noon and comes straight upstairs with lots of western dresses for me, including inner wears. "Can you try them on?" He instantly vanishes again to the ground floor.

Trying one of them on in front of the mirror, I find the dress is a perfect fit for me. This man has beautiful taste. Another thought curls inside my mind. I should have asked him to bring some Indian clothing for me, preferably sarees. A saree could cover my face from the vigilant eyes of the informers. A white woman and in western clothes could be distinguished easily in a sea of people. I imagine the rush of devotees in Varanasi. Bibi had told me that it is a perfect place to remain hidden. So many female devotees flock to the holy city, and many of them keep their faces covered.

"Beautiful."

I swing back, and Harry is standing there, watching me with a charming smile, one hand in his pocket. My heart thumps inside my ribs. I should ask him to help me travel to Varanasi. But Harry comes close to me, and his hand comes out of his pocket—a ring box in his hand. Before I can say anything, he kneels and asks, "My dear Amy, will you please marry me?"

All of a sudden, I become a statue. Am I in a deep slumber and dreaming? Dreams are never real. Can't be right. Silence swells in the room. Harry is still in the kneeling position. "My knees are hurting, Amy," he says. His smile is now blended with a little anxiety.

"But I am already married. I have a husband," I mutter.

"I know. Your so-called husband is a monster. He is looking to finish you with any false allegation he can get against you. He doesn't deserve you. And don't worry, Amy, I will take care of everything. Leave that all to me."

I have little doubt about the capability of this strong man. I slowly nod, as if he is keenly watching the movement of my head. Taking out the diamond ring from the case, he slips it onto my finger. I had thrown away my wedding ring the day I had left Colin's home. I hug him tightly and plant kisses on his lips. Tears roll down my cheeks and drip inside his mouth.

"You will not go out from this place. No one will come looking here, and only a few trusted servants work here. I have to go to the city. A consignment is coming from Calcutta. I import goods from England."

I agree with a smile, like a devoted wife.

I can't wait to write this in my diary, but then I recollect I have left it in Bibi's house. Thank God, all my writings would've been lost in the Gomti River. I can still get them and let Bibi know I'm safe in Harry's bungalow. I would love Bibi and Madhuri to witness my wedding with Harry.

Walking over to the edge of the river in the afternoon, I sit down on the bank and watch boats playing in the water. I am thrilled today. Since the days I was in school, I have dreamt of a prince in my life. Every girl has this dream. Today I have achieved this. I remember Mata Radhe's statement. *You might plan anything, but finally, it is God whose planning matters.* Moments ago, I was planning to go to Calcutta and board a ship to London. Everything has changed now. Wind gusts, and a massive wave slaps on the riverbank. Suddenly a conflicting emotion crashes into me. *How do I get a divorce?*

Antonia's letter could've helped me. Why didn't I get it from Sona?

CHAPTER 27

1 August 1857 Night
Brigadier Colin Lawrence

It was past midnight. Colin had no time to sleep. He was preparing to make a voyage to Calcutta from Lucknow, through the Gomti and the Ganga. Lots of preparation was required to carry a dangerous and angry caged lion.

Rupen Naik. Defeated and imprisoned by the British.

That was a prolonged fight. Rupen was the man who sieged The Residency and kept hundreds of British families in real terror for the last seven days, shooting shivers into the spines of every English man and woman in northern India. During the siege, the news of the Bibighar massacre took rounds, boiling the blood of many, and causing anticipation of another massacre in Lucknow. If Bibighar saw the butchering of hundreds of women and children, The Residency had the threat of thousands—not only women and children, but also capable English soldiers had been made captives. Major General Henry Havelock arrived at Lucknow after recapturing Kanpur and was planning to storm The Residency. This could have witnessed unprecedented bloodshed from both the sides, but the victory was not yet guaranteed to the East India Company.

Major General Sir James Outram soon superseded Havelock, who changed the war game completely. He bought time with the rebels, prolonging discussions in the name of negotiation. Those whose families were under siege lost patience. Havelock was one of them; hence his plan to storm the blockade. People warned Sir Outram that these delaying tactics could cost thousands of lives. An annoyed Rupen could order his soldiers for butchering the captives.

Rupen was Colin's dearest friend before the war, his companion in all those glamourous evenings. Therefore, Colin was able to provide Sir Outram with valuable insight on Rupen. His strengths and weaknesses. Rupen was a devotee of Lord Shiva and Goddess Kali. Devotees of Kali always respected women and would never take their lives.

The decision not to harm women—was it a strength or a weakness?

Colin had heard from Rupen many times when their friendship was at its highest peak about his pride in protecting the weaker sex, as he often described it. Men who were not mentally stable or vulnerable inside often attacked women. Colin felt a meaningful smile on his own lips. *This was your weakness, my dear friend. Your decision not to attack the females inside The Residency cost you Nawab's kingdom. The Bibighar massacre is nothing. A massacre at The Residency with the lives of thousands of British women and children could have sent shivers to the queen's bones in London. The East India Company could have thought of packing its bags and setting for a permanent return journey, back to England. Your Nawab could have become the emperor of the entire country, replacing the Emperor Bahadur Shah Zafer in Delhi.*

When all the efforts from the British side failed, the siege continued throughout the week. Major General Outram planned attack on multiple levels. Colonel John Inglis, who was inside The Residency, had few soldiers and ammunition. He was advised to be ready for instruction for a surprise pushback from inside. Another team prepared to come in the ferries in the Gomti and hit from the side of the river.

Was this double attack enough to defeat Rupen?

Outram planned a third, and in his words, *an ischemic attack*, which would stop Rupen's heart.

On Colin's suggestion, the British army bribed the Indian sepoys who guarded Rupen's family. His wife and two daughters were somehow kidnapped and made captives. The negotiation table became hot and tempting for Sir Outram. He could play the captive cards much better with Rupen. But when Rupen didn't care about the detainment of his family, Outram lost his patience. It was almost the last straw on the British side.

Did Colin's idea prove ineffective?

This night would be one that Colin would remember forever. A night that could decide whether the British continued to rule over India or pack their baggage and go home. He was always on the side of Major General Outram. Colin sent a man to Rupen with a personal letter.

Your family is dear to me, my friend. You may disregard their safety as a true patriot, but they will be the ones who love you the most. I am standing in between a rock and a hard place. But I have negotiated with the Major General on your behalf. Believe me, this goes totally to your benefit. Just release a hundred women and children, and I will personally come to you with a gift, i.e. your wife and two daughters. The three jewels of your family. This is a personal promise. This way, you are getting back your family, and after this, thousands are still captive inside The Residency. You are the winner in this. And I am with you. I hope the war soon is over, and each side goes back to the conditions they were in before the rebellion. You rule the kingdom as the Chief General of Nawab's army. We can again have colourful evenings together. Your close friend, Colin Lawrence.

He folded and sealed the envelope. "My dear friend. I do not know how you could charm women. You have provided lots of pleasure to me, but after Amelia met you, I lost her. Still, I am helping you. Giving you the benefit of doubt."

Colin waited with bated breath for the reply of Rupen. More than the life of Rupen's family, his own image in the eyes of the Major General and career in the army was important. If his friendship with Rupen had brought unrest in his family life, which he wasn't sure, then let that friendship help him in his career path. A senior position meant more money and the opportunity for another marriage.

Rupen assured to release only fifty women. Outram agreed.

One thing Colin didn't understand. How would the Major General lodge the ischemic attack?

As per the agreement, Colin went to meet Rupen unarmed in a horse cart. Another cart followed with Rupen's wife and daughters. The Major General was personally present just before Colin left to meet Rupen. Colin wanted to meet Rupen's wife and say hello, but Outram advised otherwise.

Rupen had assured Colin's safety. Could Colin trust such a friend who he believed had ruined his marriage?

Rupen had already released fifty captives and was awaiting his family. Colin clambered out of his cab and hugged Rupen. He was about to go to the other cab, but Rupen said, "Friend, please be seated here. I will go and welcome my family myself."

Colin was immediately served with coconut water, the traditional way to receive a valuable guest. He was under lots of tension. Finally, he could achieve something to show his contribution to the war.

Rupen was coming back from the cab, holding a large plate. Colin instantly sprang up from the chair. The coconut water glass fell from his hand. His heart pounded in horror against his ribs. *Is this what the Major General called the ischemic attack?*

Three chopped heads were sitting on the plate in Rupen's hand. His wife and two daughters.

General Outram has sacrificed my head for a decisive win against the rebels. Do I deserve this reward for providing him with information about Rupen's family and how to approach his bodyguards?

Colin had started counting his last breaths when Rupen approached. "General Outram has betrayed me, I swear." Colin had folded his hands. "I was told your family is safe inside the second cab. Please believe me."

Rupen's gaze was fixed on a sweating and shivering Colin.

"I was planning to treat you as my guest for bringing my family back to me. We Indians treat the guests like a God. I believe that you haven't killed my wife and daughters. But I can't extend that respect anymore. Not with chopped heads of my dearest souls sitting before me. You may go back. I will instruct my soldiers not to harm you. And tell your coward General that I am strong enough to resist the temptation of taking revenge on the captive women and children."

It was like his second birth. Colin returned from the cave of the maimed lion in one single piece. The time was right when the Chief General of the enemy was mourning. Major General Outram had already mounted the attack.

Ischemic attack.

The Residency was freed within hours, and Rupen was captured, alive. Dreams of an independent Awadh kingdom by the Nawab and his trusted army went to the ashtray. But Colin could not recover quickly. He had no guts to confront General Outram. Surprisingly, the General gave him another assignment—carry the caged lion, and move him to Calcutta.

**2 August 1857 Morning,
A Military Ferry in the Gomti River**

"Call me Sir Colin Lawrence, not just Mr. Lawrence, Mr. Naik."

Rupen Naik, hands tied behind his back and legs tied to the wooden railing of the cabin, straightened his back and stared into his eyes. "Where are you taking me?"

"Hell." Colin's eyes danced with mirth. "You are Nawab's…" he paused and laughed again, "the great Nawab Wajid Ali Shah's Chief of the Army! You should know each nook and corner of his territory! Don't you understand we are on a ferry in the Gomti? Oh, sorry, sorry. I am so sorry, Mr. Naik. This was Nawab's territory only until yesterday. Until his Chief of Army became a prisoner of war in our hands. In the hands of the mighty British army. The mightiest in the world."

"Do not fool me, Mr. Lawrence…"

"Hm hmm, no more Mr. Lawrence, Sir Lawrence. I, no I mean, we, the British, are the ruler of your land. You black—sorry, my slip of the tongue—you uncivilised brown people are henceforth our slaves."

"Your army is not the British army, Mr. Lawrence. It is a militia. The East India Company has practically become a warlord. Mind it, Mr. Lawrence, we are not fighting against the queen of England. Do you understand why Nawab Wajid Ali refused to talk to your Governor? Because he is a sovereign king and can speak with only another sovereign. Your governor is not a monarch. You mind your language, Mr. Lawrence, you are talking to a Chief of Army, and you are not so senior."

Colin didn't reply. A defeated tiger must snarl but is still harmless as long as it is in captivity. His gaze scanned Rupen sitting on the floor before him. His eyes were closed as if he had shifted to a different level beyond his reach. Wind from the Gomti buffeted his long, dark, curly hair across his face and neck. The man was powerful with broad shoulders, arms, and chest muscles ripping through the torn shirt. Envy burnt through his nerves. No doubt Amelia was staring at this handsome man on the very day Nawab Wajid Ali threw a reception in her honour, forgetting all modesty and respect to her newly wedded husband.

That was supposed to be his first night with Amelia, the night he had planned for a long time. He would undo all the wrongdoings he had inflicted on Antonia, his first love. He had planned to see the reflection of a modified and loving Colin in the eyes of his new bride. To impress her and get true love from her. This man Rupen spoiled all his dreams. He would have never hit Amelia on their first night and ruined her very first impression. After that, she could never love him from her heart, forcing him to lose patience and hit her again and again. The foundation of his new love started in a fit of jealousy toward Rupen. He should have never come to greet Amelia on the pretext of welcoming her to the kingdom of Awadh. He should have never sent gifts to his house, to Amelia.

Amelia's decision to flee created a never-ending dark void that consumed everything, leaving him empty. His hollow soul crept in the shadows of the lost hope of a lingering love he had dreamt of having with her. Trying to find her and start afresh. A new and meaningful life. He could not, even in his wildest dreams, think of Amelia warming another man's chest. Hopefully, he would find her again with her purity intact, unpolluted. He inhaled deeply. The thought of another man with Amelia inflicted multiple stabs in his heart. Fleeing the home could be forgiven. But making love with another man!

"Breakfast, Sir." The sepoy was standing at the cabin door holding two plates of Indian breakfast. The aroma from the hot *puris* intrigued Colin's palate. He had boarded the ferry at Lucknow early this morning with the responsibility of escorting the captured Chief General of the Awadh kingdom through the river route until Calcutta. No ordinary army officer could have been given the responsibility of guarding a star prisoner like Rupen in a high-security military ferry.

Colin glanced at the sepoy holding the plates, envy against Rupen still raw inside him. This handcuffed man sitting in front of him had starved him from his love. Now was the time to give him a taste of real starvation. The sepoy's gaze was fixed on Rupen's calm face and closed eyes. He was not asleep, must be hearing everything, feeling the aroma in his taste buds. Calculation played in his mind. Despite the Sepoy Mutiny, the British side was still depending upon the Indian sepoys. Many of them were still loyal to the East India Company. The sepoy standing with the breakfast plates must have regard for the army-head of the kingdom. He could not show himself in poor demeanour.

"Keep them on the stool, both the plates." Colin took out the keys from his pocket and removed the handcuffs so that Rupen could eat.

"Breakfast has been served, my friend," Colin said softly. So many times he had addressed this man as 'my friend' before things took an ugly turn when he started casting his eyes on Amelia, and then this bloody mutiny. "This is an Indian style breakfast. We have chosen to keep his highness Nawab Wajid Ali's General happy. Please join me in eating."

The sepoy left.

Rupen was hungry since last night.

Colin's gaze went to Rupen. Sitting cross-legged on the floor, Rupen was chewing pieces of yummy *puris*, focussing on the food plate.

So many times he had visited Rupen's home along with Antonia, he had lost count. Rupen and his wife welcomed them every time with open arms and treated them like valuable guests. That was after he used Antonia and got an untimely promotion due to the extra sympathy his boss showered on him. As a new high-ranking officer in the British army, he got the opportunity to meet the Chief General of Awadh, and a new friendship bloomed. Rupen's wife also became Antonia's close friend—going to the market together and having women-only parties when both husbands were busy with their jobs.

Rupen was very protective of his wife, even though he had a courtesan concubine and he was also bringing sexy call girls to his men-only colourful evenings. But Colin believed Rupen's wife might have influenced Antonia against sleeping with the boss. After Antonia's death, Rupen had never invited him to his home again. Rather, they always met somewhere outside.

The *puris* was yummy. Colin took a break from his wild thoughts and enjoyed his breakfast. "Do you need more, my friend?" he asked, this time without a sneer.

Rupen raised his eyes and met Colin's gaze. "This was enough for me. Thank you." He seemed to be enjoying the food, trying to hide his sorrow.

Only yesterday he had been served with the chopped heads... Colin was unable to think any further.

A shock wave passed through him.

"Are you all right?" Rupen asked.

Colin came back to the present, sweat beading on his skin and heart thumping against the ribs. Rupen was a real man who could sit with a quiet mind even after so much disaster in his life. This was the story of just yesterday, still raw. Rupen was the real winner, even in his defeat.

Colin met Rupen's gaze. "You must be worried for your family. Whatever happened was not good. Outram was disturbed by the Bibighar massacre, but this was not the way to take revenge."

"He is weak and a coward. Rebels didn't massacre. Rather, it was done by a heartless person to demoralise the war of freedom. And I am least worried about my wife and two daughters who have been martyred in the war. Their souls have already arrived in heaven. That is the place for patriots. I am happy my wife and brave girls haven't taken the wound on their back, and I am sure they must have looked into the assailant's eyes. I am proud of them."

Colin got up and removed the chain from his legs. "You can now sit or sleep comfortably." He was sure Rupen didn't know how to swim and wouldn't jump into the river.

Colin came back to his own cabin and tried to get a nap. Last night he had not slept—nor any other army officer in Lucknow, because of the *Operation Ganga Head.* Colin knew the name of the undercover operation. He was even partly instrumental to some extent in organising the kidnapping of Rupen's wife and two beautiful minor daughters. *Everything is fair in love and war.* It was both war and a matter of love for him. But killing them was not his decision, nor he was even aware of that. The operation could have been successful even without such a horrendous act. This was no way to take revenge against the

Bibighar Massacre. Major General Outram should have understood the dynamics of Indian politics. The country was ruled by hundreds of kings and nawabs. The Sepoy Mutiny had no single leader, even though rebels had announced Delhi's Bahadur Shah Zafer as the de facto Emperor of the whole of India. Rani Laxmi Bai was leading the rebels in her kingdom Jhansi. On the other hand, Nana Saheb and Tatya Tope were basically responsible for the Bibighar Massacre. Even British forces had done similar crimes in Delhi. Colin closed the window to block the sunrays and pulled the sheet above him. The ferry would take more than a week to arrive at Calcutta, and he had plenty of time to ponder about Rupen and Amelia. Colin needed some time to rest and soak in the calm peace of nature. The river breeze whispered like a lover, planting sweet kisses on his cheeks.

Barely a minute of sleep came to him before some roadblock stood in the way—an awareness that something was close but hidden, yet he could not fathom what it could be. The Gomti was quiet like an obedient and caring wife, a wife he had always imagined but was like a mirage. He remembered how Indians treat rivers in the feminine gender, and sometimes even as a goddess. The Gomti would join the River Ganga. It is, in fact, Ganga's tributary. He changed sides and attempted to sleep again. Something was missing. Varanasi would be on his way after the ferry entered the River Ganga, which the Hindus worship also as a goddess. Ganga is a female. A woman, a special woman. Yes. Ganga was the name of Rupen's wife.

God! How was he such a fool?

He could not decipher the code *Operation Ganga Head*. It was planned to chop off the woman's head and serve to her husband on a silver plate. Disgusting. And what about the teenage daughters? Their lives should have been spared. The horrible images of headless bodies floated before him. He couldn't close his eyes. Colin jerked up from his bed and jumped onto the floor. Yanking the door open, he ran out.

The Indian sepoy who had served him breakfast was the first individual he met, as if he were standing and waiting for instructions. "Sepoy, what is your name?"

The sepoy was just opening his mouth to reply, when impatience shot through him. "Whatever be the name, don't mind. Go and unlock General Rupen Naik's cabin. Mr. Rupen Naik. Understood? Take the keys." Colin again retreated to his cabin. Hopefully, he would feel a bit better. He was sure Rupen could not flee such elaborate security arrangements. Let him get some fresh air off the Gomti. And he couldn't jump into the water. He knew Rupen couldn't swim.

Enjoy your last freedom, my friend. You will remember me inside the four dreaded walls for decades after this.

A knock sounded on the cabin door. The sepoy must have returned from executing Colin's instructions. After getting some rest, he would then meet with Rupen, his ex-friend Rupen Naik, on the decks of the ferry. Time to relax before arriving at Calcutta—the poor fellow's gateway to his next destination, which could chill anyone to his bones.

The sepoy pushed the door ajar. "Sir, you will lose your sleep because of the key."

"What nonsense? How dare you..."

Shoving the door ajar, the sepoy stood near the cot, a confident smile beaming from his lips and gaze focussed on Colin. A sudden stab of panic whispered a foreboding chill into his chest. "What about the key?" Colin said slowly, holding his gaze. This sepoy might have changed loyalty from the British to the rebels!

"Mr. Lawrence, sorry to disobey your commands, please forgive me."

Colin jerked and sat up. No Indian soldier would address him by his name. "You speak English like a perfect Englishman? What is your name?"

The sepoy smiled. "What is in a name, Mr. Lawrence? You may call me any name. I will take this opportunity to say a few things to you. To educate you."

Colin stared at him; his head was empty.

"You have lots of sympathy for your friend—sorry, ex-friend Rupen Naik."

"How did you know?"

"I was eavesdropping in the morning, after serving you breakfast."

"Eavesdropping?"

"Sorry, bad manners. But what to do? I thought I would show you the right path. I have some information which you will love to have."

Silence hung between them for a few minutes. Colin's heart was thumping in some unknown fear. He was missing something. How could a junior sepoy talk to him, meeting his gaze?

"You are sad Rupen's wife was killed in Operation Ganga Head. Do you know he has a lover, who is a courtesan in Lucknow?"

"What is great in that? Every nobleman has one or more concubines! That is the norm of the well-to-do individuals."

"You do not know after that. Please focus on what I am going to reveal. Sehnaz is one of the most beautiful courtesans in Lucknow, and intelligent, too. A great poet and expert in managing the information network of the Awadh army. Rupen was not a fool to visit her regularly. She was getting a handsome salary from the royal exchequer. And the other important news if you do not know, your wife Amelia was also a secret lover of Rupen. She was meeting him secretly on the pretext of shopping when you were busy with your loyal service to the East India Company. She was the woman who had sourced the map of The Residency and handed it over to Sehnaz."

Colin's breath hitched. *So far, I had a doubt on you regarding Amelia, my friend. But you are a poisonous snake, Rupen!*

"Now she is hiding somewhere in Varanasi, and your dearest wife Amelia is warming Indian nobles' beds in God knows where. She is also now a courtesan. Rupen Naik was a playboy, and he played the game very well. Once freed, he can create havoc."

A disgruntled Colin sat up straight, anger stirring in his blood. *Amelia with Rupen in the same bed?* He recollected the reception evening hosted by the Nawab. Amelia's gaze hovering around this Rupen. Why would he be sad with the demise of his wife when he had so many women? White included?

"How do you know all this?"

"I work closely with Major General Sir James Outram. And I have been trained in London in military intelligence. My name is Dhiraj Rao, disowned by my patriot father, who has decided to entrust his throne to my stepbrother."

A mild breeze gushed through the window and tingled Colin's skin, anxiety ebbing out. "So, you are a prince. Which state?"

"Doesn't matter. Take care, Mr. Colin. Get some rest. See you again on this ferry." Dhiraj got up to leave.

Colin jumped out of bed. "Many thanks, Your Highness." He bowed slightly.

"I am travelling in the guise of an ordinary sepoy, please call me by my name," Dhiraj said.

"Right, Your Highness."

3 August 1857 Afternoon

"I am not responsible for those massacres. That was done by a Muslim woman, a mistress of Nana Saheb. She was Begum Hussaini Khanum who ordered sepoys to butcher all women and children. I condemn the act, but that was beyond my jurisdiction. I had sieged The Residency, and you know very well, Mr. Lawrence, no woman or child has been harmed."

Rupen stared straight into his eyes.

"You have a mistress, Sehnaz. Is that correct?"

"Yes, you are right. But you already know this." A smile unfurled on Rupen's lips.

"Where is she now?"

"No idea. I don't have any contact with Sehnaz because of the war. Definitely not in Lucknow, but I have no idea her whereabouts. I don't know if she is dead or alive."

Colin got up from the chair and looked around to see if anyone was eavesdropping. Prince Dhiraj was standing, but at a distance. Coming back inside, he said, lowering his voice, "Have you ever slept with a white woman?"

"What are you talking about? Which white woman?" Rupen narrowed his eyes.

"I mean, Amelia, my wife. She has fled."

"I had met her in a jewellery store once in Lucknow, in the good old days, when you were my close friend. I never betray my friends. After that, we have never met."

"Huh." Colin sat silently. He didn't know whom to believe. Dhiraj Rao or his ex-friend. Anyway, they are all in the past now.

A long silence swelled in the cabin.

"Where is Nawab Wajid Ali?" Rupen asked.

"He has surrendered to the East India Company and now is in Calcutta. He is about to sign an agreement to cede all his rights of Awadh kingdom to the Company. He will receive a nice pension and a large luxury bungalow on a ten-acre land. His days in Lucknow are finished. He can spend his time writing poetry and organising dance ceremonies, his hobby."

Rupen's forehead crinkled. "And me? What about me?"

Colin flashed a sardonic smile; he was awaiting this moment.

"That is not good news, my friend. Unfortunately, not my decision. It is Sir James Outram, Major General."

Rupen's muscles swelled through his torn shirt, his eyebrows crumpled in frustration. "Please, Mr. Lawrence. Whatever it is, I need to know."

"Severe punishment. *Kala Pani*. Black Waters. Andaman."

Silence thickened between them again. Colin avoided Rupen's gaze.

Colin started again after few minutes. "That is an island in the Bay of Bengal. The British are building a jail there to house all the rebels, a severe punishment for challenging the mightiest military of the world. You, in all probability, will spend the rest of your life there in prison."

Rupen gave a long and measuring look. "I would rather prefer death..."

"That is again, not my decision. As soon as we arrive at Calcutta, you will board a ship. I will not accompany you any further. However, I can do you one favour."

Rupen regarded him for a few minutes.

"I have brought a pen and paper for you to write a farewell letter to Sehnaz. I assure you I will never open the letter. Just write on it where I will find Sehnaz, and I will deliver it to her myself."

"You will not punish her for the map?"

"No, my friend. No one will know I have met her, a complete secret. You have lost your wife. I will make sure that your lover is not harmed—a gentleman's words. You have to trust me."

Because where I find Sehnaz, I will find Amelia.

CHAPTER 28

**10 August 1857 Morning,
Varanasi-Outside Kaal Bhairav Temple
Brigadier Colin Lawrence**

"Who can stop a British officer from entering into the temple? We are going to be the real de facto ruler of this country."

"You are right, Mr. Lawrence." Dhiraj smiled at him. "Please remain in the carriage until I come back." With the commanding movements of a prince, he clambered out of the horse cart, leaving Colin alone near Varanasi's Kaal Bhairaav temple on one side and the River Ganga on the other.

Colin let out a laugh, a closed horse carriage was an excellent place for a bit of soliloquy. Stretching his legs to the front seat, Colin tilted his head for a nap while Dhiraj went inside the temple. The last few days had been frenetic. The East India Company might have been planning a celebration—which looked indubitable now after occupying Lucknow and Delhi both—but Colin's war was still incomplete, or partially incomplete. Getting rid of Chetan had put an end to Sona's death worry. Hopefully, the day was not far when he would get another love who would listen to his mind.

With a mild breeze from the River Ganga ruffling his hair, a faint, distant memory haunted Colin. The only woman who had ever tingled his hair was his mother. Neither of his two wives ever loved him. He was no longer interested in getting Amelia back. A woman who could warm the bed of many people was not capable of either making or getting love from him.

Dhiraj, Prince Dhiraj, must be right. He knew what Colin hadn't even thought of in his wildest dreams. He also knew Colin's first wife was dead—had committed suicide. That was what the world knew. In Dhiraj's analysis, though, it was a murder. Colin wondered how far this man might have gone. He vividly remembered the statement of police after the post-mortem, their suspicion that it could very well be homicide.

"Police files are closed, but they can be reopened when new shreds of evidence are found," Dhiraj had told him on their way from Calcutta to Varanasi. "The fingers have been pointed at you, Mr. Lawrence, possibly by your second wife, Amelia. And she could have gathered shreds of evidence with help from Sona."

The last sentence replayed in his mind again and again—*Amelia must've gathered evidence with the help of Sona.* Chetan mentioned Antonia's letter. Did Sona give that to Amelia as a parting gift—a deadly weapon against Colin?

In fact, Brigadier Thomas had woven such a spider net around Colin before his own death. The more he was trying to free himself, the more he was being trapped. Amelia was not that clever to source the map of The Residency and provide it for Sehnaz. But if Sehnaz were to be taken for investigation and she were to give a statement in favour of Amelia, that could trap Colin further. Amelia could provide evidence against him as the alleged murderer of Antonia.

When Dhiraj came back, Colin at first could not recognise him. Wearing a plain silk cloth around his waist and with a bare chest, he was looking like a Brahmin priest. His broad, muscular chest and strong arms all covered with gold necklaces and armbands displayed his royal appearance.

"Let's go to the temple," Dhiraj said, standing near the cab door.

Colin clambered out of the cart, and they both arrived at the gate of the temple. "It is good you are in civilian clothing, Mr. Lawrence. You may now go inside. I will visit the Kashi Viswanath temple and pray to Lord Shiva. I will leave you here alone."

"Right. Hope with God's blessings you will get back the throne you so well deserve."

Prince Dhiraj Rao retreated with a smile on his lips. This was a rare scene for Colin, as Dhiraj always had a serious face.

To Colin's dismay, no one paid him any attention or saluted him as he entered the temple. *Ah, but I am dressed as a civilian*, he remembered. A few priests greeted him, and Colin smiled politely with nervous butterflies in his stomach. Even though he had never seen Sehnaz, he knew how courtesans dressed. It wouldn't be that difficult to find her among so many people.

Monday being an auspicious day for the Hindus, hundreds of men and women gathered in the temple. Standing amongst the devotees, his eyes scanned the crowd, but he couldn't find the woman.

A realization suddenly snared at him. *I am such a stupid. How can a woman dress vulgarly in a place of worship? She must be wearing what all other women are wearing.*

Finally, he asked a priest if he knew any Sehnaz. The priest stood silently and regarded him.

"Sehnaz." The priest scratched his head.

A glimmer of hope flashed before him. Sehnaz must be here. Rupen had said she was staying inside the temple, in rooms for the outstation devotees. His attention was diverted by the coachman of his horse carriage, who after finishing rituals, was exiting with a plate full of flowers. He saw Colin but immediately glanced away as if he had never seen him. Surprise pinched Colin, but only for a moment. The stupid fellow didn't know how to show respect to the officers of the British army. His gaze went to the priest standing before him.

"Sehnaz, means a Muslim name?" the priest asked.

"Yes, you are right. So what? I was told she lived inside the temple."

The priest grinned. "Yes Sir, but how can a Muslim be a devotee of a Hindu God?" He went away and attended other devotees.

Colin had to refrain from slapping his palm over his forehead.

By noontime, the devotees had slowly thinned out. Colin found no way to trace a woman in a city like Varanasi where thousands of devotees from across the country flocked in the hope of salvation. How could Colin attain his own *salvation* unless he found this woman?

Sehnaz might have changed her name and gotten a Hindu woman's getup. Or she might have changed her location completely, and it would have been impossible for Rupen to know that detail. He could even go back without delivering the letter. He didn't owe a reply to Rupen. But his goal was different. Amelia, his gateway to break free from the spider net. Getting rid of that ungrateful wife could free him from Antonia's ghost.

Could Colin implicate Amelia in the map stealing allegation?

An idea suddenly appeared in his intelligent brain. Standing on a location which was almost equal distance between the temple deity and the main gate, he pretended to talk to someone loudly. "I am here to deliver a letter to Sehnaz from Rupen..." and watched from the corner of his eyes. No one approached him. He repeated it a few times, but without success.

Finally, Colin decided to go back and ask Dhiraj for help. He was about to leave the temple when he noticed a woman following him. Or it appeared so. The moment he was about to cross the gate, he slowed down so that the woman could surpass him.

"I know Sehnaz." A whispering voice tickled his sense.

Colin stopped; electricity crackled between them. Did his trick work? Colin eyed her. She wiped the perspiration off her brow.

"Please meet me outside," the woman muttered again and went ahead. She stood alone near a food shop full of customers. "Where is the letter? I will deliver it," she said, meeting his gaze, something unknown burning in her eyes.

"I am sorry, lady." Colin held the sealed envelope with Rupen's handwritten address displaying like a trophy. "Rupen is my close friend, and I have committed to deliver the letter to Sehnaz only and get some message from her. Rupen and I were meeting regularly in the courts of Nawab Wajid Ali."

Something inside him said this woman might be the one he was looking for. He decided to play diplomacy. "Have I ever seen you in Nawab's court, lady?"

This was enough for the fish to jump out of the water.

"Sir, I am Sehnaz. I had to take a Hindu name; otherwise, I couldn't have stayed in a Hindu temple." She was bug-eyed.

The letter is the key to getting more out of this woman. "How do I know? I have information that my wife Amelia was with Sehnaz and both were sailing together in the Gomti and Ganga. She was the one who had stolen the map of The Residency and made the siege possible."

The woman's jaw dropped, and she looked like she was about to run away. "Amelia, your wife?" she said nervously. "You are Colin Lawrence! She told me you are not her husband and there are other people with the surname Lawrence."

Colin squashed the wicked smile threatening to curl on his lips. *Yes, this is Sehnaz. Look how scared she is!* He contorted his face into a counterfeit look of concern. "See how that woman lied to you? Where is she? The police are looking for her, and she will be convicted for the siege of The Residency. Is she also here?"

Her eyes darted in all directions before landing on Colin's. "I, I mean, we tried to become good friends. But because of the war, we could not trust her as she is white and British. Left her in Sultanpur. I do not know if she is still there. But she had not given me the map. The map was with me even before I met Amelia. She should not be convicted for work she has not done."

Colin regarded something in silence. If he accused Sehnaz, then Amelia would not be convicted, and she may use Antonia's letter to send him to the noose. Dhiraj had mentioned that police were poking around Antonia's death again. He needed to get rid of Amelia.

He placed a hand over his heart. "You know how many people have died because of the siege? Rupen is responsible for all of that, and now I am trying to save him. He was a close friend before the Sepoy Mutiny began. If Amelia is acquitted of the charges, then it might come to you. I have promised Rupen to help you. There is only one way. You will write a letter saying it was Amelia who gave you the map. You need to kill someone to save yourself."

Sehnaz stood still; something was warring inside her mind. Colin stood patiently.

Suddenly, all her nervousness was gone. She straightened her spine and calmly said, "I can't. I am already repenting from leaving Amelia alone in Sultanpur. I would rather be convicted and hanged, but I can't accuse an innocent woman and send her to the noose. I will never do it. Please take me with you, Sir, if you wish, and get me arrested."

Colin gave her a long, measuring look. Sending Sehnaz as a convict for the stealing of the map would be counterproductive for him. The map of The Residency was the only card with him now to eliminate Amelia. Scratching his head, he inhaled deeply. There was hardly any time left. Chetan has been eliminated, and Sona's death was no more a threat to him. Then... Sona. An idea shot through him. *Sona!*

"I have an idea, neither you nor Amelia would be convicted. Anyway, Amelia is my wife, and I love her. And being the love of my dearest friend General Rupen Naik, I can't harm you, either. Now there is only one way out—Sona."

"Sona?"

"She was a maid in our house; she died a few weeks ago while delivering a baby. If you write a letter and say it was Sona who had given the map, all our problems will be solved. A dead woman cannot be hanged, you know." Colin laughed. "I will leave you here. I do not want the police to interrogate you. I can make up a story that you jumped into the Ganga and died. You can spend the rest of your life with another name.

Anyway, you were a courtesan, and you must have changed your parental name. Another change. How does that sound?"

Sehnaz gazed at him. Colin noticed the reflection of a devious man inside her glistening eyes. "I have no time," he continued. "Another officer is travelling with me. If he comes here, he will insist on arresting you. And do you want Rupen's letter or not?" Taking out a plain paper and pen from his bag, he gave to her.

Sehnaz sat down and started writing.

Colin dictated what to write and exchanged it with Rupen's letter. He was about to leave when Sehnaz asked, "Where is Rupen?"

He swung back. "I hope he wrote it in that letter. In case he didn't, he is being sent to the Black Waters in Andaman. *Kala Pani*, you know? Life in prison."

Sehnaz held her head and sat down with a grunting, "Hi, Allah."

A mischievous idea thrilled Colin. He came back to her and bent down. "You know, Sehnaz, who killed that maid, Sona?"

Sehnaz lifted her head and gazed into his eyes. Blood had already drained from her face.

"I, me, I am responsible for Sona's death." Colin stood and loped toward the horse carriage, holding the ticket of his ultimate victory, something that he should keep away from Dhiraj for the time being.

He was about to reach the carriage; he noticed the coachman hurriedly going somewhere. He shouted at him to come back. The coachman did not pay any heed and vanished in the rush of pilgrims. Realizing something was odd, Colin walked to the carriage. The door was closed. That meant Dhiraj had yet to come back from the temple. He raised one foot to place on the wooden step of the cab, and suddenly his gaze fell to the blood dripping from the inside, flowing to the ground and creating red mud.

Colin yanked the door open. Dhiraj, Prince Dhiraj was lying there, his body shivering and a knife wound on his chest winking at him. He noticed writing on the cab wall: *Punishment for betraying the motherland.*

Colin shook Dhiraj. "Prince, are you all right? Who did this?"

Dhiraj opened his eyes a little, his lips quivering. "That, that man, no coachman. A soldier from my kingdom. My father's." His eyes remained open, but his lips stopped moving.

With Sehnaz's letter in his pocket, Colin started running to the jetty where the ferry had been anchored.

CHAPTER 29

10 August 1857 Afternoon
Sehnaz

That was the day Sehnaz had been dreading most. She became lonely in this world. Colin's message regarding the exile of Rupen Naik to the Black Waters of the Andaman Islands was like a bullet that tore into Sehnaz's ribs and settled there, neither killing her nor letting her live. Had Rupen been sent to any other prison, she could have plotted to rescue him. This rebellion was lost, but that didn't mean another war couldn't start. Sehnaz could keep in touch with other kings of North India or even Maratha to prepare for another war against the British.

That fateful evening, Sehnaz was leaning on Sheru's chest and weeping. The man who at one time was like a servant to her had gained lots of respect from her. He had the valour which could have taken him up the career ladder to some senior position had he not deserted the British army. From the prior relationship between mistress and servant, they had become more like friends, which was not usual.

"Soldiers do not lose heart, ma'am," Sheru said while placing a palm on her shoulder. "They continue to fight until the last breath. I am still on the same duty that Rupen Sahib had given to me, and I will continue it."

Sehnaz buried her face again in his chest. Sheru's scent mixed with Sehnaz's tears created a potion that slowly engulfed her soul.

Sehnaz didn't realise that her saree had slipped from her shoulder, exposing her blouse.

After a while, she felt Sheru's fingers slowly crawling on her back and trying to cross her armpit. She didn't mind, as his fingers stopped there. His chest was slowly heating up, and she could feel his shallow breath on her hair. Fingers started creeping again toward her front, slowly pressing her soft bosom and gently squeezing her nipples.

A fire cracked in Sehnaz's veins. Raising her head from his chest, she looked up. Sheru's eyes were full of passion. The poor soldier had been away from his family for many months. Sheru's blood must have been starving to be with a woman. His hot breath hitched. Blinding desire swelled as her tongue moved out and touched his lips. Moments after, her breasts sprang out as Sheru unhooked her blouse.

Suddenly, the holy conch shell in the temple sounded three times, shooting shudders through Sheru's muscles. It was so strong that Sehnaz felt it in her bones. He bounced out of bed, and Sehnaz fell on the floor. "I am, am, s...sorry, ma'am. Pl-please f...forgive me," he said, voice shivering, "I have committed a sin. I must do penitence."

Sheru sidled from the room. Slumping on the bed, Sehnaz buttoned her blouse. She was sure Sheru must have gone to the temple to ask for forgiveness from the deity, Lord Shiva. She should have been careful. Rupen's sudden disappearance had created a massive void in her mind, and she was in a dilemma on what she should do: go back to Lucknow and start again as a courtesan, or stay in Varanasi forever. Having no permanent home or a family to go back to, staying with Sheru and pretending to be his wife gave her a false sense of security—the security a wife sought from a husband. Sheru had never even attempted to cast a brazen glance at her.

Did the deity of the temple forgive Sheru?

Nearly an hour later, Sheru came back—at the time they usually went together to the temple food hall for dinner. Sehnaz sat without saying any words. Sheru had admitted his fault, and there was nothing for her to be shameful of.

Sheru started packing his bag in a hurry. Before Sehnaz could react, he stood up with the bag. "Lord Shiva has finally awakened my wisdom. I will go and stay away from here. That way, your modesty is safe from my lustful eyes."

Remorse washed through her. "You could never cast a lustful glance, Sheru. Whatever happened was a moment's weakness, neither of us is responsible for that. We have a safe roof above our heads. Where will you live now, roadside? Under the open sky?"

Sheru's eyes were focussed on the floor. "We lied about our identity. We were fighting with the enemy, and we had a mission. Lying for the sake of the motherland is not a sin. Now that the war is over, is there any justification in living like a false couple? You may stay here for a few more weeks. I will come to the flower shop in front of the temple every day after I finish my work, and if I have any news about the rebellion, I will pass it on."

CHAPTER 30

12 August 1857 Afternoon
Sehnaz

Every day, beggars came to the temple gate asking for money and food. Sehnaz had gotten used to the scene. In fact, she had hardly any work nowadays since Sheru started staying elsewhere, leaving her alone. Every day, he would go out looking for a job as a casual worker in the jetties, where goods boats arrived regularly from Calcutta. Sehnaz lived alone as Sanju in the Kaal Bhairav temple. Buying some food from the nearby market, she would distribute it among the beggars who came to the temple gate.

Sehnaz was almost withdrawn after the defeat of the rebels and Rupen having been sentenced to life imprisonment in the Black Waters prison of the Andaman Islands—a place she had never heard of. It was somewhere in the mid-ocean or Bay of Bengal. He should have been a martyr in the war—or the death punishment would even have been far better than a life in Andaman. A hollowness ballooned through her.

Sehnaz was sitting on the stone floor of the temple compound. The chorus scream of some priests forced a sudden break to her thoughts. A beggar had trespassed inside the temple. What a strange rule. Devotees come to God and beg for anything on the earth, but the real beggars are not allowed to even see the statue of God.

"I am not a beggar, please listen to me, I am not a beggar," the trespasser shouted back. "I am a soldier. Please believe me."

Sehnaz sprang to her feet. *Soldier? How can you treat a man fighting for the country as a beggar? Only because the Indian side lost the war?* Frustration bubbled through her. The priests had surrounded a man in torn clothes and an unkempt beard. She struggled to recollect how to address a Hindu priest. "Hold on, *Panditji*." She lurched toward them. The priests knew her as Sanju, a wealthy woman, so they respectfully dispersed when she intervened.

The man did look like a beggar. Wide shoulders and muscular biceps bulged through his torn shirt, which looked like some uniform. He was praying with closed eyes, "O Kali Ma, you saved me so many times in the faces of sure death. I owe my lives to those dead soldiers. Please help me. They need religious rites. Their families need to know about their deaths."

Sehnaz stared at him. Even though she was a Muslim, after living more than a month in a Hindu temple, she knew this was Shiva's temple—a god, not a goddess.

"Hi, I am Sanju, a pilgrim from Lucknow and staying in the temple compound. You said you are a soldier. What is your name?"

"I am Chetan, ma'am." A desperate look shadowed his face. "I am not a beggar, ma'am. I am not asking for anything. And I am also from Lucknow, was working in The Residency when the rebellion happened."

This has happened to all those who were working for the British and deserted them to join the rebels. No one was paying salary to these people. Sehnaz thought of Sheru, who was working every day to earn a living.

Sehnaz took out some money from her purse. "Please take this and go to the market. Get yourself shaved first. The Ganga River is nearby, take a nice bath. I have given you enough money so you can buy new clothes. And yes, lunchtime is over. No food will be available in the temple now. Please eat something before coming back here."

Chetan again bowed his head. "Ma, you again blessed and appeared before me. Thank you, Ma."

"I am not a goddess, Chetan. And this's not a Kali temple, either. I know a man who will come here in the afternoon. I am sure he will help."

"I know, ma'am. But the goddess always helps through somebody. And today she helped through you. She spoke to me through you. Otherwise, how come you are present when I was about to be thrown out? I have gone to many temples asking for help, and everybody thought I was a beggar."

A cool wave passed through Sehnaz's nerves. She felt her own smile. "You are right, Chetan. Everything in life has a purpose."

Chetan left the temple in a hurry. Sehnaz slumped to the floor, leaning against a stone pillar. *If God is helping this man everywhere, why am I in such a situation? Is this because I am a Muslim, and the deity here is a Hindu God? But I have heard the priest was saying God is one irrespective of religion.*

Sheru would never come back to the temple. For the priests' information, her husband had gone out of Varanasi for some work and would be back after weeks. She must meet Sheru outside the temple; God knows what news Chetan had brought.

Sehnaz glanced up. The evening ritual of the temple was about to begin in an hour. This was the time Sheru always came to meet her in the market, even if he had no news about the war. Noticing a clean-shaven man in white clothing entering the gate, she understood—that was Chetan in a new avatar. He was coming toward her with a weak but grateful smile on his face. Sehnaz stood and indicated for him to meet her outside the temple.

They settled on a stone platform built on the bank of the River Ganga, overlooking both the river and the Kaal Bhairav temple. Sehnaz glanced around. Sheru should be there at any time.

"You left your job with the British army and joined the rebels?"

Chetan's eyes were focussed on her, as if thinking hard on what to say, sitting with his legs folded in meditation pose.

"Nothing like that, ma'am. I believed—" he struggled to find words — "I thought, I should not betray the hand that is feeding me. Joining the rebels is like betraying. Unethical. Sin."

Sehnaz regarded him for a few minutes. Silently. *I am helping a man who is still on the side of the British?* "Even though the whites are regularly betraying the nation that is still regularly feeding them, filling up their coffers?"

Sheru was there when Sehnaz shot the last sentence. Curling his fingers tightly around the knife handle on his waist, he inched closer. "You traitor of the country! Don't you know thousands of patriotic soldiers have already died defending the freedom of their beloved nation, and you are still a trusted British dog?"

Chetan stood with folded hands facing Sheru. "Sir, I do know. In River Gomti. I was floating, trying to save my life. I have seen the dead soldiers the British have killed, and I brought them here for decent and religious cremation and rites."

"You were floating? Why?" Sheru asked.

"Colin Sahib had arrested me and was taking me back to Lucknow. I would have been punished for something I didn't do. They think I have killed Sona, my wife. I jumped out of the boat to save my life."

Colin? Sona? Those two names rang the bell hard with Sehnaz. "You mean Colin Lawrence? The Brigadier General? Sona is, sorry, was his maid?"

"You are right, ma'am. Sona was my wife. How could I murder her? She was the mother of my only daughter."

"You have been framed," Sehnaz said. *He got me to sign a letter implicating Sona as the conspirator for stealing the map of The Residency before admitting he killed her himself.* "It is difficult to predict the man. How did you jump? Weren't your hands tied?"

Chetan narrated his story—how and why he jumped from Colin's ferry and how he found the boat having dead bodies of Indian soldiers.

"I promised the goddess to cremate the soldiers with full respect and religious rites. So I did. I have even found addresses of a few. Their families should know that they are martyrs. How do I organise to send people and give them the bad news? I do not have money."

"Sit down, Chetan." A meaningful smile curved around Sheru's lips. "Sehnaz ma'am and I will organise that. It will take time. But we will do it for the patriots. I would love someone like you to take care of me if some day I die in the war."

"Clever man. Colin." Sehnaz smiled. "He wanted you to jump into the river; he thought you would die. John Nicholson is a ghost to scare you. Taking you to Lucknow could have proved that someone else had killed Sona. Colin himself. He shot two birds with one bullet. Saved his own ass and implicated her for stealing the map. For British authorities, Sona's life is less important. But punishing someone who has stolen the map is a high priority. Implicating her would direct the cannon at the poor dead woman, and the East India Company would rather be happy that she has been killed. He might even take the credit for himself."

Something unknown was going through Chetan's features. He crooked his brow. "Sona was telling me Colin Sahib had probably killed his first wife, Antonia. She had a letter of Antonia ma'am. I do not know what is written. But the letter is at my home. In Lucknow."

Venom raced through Sehnaz's veins, and she lurched to her feet. "Got it. Now is the time to finish that bastard." News of Rupen's exile punishment was still raw for her. "I made a mistake in abandoning Amelia in Sultanpur. I should go and find her there. She is another harassed soul, and Colin could have butchered her by now. Like he did with his ex-wife. And Sona."

"Amelia ma'am?" A strange look crossed Chetan's features. "I have seen Amelia ma'am in the Shakti Ashram of Sultanpur," Chetan whispered to Sehnaz.

"What did she say to you?"

Embarrassment ran through his eyes. "I could not. I was a security guard there but was not allowed inside the ashram complex. Because, because..." He avoided her gaze.

Sehnaz blurted out a laugh. "You are blushing, Chetan. I know, women in the Shakti Ashram mostly stay nude. Did you see Amelia without clothes?"

Hesitation clouded his eyes. "I, I, she, yes, she..."

She was about to say something, but a dark shape loomed on the pathway. Sheru had already noticed, and his hand was tightly grabbing the pistol on his waistband.

"Stay where you are." Sheru's voice was suppressed but commanding. "I will shoot you."

The man stopped immediately and raised his arms above his head.

"Keep like that and proceed."

"I have brought a letter to ma'am," the man said in a low voice. "Letter from Lucknow. Confidential. Urgent and important."

"Show the letter." Sheru lowered the pistol.

The man gave the letter to Sehnaz and quietly went back.

This was information from her trusted source. Colin had altered her confession letter to include Amelia's name, implicating her to have teamed up with Sona to provide The Residency map to the rebels. The trap had been laid, and no one could save her from the noose.

Lifting her head from the letter, she first glanced at Chetan and then Sheru. "There is no time now. We need to rush to Sultanpur."

CHAPTER 31

12 August 1857
Amelia

I have never been thrilled so much. Not even when my wedding was finalised with Colin; he was the prince of my dreams until I found the real picture. After Harry rescued me from the storm and proposed, I'd contacted Bibi and she arranged to keep me in a secluded place. Harry planned to take me to Calcutta after the wedding.

Going to a church to marry Harry is out of the question. I am still the legally wedded wife of Brigadier General Colin. No one in England can even think of marrying again without formally obtaining a divorce if the husband is alive.

"Divorce?" Mata Radhe laughs. "Women here do not have that choice. They either blame their fate or the unknown sin they might have committed in the previous birth if they get a bad husband. Most women are mentally prepared to undergo the penitence so that their next life will bring them a better man. Those who dare run away from the marriage will face some unknown future. You chose the latter."

That has not been easy. I cannot hide my identity for long. Churches will no doubt find out I am the estranged wife of a senior British army officer. The heat of the Sepoy Mutiny is still circulating on both sides, even though the rebels have lost. The fire is yet to be extinguished and may flare up at any moment. The British have started taking revenge at the slightest pretext. Harry's information is not wrong. I might be implicated for a crime I have never done; the allegation is enough for facing a court-martial and a possible death sentence. I do not wish to be the first woman or even the first white woman of this country to confront the noose for supporting the rebels.

Mata Radhe comes up with a unique idea. No need to go to a church. The wedding will be solemnised in the Shakti Ashram, and she will be the priestess. For one day at least, nuns will be asked not to stay naked so that Harry can come inside the temple. Even though I have no intention of changing my religion and becoming a Hindu, I am still thrilled. I will be the first woman in the world whose marriage will be solemnised by a woman priest.

Bibi Khanum is thrilled, too, as if this is her daughter's wedding. It is rare for a courtesan to go back to the normal society and be someone's wife. She makes all the arrangements, like buying jewellery and a wedding dress for me. Everything happens, but quietly.

A dream has come true. Finally, I am all set to start a new life with the man of my dreams. Harry has even suggested I take a new name and change my identity. I will live far away from here, in Calcutta. Once everything about the mutiny cools down, I may sometimes come with Harry to Sultanpur and stay in the heaven-like island palace he has built. I could meet all my friends here—Bibi Khanum, Mata Radhe, Madhuri, and who knows—one day I might meet Sehnaz, too. Harry has no problem with me spending some time in Shakti Ashram in a free environment. I have discovered it is empowering and relaxing.

Harry is also interested in me helping him with his business—not as a wife, but as a business partner. Once I decide my new name, he will set the papers for the partnership. I will earn money by using my own capability.

Who said married women do not have independence?

14 August 1857
Brigadier Colin Lawrence

East India Company could not have gotten a better committed employee than Colin—a dedicated soldier who was both honest and also superefficient.

Was the universe finally giving Colin more than he bargained for?

How many people could admit their own wife was the culprit and be willing to hand her over to the law enforcement for the most severe sentence? Exemplary punishment would force people to think a hundred times before even remotely supporting any rebel activity. Colin had also received appreciation for capturing General Rupen of Nawab Wajid Ali Shah, who was the mastermind of The Residency siege, avoiding another Bibighar Massacre. Not many officers would have dared to go inside the lion's den carrying the headless bodies of his wife and daughters. He had also captured Chetan, whose wife was alleged to have taken the stolen map organised by Amelia and given to Rupen's lover Sehnaz. Authorities are happy Chetan died jumping into the river. There was no need to waste valuable energy carrying out a trial when it was known he was the culprit in hiding his wife's nefarious activities.

Colin had been nominated for the highest award from the queen of England. He was now on top of the world. He had even planned to get a unilateral divorce so that he could marry a decent and obedient girl. He had his eye on the daughter of a junior clerk in Madras. A girl who was not highly educated like Amelia, but educated enough to maintain a household and obey the husband—the qualities of a good wife. No doubt Amelia was the one with more beauty, but he could compromise a little bit for a more obedient woman.

Colin started the travel to Sultanpur, along with a few soldiers. A telegram had already been sent to Sultanpur cantonment with instructions to guard all routes, especially the river routes so that a white woman could not escape. Any white woman surrounded by natives was to be stopped but not arrested. He wanted all the thrill for himself. He would love to see the shock in the eyes of a disloyal wife who would be punished in the most innovative way—a murder that the law enforcement would do based on the mighty trap he had prepared so meticulously. He had avenged his first wife Antonia before. But that was not the correct or foolproof way. Although police concluded that as a suicide, Dhiraj mentioned they might be reinvestigating. And now Amelia had some material which could implicate him. He thought he had destroyed Antonia's letter. But Chetan admitted Sona had the letter, and now Amelia had obtained it, Colin was sure of it. Now he was about to kill two birds with one stone. She would get punishment for her disloyalty, and also her statement against him would not be trusted.

Coming to the deck as the ferry approached Sultanpur, Colin noticed a beautiful mansion on a tiny island in the Gomti River—close enough to the shore that one could swim across, yet still connected by a small bridge. The colours of the island were very different: the mellow yellows of the mangoes, red hues of lychee, and the well-maintained green lawn fused into one palette. Must be owned by a wealthy local businessman or a royal family member. He planned to buy the mansion once he got promoted and received the awarded prize money. Indians had no right to live in such lavish mansions, whether a royal or a businessman. They should start learning to live as second-grade citizens, in a land occupied by the white British.

Thwarted to the imagination of his would-be third wife, Colin took out her photo from his pocket. He had gathered all the information about the young girl. Agreeing to marry Amelia was a colossal mistake. It was almost impossible to get information about her as she was living in England at the time. He was happy that luck started smiling at him after the Sepoy Mutiny.

His gaze went to the clear blue sky. Everything looked beautiful. When a small patch of dark cloud appeared at the distant horizon, Colin blurted out a laugh. Amelia was always scared of this. She must be watching this from the terrace of some goddamn *kotha*, and a dark foreboding must be taking control of her nerves.

Come on, darling, this time, your foreboding will be correct. The sin of ungratefulness will be punished. A matter of days only. What have I not done for you? Provided a wealthy life with all sorts of luxuries and the respect of society. Still, you prefer the company of the wretched Indians?

14 August 1857
Sehnaz

This was not unusual for Sehnaz. She even expected this and prepared accordingly for sailing to Sultanpur. Chetan dressed as a *maulvi* and Sheru as a Brahmin who was travelling with his *purdah*-wearing wife, Sanju. She was particularly afraid of Colin, who could quickly figure out Sanju was the same as Sehnaz.

Lifting the veil slightly, Sehnaz noticed: one police inspector, British, and two havildars—both Indians went on checking everything on the ferry.

"I am Sheru Pandey, a Brahmin, coming from Varanasi to do some religious rituals for my clients." Sheru extended his hand, pretending to bless the police fellows. "Let God give you long life, wealth and health." He recited a Sanskrit verse.

Sehnaz chuckled silently under her veil. Police went past Sheru and checked on other passengers. Her gaze went to Chetan standing at a distance—his sweating face and tense eyes. Calling on Sheru, she said in a loud voice, "Maulvi Sahib is not well. I think his fever is coming back. Please go to him and give him some water." Then she whispered in his ear, "Tell that stupid to behave normally. Or else we all will be caught."

When the inspector gave the go-ahead after completing his work, Sehnaz quietly asked the Indian havildar what the matter was. His answer did not surprise her but instead confirmed her assumptions. They were after a white woman accused of a war crime who might be trying to escape. Brigadier General Colin was arriving from Lucknow to take her into custody.

Will Amelia survive this trap Colin has laid?

Sheru came to her when the police left the boat. "I do not think we will be successful in our endeavour." A strange look crossed his features. "It might be possible Colin is already here with his team, and soon the British spies will find out where she is hiding."

A thick tension flowed between them.

"She was in the Shakti Ashram," Chetan said, "we can find her."

"Finding her is not an issue, but taking her out from here certainly is. Looks like they have guarded all the routes. Really tough for a white woman to move in disguise. Not even in a veil," Sehnaz said.

"Why not a *purdah*? Didn't you notice the police didn't ask you to lift your veil?"

"They are looking for a British woman, and only my face is covered, not my arms. The police are not stupid, they could notice my skin colour. I am not that much concerned about finding her."

"What are you worried about?"

"That cursed map. Chasing Amelia like a ghost. If only Chetan could fetch Antonia's letter from his Lucknow home. Enough to send Colin behind bars for the murder of his first wife," Sehnaz mused.

Dead first wife could save the life of the second wife. Is it possible?

"Not possible. Hardly any time, ma'am." Sheru looked tense as Chetan watched with a mixed expression. "Colin could shoot Amelia when he sees her. He is a clever man and knows taking her to court could have any result. I mean, he knows Amelia is also intelligent and will not leave without a fight."

Sehnaz blew out a chestful of air. "I shouldn't have forsaken her. I know how it hurts when your own husband becomes your enemy." Sehnaz sobbed.

It was almost dusk when they disembarked from the boat. A few other ferries were also allowing their passengers to get off. When a small crowd of ferry passengers walked through the jetty holding their luggage, Sehnaz noticed Chetan was not with them. The group was not that large, so it didn't take long to locate him. He had taken a small girl in his arms, hugging and kissing her. Moving a bit closer, she noticed an old woman holding a box was keenly watching them.

Chetan introduced the old lady. "Auntie used to keep my baby when both Sona and I were on duty at Colin's home." Tears streamed down his cheeks.

The lady beheld the reunion of father and daughter, tears of relief pooling in her eyes. "That night I was feeling restless as if a banshee were singing somewhere in the bushes. Next morning, neither Sona nor Chetan came back home. I usually go to work outside after Sona returns. I waited for hours. When I heard a knock on the door, it was neither of these two. I was scared to see police on my doorstep. They searched my house and asked where Chetan was hiding. I had no clue what was happening and no courage to ask questions to the police."

"How did you know that Sona had died?" Sehnaz asked.

"Another neighbour told me. I couldn't believe it. He said Chetan had killed her after he saw her sleeping with Colin Sahib, and he fled out of Lucknow. The police were looking for him, and he will get death punishment if caught."

A thick emotion bubbled inside Sehnaz. "How did you know you would find Chetan here, in Sultanpur?"

"I did not know. Last week a man came and told me that Chetan had jumped to the river and taken his own life. When Colin Sahib was bringing him back in a boat. The man said he had been sent by Sahib himself. He even advised me to leave the baby in an orphanage. I knew Sona has a sister who lives here, in Sultanpur. She is a widow and has no child. I came to look for her. I do not know where she lives. But I thought to give it a try."

"The man came just to tell you that Chetan had died?" Sheru's eyes narrowed.

"The man asked about a letter. Sona had kept a letter written by Colin Sahib's first wife. She had told me the man had killed the poor woman as she did not obey him. I told the man I am illiterate and do not understand about letters."

"Letter?" Sehnaz glanced at Chetan. "That letter could have saved the poor woman, Amelia. But now that is impossible."

An inscrutable smile curved the lips of the old lady, beyond the comprehension of Sehnaz.

"I understood it was not the police but only that man who was asking about the letter. I went to Chetan's house and found a letter in a box. I do not know if that is the letter written by Colin Sahib's ex-wife, but that is the only letter I found, and it is with me." Opening her travel trunk, she took out the envelope.

Sehnaz almost pounced upon her and snatched the letter from her fingers. Tearing open the envelope, she peeked inside. Her jaw stilled as she unfolded the piece of paper. She glanced at both Sheru and Chetan. "I know Sheru cannot read English. Chetan, can you?"

"No, ma'am."

Sehnaz's heart was beating hard against her ribs. None of them could read. Chetan suggested they approach some English officer in the city and ask to read it to them.

She dismissed the idea. "You mean the lamb will go to the butcher asking for help?"

"We should not stand here any longer. Another ferry is approaching the jetty, and the police might be here again soon. They might even suspect us standing together like this. We are not yet out of danger." Sheru's gaze wandered along the Gomti.

The five of them started walking. Chetan's daughter had not let go of his hand since they had reunited.

"We all will go to the location where we had gotten shelter last time," Sheru said.

On the way, Chetan pointed out a road. "This goes to the Shakti Ashram."

They came across several groups of soldiers moving around. A strange feeling washed through Sehnaz. The mutiny was over, and the British had already won the war. Nawab Wajid Ali was in Calcutta, imprisoned inside a palatial house, with full royal honour. *What are these soldiers doing here?*

Darkness was slowly closing in, robbing her of her best senses and replacing them with paralysing fear. Her lover had been sent to the Black Waters prison in Andaman Island, and finally, the predator was about to pounce upon Amelia, the woman who could have been her best friend. The woman whom she betrayed because of some unsubstantiated doubt.

Amelia's time has run out. Who can save her now?

CHAPTER 32

15 August 1857
Amelia

I am all set for the day. Today Amelia will die, and a new woman will take birth, with a new name I do not know yet. Without changing my identity, I cannot live in British-India. My name is blacklisted as an abettor of a serious war crime, a crime I never committed. Who can fight against the mighty British empire?

I am not the only one dressed up for the wedding; all the nuns here are also wearing clothes for today. There will be many firsts happening here: first wedding ever done in the Shakti Ashram, where the priest is a woman, and the marriage of a Christian couple solemnised by a Hindu nun. Finally, there will be another first. Harry, a male, will be welcomed in the ashram. I chuckle. How fun it would have been if all the nuns could attend the wedding naked. I know Mata Radhe will not let that happen. Nuns shed clothes here only in the presence of other women, *Daita* the only exception.

I stopped performing before audiences when the rebels lost the war. I know I will be hounded, and if found, will be taken in by the police. Bibi Khanum gave the strictest instructions: I am confined to my room, at best to my balcony. In the late evenings, I take a stroll on the backyard lawn, facing the Gomti River. That is the time when dance performances are over, and no patron is allowed in the *kotha*. Yesterday evening, I packed my suitcase and said a final goodbye to the *kotha*. I came to the Shakti Ashram through the secret tunnel. Once I become Harry's wife, he will take me from here. Forever. We both will go to Calcutta and stay in his farmhouse. Away from the hustle and bustle of the busy capital city.

As I am ambling in the garden facing the river, my gaze goes to the ferries playing throughout the waterway—lots of goods boats. Everyday life has again started now that the war finished. I glance at the jetty where people are either embarking or getting off the ferries, a phalanx of soldiers with rifles on their shoulders watching them.

A cool whisper threads through me. Are they keeping an eye out for if I escape? I am the culprit in the eyes of the new de facto ruler of this land where the nawab is no longer the king. A fear surges in my chest. Can the big shots like Harry, Mata Radhe, or Bibi save me?

My gaze automatically goes to the bright sky, at a small patch of white cloud somewhere near the horizon—confidence blooms. Today is my lucky day. All my life I have been looking for a day like this. My heart fills with joy.

I saunter into Kali temple and find both Mata Radhe and Bibi Khanum standing in a corner. Whispering. A sudden thickness in the air touches my skin. I have always seen Mata Radhe in a jolly mood. She would comment sometimes, "No family, no tension. Only reason monks and nuns stay single.'"

Which anxiety is darkening her eyes?

I run outside toward the same location where I noticed the patch of white cloud in the clear sky—the symbol of fortune. A light gust of wind washes over my skin, teasing me. *You are unnecessarily worrying, Amelia. Today is your luckiest day.* I know I am safe here in the Shakti Ashram. I return to where both ladies are still standing, as if awaiting me.

They are looking at me. I swallow.

Bibi Khanum comes to me, rests her hand on my shoulder, and then hugs me. Tightly. A mother's warmth passes through my skin and touches my heart. Her warm breath touches my face. Pulling back, I stare at her. Her eyes are welling—they might overflow anytime.

I free myself from her hug. "What is the matter?"

Mata Radhe is standing beside me. I look at her, questions on my mind.

"You have told me so many times you wanted the same position as men. Independence. Having your own status. Earning an income. Not confined to the four walls during the day," she says.

I still do not understand and turn my gaze toward Bibi. She explains.

"Harry is not coming. His family is pressuring him to call off this wedding. Not to marry a courtesan. Not to a woman who is already married and not gotten a divorce."

"He knew this." I try to control my eyes from flooding. "He knows I am a courtesan. He knows I can't approach my so-called husband for a divorce."

"I know. That is not correct. Harry fears the wrath of the East India Company." Bibi pauses. "I think we need to give it some time. The British are in revenge mode now. They have even started destroying historical structures in Lucknow in retaliation against the rebels. Please do not lose heart."

I'm still thinking of that white patch of cloud, unable to make out what is happening. The wedding was too good to be true. I should have never been in haste in accepting Harry's proposal. I am disheartened but not broken. A sweltering heat flushes up my chest, and then my face. Coming out of the temple, I trudge toward the front. I don't know why—a sudden desire to remove all my clothes and throw them into the bush sprouts inside my guts. When I start unbuttoning my blouse, my gaze goes to *Daita*. He is ambling toward me in his trademark tiny piece of cloth covering his groin. Today, I will take advantage like other nuns and let out some steam sitting on his lap. But the temple corridor is not allowed for that. We need to go toward the caves and do whatever we like.

Daita is saying something, but I can't understand him. Looking around, I notice Madhuri.

"Do not remove your clothes," Madhuri warns and sprints toward me. "Soldiers have surrounded the hill. Please go inside. We will again go back through the tunnel. To the *kotha*. With your suitcase."

Before swinging back and running inside, I take a quick glance at the foot of the hill. Hundreds of soldiers have already surrounded the area—a siege. I wonder if the Sepoy Mutiny has started again.

"Do not stay here, Amelia. Let's go back to the *kotha*." Madhuri holds my arm. Her voice low. Quiet.

"I am sure so many soldiers are not coming for just one unarmed woman. There must be something else. Someone might be hiding in the bushes." My gaze goes to the steps of the hill. A known face, along with soldiers, is striding up the steps. I freeze. My heart kicks—Colin with a pistol in one hand and handcuffs in the other. A hot rush of adrenaline thumps through me. I cannot escape anymore. The time has come to face him. I must confront him and say that my love for him has been dead for a long time. Will he give me a divorce?

Colin meets my gaze. I can clearly see his trademark supercilious smile. A smile that shoots shockwaves deep inside my heart.

"You have given The Residency map to the rebels. Hundreds of men and women were killed because of the siege. I have concrete evidence for a court-martial."

That man can create any false evidence to send me to the noose. Knowing that my time has come, I swirl back and run. I am ready to die, but I do not want to stand in a court and listen to how I have betrayed my own countrymen. I do not want to go through that hell. So many thoughts run through me within seconds. I have two paths: face hanging through the so-called judicial process, or...

I choose the second and run to the top of the hill through the narrow zigzag path with a wall of hedges on both sides—the location which has been my favourite spot to view the Gomti. I know Colin will take the time to find me. But he has a group of well-trained soldiers. Many of them are Indians. They must have knowledge of local landscapes. I stand just below the crest. No one can see me from a distance.

Madhuri is just behind me. "Why did you come here? Where will you go now?" She breathes hard.

I suck in a deep breath. My brain stops when I hear boots crunching over the dry leaves. Colin must be pushing his way to the crest. I have only a few seconds to decide.

Should I die now or die in prison with the help of the hangman?

There is hardly a chance to survive. I think of doing the last prayer as a true Christian. But all I can see in my mind's eye is the statue of the goddess Kali. I pray.

Ma, if I jump from the hill, I will consider it as your wish. You, the goddess, the symbol of infinite energy, have finally lost to the power of a man. Amen.

I take my first step to the crest and within no time arrive at the fork leading to two different peaks, one taller than the other. I stride to one of them when I hear Colin's voice. His sardonic laugh. Closing my eyes, I take a pause. I still have time to jump. I want to feel my life, at least a few more seconds.

I hear a commanding male voice.

"Mr. Colin Lawrence. I'm the magistrate of Sultanpur. Please stop immediately and surrender to me."

I do not believe what I have just heard. It might be the internal sound a dying person hears. Is my mystified brain playing with me?

"Stop, Mr. Colin. You can't kill that woman. Please surrender," the man yells. "I have evidence you have murdered your first wife. I have the warrant to arrest you."

The world freezes. I still can't see the man who is calling himself magistrate. But I do see Colin. He is standing with his mouth agape, eyes widened. Madhuri is standing a few steps below me with her mouth open. I am at a loss to understand how this could happen. The magistrate closes in, with two known faces behind him. Sehnaz and Chetan. Slowly I climb down. I will survive.

Thanks, Ma Kali.

"Mr. Magistrate," I scream, "I have never done anything against the British. All I have done is flee my husband's home as I believed he might kill me."

The magistrate stops and stares at me.

Colin takes this as an opportunity. Suddenly leaping onto the steps, he flounces to the crest. The magistrate along with two constables follow him. But before they can reach him, Colin vanishes. The magistrate runs to the ridge and looks down.

I hear someone down the hill, yelling, "The man has been splattered to death."

CHAPTER 33

15 August 1860
Amelia

My diary—Amelia Elliott Spencer's diary.

This is my story. I am now an independent and liberated woman while most western women don't even know what 'liberated' means. I am sitting in my luxurious island mansion in the Gomti River, near Sultanpur. Sultanpur was the capital of the Awadh kingdom, ruled until 1857 by Nawab Wajid Ali Shah. He is now in exile in Calcutta, and the British are now the de facto ruler of his state along with many other Indian kingdoms.

You must be wondering how I am living in the mansion owned by Harry, even after he called off the wedding. Yes, that dream wedding never happened, and I do not blame him. I was attracted to his physique, his affection for me, and the way he rescued me from the stormy river when the boat capsized. But he is probably right in his decision. His family gave massive pressure against marrying a courtesan. The fear of British revenge was also too much to bear. Despite all this, we are good friends.

I inherited Colin's estate as his widow, which I gladly accepted. The man who killed his ex-wife and ruined my dreams at least owes his wealth to me.

Discarding Colin's surname 'Lawrence,' I became Amelia Elliott Spencer—Spencer is my mother's maiden name, and Elliott is my father's surname. Even if I marry in the future, I have decided never to take the husband's last name. I believe that is the first weapon in the hands of a patriarchal family to destroy the identity of a woman. I have sent a letter to my parents detailing what happened with me, without mentioning that I had become a courtesan or my experiment with nudeness in the Shakti Ashram.

With my inheritance, I bought Harry's palatial house on the island when he decided to move to Calcutta permanently. When he knew that I was an interested buyer, he was willing to gift it to me. But I do not want any charity, even if from Harry. I want to walk with my head high.

The East India Company, after defeating the rebels in the famous Sepoy Mutiny, could not rule the country. It had to transfer the power to the queen in August 1858, when the Government of India Act was passed in the British Parliament. The government in England blamed the Company for misgovernance and not correctly handling the rebellion, which could have been averted in the first place had the local British officers treated the Indians with compassion and respect.

The new government in India has taken several developmental works. The most important one is setting up schools to spread English education. I was successful when I approached the government to set up a school in Sultanpur. I have been appointed as a teacher there. Obviously, the headmaster is a man. Students are mostly boys. But a few educated and wealthy Indians send their daughters to the school, also —like Chetan's daughter. I have an adult female student, Sehnaz. She is no longer a courtesan and is living with me.

I am no longer a courtesan, either. I don't dislike the profession, but it's not for me. They were helping the rebels against the British in the Sepoy Mutiny. The British have left no stone unturned to discredit them. They propagated that the courtesans are prostitutes. In my words, they are dancers, singers, and some are even excellent poets. They maintain freedom in a man's world, which is not easy for a woman. They do not like married life.

I remember what Mata Radhe had told me so many times, *The moment a woman marries, the first thing she surrenders is her freedom.*

Yes, like any other average human being, the courtesans fall in love and also sleep with the men they love. Not for money. They have all the qualities of a strong and independent woman. They do not subjugate themselves to male domination.

15 August 1857. That is the memorable day when I got my freedom: freedom from a monster husband, and freedom from male dominance. After everything was over, Mata Radhe sat for an hour-long meditation while I sat cross-legged by her side. I felt an aura radiating from her. Opening her eyes, she told me, "Ninety years from today, the country will attain complete freedom. Until then, the British will rule this land."

I calculate. 15 August 1947. Will I ever survive for ninety years?

Anyone who is reading this after ninety years from now, please check if India has gotten freedom from the British. If so, when?

Chetan has married Sona's widowed sister and settled in Sultanpur. He is working as my security guard.

I must devote a respectable space in my diary for the *letter*. The letter written by Antonia, which saved my life. I'd gotten it from the magistrate after Colin's death. The woman had fought against her oppressive husband and finally lost her life. She had written the letter to the Governor General of India, who was the head of East India Company.

To,

Lord Dalhousie

Dear Sir,

I do not know whether this letter from an ordinary English woman will find its way to your kind notice.

Sir, I beg my life to you. My life is in danger. The very same man who has vowed to protect me and love me until death do us apart, now wants to clear the way so that he can get another woman in his life. Sir, I have served my husband Mr. Colin Lawrence as an obedient and loyal wife. I have made all efforts to keep him happy. But I could not agree to become a whore. He wants me to warm the bed of his senior officers so that he can get faster promotions. Any woman with self-respect shall resist this. I am not an exception. But now, he has threatened to murder me and hang me from the rafters to look like a suicide.

Like any other wife I also want my husband to rise in his career, in the army of the East India Company. But he should be promoted because of his service to the company, not at the cost of his wife's body. I have tried to send a letter to you before this, but unfortunately Mr. Colin found out and destroyed the letter. He has instructed the security guard not to let me outside of his bungalow—the house, which was a home to me, but is a hell now. If my life ends before receipt of this letter, please enquire of my husband. I would hate for another woman to endure a marriage to him.

Your kind attention can save a helpless woman's life, Sir.

Yours Truly,

Mrs. Antonia Lawrence

The Residency, Lucknow

The letter—which could've saved Antonia's life—finally saved mine, and I will preserve the same as her memory. Let her soul rest in peace in the heavens.

I have preserved some costumes from my days as a courtesan. Out of that, my favourite is a pink-coloured bodice. Sehnaz knows this. She has managed to create pink colour by mixing different inks, and on the cover page of my diary she has written, *The Pink Mutiny.* This contains my story since I arrived in Calcutta in the brides' ship until now, all the thrilling memories.

Sehnaz always says, "Rebels have lost the war to the British. But you have won the mutiny against all those who do not treat women well."

"No, Sehnaz, this rebellion was just the beginning of the freedom struggle." I remember Mata Radhe's prediction.

The pages in the diary are about to be finished. Sehnaz has brought paper from the market and is binding another book for me.

Today I noticed she was packing her bags, preparing to go somewhere. I have never thought of a life without her. She said she is going to the Andaman Islands in the Bay of Bengal, to the Black Waters Prison. Rupen is spending his life behind bars there. I understand her pain, and I said to her, "Please wait. We both will go there with full preparation and a strategy—a plan to liberate him either legally or whatever way possible."

I notice I am on the last page of my diary called *The Pink Mutiny*. And now, I am opening the other book Sehnaz has made for me and on the cover page am writing *The Black Waters*. I just raised my head and noticed the most precious sight ever, a million-pound smile.

My next destination is The Black Waters.

LETTER FROM THE AUTHOR

Thank you so much for reading **The Pink Mutiny**. I hope Amelia, Sehnaz and Chetan's story appealed you. Even though this is a work of fiction, the Sepoy Mutiny of 1857 was very real and a famous historic event of the British-India history. Historians have underestimated the role of courtesans in the freedom movement, as that was a male dominant age and courtesans were all women. After researching a lot about them I found that famous courtesans of Lucknow in Nineteenth century were more of singers, dancers, poets. But their role in the rebellion angered the British rulers, and they got a bad name as sex workers. They were leading independent lives in an era when the word 'liberated woman' was not in use. Some courtesans also were taking part in advising kings and nawabs about their royal functions.

If you enjoyed this book, **I'd be grateful to see your review.** I love getting the feedback, and your review will help other readers discover the book.

If you love Amelia and Sehnaz, their story is not yet over. You will find them again in **The Black Waters**, which is the sequel. If you sign up below, I will send an Advance Review Copy (ARC) for free when the book is ready for publication, or even before that.

Email Sign Up
https://blisspublishing.com.au/sign-up/

You will never receive emails unless there's a new book to share, and I will never share your email with anyone else. You can unsubscribe any time by simply an email with the word "Unsubscribe" in the subject field.